Coot and the Gophers

Coot

and the

Gophers

Sixth in the Prairie Preacher Series

P. J. Hoge

iUniverse, Inc.
Bloomington

Coot and the Gophers
Sixth in the Prairie Preacher Series

iUniverse books may be ordered through booksellers or by contacting:

iUniverse
1663 Liberty Drive
Bloomington, IN 47403
www.iuniverse.com
1-800-Authors (1-800-288-4677)

ISBN: 978-1-4620-5427-5 (sc)
ISBN: 978-1-4620-5464-0 (hc)
ISBN: 978-1-4620-5428-2 (ebk)

Library of Congress Control Number: 2011916642

Printed in the United States of America

iUniverse rev. date: 10/07/2011

1

Carl Kincaid turned over in his bed to try to find a more comfortable position. He looked over to his roommate, an old duffer in his mid-eighties also on oxygen. Carl thought to himself, 'There is enough oxygen in this room to blow the whole damned place to kingdom come. And that probably wouldn't be the worst idea any one ever had.'

He raised his hospital bed to he sit up and look out the window. He could see the first signs of morning caressing the prairies. It was quiet in the house and he could hear some overactive meadowlark singing its heart out.

It was a pretty place, if it wasn't where it was. From the bedroom window, he could look over the yard north of the house and toward the windbreak. The lilacs were finished blooming but the foliage was still deep green. He could just make out the edge of the road into the Schroeder farm and the corner where it attached to the main gravel road to Merton, North Dakota.

'How in the hell did I end up in the middle of this God forsaken country?' he wondered to himself. 'Sharing a room with an old guy who can't be happy about anything and living with people I only met a few weeks ago.' He actually knew how it happened, but it made no sense at all. In his whole life, he had never been so irrational.

He watched as the Schroeder's black and white dog Elmer ran off on the trail of some gopher. He ran over to the hole and started to dig furiously.

'Damned fool,' Kincaid thought, 'Like he really thinks he can dig him out! Not a chance in hell.'

Bert Ellison started to cough and almost lost his oxygen mask. Kincaid watched until the old man quit and he was sure that the mask was still on. Once the old man coughed so hard that Kincaid got himself over to his bed to replace the mask. Bert never woke up or if he did, chose not to acknowledge him.

Kincaid could get up and move around but was still very weak from his surgeries. The FBI agent had taken a bullet in the upper back/neck region that damaged an artery and some blood vessels. Of course, he was no spring chicken himself and had smoked for forty of his sixty-three years. That didn't help the situation.

Some violent psycho, scam-artist-turned-preacher who specialized in blackmail and extortion took a shot at him. Well, that wasn't really true. He tried to kill his own little girl who was just a toddler and Kincaid saw him point the gun at her. Without thinking, he threw himself on top of her like a Secret Service agent over a President and knocked her to the floor. Carl was about six feet tall and weighed about two hundred forty pounds. He could have killed the tiny malnourished thing if he landed wrong. The bullet traveled through him and landed in her hip. She ended up with a flesh wound, a hairline fracture of the hip and a lifelong fear of flying men, no doubt.

Kincaid twisted his pillow around, trying to find a way it was comfortable. Poor little kid. Usually in his work, he had little to do with the victims and rarely saw them for more than a second after the case closed. This case was not like that. In fact, nothing about this case was normal.

The case was brought to the FBI by a Boston Special Detective, Ian Harrington. There had been an apparent suicide who was buried in an indigent cemetery there. Simple enough, until a family member called and questioned the circumstances of the man's death. Before long, it turned into a multi-state fiasco with big money in off-shore accounts and unmarked graves in backyards. There was an old crazy evangelist and his son-in-law, a deranged tough guy with visions of grandeur named Ezekiel.

There were connections of this lunatic evangelist to Texas where Kincaid worked. So he was the lucky devil upon whose desk the case file finally landed. It also turned out to be his last case. Because of his injuries, he was unceremoniously retired from the FBI.

The case had also taken the career of Harrington, the young Boston detective in his early thirties. Kincaid wasn't a religious man, but he thanked God that it hadn't happened to him when he was as young as Harrington. It was bad enough at his age.

One of the crazy preacher's kids, Zach Jeffries had come down to Texas with Harrington. He was a pediatrician, probably a good calling for a petunia like him. He was a good enough sort, but was pretty soft by Kincaid's standards.

The psycho that shot Kincaid was married to Zach's lunatic sister. Naomi was a real piece of work to Kincaid's mind. She is the one who shot Harrington. The abused and neglected little girl, Miriam, was the daughter of Ezekiel and Naomi.

Kincaid woke up in the hospital after surgery in his bed trying to figure out what he was going to do with himself. If only he had his revolver, it would've been an easy decision. Who in the hell came down the hall? Petunia!

He had come to the hospital to see Miriam. He was going to take care of her since he was next of kin. Harrington was also in the same hospital. Harrington had become Zach's friend, so it was logical that he would see him.

Kincaid almost choked when he looked up and saw Zach peering at him from his bedside. "Petunia?"

"Yah, how yah doing?" Zach had asked, with a friendly smile.

That was just the beginning of the surprises that followed. Zach and his friends all came to visit and keep vigil with him as well as Harrington and Miriam. They were always there and watched over him like he had been a member of their family forever. He never saw the beat of it.

When Kincaid developed a bleeder in his lungs which required another surgery, he thought he was going to die. For the first time, he felt mortal and he didn't like it one damned bit. It wasn't a pleasant situation for a man who managed to keep his life small enough to easily control.

Carl had married when he was a young man. He loved his Cecelia. She was way out his league and he knew it. For some unknown reason, she loved him. They were very happy until the car wreck a year later that took her life. He never got over loving her. He knew he would never find another woman like her again, ever.

He threw himself into his work and the FBI eagerly used his time. The next thing he knew, the years had gone by. It was no longer that he would never find another Cecelia; hardly any woman would look at him twice. He never owned a home, drove a beat up old car, his immediate family had all passed away and all he had his demanding job. He thinning hair was almost white and he wore it in a short cut. His broad shoulders had migrated south and stopped above his waste. His brown eyes hid behind bifocals and his smile had long since disappeared, replaced by a sarcastic scoff.

He always laughed at people who had hobbies or interests; thinking it a waste of time. He had a big bank account and a few worn suits. Pretty pathetic, but none of that bothered him until he thought he was going to die.

Kincaid reached the lowest point in his life that day in that Louisiana hospital. He realized he had no one to leave anything to or even take care of his funeral arrangements. He didn't think it really mattered. Only a handful of loyal coworkers would even attend, if they weren't too busy.

Then the Petunia showed up. Zach teased him and cajoled him, but mostly treated him like a real friend. Having figured what kind of a guy he was, Kincaid thought he was about as honest as anyone could be. Watching how he took responsibility for his niece, he figured he could rely on him. They talked for only short time before he gave his power of attorney to Zach to handle medical decisions or to bury him if need be. He didn't figure it was a smart thing to do, but he didn't waste time checking the condition of the only life-line thrown to him.

During his recovery, he got to know Zach's friends. There was this preacher, Byron Ellison and his best friend, Elton Schroeder. He also met Suzy, Zach's fiancée and Ruthie his sister. Then he met Detective Harrington's family; Maureen, his mother and Matthew his priest brother. All fine people to be sure, but way too goody two-shoes for his blood. They were mostly petunias, except for Maureen. He thought she was like a rose in the petunia patch.

After ten days, the doctors announced that he could go home in a week or two, but that he would be in a wheelchair and on oxygen for some time. He couldn't be on his own and needed care. He told Zach he'd go to a nursing home, but Zach wouldn't hear of it.

Zach and Elton drove to Texas and closed up his apartment. Then they shipped all his things to North Dakota where they lived. The rest of the family took Miriam home when she was well enough to travel, but Zach and his sister stayed behind with him. That was really something. He couldn't believe anyone but a real sap would do that.

As soon as he was well enough to travel, they took him to North Dakota where he was going to live with Elton's family until he healed up enough to be on his own. Zach had a second floor apartment so Kincaid couldn't be there. As much as he hated being an invalid, he had to say it was damned nice of these folks to care for him. They were still a bunch of petunias, but a decent sort of folks. He hoped the petunia-ness wouldn't rub off on him too much before he got well enough to leave. He wanted to go back to his non-life.

His roommate, Bert coughed again and this time did knock his oxygen mask loose. Kincaid clambered out of bed and over to Bert. Kincaid slipped the mask back over the old man's face.

Bert opened his eyes and said, "Mighty kind of you. Now get your ass back to bed so you don't fall over. Damned certain I can't pick you up."

"You got it," Kincaid chuckled. The Old Goat, as most the folks in the household called him, was certainly not known for his kindly manner, but he had a lot of spunk. Kincaid liked that.

Back in his bed, Kincaid watched stupid Elmer still digging his heart out after that gopher. 'Wonder how long he is going to dig before it dawns on him he might as well give it up?' He closed his eyes and drifted off to sleep.

2

Carl woke up again when he heard Elton's daughter, Pepper's alarm go off. He got himself dressed before he went out to the kitchen in his wheelchair. He knew the whole family except the Grandpas would be rumbling around.

He wheeled into the kitchen and all the morning confusion. Grandma Katherine gave him a big smile, "Coffee?"

"Yes please," Kincaid said and drove his chair over by the table to the place they deemed his spot.

He saw Elton putting cream and sugar in his coffee mug and criticized him, "Hell Magpie, you got so much garbage in there, I'm surprised you can taste the coffee."

Elton never even looked up from his culinary task, "I've made more and better coffee in my life than you have ever tasted, Kincaid. North Dakota Lutherans might not know much, but we do know our coffee."

Kincaid loved bantering with him. Elton was quick and a formidable foe in the insult department, though Kincaid thought he still held the edge in sarcasm.

Elton finished fixing up his coffee and looked at him, "Why are you bellied up to the table already? Think you'll get fed before the rest of us?"

"Might just at that," Kincaid grinned. "You're foolish to leave me in the house with your women."

Elton smirked, "Not in the least. There is no way my Nora's head could be turned when she has someone as dapper as me?"

Nora raised her eyebrows, "Keep it up and you both are going to be paying room and board to Elmer!"

"Wow, Mom!" Pepper giggled, "You got guys fighting over you. Pretty neat!"

"And neither one of them are worth putting on makeup for," Grandma stated.

Carl looked at Elton, "These women get vicious, right off. Don't they?"

"Yup, that they do. It's wise to keep agreeable around them," Elton nodded.

"Oh Dad," Kevin joked as he came in, "You're as disagreeable as they come. Mom hasn't kicked you out yet."

"She's come mighty close, Son," Elton grinned, "Mighty close."

"How's the wheelchair working for you, Kincaid?" Kevin asked as he checked the battery connection. "I figure it needs to be recharged every other day or so, depending on how much you run around. See this gauge? When it is at this point, you need to recharge it. I got a spare battery all charged up for you in the garage."

"Thanks Kevin," Kincaid said, "You did a fine job on fixing this up for me. Sure beats having to use my arms."

"Well, I can't see how turning the wheels would be good for your bad arm pulling on those blood vessels. Anyway, if you have any trouble with it, let me know. I might not be able to fix it but I can help you feel bad about it!"

Kevin was a good kid. Kincaid got a bang out of him. He was the second oldest of Elton and Nora's kids. He was a real clown, but he had a serious side and was quite responsible. He constantly teased his sweet young wife to near torment but she just smiled at him. Carrie was expecting their first child and Kevin was like an old hen keeping an eye on her; however, that didn't stop him from giving her grief every minute. They lived in the house that used to be Engelmann's. It was situated between the church parsonage and Elton's place. They came over twice a day to help with chores. Some of the milk cows were theirs and they shared in the milk, cream and eggs.

Pretty soon the milkers headed off to the barn and Carl rested at the table while the ladies made breakfast.

"Bert coughed quite a bit toward morning. Does he always do that?" Carl commented.

Nora listened carefully. Elton's wife was a beautiful, graceful woman with a gentle, thoughtful nature. She gave him a worried look, "No, he's probably getting pneumonia again. He just got over it. Poor man. His only lung has put up with a lot over the years. It must be mostly scar tissue by now. Did he keep you awake? Maybe we need to rearrange things so that you can get more rest."

"Not necessary," Kincaid returned, "It don't bother. This way, I can keep an eye on him. Sometimes he coughs his oxygen mask off, I put it back on."

"You don't need to do that. You are here to recuperate, not be a nursemaid to someone," Nora objected. "We'll move you."

"No way. I'm not an invalid," Kincaid said abruptly. "It makes more sense for me to do it. Hell, I'm a few feet away from him. You guys are wandering around all night as it is. I heard Elton up with Lloyd again."

Grandma nodded, "That's almost a nightly occurrence. Elton has the best luck talking him into going back to bed of anyone. He ignores me, though he listens to Zach pretty well."

"Where is that petunia?" Kincaid asked.

"He had surgery early this morning. It'll be good for him to get back to work. He can't leave his practice too long you know," Nora explained. "A lot of folks count on him. He is an excellent pediatric surgeon. He'll be back tomorrow if his patient is doing okay."

Grandma Katherine, a tiny little lady who was about four foot ten, put some boiled potatoes with their jackets on, in front of Kincaid. "Here young man, earn your keep. You peel these potatoes so I can fry them for breakfast."

The former FBI agent's mouth must have dropped open a foot. "Huh?"

Grandma giggled, "Here, I'll show you. Put the peelings in this bowl and the potatoes in this one. They're easier to peel boiled than raw."

Kincaid picked up a potato reluctantly and took a knife in the other hand, looking very bewildered. She took it from him without a word, showed him how to do it and handed the potato and knife back to him.

Kincaid finished the potato and gave himself a congratulatory smile. "Bet Magpie doesn't do as good of a job as me. I bet he's never peeled a potato in his life."

Grandma Katherine patted his back, "Sorry, you'd be wrong. He is actually a very good cook. But with a little practice, you could become a fine cook yourself."

"What if I don't want to?" Kincaid asked.

"There's always dry cereal!" Katherine giggled.

Kincaid finished the potatoes and then even chopped the onion for the fried potatoes. He watched as the women fixed a breakfast of ham, scrambled eggs, fried potatoes and homemade bread toasted. They had four kinds of homemade jellies and canned peaches.

"You guys have so much food, I can't believe it." Kincaid pointed out.

Katherine put the plates around the table, "Well, Sonny, everyone works and needs a lot of energy. You have to put fuel in the tractor, or you don't get much plowing done."

Kincaid nodded, "Makes sense."

The kitchen door opened and the entire crew came back in the house. Kev and Carrie took off for home right away, but Pastor Byron and his little girl stayed for a cup of coffee. Byron's youngest daughter Ginger came over every day to milk cows because it was good exercise for her hands. She had to rebuild the muscles that had been destroyed by chemical burns earlier that year. The tomboy had trouble getting around on her own because her vision was also damaged by the chemicals. Her peripheral vision was very poor and her long distance vision fluctuated daily. However, it was beginning to improve.

Ginger went right over to Kincaid, "Guess what? I talked to Harrington, Badge 11918 last night on the phone. He called to talk to Ruthie, but I got to say hi. He said to tell you hello. So, hello."

"Well, hello back to him," Kincaid smiled. "Is Harrington ready to come out for Zach and Suzy's wedding?"

"I think so," Ginger was very serious and sat on the chair next to Kincaid, "But mostly, he just wanted to talk to Ruthie. I think he wants her to be his bouncer."

"Bouncer?" Kincaid was curious, "What's a bouncer?"

"You know, like my Daddy always says to my Mommy, 'I want to bounce something off you.' You know, like Suzy and Zach do. I think that is what Ruthie and Badge 11918 are going to do. Did you have a bouncer?"

Kincaid was chuckling, "Yah. Long time ago."

"What happened to her?" Ginger asked Kincaid still unaware he was about to be interrogated by the best.

"She died in a car accident."

"Oh, that's sad." Ginger looked at him seriously, "Did you cry a lot?"

Kincaid was taken back but answered, "Yes, I guess I probably did."

The little girl patted his hand, "That's okay, as long as you didn't be a blubber baby. I don't like them much."

"Neither do I," Kincaid had to agree.

"But if you don't cry at all, you get filled up with tears and then your nose runs and you get a headache," she announced. "So, did you find another bouncer?"

"No, I didn't, but I didn't look for one either," he answered with a grin.

"Ginger," Pastor Byron reminded his daughter, "Mind your own business. You shouldn't be so nosey."

Ginger was indignant and shook her mop of mahogany curls, "I am not being nosey. I'm his friend and I need to know his stuff. I'll tell him my stuff so he knows. Okay, Mr. Kincaid? I just turned seven and I wrecked my hands and eyes pretty good. Smitty fixed them up. I call him Smitty, and so do Andy and Uncle Darrell but everyone else calls him Zach."

"Not everyone else," Kincaid laughed. "I don't."

"You don't?" Ginger was surprised, "Do you call him Smitty, too?"

"No. I call him Petunia."

Ginger rolled her eyes, "That's a silly name. Why do you call him that?"

"Because, ah, I guess because he's not rough and tough."

"Well who wants their friend to be tough? I want my friends to be nice. Don't you?" she looked at him quizzically.

"I don't have many friends," Kincaid explained.

"I can see why. You need friend lessons and then maybe you will get another bouncer. Then you won't be so grumpy all the time," the little girl said matter-of-factly.

"Watch it Ginger," her Dad said, "You be careful so you don't hurt his feelings."

"She's not," Kincaid said, "But she sure doesn't beat around the bush."

"Why would I want to beat a bush?" Ginger went on, "I would rather dig in the dirt. I love to dig. Me and my little brother Charlie dug a lot until my Dad put the kibosh on it. Did you ever have a kibosh on something? That means if you do it; you get killed. When my Dad kills us, he makes us think; but when Uncle Elton does, he skins us. And if you are really, really in trouble, he will skin you alive! But I know a secret. He only skins on Tuesdays, so just be really careful that day." Her hazel eyes got huge as she explained everything to the man. "And Aunt Nora just thinks about it, but sometimes you don't get any treats while she is thinking and my Mommy, she goes to her wits end! When she gets there, she has red lights come out of her eyes like the devil! Then it is usually a good idea to find Uncle Darrell and he'll save you. He is mommy's brother and he knows how to get her back from the wit's end. If you forget any of this, you can call me or my brother Charlie. We will explain it to you again. Right now, Charlie is pretty busy teaching Miriam. You know, she doesn't know about any of this stuff either and she is full of jelly."

By now, Kincaid was dying trying to control his laughter, "Full of jelly? How's that?"

Ginger nodded spoke with great gravity, "Mommy and Daddy both said we have to be careful of her because she is frad jelly."

Byron corrected her, "You mean fragile, Ginger. Now take a deep breath and let Mr. Kincaid relax a minute."

"I don't think he wants to relax Daddy. He has a lot of work to do before he can get over being so grumpy. Mr. Kincaid, do you know anything about dirt? I'm a pretty good thinker about dirt. I have collected dirt from all over the place. You know, it is all different. I learned about new dirt called silk the other day."

Elton interjected, "I think you mean silt, Ginger."

"Yah, that's it. I can remember because it is smooth like silt, silk." Ginger explained.

"Come on Ginger," her Dad said. "We had better get home because Mom will have breakfast. Thanks for the cream and eggs, Nora."

"How are things going at your house?" Nora asked.

"Fine," Byron replied, "Miriam had a nightmare again last night, but I got her calmed down and then Ruthie rocked her until she went to sleep. It wasn't a real bad one and she was all over it within twenty minutes."

"I wonder how long that will go on," Elton asked.

"Don't know. Seems to have no connection with how her day goes," Byron observed. "Hopefully, it will cease soon."

"Do you have bad dreams, Mr. Kincaid?' Ginger asked, "I only do once in a while. Once I dreamed that Charlie and I were digging in

Daddy's cemetery and he caught us and took away our shovels for a whole year! Then I cried."

Kincaid chuckled, "I heard you guys did dig in the cemetery once. Is that true?"

"Oh yes," Ginger spoke in a loud whisper. "Did you know that my Daddy can get so mad that his lips turn blue? I would have been a goner if Uncle Elton hadn't come along."

"He saved you, huh?" the man laughed.

"Yah, Uncle Elton laughed and called me his gopher. I think that Daddy was mad at him then, but they don't ever get too mad at each other. Not like Charlie and I do. We get really mad sometimes. Mommy and Daddy said we can't do that to Miriam until she gets over her jelly. I mean frad jelly. But then I think we can. So we are trying to remember everything, so that when she is over it, we can give her the business."

"Ginger, Ginger," her Dad said, "Come on home. I think that hot cocoa went straight to your head. You are all wound up."

Ginger looked at him very seriously, "Daddy, what's it like when I'm not wound?

"I don't know. I've never seen it," Byron took his daughter by the hand.

3

Pepper and Elton brought the Grandpas to the table and soon everyone held hands in grace. Pepper said it this morning and they all ended with amen. Kincaid had never been in a family that actually said grace before every meal. He was amazed but very glad all he had to do was say amen at the end.

When the food was passed, Grandma announced Kincaid had helped make the fried potatoes. Annie tasted them right away and commended his fine work. Pepper thought he should be the potato salad maker. Elton just sat their grinning from ear to ear.

"What's so funny, Magpie?" Kincaid asked, wondering about the wisdom of delving into it.

"Nothing," Elton smirked, "Will you be quilting this afternoon?"

"Shut up, Schroeder!" Kincaid blustered.

"You probably shouldn't be talking to my son that way," Grandpa Lloyd said, "I'd have to get mad at you. I know he can't fix a car worth a damn, but he really tries hard. Say you're sorry and we can forget it."

Kincaid looked at the confused old man and then smiled, "I'm sorry, Lloyd. Elton, I'm sorry you are a jackass."

Grandpa Lloyd looked at Grandpa Bert, "Did he say he was sorry or not? I'm not sure."

"Close as it will get from that grouch." Grandpa Bert tattled. "Hey, Nora, he comes over to my bed when I'm sleeping and stares at me. Do you think that is normal? Maybe he needs a head doctor or something."

'"He was checking to make sure your oxygen was on. You're coughing a lot last night," she answered. "He was helping you."

"Help? You think that's help," Bert grumbled. "Well that's your opinion. I'm not so sure it is doing me any favors."

"I suppose I could unplug the machine," Kincaid pointed out. "It would be a lot more pleasant around here."

"Maybe for you. What makes you think the rest of them like you any better than me?" Bert snapped back.

Elton started to laugh, "You both got a good point there. But neither of you are going anywhere and we're all stuck up with it. So cope. I think you guys need a break from each other. What do you want to do today, Kincaid? Want to get out of the house for a while?"

"Yah, might be a good thing," Kincaid glared at Bert. "I need some fresh air. What's everyone doing today?"

"I have to go to work this afternoon," Annie said. "This morning I'm going over to Ellison's with Pepper to do the girls therapy before she leaves for work."

"I have to be to work at ten," Pep explained. "Chris will pick me up from work. I won't be home for dinner. We're going out with Eddie and Denise for burgers and a movie."

"I'll hitch up the team to take you to town," Grandpa Lloyd offered through his Alzheimer's confusion. "Me and Katherine will go along. Don't you think Katherine? We haven't been to a picture show in a long time."

"Thank you Lloyd, but I'm not feeling up to it tonight. Otherwise I'd love to," Katherine patted her husband's hand.

Lloyd smiled sympathetically to his wife, "I know, Katie. I'll stay home with you. You kids go on without us. The wife needs me, but I'll have Elton hitch up the team for you. Right, Elton?"

"I'd be happy too, Lloyd," Elton nodded.

"There Pepper, don't fret," Grandpa Lloyd reassured her. "We'll try to make it when Katherine is feeling better."

"Thank you Grandpa," Pepper smiled, "You always take good care of us kids."

The old man sighed, "I do my best."

Kincaid was lost in thought. This watching out for others thing must have been something that man had done all his life. No matter how befuddled he got, he still tried to make sure he was watching out for his family. No wonder Elton thought so much of him.

Then Grandpa Bert spoke up, "I'm going to Merton today."

"Why is that, Bert?" Nora asked, "Do you need something?"

"Earplugs. I can't sleep with this guy snoring all night in my room," Bert was relentlessly determined to get Kincaid into hot water. "Sounds like a buzz saw. Kept me up half the night!"

Kincaid was going to smart back to him and then thought of how Elton handled things. He decided to see if it would work. "I'm sorry, Bert. I won't snore tonight."

Bert was shocked, "Well, I'm glad we got that straightened out! I'd appreciate it. But mind you, this is your last chance!"

Kincaid thought to himself, 'feisty old fart', but said, "Got it."

He was pleased that it did stifle the old man's grumping for a bit.

"I'm going to the shop today. I have to help Kev with that transmission. You can ride along if you want, Kincaid," Elton offered.

"It would be better if he rode with us over to Ellison's. I could put your therapy in with Ginger and Miriam's. We could have a full time exercise class. I know the little girls would like it. Then you wouldn't be gone so long like if you went with Dad," Pepper asserted.

"Or you can stay home. I can show you how to snap green beans. Nora and I are going to be storing up a pile of them and could use the help," Grandma suggested.

"I was thinking of taking a nap," Kincaid raised his eyebrow.

"Right after everything else is done," Grandma said. "Now, let's get moving around here. We are burning daylight."

"CREEACK!" Elton. laughed making the motion of a whip cracking.

Within an hour, Kincaid found himself in Pastor Ellison's dining room as part of the exercise class. Mortification would not exactly explain how he felt about it. Humiliation was in there too, and nausea. A lot of nausea and total embarrassment!

Annie and Pepper had the little girls, Miriam and Ginger joined by Ginger's mom, Marly and Miriam's aunt, Ruthie. They were all doing exercises. The only man in sight was Kincaid. If one of those girls, just one, had worn tights and a tutu, he would've died. Happily and eagerly.

They did the hand exercises for Ginger. Mostly it was moving their fingers and wrists and it wasn't too bad. Then they moved on to Miriam's exercises for her hip. The exercises were bad enough, but Kincaid couldn't even do most of them. That was the worst thing in the world for him, but the little girls loved it!

Miriam had been badly battered as a child so was terrified of almost everything, but she broke into a good old belly laugh when Kincaid couldn't lift his leg very high. He was happy to see her giggling, but wished she was making fun of Magpie or Petunia instead of him.

'Boy is Petunia going to get a piece of my mind when he gets out here! What the hell was he thinking? Maximum security would be a step up from this! General population wearing a tee shirt saying I was an FBI agent!'

They did the exercises for his arm. The little girls watched him as Pepper helped him go through the paces. Ginger at least made the attempt to be nice about it, but Miriam was too little and just plain giggled. She giggled so much, she got the hiccups.

When the 'exertorture', as Kincaid anointed it, was over, Marly offered them all a glass of ice tea, although he was developing a taste for cyanide. By the time Byron came over for a break from the church and greeted everyone, Carl could barely be civil.

Miriam always listened and mimicked what others did. She heard Maureen call Kincaid an old coot, and so she called him Coot. He wouldn't allow anyone else to do it, except her and Maureen. After all, he had to maintain some dignity. He would think about it later and figure out what shred of dignity there was left to maintain.

Byron asked everyone how their exercises went and Miriam pointed to Kincaid and giggled, "Coot."

Byron grinned and asked what that was about.

"Never mind," Kincaid said, "Just some dumb kid talk."

"Oh no," Ginger reminded him and then told her father every detail with great flourish, "Don't you remember when you tried to lift your leg and all you could do was grunt? Miriam got the giggles. Daddy, you should have seen her. She got the hiccups, she giggled so much."

Byron noticed Kincaid's discomfort, "Well, it is okay for Miriam to giggle because she is too little to understand but you need to remember that sometimes a person's body doesn't work so well when it gets hurt. Right, Ginger? You shouldn't laugh at someone."

Ginger thought a minute and then turned to Kincaid, "I'm sorry Mr. Kincaid. I was naughty. I won't laugh at you anymore." Then she patted his hand, "If you keep practicing, you'll be able to lift your leg high like a big kicker!"

Kincaid had to admit he was touched by her attempt at encouragement but still would have preferred to simply forego the entire experience. "Don't worry about it, Kid."

He was glad when they pulled back into the yard of the farm. He felt like going in the house and picking a fight with Bert. But when he got inside, Bert was already taking his nap.

"Not doing so good?" Kincaid asked.

"Not at all. Chris stopped out and listened to his chest. He left a message for Zach and they're going to get a different antibiotic," Nora worried. "I hate it when he gets so sick. Are you sure that you don't want to move out of the room until he gets well?"

"No. I can keep an eye on him this way. Just tell me what to do."

"I can tell you what to do," Grandma Katherine grinned. "Get cleaned up. If you need help with your shower, the girls can help you. Or we can call Marty. Then you can snap beans."

"No, I can manage my shower on my own," the man answered, and raised his eyebrow to the diminutive lady, "May I ask, what rank were you in the Army?"

Without a flinch, Grandma said, "Commandant!"

Kincaid took his shower and had to admit that was about all the energy he could muster. He was glad Kevin had put the battery on his wheelchair. He checked on Bert who was sleeping soundly. Then he went out to the kitchen.

He parked at the table across from Annie. Piled on the table between the two of them was at least a bushel of green beans. Pepper came bouncing through and showed Kincaid how to snap the beans and then kissed his cheek. "Have a good day."

Then she told everyone goodbye and ran off to her car.

About twenty minutes later, Nora and Grandma came back in with another bushel basket of green beans. They dumped them on the table.

Grandma picked up a bowl from Kincaid and he asked what she was going to do with them. "I'm going to blanche them. That is kind of like cook them a little and then plunge them in ice water. Then put them in freezer bags. When the cool off, we'll freeze them for the winter. I think we'll be canning the next batch though, huh Nora?"

"This pile should last you all winter, huh?" Kincaid asked as he motioned to the stack of vegetables before him on the table.

"No. We'll do this again as soon as they are ready. You know, there are a lot of mouths to feed around here. Keith and Darlene will be home in a couple weeks. Kev and Carrie get some, Ellisons and then all of us. It all adds up. But beans grow good and we can get a lot of them," Grandma explained.

"I guess, huh?" Kincaid muttered.

Annie looked at him and smiled. "You'll get used to it. I don't mind doing beans, but I sure get tired of tomatoes!"

"I love to eat it, but I hate putting up corn," Nora said.

"Is there anything you guys don't do?" Kincaid was getting worried.

"Yah," Nora teased, "We don't do any seafood."

Kincaid gave her a dirty look. "Humph, I thought Magpie was lucky to get a looker like you, but you're as bad as he is."

"I know," Nora smiled sweetly, "Aren't we lucky we found each other!"

Annie giggled, "You might as well give up. You won't win that argument, Carl."

4

It was about one o'clock when the table was set for lunch. Annie left with Marty, her coworker, for Bismarck. Elton had just come home to eat. The Grandpas were setting up to the table when Elton came in and gave his wife a kiss. Within minutes, they had all said grace and were passing the food. Nora had made some vegetable soup to go with Grandma's hot rolls.

"How was your morning, everyone?" Elton asked.

"Pretty good. We got a couple bushels of green beans frozen," Nora explained. "They all had their exercises and Marty was good enough to come by this morning to help with the Grandpas showers. Chris stopped by and he'll be out this afternoon to bring Bert's new prescription. How was your morning?" Nora asked.

"Good. Got that transmission done," Elton grinned. "Kevin and Rod went out to Sandvahl's to work on their tractor. It was Ken and I in the shop this morning. He is really a good kid. The more I get to know him, the more I like him."

"Is he the Preacher's kid?" Kincaid asked.

"Yes, the oldest. He just turned seventeen," Elton explained. "He said that Miriam is doing okay, but still curls up at the drop of a hat. Katie read her a story and the kid in the storybook was coloring with a crayon. When they turned to that page and she saw the picture, Miriam started to shake and curled up in the fetal position just like that. I guess Marly had her hands full to get her to calm down. I wonder what is with the crayons."

Kincaid raised his eyebrows, "Doubt we really want to know. I can about guarantee that. I wish those people could have been made to pay for what they did to her."

"Yah," Elton agreed, "I'm sure glad it isn't my job to figure out what they deserve because I couldn't think of anything bad enough."

Lloyd was extremely quiet and after a while, Elton asked, "What is it, Lloyd? What is bothering you?"

"I don't know where Katherine is. Do you think she left me?" The old man asked, nearly in tears. "I didn't mean to make her sore at me."

"I'm here, Lloyd," Katherine got up and gave him a hug. "I'm not sore at you. I am right here."

Lloyd looked at Elton, "Do you think this is really my Katie? I don't think she is."

Elton smiled, "Oh yes, Lloyd. She is your Katherine. I think that you just need to clean your glasses, okay?"

He looked at his wife, "I'm sorry. I need new glasses. Yah, now that you mention it, you are my Katie. She is a fine one, you know. Best wife a guy could have. Have you met her, Mister?" He asked Kincaid.

"Yes, I did, Mr. Engelmann." Kincaid answered, "She is really a nice woman."

"She isn't a woman," Lloyd explained, "She's my wife."

"That's right, Lloyd," Kincaid agreed. "She's a fine wife."

"Sometimes I get mixed up," Lloyd explained, "Isn't that right, Elton?"

"Yes, Lloyd, sometimes you do," Elton agreed, "But that is just because you have so many people to take care of. It would mix anyone up."

Lloyd frowned, "Don't I do a good job?"

"You do a great job, Lloyd," Elton reassured him. "You always do a great job."

Kincaid thought about it while he listened to them talk. Most of his life, he had dealt with people who only took advantage of everyone around them. They never seemed to care or show remorse. Now here was a fellow who spent his life caring about others, and he was worried and apologizing. What a mixed up mess! Maybe a guy was better off not giving a damn about anyone. 'Doesn't seem like a good pay off,' he considered.

"Oh, Honey," Nora said to her husband, "Jenny called and asked if we would babysit for Matthew tomorrow night. She and Danny want to take Byron and Marly out to dinner. I told her I'd call her back after lunch."

Elton grinned, "Tell her of course. Ken asked me to ask you if it would be okay if they stayed over here tomorrow night, because Danny and Jenny are taking out his mom and dad! I told him I'd let him know!"

Everyone laughed and then Nora said, "You know Elton; I don't think our house is any too big!"

"Just how many kids are staying over?" Kincaid asked with concern. He was never very crazy about kids, and he didn't think he wanted to be around a houseful. He was already thinking he might get a headache and require confinement to his room.

"Oh, not that big a deal, Kincaid," Elton chuckled. "There will be baby Matthew. How old is he? Three months or so. Then Miriam, Charlie, Ginger, Katie and Ken. Just the Ellison kids."

"Man, that is like six kids!" Kincaid explained. "That is a houseful!"

"Actually, though," Elton said, "Ruthie will come over too so she can help with Miriam. She is a little nervous to be with her alone yet. Don't worry. The Ellison's kids have been here so much, this is like their second home."

Kincaid looked at his coffee cup, "No wonder you freeze so many beans."

Grandma giggled, "You're so funny. I'm thinking we need ham and potato salad tomorrow night and you, my friend, can plan on cutting up the potatoes tomorrow for me."

Kincaid smiled with a hint of pride, "I'm pretty good at it, aren't I?"

Grandma grinned, "Why you are so good at it, I'll get the eggs ready so you can cut them up too."

"Well, gang, as much as I love you all, I really need to get back to work," Elton smiled, "I can help you get the Grandpas down for their nap. What about you and I plan on either going to the shop to work on the airplane or me beating you in rummy when I get home, Kincaid? Unless there's something else that you want to do."

Kincaid's mind was still pondering the house full of kids, "Whatever, Magpie. I have to take a nap though. I can't believe how tired I am."

"You did a lot this morning," Nora pointed out. "Carl, don't let us push you too much. If you're tired, just tell us."

"No Nora, I didn't do too much," Kincaid decided. "It's just that I haven't done anything in so long. Thanks Elton, I'll be ready when you get back."

Elton clapped him on the shoulder, "You need to get your rest."

That evening about four-thirty, Elton came into the house from his day's work. He changed his clothes and then asked Kincaid if he'd decided what he wanted to do.

"I guess I'll go look over that airplane," Kincaid suggested. "I'd kind of like to get some fresh air."

"Sounds good," Elton grinned and then he gave his wife a big kiss before he left the kitchen. "Hey, we should try you going down the ramp by yourself. If you can master it, then you can go out on your own. I don't imagine that you like being cooped up all day."

"Yah, I'd like that," Kincaid said, "But if I get stuck with my chair or something, the ladies couldn't pull me out!"

"No, but they would call us to give you a hoist. Unless you have been extremely ornery, in which case, we might just leave you!" the mechanic joked.

"You really are a jackass, Magpie."

"I'm glad you noticed. Well, let's see if you can maneuver the ramp."

Kincaid was able to get the chair down the ramp without tipping, but Elton suggested they put an old mattress at the end of it, in case he got too much momentum and became airborne. He had a good laugh over it, but Carl didn't think it was funny.

Kincaid followed the new sidewalk to the garage and then he noticed the concrete was fresh. "How long has this been in?"

"Oh about a week," Elton answered.

Kincaid stopped and gave him a dirty look, "Did you do it for me? Why did you do that?"

Elton responded, "Because I didn't want to carry your sorry ass."

"This is ridiculous." Kincaid started to expound, "I hardly know you."

Elton raised his eyebrows, "Believe me, if we'd known you better, we wouldn't have done it! Quit stewing over it. We can use a good walkway anyhow."

"Magpie, you're an idiot!"

"I kind of like hearing that," Elton explained, "Usually everyone says I am crazy."

"I imagine you have to get your compliments where you can," Kincaid poked.

"Too bad you don't even get that choice, huh?" Elton chided.

In the shop, Kincaid noticed that Elton had made an area where the wheelchair would fit. "This is your stanchion."

"Stanchion? What's a stanchion?" Kincaid frowned.

"It the place where a cow stands to get milked! Man, you need to get to the barn sometime! I wonder how we could get the wheelchair in there."

"Don't strain yourself thinking about it. That's nothing I have any desire to do." Kincaid was definite about that.

"You'll miss out then. Hey, you want a soda? I think I have Coke and Seven Up. Hope you like one of those?"

"I like Coke."

Elton opened two bottles and put them on the table, "Here you go."

"So, what do we do?" Kincaid asked.

"Well, we first figure out what we want to work on, read the instructions and then try to do it. Pretty simple, really," Elton said. "Then after we mess it up, we start over again."

"Do we have to work on the same part?" Kincaid asked.

"Nope. Little Charlie has to help someone because I swear that kid had eighteen arms and fifty hands. Everyone else can do their own thing," Elton observed.

"Why don't you guys tell him to stay away from this? He is too little to do this stuff," Kincaid suggested.

Elton shrugged, "I suppose we could, but how would he ever learn? He's actually not too bad at it and he can find little parts better than I can because he has the eyes of an eagle."

Kincaid watched as Elton took the parts of a window and started piecing them together. In a minute or so, he felt Kincaid watching him and stopped what he was doing. He looked at the retired agent, "What?"

"Just wondering if you're real?" Kincaid went on, "I don't figure you out."

"Well, it's real simple, Kincaid," Elton took a swig of his soda pop. "I was a loner most of my life. I'd get off work, eat and drink. I had myself convinced I liked it that way. I think I knew I didn't. Then the good Lord came along and slapped me upside the head. Next thing, I had a wife, a pile of kids and loved it. Damnedest thing you ever did see! I was amazed how nice it is to matter to someone else."

"Sounds to me like some churchie-gobbledegook," Kincaid observed sarcastically, "All fluffy and sweet."

Elton never flinched, "Yah, I guess it does at that. Preacher Man always says doing God's work isn't for the weak. I used to laugh at him, but I've found out, he's right."

"Ah, yah," Kincaid grumped, "Going to those tea parties and talking all nice is tough work, alright?"

Elton smiled, "Wouldn't know. I never tried that. Can't really see me doing that, though. I can't hold my little pinky finger out very well."

Kincaid watched Elton mimic a queen's tea party and started to laugh. "I think I'll work on this rotor. Okay? Maybe I could take it up to the house?"

"I guess you could. I'll find a small box for you to put some tools in that you might need. I'll have to ask you to keep it away from Lloyd though. He'll help you. Believe me, he will really help you!"

"He isn't very good today, is he?" Kincaid asked, seriously.

"You know, Carl, I hate to see it, but he is failing. His bad days far outweigh his good. I wish you could have met him before his mind started to go. He was always full of baloney and good advice. Sometimes, you really had to shovel to separate it, though." Elton shook his head, "Makes me sad."

"He must have been quite a guy."

"When he has his good days, he still is," Elton changed the subject, "So Bert has pneumonia again, huh? Chris came out?"

"Yah, while we were at exertorture. Chris seems like a nice guy. How long have he and Pepper been going together?" Kincaid asked.

"About six months. It seems longer than that though. They really make a good couple," Elton beamed, "And Annie and Andy—now that's something?"

"Do I know Andy?" Kincaid asked.

"No, Andy is in Vietnam. Annie is his sweetheart."

"I thought she lived here or with Pepper," Kincaid said. "You people all live here, don't you?"

Elton laughed, "Kind of. It is because we are far enough from town, so that it makes more sense to stay over here. The girls share an apartment in town, but stay out here when they are off work. Marty, my nephew, lives in the house next to Kevin's but he works at the Fire Hall like Annie does. When they work, they have to stay there. Rest of the time, he lives out here."

"So what about Zach?" Kincaid asked.

"He has a place in town he's at when he's working or on call. When he is off call, he stays out here. He has a room here too." Elton said matter-of-factly.

"So, how many people live here?" Kincaid asked.

Elton laughed, "I can honestly say I have no idea. If they get up in the morning, we feed them."

"So Darlene and Keith are your kids too?"

"Yah, Keith is the oldest boy. He married Darlene Olson. The Olson's are neighbors and fine folks. We have known them forever. But the kids will only be staying here until they get their own place in town. They'll both be working in Bismarck, so they'll get a place there. But probably not right off, you know?"

"Yah. So, which of the boys are expecting?"

"Keith and Darlene are expecting end of October and Kevin and Carrie are in December," Elton grinned. "I can't wait!"

"Good grief, Magpie! You really are a goody two-shoes," Kincaid poked. "You can't like little babies."

"No, I'm not too crazy about the newborns because I might break them, but I love the toddlers," Elton grinned. "How 'bout you?"

"Neither."

"Okay," Elton grinned. "I suppose you like teenagers?"

"Oh Lord no! I have to say though, the preacher's teenagers seems pretty good," Kincaid had to concede.

"That they are," Elton agreed. "Speaking of which, we had better get your box together so that we can get up to the house before the Ellisons arrive. My Chicken Man should be showing up pretty soon to do his chores."

"You know, I think I won't take the things to the house. I can come down here to work if I want and I wouldn't want Lloyd to get into hot water."

"That's thoughtful," Elton said with a smile, "I appreciate that."

Kincaid gave him a dirty look and they worked together to put the lightweight tarp over the model airplane. Then they headed up to the house. When they arrived, Charlie was sitting on the front steps with his elbows on his knees and his head in his hands.

"What's up, Charlie?" Elton asked as he sat down beside Ellison's youngest, six-year old Charlie.

"Nothing," totally discouraged, the tow headed lad never moved but stayed staring at the dirt.

"Hmm. Looks like something to me."

"Uncle Elton, how long will it be before the girls get over being babied?"

"Don't know. Is it getting to you?" Elton asked sympathetically.

"Yah, I feel sorry for them and all that but I want to run and dig with somebody. I have to be so careful with them all the time. They're like baby chicks!" the little boy pointed out.

"Yah that can be a bearcat. I see that. Your Dad said that Pastor Marvin's boy, Clark was going to come over to dig with you."

"Only once in a while. He has to stay home with his little sister, too," the little boy was fighting back his tears. "A guy shouldn't have to put up with that."

Elton put his arm around the little kid, "No, by George, you really shouldn't have to. What can we do about it? Any ideas?"

"I need somebody who can dig, every day. And who doesn't curl up when you yell and can get dirty without hurting their hands and can see where they're going." Charlie laid out his criteria. "The Grandpas could, but they just want to talk about wars."

"I see the problem," Elton agreed. "It's a dilemma."

"If Zach was here, he could do stuff with me. Or Harrington. Sometimes, I get to do stuff with Uncle Darrell or Kevin, but they're so busy. I am kiboshed," Charlie shrugged in despair.

"What?" Uncle Elton asked.

"You know, like when Daddy put the kibosh on my digging," the little boy explained, "My whole summer is kiboshed. If I didn't have my Chicken Man chores, I wouldn't have anything to do."

"I think we had better fix that, huh?" Elton said. "Let's see. Let me think."

Kincaid had been watching the whole thing from his wheelchair on the sidewalk and listening intently. He had never considered a kid that age would think about what he would do. He thought they just did stuff without a thought.

"You could work for Aunt Nora and help her out?" Uncle Elton asked.

"I wouldn't mind Uncle Elton, but she'll give me made up work. I want to do stuff. Real stuff. You know?" The little boy tried to explain.

"Well," Kincaid cleared his throat, "You could help me. I want to go outside but I need someone to go with me so that if I get stuck they can get me some help. I can't go outside otherwise. I was going to have Elton hire me somebody."

He did get the young boy's attention, but then he shrugged. "Like what kind of stuff would your helper do? I get too figgetty if I have to stand around."

"It is fidgety," Elton said.

"I know, figgetty," Charlie said, "Do you want to go down the road or what? I'm not allowed on the road."

"I don't know Charlie," Kincaid said. "I never thought about it because I didn't know if I'd get anyone to go outside with me."

"What would we do?" Charlie asked.

"Well, we could do the Chicken Man chores and then maybe help the ladies with the garden. We could weed and pick some vegetables. I don't know if I could dig very well, but I could try."

That was all Charlie wanted to hear! He jumped up, ran to him and gave him the world's biggest hug. "I love you, Mr. Kincaid. I could help you dig! You won't cry if you get dirty, will you?"

"No, I don't think so."

The little boy just sighed in relief, "Oh that is so good. Uncle Elton, he won't cry! Isn't that great?"

"Well, I guess it is." Uncle Elton said, "We need to check out where he can go with his wheelchair though. If you guys are going to take care of the garden, he needs to get down the rows without getting stuck. I'll talk to Kevin and we'll figure out how to get you to the garden and back. I know the ladies would love the help. But Charlie, if you are going to be his helper, you have to listen to him. He'll be counting on you."

"I can do that. He can be part of our Secret Project Club, like you and Zach and Harrington and then we all stick together. Okay?" The little boy looked at Kincaid.

"Sounds good to me," Kincaid said.

"We will both be on 'promotion' at first," Charlie explained.

"'Promotion'?" Kincaid asked.

“He means probation,” Elton explained. “We have to run this by your parents and Aunt Nora, first. Okay?”

Charlie looked down and shuffled his feet, “Why? What if they say no?”

“Because that’s what us Agents do, Charles! We have to mind the rules and regulations. A good agent never dodges the hard stuff!” Kincaid said with authority.

“Okay, Agent Kincaid.” Charlie saluted.

“You got it, Agent Ellison.” Kincaid saluted back.

Elton followed the two up the ramp. Elton knew that whether he realized it or not, Kincaid had plunged into the abyss.

5

After a serious conversation with his father and Aunt Nora, the permission was granted for Charlie to be Kincaid's helper. It was decided that he come back over with them after morning exercises and then stay until evening chores. He would help Kincaid during the day.

They'd be responsible for the weeding in the garden, picking the vegetables for the ladies, gathering eggs and doing the Chicken Man chores. They had to help Grandma Katherine in the house with her chores. Then when they had time, they could dig. They also thought they might find more chores to do later.

Charlie had to remember that Kincaid had to take a nap though and that he couldn't do stuff that made him sick. The worst thing to happen was that Grandma Katherine got put in charge of their 'promotion'! She would be the one who would say what they could or could not do!

Neither Kincaid nor Charlie was happy about that, but decided that good agents never dodge the hard stuff, so they'd do it. Charlie did whisper to Kincaid though, that any day but Tuesday (Elton's skinning day), they could do stuff Grandma didn't know about after they got their work done, if she didn't see it. They decided it would be a good plan. Charlie would be Kincaid's Goer and Getter Guy.

That night after chores and everyone had gone home; Kincaid was watching television when Elton came out from putting the Grandpas to bed. Nora and Katherine were working on something in the sewing room. Kincaid was nervous and asked Elton if there was some coffee.

"Sure, come on, I'll pour you some."

In the kitchen, Kincaid stared at his coffee cup. "How? Ah-what? Ah, shit."

Elton grinned, "Don't worry about it. You'll do just fine."

"I don't know how to talk to kids," Kincaid pointed out. "I can't stand them! I have never been around a kid a whole day in my life! Whatever possessed me to open my big trap? It must be the blood loss."

"Yah, that's it, Kincaid." Elton grinned. "Look, a kid Charlie's age is just like you and me. They're shorter and their bodies are different, but for the most part they're just like us. Don't lie to them. It's okay to kid around, but don't feed them a line. Once they figure out you're lying, and they will, they'll have no respect for you. If you don't like what they do, try to tell them why. Don't just say 'don't do that'. Tell them you can't do that because you will get hurt—or whatever. They're more apt to remember it. You rest you can figure out yourself. Just remember, they haven't been on the planet as long as we have. Sometimes that is a bad thing and sometimes it's a good thing. You'll be good at it. I have seen the way you talk to Miriam, Ginger and Charlie. You know how to be. You're a natural."

"But I don't talk all sweet like parents do," Kincaid said.

Elton burst out laughing, "Neither do I. Neither does Bert or Lloyd. Kids don't care. They know how you feel, but you have to be honest. If you screw up or say the wrong thing, apologize right off."

"Don't they think you're weak?"

"Nah, they'll think, 'gee he's a grownup and he apologizes, so then it will be okay for me, too'. See?"

Car groaned, "I don't want to do it. It makes me dizzy just to think about it. Maybe you should just call Byron and tell him to make an excuse to Charlie. I think I was nuts to even say anything. I just felt so sorry for the poor kid today."

They were interrupted by the phone. Elton answered and then grinned, "Well, hello Maureen. How are you? And how is Harrington?"

Elton nodded and smiled. "I'm glad to hear that." Then he listened, "Well, of course, he's right here. He and I were just having a cup of coffee. Nice talking to you."

He handed the phone to Kincaid, "It's Maureen Harrington."

Kincaid was flabbergasted and took the phone. "I'm going to go see what the ladies are up to," Elton said as he dismissed himself to give Kincaid some privacy.

The man had to think a minute before he said anything. He was really astounded that she had called. Finally, he said, "Hello, Maureen. How are you?"

"I'm fine, you old Coot? How yah been? Are you behaving for the Schroeders or have you worn out your welcome yet? You know, it's been four days!"

Before long, Kincaid was telling her all about his day. He told her the whole thing, the exertorture class, the old guys, Miriam and then the business with Charlie.

"I just told Elton to call Byron and get me out of this thing with the boy. I don't know a damned thing about kids," Kincaid explained.

"You big fake!"

"What did you say?" Kincaid frowned.

"I said you're a big fake. You can talk to serial killers! Don't tell me you are stymied by a little boy! That is just a lame excuse," Mo wouldn't back down. "You just do what you know is the right thing and don't pull this stuff. You want everyone to be fussing over you."

"I do not. You just don't understand, Mo. This is different from anything in my whole life," Kincaid tried to explain.

Maureen responded with sympathy, "Carl, I do understand. It must be brutal for you. I wish I could be there to help you on the path but it isn't the way things are right now. You told me you were going to hang around until that little girl got well and I don't hear that she is yet. You peeled the apple, now you'd better eat it."

"You're an old nag," Kincaid retorted.

"Well, maybe if I was treated like a filly, I wouldn't be an old nag," Mo giggled.

"What?" Kincaid asked. "I don't understand a damn thing that anybody says anymore. I wish someone would just talk English."

"Okay. You quit whining; you work with Charlie and help Miriam with her exercises, even if you have to wear a tutu. Behave yourself and help those folks who are kind enough to take care of you. I'll be out there before long to check up on you and I don't want to be embarrassed to say I know you. Is that plain enough?"

Kincaid was quiet, "Well, yah. It could've been a little nicer though."

"Okay," Maureen said sweetly, "I'm coming out there and I hope you'll take me to this big wedding dance. So don't make me have to bring a date."

"Gee, I don't think that was much nicer," Kincaid chuckled, then he got serious, "You know, Mo, I might not be able to do a dance. I might be just sitting around."

"I think that if you keep exercising. going outside, practicing standing and stuff, you'll be able to do a lot. I don't expect to be doing a jig, you know. Whatever you can do, that'll be good enough, Carl."

"Thanks Mo. How is your kid?"

"Ian is fine. He's so lonesome for Ruthie it makes me sick, but he's really trying to get his strength back so he can go see her. She seems like a fine girl. Don't you think?"

"From what I have seen, she is. She works at the church and then helps with the kids and does that exertorture! Gad, Mo, there was Miriam, Ginger, Annie, Pepper, Ruthie and Marly and then me. It was horrible."

"The heaven and all the saints! You insane man! Most men would pay big bucks to be in an exercise class with young women! Here you feel sorry for yourself. Guess that's what I get for looking for a guy in intensive care! I need to find different hunting grounds!" Mo laughed with her infectious giggle.

Kincaid chuckled, "Okay. You got me. I'll be glad I am the only guy in exertorture. But when you get here, you have to join in the class."

"I really have to hang up now. You have no idea how much long distance costs and I am on a fixed income!" Mo backtracked like crazy.

"You heard me. You have to join in class."

"Honey child, women don't wear full body girdles in exercise class. Why if the elastic let go, I could blow the side of the house out!"

"Well, Mrs. Harrington, you better figure out a way," he grinned. "Hey Mo, thanks so much for calling."

"Anytime, Kincaid." She said softly, "I missed our talks."

"Me too. Every night while I am laying there listening to Bert snore, I think of you." His eyes just sparkled in teasing delight. He could just imagine her dander going up.

"You old Coot! I have half a notion to not call you ever again!"

"Please do, Maureen. It was great talking to you," Kincaid beamed.

"Yah, I know it was a thrill for you," then she said quietly. "Take care, Carl."

"You too, Maureen."

He sat a minute after he hung up and was surprised at how he felt. He had really enjoyed talking to her. Then the phone started to buzz. He wheeled over to the phone and tried to hang it up. Elton came out of the living room and hung it up for him.

"We should probably put the desk phone back in until you can reach this, huh? This isn't very helpful," Elton offered.

"Mo said I should be standing up more and walking pretty soon, huh? Did you hear how long I have to take it easy?"

"No, I didn't. Zach'll be home tomorrow night and he can answer you that. You know you can maybe use the walker in the house and only use the wheelchair outside."

"Yah. Mo thinks I'm going to take her to Petunia's wedding dance. I think she is dreaming."

"Nothing wrong with a dream, Kincaid." Elton said, "As long as you use common sense and Maureen is very sensible. She's a good gal."

"Yah, she is, huh? She said I should give it a try with Charlie. What do you really think, Magpie?"

"I think you should. If it doesn't work out, then so be it. At least you gave it a whirl. You know, Kincaid, things sometimes turn out good like we think they will but sometimes they turn out good like we didn't think they would."

Kincaid shook his head in dismay, as Nora came in the kitchen. "What is it Carl?"

"Does your husband ever make sense?"

Nora looked at him and grinned, "No. But he tries so hard. Don't burst his balloon, okay?"

Kincaid held his forehead, "You're all nuts."

The next morning, it was threatening rain. That could really mess up the plans for going outdoors. Kincaid was deep in thought. When he had the chance, he asked Elton, "What am I going to do if I'm stuck in the house with the kid all day? I'll just die."

Elton made a face, "I'd really rather you didn't. It might give him a complex. He felt pretty bad when two chickens almost died on his first day as Chicken Man."

Kincaid glared at him, "You know what I mean."

"Yah, I'm sure the ladies will have a pile of things for you to do and if you run out, you can ask them. They are pretty good at coming up with stuff. Do you play checkers? I started to teach him a while back. You could do that. Or you could talk."

"Talk? Now why in the hell would I want to do that? I have nothing in the world to talk to him about."

"Well, if I was you, I'd be starting to think of something. It really looks like it is going to rain. Hey, I have an idea." With that, Elton ran up the stairs and came back with a couple books. "These were Andy's. One is about the biggest dams in the world. And another one is about heavy equipment. You guys can look at these."

"I don't know anything about heavy equipment!" the wizened detective panicked.

"You can read, can't you?" Elton asked.

"What am I going to say if he asks a question?" Kincaid asked in horror at the prospect.

"You can say, 'I don't know. Let's try to find out together.'"

"Won't he think I am stupid?" Kincaid asked.

Elton just started to chuckle, "Really? You don't want to answer me that, do you?"

"Dammit, I hate you Magpie."

Elton burst out laughing. "I think I'll stay home from work today. I hate to miss this."

The exertorture class was short because Marly and Ruthie had to lead them. Nora and Suzy came to help also. Pepper had stayed in town because she had to work early in the morning. Annie, of course, was at the fire hall. Kincaid was able to stand longer than the day before and Miriam didn't giggle quite so much. At least, she didn't get the hiccoughs.

Kincaid tried to convince Charlie that he should join in. Charlie raised both his eyebrows and just shook his head no, very slowly and deliberately. Kincaid had to admit, he didn't blame the kid.

Ginger was in a good mood and talked nonstop about her conversation with Harrington Badge 11918 the night before. Finally, Marly told her to take a deep breath. Well, she did. All that happened is it refueled her for another twenty minute soliloquy.

Byron joined them for the coffee break and then called Kincaid aside. "I talked to Elton this morning. He said you were worried about today if it rains. Look, here's a book that Ken had in his room. He and I talked about it the other day and he was going to give it to Charlie. It is about building dams. Sort of the construction end of things, but also explains about water flow and all that kind of thing. It might be just the ticket for you."

"I suppose Magpie couldn't wait to tell you how nervous I was, huh?" Kincaid pounced.

"No, he didn't, Carl. I called him about something totally unrelated and he simply mentioned that you didn't know what you would do if it rained. He never even said you were nervous about it. Kincaid, adults have to think ahead about things like that. Like how are you going to keep kids quiet in the car on a long trip and what to do during a rainstorm? Don't get all paranoid." Byron reassured him. "I'll tell you a secret. You can always feed Charlie. Chocolate works pretty darned good!"

"Thanks," Kincaid smiled. "I guess I am just overly nervous."

"You got Nora and Grandma. You're in good hands," Byron smiled. "Well, I have to go write a sermon. Preferably one that will keep the congregation awake through the whole thing."

"You know, Byron," Kincaid said seriously, "I won't be going to church. I hope you don't get your feelings hurt."

Byron grinned, "That is entirely up to you, my man. I'm not the church police."

"No hard feelings?"

"I'll make you a deal. You don't have to go to church and I don't have to be arrested by the FBI? Will that work?"

Kincaid smiled, "Works for me."

The group got home and in the house before the rain started. Then it poured. Little Charlie took off his coat and stood by the front window. His bottom lip came out and he was fighting back the tears.

Kincaid felt almost the same way. He really didn't want to start things out this way, at all. Why did things like this happen to him? 'Okay Mo! It was your good idea and where are you? Clear across the country!'

Kincaid looked at the kid and then drove up to him. "Well, Charlie. It looks to me like we're going to have to go to our contingency plan."

Charlie turned to look at him, "A Tingy plan? What's that?"

"A contingency plan. That is the plan you have when you can't do your first plan. It is like a backup plan," the older man explained.

"What is our some-tingy plan?" the little boy asked.

"Contingency." Carl repeated, as he thought to himself, 'Yah, what is it?' "Well, I was thinking we could do some dam planning."

Charlie's eyes got huge and he made a face. "You'd better not let Aunt Nora and Grandma hear you say those words. You'll get skinned for sure."

"No Charlie, I said dam planning. You know, planning dams."

Charlie sighed with relief, "Oh that. Well, all you have to do is go outside and dig where the water runs and make it stop. It'll make a lake. That is how you do that."

"I was thinking about this book. It is about how to build dams. It tells about which way water goes and how deep to make the overflow and all that kind of stuff." The older man explained.

"What's an overflow?" Charlie asked.

"Come on, let's go look at this book Ken lent us. It looks like a good one. Wanna try?" Kincaid asked.

The young boy nodded and they went to one of the dining room tables and got comfortable. Soon, they asked Nora for paper and pencils and spent the entire morning drawing, planning and looking at the book.

When Elton came home for lunch, he went in to look their project over. "Uncle Elton, Mr. Kincaid showed me all sorts of stuff. How to build dams, dig them and where to put them! It is way cool. Way, way cool! Look at our plans. We worked all morning! We are going to go to the library someday and get some more books. This is the best some-tingy plan."

"That's great, Charlie. We'll have to take a trip to the library." Then Elton patted Kincaid on the back and gave him a big grin. "You seem to have done a fantastic job, Kincaid. Good work."

Kincaid could not, or would not, ever tell Elton how much that meant to him, but it was a lot. He knew he would tell Mo, however. It really was one of the nicest things that ever happened to him.

Lunch was good. Everyone was looking forward to Zach coming home that evening. Then the babysitting crew would arrive. The ladies told Charlie and Kincaid they would have to work for Grandma in the afternoon to help with supper. Charlie didn't want to, but Kincaid pointed out that good agents always did their jobs, even the hard stuff.

After the Grandpas got settled for their naps; Charlie and Kincaid cut up the boiled potatoes and eggs. Then while Kincaid was chopping onions, pickles and celery, Grandma showed Charlie how to mix the sauce for over the potato salad. He helped her put in mustard, mayonnaise, cream, vinegar, salt and pepper, a dash of horseradish and a bit of sugar to bring out the flavor. Kincaid tasted the mixture and gave his approval. Charlie was proud as a peacock. And secretly, so was Kincaid.

Since Kincaid couldn't go out in the rain without getting stuck, Grandma decided to have him help her clean the garden lettuce, while Nora helped Charlie with the Chicken Man chores. By the time Uncle Elton drove back in the yard, the ham dinner was ready and the chicken chores were done.

He came in and Charlie forgot himself and gave him a big jump up hug. Elton caught him in his arms. "Did you have a good day, Charlie?"

"Oh yes, Uncle Elton. It was great and I cooked the sauce for the potato salad by myself, except for Grandma's help. Kincaid tasted it and said it was good!"

"Well, that's just fantastic Charlie. I'm proud of you!" Elton set him back on his feet and then kissed his wife.

The door opened and Zach came in. Charlie did one more jumping hug. He was talking a blue streak and within about two minutes, had updated Zach on their entire day. Every detail.

Zach beamed, "I'm glad you're happy Charlie. How did Kincaid survive?"

Carl looked up and smiled, "Very well thank you. We did good, didn't we Charlie?"

Charlie looked at Grandma Katherine, "Did we do good?"

"You did for sure, Charlie. I was proud of you both." Grandma patted him on the back. "Now, maybe you'd let Zach get his jacket off."

Zach set Charlie down and the little guy tried his best to carry Zach's bag, but it was too heavy for him. Kincaid rolled over and helped the little guy put it on his lap. Then together they took it to the bottom of the stairs. Zach would carry it up himself later.

Zach was listening to Bert's chest when Chris drove in with his new prescription. The two discussed his condition and then decided on what level to set his oxygen on the machine.

A few minutes later, the Ellison's drove in with their crew, all with their overnight bags and then Danny and Jenny arrived.The focus of attention was little Matthew. He was a three month old baby boy who was a smiley kid. He had dark hair like his dad and a few freckles like his mom.

Jenny giggled, "I don't know how those freckles sneaked in there?"

Ginger raised her eyebrows, "I hope he doesn't get too many like Uncle Darrell and I did."

"You have beautiful freckles, Ginger," Jenny smiled, "Don't you ever forget that."

"I know, Aunt Jenny. I won't try to take them off anymore, ever." The little girl stated adamantly.

Soon, the two couples left for their evening and the rest settled into their routine. Some went to do chores. Grandma, Nora, Katie were soon joined by Suzy in the kitchen. Miriam found a comfortable spot on Kincaid's lap in his wheelchair and was content there.

After chores, they all had a fine dinner and Kincaid and Charlie were toasted as fine chefs. Then everyone played checkers or Go Fish. They took turns holding baby Matthew. Even Kincaid held him for about a half a minute.

Then it was bedtime. Suzy and Zach went for a walk, outside. Nora had moved baby Matthew into their room in the crib with wheels. Ginger and Miriam were asleep in the nursery on the daybed. The other folks were all in rooms upstairs.

Everyone was settled down to sleep when Zach and Suzy finally said goodnight and she went home. Kincaid heard her car pull out of the yard and Zach close the kitchen door and set the Pa Bell.

Then the door to Kincaid's bedroom opened, Zach came in to check Bert and listened to his chest. Bert never woke up for the exam. Kincaid nearly scared Zach half to death when he asked, "How's he doing?"

Zach shook his head. "Not so good, but this new antibiotic should knock it. How are you doing? Are you settling in okay? I heard from Suzy that you don't like the exertorture classes."

"Yah, Petunia. You owe me one for that! I know it's hard for Pepper to do the work for everyone. Hell, this outfit could just about keep a therapist going full time."

Zach smiled, "Yah, and she just got finished with her Dad's. He was an impossible patient."

"I can see that. Hey, have you heard how long I'll be laid up?"

Zach shook his head. "We have an appointment for you on Tuesday. Then we'll know more. Why? You getting restless?"

"Yah. I really am. These folks are great, but this isn't me. I'm not used to this. I'd like a whiskey."

"I know. I don't think it would be a good idea yet. We can ask about that on Tuesday, I promise. Right now it would just make you pass out."

"Ah, that wouldn't be good. Zach, how does Elton do it?" Carl asked earnestly.

"Do what?"

"Wander around half the night and then work all day? He's up with Lloyd every night. It would kill me."

Zach nodded, "I know. I'll get up with him tonight. I already promised Elton I would do that, but he is such a mother hen. Then he gets up to see if I'm okay being up with Lloyd."

"Is he for real?" Kincaid asked, sincerely.

"What do you mean, Kincaid? Lloyd or Elton?"

"Elton. I mean, he told me that he was a confirmed bachelor for years and never when to church in his life. Now look at him? Was he lying then or is he lying now?"

Zach shook his head, "Carl, if he had been a good guy all his life and then started drinking and running around, would you think he was faking it?"

Kincaid thought, "No, I wouldn't."

"Well, why do you question it the other way around?"

"Don't know. Guess I never thought about it. You know the FBI deals mostly with those who went from good to bad. Not bad to good."

Zach nodded, "I'm here to tell you, the other way works too. Elton is for real. He is about the realest you'll ever find."

Kincaid thought, "You know, I'm glad to hear that."

7

It was three-thirty when the lightning struck not far from the wooden farmhouse. The storm was directly overhead and the thunder was deafening. Hail beat down on the house and made a terrible racket. Miriam screamed when the lightning cracked a tree in the windbreak surrounding the house and Elton and Zach ran to her room. Matthew started crying and then Ginger joined in. Charlie came down the steps without his foot touching a single step. He was in Ruthie's arms so fast that she didn't know how he got there!

Elton and Nora directed everyone to the basement until the storm was over. It was an ordeal. Ken and Zach helped the Grandpas and Elton helped Kincaid. The ladies made up a nest for them in the southwest corner of the basement, the safest place to be in case of a North Dakota tornado. There were a couple old chairs and an old sofa there for just that purpose. Nora kept a pile of blankets, some pillows, a flashlight and lantern handy.

Zach had his hands full trying to calm Miriam, but she was curling up into the fetal position. Elton took her to calm her. Ginger just trembled until Zach took her on his lap. Nora was holding baby Matthew. Charlie was trying to be brave, but it wasn't working out too well. Kincaid noticed and asked him to come help him.

"I can't walk if I need something. Could you help me out, Charlie?" Kincaid asked.

Charlie looked at him and debated if he wanted to do that or just cry. Finally, he went over to the man. "Okay."

"Could you sit on my lap? Don't tell anyone, but I'm afraid of storms. How 'bout you?" Kincaid asked.

Charlie shrugged, "Sometimes. I'll try helping you be brave."

"That'd be great, Charlie."

Before long, Elton had Miriam calmed down enough so that she at least was no longer whimpering and Nora had baby Matthew taking a bottle. Curled up in Zach's arms, Ginger was back to sleep. Ken made progress convincing Grandpa Lloyd that he didn't have to check the cows. Grandma Katherine was making certain that Bert's oxygen stayed on. Katie and Ruthie helped out wherever they could. It was a miserable night.

When the sun came up Saturday morning, there was a bedraggled bunch of folks that emerged from the basement. Kevin arrived early and helped the men bring the Grandpas upstairs. The Grandpas went back to bed, no worse for the wear.

"How was it at your place?" Elton asked, "Any damage?"

"Nothing major. Just a bunch of wind. My picnic table only has three chairs now. The hail took the care of Carrie's garden. I noticed yours doesn't look too good either," Kevin reported. "It is still raining cats and dogs out there. I'll go down and start on chores."

"I'll come with," Ken offered. "I just have to throw my jacket on."

"Thanks, Ken," Kevin said. "How did everyone fare?"

"Matthew was fine once he got settled back down," Nora giggled. "He must be a Schroeder for sure. Once his belly was full, he went back to sleep."

"Good boy," Kevin chuckled. "Carrie won't be over this morning. She is upchucking again. I think it was something she ate but she says no. She hasn't had a bout of morning sickness like this for a while now."

"Let me know if she doesn't get it under control," Zach commented. "I can run over to see her."

"Thanks," Kev said, "Well, come on Ken."

Miriam had been watching the whole thing and started to whimper when Kevin started to go to the door. "Son?"

Everyone stopped, shocked at Miriam's little voice. Kevin turned around, "I'm sorry Miriam. I didn't even give you a hug! How naughty of me."

She held out her arms to him, "Son."

"Okay," he smiled, "Come here Sweetheart. I have time to hold you for a minute. Maybe Dad can get dressed while I do that."

"Uncle," Miriam said, and then hugged Kevin's neck as tight as she could. After a minute she looked at him and made a noise like thunder, "Boom, boom, boom."

"That's right, there was a big thunder storm last night," Kevin consoled her. "Wasn't there? But everyone is okay and it was kind of fun to be in the basement, huh?"

Miriam studied his face a minute and then softly said, "No."

Kevin hugged her, "I guess not, huh?"

Then she hugged him again and held on tightly.

The rest of the folks got ready to help milk, but Miriam made no move to relax her grip on Kevin. When they tried to extract her from him, she just gripped harder. Zach tried to convince her that Kevin would be right back and Elton offered to hold her, but nothing changed her mind.

Finally, Kevin said, "Have you got a jacket for her? I'll just take her along. There are enough of us, so I can hold her this morning. Okay? Maybe she would like to see the cows?"

"I don't know Kevin," Elton said, "Last night was very upsetting for her."

"Well, if she gets upset, I can bring her back up. Okay?"

"Okay, Son," Elton said after appraising the situation.

Miriam patted Kevin's neck and said sweetly, "Okay, Son."

Byron drove in as they were almost at the barn. The rain was pelting down so hard it was almost painful, but Miriam never flinched. She buried her head in Kevin's jacket and kept Mr. Bear buried between her and Kevin.

In the barn, she clung to Kevin as the cows went into their stanchions. Elton milked Percifull, Zach helped Ginger milk Petunia and Byron helped Charlie with Snowflake, but he mostly did it himself. Kevin and Miriam operated the cream separator. She did let him set her down on a milk stool in the milk room, while he dumped the pails in. But she was only about two feet from him the whole time.

During their coffee break, she had hot chocolate like Ginger and Charlie did, but she sat on Kevin's lap. After coffee break, he wanted to help clean the barn and told her, "You can go with Byron and look at the horses. I'll be right here. Okay?"

She shook her head no.

"How about Uncle Elton take you to see the baby calves?"

She shook her head no.

"How about Zach takes you to see the piggies?"

She shook her head no.

"How about I hold you?"

She smiled, "Okay, Son."

Soon they were all back at the house. Jenny had picked up baby Matthew. Grandma and Nora had put the kids' things together so they could go home with their Dad. Miriam still had not let go of Kevin.

When it got to be time for them to go home, Ruthie said, "Come on Miriam. We have to go home now. Kevin is tired and he needs a nap."

Miriam looked at him in surprise. "Son nap?"

Kevin pretended to yawn, "Yes. I need a nap. Do you want to go home now and we can get together later, after my nap?"

Miriam shrugged.

"Miriam, when Carrie's tummy gets better, do you want to come over to visit at our house? Maybe we could have cookies or something?" Kevin asked.

"If you want to," she said, but it was obvious that she didn't care. She wanted to stay with him, now.

"No," Kevin said, "It is if you want to."

She looked at him and then shook her head no.

He smiled, "That's better. Okay, we won't do that. How about Uncle Byron can bring you back over so we can milk again soon?"

Miriam hugged him again, "Okay, Son."

Then she went to Byron and waved good bye like any other day. After they left, everyone looked at each other. Kevin shook his head, "I wish I knew what to do with her."

Zach smiled, "She talks to you more than to anyone else. I mean, if you can call it talk. But you are about the only person she will say no to. That's really progress for her. She used to do whatever anyone said."

Kincaid made the observation, "I think some of that comes from watching the other kids. If someone asks them something and they say no, they don't get beaten. Maybe she decided it's safe to do."

"Safe is the operative word," Nora said. "I think she's beginning to feel safe with us. She hasn't been beaten or neglected since she has been around us. Maybe it's just a matter of time. Even with the painful therapy, she isn't afraid of Pepper."

"Wow! Talking about safe! What was that storm last night?" Kincaid asked. "That was awful. I know it scared the hell out of me."

"Yah, the weather can really raise hell when it sets it mind to," Elton agreed. "Those tornadoes are nobody's joke. Last night was a good lesson. We need to figure out a way to get the old guys downstairs in a hurry."

Zach said, "My guess is that Bert will be in the wheelchair when Kincaid is done with it. And with Lloyd, it's a matter of convincing him. We actually got the whole gang downstairs in short order last night."

"Zach," Elton said, "If there had been a tornado, we'd all have been blown to kingdom come. We need to get a system."

"Guess you're right, Elton. Right after breakfast, we'll work on it. Okay?" Zach agreed.

"Okay, son," Elton chuckled. "I think Miriam thinks that is Kevin's name!"

"Well, you call him that all the time," Kincaid said.

"Nah, I don't," Elton said. "Do I?"

The whole family nodded, "Yup."

"Really? Do I call the other boys that?" Elton asked.

Nora answered, "Once in a while, but not all the time like you do Kevin."

"Oh brother," Elton held his head. "I suppose I hurt someone's feelings. Did I?"

Nora smiled and shook her had no, and then Kincaid laughed, "Well, you sure aren't hurting mine!"

"Yea gads!" Elton laughed, "If I'd a kid like you, I don't know what I would do!"

"No worries, I'd have run away from home when I was a toddler."

8

Zach checked Bert's lungs and he actually seemed a bit better. "I think it was a combination of moving around all night and the new antibiotic. Looks like we dodged the bullet one more time!"

Bert gave him a dirty look, "Don't get the idea that I'm going to stay up all night like Lloyd does!"

Zach shook his head, "None of us could stand it, Bert. But we may have to keep your bed up higher at night when you sleep."

"How will that work? I'll fall out of bed," the old man grumped.

"How about sleeping in a recliner?" Kincaid suggested.

Bert gave him a dirty look and snarled at him, "When you get a good idea, I'll let you know. Until then, keep quiet!"

"Man, I can't believe Byron is such a nice man and he's your son, you old goat." Kincaid grouched back.

"Truthfully," Elton grinned, "I can't stand either one of you!"

Both grumpy men snapped at Elton in unison, "Who cares?"

Elton frowned, "Well, if that don't beat all."

"What are you going to do today, Zacharias?" Elton asked.

"I'm going to pick up a new prescription for Lloyd." He raised his eyebrows to Elton, "You know, another vitamin."

"Oh," Elton nodded knowingly, "Good idea."

"I'm not taking any more pills," Lloyd grouched, "They just make you sick. Right Elton?"

"Not really Lloyd, sometimes they make you stronger."

"I'm already strong," the frail octogenarian stated emphatically.

"I know you are, but you'll be stronger."

Lloyd scrutinized Elton and said, "To my notion, you should be taking them."

Elton looked at him blankly, "Yah, I guess you're right about that. Well, I'm going to the garage to work on the airplane."

With that he abruptly got up and put on his jacket. Zach looked at Nora and she shrugged. It was very unlike Elton. Zach put on his coat and followed him out.

When he opened the door to the garage, Zach saw a sight he couldn't have imagined. Elton was sitting on a stool, bent over the workbench and weeping into his folded arms. Zach didn't know if he should just leave or if he should talk to his dear friend. He felt like he was invading his privacy.

Elton wiped his eyes and Zach knew he had heard him. It was too late to leave now. He went over to him and put his hand on his shoulder. Elton blew his nose and tried to act like everything was okay, but it only lasted a half a second. Then he just started to cry again.

Zach patted his back, "Do you want me to get Nora?" he finally asked.

"No," Elton answered. "I'll be okay. Sometimes, Zach, I just can't take it. I get so tired. It is constant. Jesus have mercy, if it isn't one of them, it's the other. I'd like to just once have them say, 'Okay, I'll take that pill'. But God bless them, they don't. They bicker and squabble steady. I love them all, but I want to run away. I'm really on my pity pot, huh?"

"No," Zach said, "Hey, want a Coke?"

"Yah," Elton nodded. "I guess I didn't get enough rest. I just want everything to be okay. You know? Just one little damned thing to be okay. It seems like everything is a miserable mess. Sometimes, I feel like I'm being ripped apart. I don't like being like this."

"Elton, this is the first time that I have seen you fall apart," Zach assured him. "You are a brick, but you are a human. You didn't get much sleep last night, or any night before. You have everyone demanding your attention and time. You never tell them no. You never say, 'leave me alone'."

Elton took a gulp of his Coke, "I think I just did. Hell, Kincaid is probably wondering what the hell's wrong with me. When Lloyd said he didn't want to take his pill, it was like the straw that broke the camel's back."

"Elton," Zach pulled up his stool and looked directly at his friend, "You need to pace yourself. You can't keep this up. You've been on the move since the first of the year. I know how you feel about the old guys, your kids, your friends and your work . . . but you need to think about yourself. You aren't a spring chicken anymore. You usually get about five hours sleep a night, and that's not all in one stretch. You go like a maniac all day long. Your body needs to rest up. You're always worrying about something. Man, you need a break. Sometimes, you need to just sit."

"I can't stand that. And I do sit, Zach. Hell, I hardly worked all week."

"Yah, when you walked the floor with Miriam, took her to the doctor, checked on Bert, calmed Lloyd down, spent time with Kincaid, helped babysit, helped out any number of people and I bet, hardly had any time with Nora at all."

Elton turned abruptly, "Did she complain? Am I neglecting her?"

"Down boy!" Zach said, "No, she'd never complain. She's almost as bad as you are. But you can't be worrying about everyone else and still have time for each other. What are we going to do to change things?"

Elton sat straight up, "We aren't doing any old people's home!"

"No, Elton, don't get yourself all wound up. We're not going to even talk about that. If these new pills work, we can get Lloyd to sleep again at night. And as far as Bert is concerned, this is going to be his new reality. One day, Elton, he is going to pass over. His remaining lung is worn out. There's no way around it and I wouldn't want to move him."

Elton started to cry afresh, "Poor Byron. It'll be so hard for him."

Zach shook his head, "Byron hell! You're the one that is going to beat himself up for it. Pepper is right about that! You are such a realist about most things; I can't imagine why you do this to yourself. You know how frustrated you get when the old guys won't take care of themselves. That is the way the rest of us feel about you! All your kids; everybody, we all watch you just wear yourself out. Now, will you do us all a favor and take it easy once in a while?"

"Just what should I quit doing, Zach? I can't let Lloyd wander, I can't let Bert choke, I can't let Kincaid go off the deep end and I can't let Miriam curl up in a ball! What am I going to do?"

Zach looked at him and shrugged, "Delegate and take a nap."

Elton's shoulders fell and he rolled his eyes. "The last time I did that, you kids remodeled the house!"

Zach sighed, "It was supposed to make less work for you and instead, you just got more people to fill it up!"

Elton grinned, "But it sure is nice to have a meal without carting all those darn tables up and down the stairs. Now, what are we going to do with the downstairs for our tornado shelter—thingiemabob?"

About an hour later, the men came back to the house. Elton had picked up the rotor parts and some tools so that Kincaid could work on them in the house while it was raining. In the end, the men played cards until lunch time. Then, in the afternoon rain, everyone took a nap. It was wonderful and when they woke up, Grandma mixed up a batch of chocolate chip cookies. It turned out to be a wonderful day.

That night at chores, Byron said that all the kids took a long afternoon nap at their house too. Marly made M&M cookies when they woke up! Apparently it was the only way to spend a rainy day.

That night, after chores, the Ellisons had dinner with Schroeders. Marly brought over Bert's favorite corned beef and cabbage. Bert insisted to Kincaid for twenty minutes about that it was not an Irish dish, but Scandinavian. They had to give it to Kincaid; he really tried not arguing with Bert, but to no avail.

Finally, Miriam cuddled up in Uncle Elton's arms and said, "Goat."

They all giggled.

"I think my little Miriam is a smart cookie," Elton said with pride.

"Smart cookie," Miriam smiled. "Chocolate."

Charlie remained two inches from Kincaid all evening and then said to him, "Are you going to sit by me in church tomorrow? I can ask Mom if it would be okay. She won't let Zach sit by me anymore. He causes too much trouble."

Zach choked, "Excuse me? Who causes trouble?"

Charlie kept right on talking like he hadn't heard a word, "But since I have this job of taking care of an Agent, I think Mom will let me. You won't cause any trouble, will you?"

"No, I wouldn't Charlie," Kincaid said, "But I won't be going to church?"

"Why not? Don't you like me? Don't you want to sit by side of me? I promise not to make you get giggle. I'll be good, honest."

"Charlie, it has nothing to do with you. I just don't want to go," Kincaid explained.

"Why not?" Charlie asked.

"Charlie, don't bug Mr. Kincaid. It isn't any of your business," his Dad directed.

Then Ginger piped up, "Will you throw up like Smitty and Ruthie? Ruthie goes to the Catlick church because it doesn't make her throw up like our church does. I told Daddy not to let Mrs. Meyers sing, but he just doesn't listen to me. Somebody else should tell him too. If a grownup did, then he would listen. Can you go to the Catlick church without throwing up, Mr. Kincaid?"

"I don't throw up in church. I'm not going to the Catholic church either."

Ginger crossed her arms and asked indignantly, "Are you mad at God?"

Kincaid started to laugh, "No, I'm not."

"Well, I think you should go then just to say hi. See, it's like having coffee with Him. But I don't think He drinks coffee, does He, Daddy?"

Byron shook his head and uncrossed her arms, "Settle down. Mr. Kincaid might just want to stay home and rest tomorrow. He isn't feeling well yet, you know. Now you mind your own business."

"My friends are my business," Ginger said, "Right Mr. Kincaid?"

"Yes, Ginger," Kincaid agreed, "But I want to rest tomorrow."

Charlie looked at his Dad. "I'm staying with him. You know, if he needs something while he is resting, I have good legs. I'm his Goer and Getter Guy."

"You're coming to church," his Dad said. "You can see Mr. Kincaid right after church. Now that is the end of the discussion."

"Alright, Daddy. But if Mr. Kincaid falls down and dies because he can't get water because you made his Goer and Getter Guy go to church, you'll feel really bad," Charlie pointed out.

"Oh for crying out loud!" Kincaid said, "I will go to church! You have quite a racket going here, Ellison."

Ginger turned to her Daddy, "What's a racket got to do with going to church?"

"Now I know why alcohol was invented!" Byron groaned.

"So," Ginger said as she turned her sights on Ruthie, "Who's going to drive you to the Catlick church?"

"I'm going with Betty and Doug Schulz. They're going to pick me up for Mass," Ruthie explained.

"Do you guys have to clean up a mess at the Catlick church? We have someone clean them up for us at our church. We have to listen to Daddy talk," Ginger explained. "I can come along and help you clean up the mess. It'd be more fun."

"The Catholics call their church Mass—not mess. We sit and listen to a priest talk, just like you listen to your Dad," Ruthie explained.

"Then why do you throw up at our church?" Ginger asked.

"Well, I probably wouldn't," Ruthie explained.

"Okay, then you can come to ours."

"But I'm a Catholic, Ginger," Ruthie explained. "You're a Lutheran."

"What are you Mr. Kincaid?"

"I'm confused," the older man rolled his eyes.

"You kids are driving me to my wit's end," Marly said, "Now be quiet."

Charlie patted the back of Kincaid's hand. "Now watch, Mom's eyes will start shooting red pretty soon."

Kincaid laughed, "I can see why Zach got into trouble."

9

It rained all night, but there was no storm. Bert decided he was going to church if Kincaid was. He wanted to check on him. Chris and Zach got the old gents showered and ready for church.

Nora and Katherine had roast beef in the oven and Lucille was bringing one also. Marly was bringing apple pies for desert and Elsie and Julia were bringing baked mashed potatoes. The other women were all bringing vegetables, hot rolls or salads. All in all, it sounded like it would be a wonderful meal.

Kincaid was in awe. He had never seen so many tables and place settings for a family gathering. "It looks like a convention! How many people will there be here?"

"About forty, give or take," Elton answered. "It's just the clan."

"You're related to all these people?" Kincaid's mouth fell open.

"I told you, Kincaid," Zach said, "This is the clan. We're not blood relatives, we're family."

"Oh yah, I remember you babbling about something like that. I didn't pay much attention to you."

"I know. Now, don't you wish you did?"

Kincaid looked at the dining room, "No. Don't think so. Will I know any of these people?"

"Oh sure," Elton said as he helped take the plates out to put on the table. "There will be Kevin and his wife, Ellisons, Danny and Jenny, and some you haven't met yet. Like my brother, Eddie."

"Now, he's you real brother?" Kincaid asked.

"Yup," Elton answered, "There's a bunch of Marly's real family. Heck. You know my nephew, Danny, is married to Marly's sister, Jenny. And Marty is engaged to Nora's cousin, Suzy's sister."

Kincaid shook his head, "I'll take your word for it. It sounds nuts. Like something a bunch of pansies would do."

"Oh hell, Kincaid," Elton laughed, "Even the Mafia has conventions!"

Kincaid had to laugh. "Yah, I guess. Do you think that Miriam will be scared?"

Zach furrowed his brow, "We worried about that, but you know, she knows a lot of people already. She can find someone to be comfortable with. Look how many people came in and out at the hospital and she never freaked about that. I sure wonder what gives her the bad nightmares."

Kincaid shrugged, "I think she dreams about her Mom. You know, I don't think that she was ever around her Dad enough to really connect with him. He probably just ignored her or whacked her. But her Mom, that was different. She was with her a lot and Miriam relied on her. Her Mom gave her the only good she ever got, but threw in enough terror to keep her scared to death. I doubt she ever knew what to expect from her. That is why she likes men better than women."

Elton and Zach both stood there with their mouths open. Finally Kincaid said, "Well, what do you think? I'm stupid?"

Zach said, "No, but that's very insightful. I think you're right. She really does seem to trust men more than women, even the gruff ones. Huh?"

"You really don't think that I know anything about people, do you?" Kincaid asked.

Elton nodded at him, "No, I knew anyone who was a good FBI agent had to have a good read on folks, but I'm surprised that it escaped the rest of us. There is no doubt that she prefers men. Her Mom was really a mess."

"Yah, my guess is that she was not only beaten, but I wouldn't be a bit surprised if her old man hadn't molested her after his wife died. The situation has all the earmarks of that." Kincaid said matter-of-factly. Then he looked at Zach, "Oh God, I'm so sorry. I didn't need to say that. I forgot she was your sister."

"No, you're right. I thought that myself. In fact, Ruthie and I even talked about it. It would explain a lot. Anyway, I'd rather not think about it anymore. I hope we can get Miriam back on track," Zach said.

"We can. She is doing really well," Elton tried to encourage his friend, "She'll be out digging with the rest of those gophers in no time!"

"I hope it quits raining soon," Kincaid said as he drove around the tables putting the silverware out, "What am I going to do with that kid? All he thinks of are dams and lakes. I am warning you Magpie, you might wake up one morning and find your entire pasture turned into a lake."

"It wouldn't surprise me a bit."

Before long, Kincaid entered Trinity Lutheran Church walking rather than taking his wheelchair so Chris and Pepper went with him. He entered the door of the church and Byron was there greeting his congregation.

"Hello, Carl. Hope you'll forgive my kids. I really have to get them to stop doing that," Byron apologized.

"Admit it. You pay them to do it!" Kincaid growled. "Extortion!"

Byron laughed, "Well, I hope it isn't too bad."

Charlie was waiting patiently for Kincaid to get seated before he came up to him. Pepper gave him a squint-eyed look. "Okay, Charlie, but Chris and I are right here on the other side. You mess up once just one time and I'll have your hide!"

Charlie's face filled with horror. He grimaced to Kincaid, "I think she means it, huh?"

Kincaid nodded, "Sounded like it to me. We'd better behave."

Charlie was in total agreement.

Marly and Katie sat with Grandpa Bert and Lloyd and Katherine sat with Elton and Nora. Zach and Suzy carried Miriam and Ginger sat with her Uncle Darrell and Jeannie.

Kincaid studied the group. 'Good grief, these people all have someone they are watching out for. Don't they ever just do something without worrying about someone else?' Then he looked next to him and realized they were looking out for him too. When you are the one on the beholding end, things don't look quite the same. He had to agree, it was nice of Chris and Pepper to sit with him. They didn't have to, but there they were. Amazingly, they still seemed content.

Church was never something that Kincaid liked, but truthfully, he hadn't gone to one in decades. He had to admit that it felt kind of good although he didn't know why. What he heard of Byron's sermon was good. He had figured it would be.

Charlie was mostly good throughout the service, helping him stand up and sit down for the liturgy and stuff. The little guy knew it like the back of his hand. His biggest problem was long prayers and the sermon. His prayer attention lasted all the way through 'Heavenly Father' and no further. He was long gone before anything close to amen. Then his legs needed to be scratched; it must have been a weird allergy of some kind. The sermon attention span lasted even less than that.

Charlie produced a string from the bottom side of his jacket. Kincaid was concerned it may have been the thread that held the jacket together. He was relieved that is wasn't. It was the thread from the hem. Before the service was over, Charlie had unraveled the entire hem all the way around the bottom of his jacket. He carefully rolled the thread around his finger and put it in his pocket, as if it was the thing to do.

Kincaid had a growing respect and deep sympathy for Marly. How that woman could function; apparently without drugs, booze or fits of rage, was beyond him. He wondered why people were ever surprised that mothers sometimes killed their offspring. After a couple days with Charlie, he wondered why more of them didn't.

Charlie wasn't a bad kid. He was actually a good kid. He just was a kid. Kincaid wondered how a sweet little baby like that Matthew could turn into a Charlie and then into a teenager! Yea gads. They were the worst of all creatures. It was fascinating that some of them actually turned out okay as adults. By the time the service was over, Kincaid had hardly heard the sermon, but had done a lot of thinking about the evolution of mankind!

After church, Marly came over and asked Charlie if he had behaved.

"Sure Mommy," he said as sweetly as he could.

Kincaid was certain the kid wasn't lying. He thought he was being good. So you pull on a stupid thread and your jacket hem falls down. Nobody cares about that anyway.

Marly looked at Kincaid, "What do you have to say?"

"I take the fifth. I'm sure he meant no harm."

Marly gave him a funny look and then took Charlie by the hand. It wasn't until they reached the bottom of the front steps that Kincaid heard Marly yell, "What did you do to your hem?"

Pepper asked him why he was giggling, and he said, "Oh, I think that Marly just noticed that her son remodeled his suit jacket."

"That little skunk!" Pepper said, "You knew about it! Why didn't you stop him?"

"I honestly didn't know what he was doing until it was too late. Then I decided it would be best to just act like I didn't see him," Kincaid tried to explain.

Pepper turned to Chris, "We are never having children! Got it?"

Chris chuckled, "Got it, Hot Pepper."

10

Dinner was more fun than Kincaid would have predicted. He knew enough people to feel comfortable. They were a relaxed bunch of folks. No one tried to impress anyone else.

Another thing that struck him was that everyone was given respect to be listened to and not talked over, whether it was a little kid or a senile old man. The group included people from all walks of life. There were physicians, farmers, teachers, secretaries, mechanics and cheese makers. He and little Charlie were the only FBI Agents there, albeit Charlie was a Very Special Agent.

Coot listened to Charlie explain to the men how to build a dam almost verbatim from the book. Soon, Charlie, Danny and Darrell were involved in a deep conversation about water flow. Danny and Darrell used irrigation for some of their fields and the process was similar. Kincaid was amazed how much he himself actually understood when they were talking about backflow valves. The men both offered to lend them books on the subject.

'I have to get out of here, and soon! These petunias are getting to me!' he thought to himself, as he helped himself to another piece of Marly's apple pie.

He thought that he should plan getting into an apartment soon; until he heard the ladies talk about how to make Hot German Potato Salad. Having recently become a bit of a connoisseur of potato salad, he was soon engrossed in their conversation.

Miriam did very well. She ate her lunch with her high chair wedged between Byron and Elton. By desert, she had moved over to her 'Son',

Kevin. She stayed with him until she fell asleep and he put her down for her nap.

That pleased Kincaid. She had landed in a good place. She'd be okay here. He felt he could leave and be confident that the little girl would be fine.

After dinner, the little boys raced with Andy's cars and Ginger couldn't play with them because she couldn't see well enough yet. The young adults had divided into groups and were playing cards. Kincaid saw her sitting on the sofa looking bored and sad.

He drove over to her, "How are things going for you today?"

She shrugged, "Pretty good. I'm just sad because I was so dumb and messed up my eyes. Now I can't race the cars with the boys so good. Clarkie Olson brought over his new race car and it is way cool. Even Maddie Lynn is a good racer!"

"I hear that your eyes are getting better, though," Kincaid asked.

"Yes, Smitty says I have to be patient. Have you ever been patient?" Ginger asked.

"Yah, but I don't like it very much."

"Me and Andy don't either. Daddy says we need to be patient because God is teaching us something. I wish He'd just tell me what it is and then it wouldn't take so long!"

Kincaid laughed, "I agree. So, how's the dirt collecting coming?"

"Oh, Mr. Kincaid," Ginger got excited, "I got a package from Andy and he sent me some Vietnam dirt! Have you ever seen that?"

"No, I don't think I have. How does it look?" Kincaid asked. "I always thought dirt was pretty much the same all over."

"I did too until Jeannie told me about it." Ginger explained, "See, it is like God has a lot of recipes for dirt. Some have this and some have that. It depends on what is in it. The dirt that Andy sent from Vietnam has a lot of dead plant stuff in it. That means that it would grow other plants really good."

"Really?" Kincaid replied, "I didn't know that."

"Yah," Ginger went on, "If you ever need to know anything about dirt, I can give you a bunch of stuff to think about. I bet you could be a good dirt thinker, if you wanted."

"Maybe so," Kincaid smiled, "So how big is your collection of dirt?"

"It is getting pretty big. Some of the people that go to Daddy's church bring dirt for me. I have mostly dirt from America. But I have some from Canada and Vietnam. It'd be fun to get it from all over, but Daddy says we'd have to build a new shelf."

"Let me see if I can think of anyone I know who could send you some. I have a friend that goes to the Grand Cayman Islands for work. I bet he would get you some from there. Should I ask him?"

"That would be way cool. Where are the Grand things?"

"The Grand Caymans are islands that are south of the United States," Kincaid explained.

Just then Jeannie Frandsen, who was Uncle Darrell's fiancée and the teacher who was tutoring Ginger over the summer, came by on her way to the kitchen.

"Jeannie," Ginger asked, "Mr. Kincaid said he could maybe get us dirt from the Grand place."

"Grand Caymans," Kincaid explained.

"Oh, wow!" Jeannie smiled, "That'd be wonderful. So, you're the man who got Charlie all excited about water flow, huh?"

"Yes, but it was really Elton and Byron. They gave me the books."

"I'm going to the library tomorrow," Jeannie explained. "I have to get this little Munchkin here some more books on dirt. I can try to find you some more on dams and water, if you'd like?"

Jeannie was a sweet girl, with a warm smile and winsome way about her. Talking to her for a few minutes, she made you feel like you had known her since childhood.

Kincaid smiled, "I'd appreciate that. Hard to say how long it is going to rain and I don't know what else to do with him."

Jeannie grinned, "I think you do fine with him. As long as you can find him something he is interested in, it makes everything a lot easier. I know if children are interested in something, they learn twice as fast."

"Jeannie says I'm a good thinker about dirt. Right, Jeannie?" Ginger asked.

"Right on, Ginger. Now she's learning about geography, science, reading and even math. Right? Tomorrow we'll have to look up everything we can find about the Grand Caymans, okay?"

"That'll be good," then Ginger got serious, "I know you can't be in my class, Mr. Kincaid. So, I'll learn about that Grand place and then tell you all about it. Okay? Then you can know too. That is what friends do for their friends."

"That's real nice of you, Ginger." Carl smiled. "Real nice."

Kincaid went in to check on Bert. His oxygen mask had slipped off and he was putting it back on when Zach came in. "How's he doing?"

Kincaid said, "His mask came off. He was probably coughing again."

"Thanks for checking on him," Zach smiled.

"Why do you thank me? You're checking on him," Kincaid was curious. "I noticed these folks all thank each other all the time, like about stuff you never think of. Why do they do that?"

Zach shrugged, "Elton and Byron both say that it always feels good to hear it. I noticed it really works well with the kids! They love to be thanked or told they do a good job, but you already know that."

"No I don't," Kincaid frowned. "How would I know that?"

"Don't know, but you do it. I've seen you do it. You're really good with kids."

"I guess I just try to do like Elton does, but I'll never have the patience that he does," Kincaid shook his head. "How did he get like that?"

"I think he just truly likes them. He says that he likes most kids better than most grownups!" Zach grinned.

"Since I got to know these kids, I might agree with him."

Bert coughed again and the men both watched until he settled down. Then they went out of the room. In the hall, Kincaid said, "How long do you think it will be for him?"

Zach kind of frowned, "Probably not long, I'm afraid."

"What do I do if he dies at night while I am alone with him? I've wondered if I was supposed to do something or something?"

"Would you feel more comfortable if you had a different room?" Zach asked.

"No. I told Nora no, too. I can keep an eye on him at night. No need to have the rest of you roaming around anymore than you already do. But is there something I should know?"

"Not really. You've seen how I rub his back and try to get him to cough? But other than that, just yell. Either Annie, Pepper or I can help you. Seriously, there'll probably not be anything anyone can do."

Kincaid looked down in his lap, "I actually kind of like that feisty old geezer."

"We all do. But, he's been ready to go home for a long time," Zach pointed out. "Ever since his wife died. He's just hanging around to help with Lloyd."

"How long will that go on with Lloyd?"

"That could go on for a very long time yet, but it will just keep getting worse. I'm more worried about Elton than Lloyd. That crazy man is wearing himself to a frazzle. He never tells anyone no. Ever." Zach said.

"I noticed that. He thinks he has to be there for everyone," Kincaid pointed out.

"Yah, but he has to take care of himself, too."

"Shit Zach, you know this taking care of people is more work than just minding your own business. Isn't it?" Kincaid observed.

"Yah," Zach agreed, "People like you and me, we notice it. These people have done it so long, they don't know the difference. But I'd rather be like them than like I used to be."

Kincaid laughed, "Well, they'd sure put the FBI out of business, except maybe Charlie!"

"I love that little guy. You know, he is going to be the ring bearer when Suzy and I get married," Zach shook his head. "Very bad decision."

"Not the most brilliant move. Hell, he'll probably unravel the wedding veil before he gets to the altar! I have to see that wedding!"

Zach looked at him, "Hey Kincaid, you still got your firearm?"

"Yah, why?"

"Bring it to the wedding, we might need it!"

The men both laughed and then joined the rest of the group for another piece of dessert and coffee.

That evening after chores and the Grandpas were in bed, the family lingered over a cup of coffee. Pepper was all weepy because Chris was leaving in the morning for Grand Forks. He would be gone until a big dance that was planned for Nora's aunt and uncles fiftieth anniversary. Nora and Elton were going to celebrate theirs at the same time. Chris would be back for that.

"Pepper, it's only three weeks. You can make it that long," Nora smiled, "Look at Annie and Andy? He still has over seven months in Vietnam."

"I know Mom, I'm being a baby but I'm going to miss him," Pepper took Chris' hand. "We hardly ever get to see each other."

"Yea gads," Elton laughed, "Between you guys and Zach and Suzy, I don't know who is worse."

Chris and Zach both answered in unison, "You and Mom!"

Elton frowned, and then grinned, "Gee Nora, I think they're jealous!"

Pepper kissed her Dad's cheek as she and Chris went outside. "Whatever!"

Suzy said, "Zach and I are going for a walk too. Which way are you guys going?"

Chris grinned, "Whichever way you don't!"

The two couples went outside giggling. Grandma shook her head and laughed, "That is one thing that never changes throughout the generations."

"What is that, Katherine?" Nora asked.

"Just how silly people in love can be!" She gave every one a hug and went to bed.

"Want some more coffee, Kincaid?" Elton asked.

"No. Oh heck, why not?"

"Yes or no?"

"Yes," Kincaid smiled at the couple. "I want to thank you for the fine dinner today. I had a great time. Your clan is a nice bunch."

Nora gave him a warm smile, "Well, thank you Carl. We feel very fortunate to have them. They all liked you. I was pleased that Miriam did well today."

"She really did!" Elton said, "What did you think, Kincaid?"

"Yah. I thought she did. She sure likes Kevin. These kids are something else," Kincaid smiled, "I like that Junior Oxenfelter and Little Bill Anderson. He is Doug and Julia's kid, uh? Now, Clark is Pastor Marvin's kid, huh?"

"Yes, Junior is ten and Bill is eight. Clark is more Charlie's age. He is six and his little sister is Maddie Lynn. She is just four," Nora said. "It would be good for her to play with Miriam. They've been together a couple times, but Maddie loves coloring and color books."

"Yah, that wouldn't go over well," Kincaid agreed. "Will Miriam have to get over that before she goes to school?"

"Yes, she will. Jeannie and Marly took all the crayons out of their house but schools have them all over. Besides, it would be impossible to keep her away from them. I don't know what we're going to do with her,"

Nora said. "However, her potty training is coming along very well. She'd be better, but she can't get around without help. Kevin got her to sit in her wheel chair for a while this afternoon. She was okay as long as he was pushing it, but she didn't want to drive it herself."

Both men nodded. "Well, she hasn't been here that long really," Elton pointed out. "I think she's done very well since the hospital."

"I know I was amazed when I got here last weekend. She was so withdrawn down there. She's made amazing progress. I bet Mo and Harrington will be shocked," Kincaid said. "When do you think they'll be out? You know, Mo keeps talking about Zach's wedding dance. I heard the dance is upstairs in the hayloft. I won't even be able to get up there. Let alone dance."

"Kevin, Darrell and I worked out something. Don't worry. We are planning on having a trial run for Heinrich's big anniversary dance," Elton grinned.

"I hear it's your anniversary, too. How long you two been married?"

"Fourteen years," Nora smiled. "And good years too!"

Elton grinned, "Eat your heart out Kincaid!"

"I was working for the last fourteen years," Kincaid retorted.

"So was I!" Elton laughed.

"Well, when you two get done bickering, you might want to talk to Elmer. I think the rent is his doghouse is going up!" Nora got up, "I'm going to watch television."

Elton waited until she left the room and then said to Kincaid quietly, "Carl. If you want to use to the phone to call Maureen or anyone, feel free. You know, she called you the other day, so you kind of owe her a call."

"How would I pay you?"

"No need. Just tell the Harringtons hi for me, okay?" Elton stood up. "Oh, their phone number is in the box here. I can hand you the receiver and when you are done, just let me know. I'll hang it up for you. Remind me to get a desk phone tomorrow. That would be easier than this wall thing."

Elton handed him the phone and number box, but never looked at him. Kincaid appreciated that. He was more than a little embarrassed, but he really did want to talk to Mo. Just to see how Harrington was, of course.

11

Father Matthew Harrington answered the phone. He was Mo's son and Kincaid had met him while in the Louisiana hospital. He seemed like a good guy. He was a year younger than Ian, the Boston PD detective who was injured in the gunfight that took Kincaid's career.

"Hello Matt," Kincaid answered, "How are things going? This is Kincaid."

Matt chuckled, "I know who you are! How are things going on the prairie?"

"I asked first."

"Pretty good out here on the East coast. Ian is getting his strength back, but very anxious about what he is going to do with himself."

"Are the nerves healing up so he can go back to work?" Kincaid asked.

"No. The doctors doubt that they will. They were pretty much decimated. He has movement in that arm, but it's very slow and deliberate. He won't be able to go back to work with the police department. He is finally coming to grips with that, but he hates it," the priest replied. "How you doing?"

"Alright. I'm antsy to get away from all these Petunias but they 've been really decent to me. I miss my whiskey and talking to someone who's lying through their teeth playing some con!"

Matt laughed, "That is a first. Most folks are the other way around."

"You're just as Petunia as these guys," Carl groused, "Hell, I even went to church today!"

"Oh, that was it!" Matt chuckled.

Kincaid was defensive right away, "How did you hear about that?"

"The radio said that were huge earth tremors in the Dakotas!" Matt teased.

"Even if you do wear that stupid collar, you're still a jackass!" Kincaid retorted.

"So, did Byron's church survive?" Matt asked, trying to contain his laughter.

"Yah. I sat with his kid. The little guy unraveled the hem of his suit jacket all through the sermon," Kincaid related with great glee.

"You should've stopped him," Matt suggested.

"Nah. It kept him quiet. He just turned six and as he says, he gets figgetty."

"Sounds to me like you're an enabler," Matt chuckled. "Do you want to talk to Ian?"

"Yah, wouldn't mind if he is handy. I'm on Magpie's phone, so I can't be gabbing all night."

"It was good talking to you. Here he is."

"Hi Kincaid," Harrington said, "How are you doing?"

"Okay. I told your brother I have to get out of here pretty soon. I'm going soft. Man, I even helped freeze green beans the other day!"

Harrington laughed so hard he couldn't even talk for a minute, "I'd have paid big money to see that! And that's a blasted fact."

"So, you doing basket weaving?" the older man asked.

"Pretty much. I've been trying to get my muscle tone back. I can walk pretty good now and all that. Don't know if I'll be able to dance for a while yet. I need to at least be able to walk up the aisle for Zach's big wedding."

"Yah, you know Charlie is going to be ring bearer," Kincaid pointed out. "Zach asked me to bring my gun to the service, just in case!"

"I just hope he doesn't run and jump up for my hug. He darned near knocked me over before. Now, I think he'd flatten me!"

"Preacher is trying to break him of that. He does pretty good now. At least, he will ask first. He stays with me all day, you know. He was bent out of shape because the little girls can't dig, so he 'helps' me. He's my legs! I tell you, it's an experience," Kincaid said with pride.

Harrington agreed it would be, "But he's a good kid. I talked to Ginger the other day. She still remembers my Badge number! Can you believe that? How is Miriam doing?"

"Ginger is one bright little kid," Kincaid agreed, "And she talks almost as much as Magpie. Miriam is making progress. You'll be surprised. She still scares easily and curls up like a ball. Still terrified of crayons."

"Poor kid. Well, Mom's here now, if you want to talk to her. I'm sure she'd like to check up on you."

"Thanks, oh! Elton says hi. I'll tell the kids hello for you," Kincaid tried to act cool. Why was he so nervous about talking to her? That was so unlike him.

"Hello, you old Coot!" Mo giggled, "How nice of you to call!"

"You know, Motor Mouth," Kincaid pointed out, "You really started something with that Coot business. Miriam calls me all the time."

Instead of feeling bad about it, Mo seemed to take it as a compliment. "Good for her! I talked to little Ruthie when she called Ian a bit ago and she said the Wee One is doing well. She said she got the giggles when you were at exer—what is that you call it?"

"Exertorture. Yes, she did. Giggled so hard she got the hiccoughs. Served her right!" Kincaid grumped.

"Oh, settle down, you love it!" Mo laughed. "I hear that you and this Charlie unraveled his-,"

Kincaid interrupted, "Hey look! I had nothing to do with it. He did it all on his own. I didn't even know what he was up to until he was almost done."

"Did you try to stop him?"

"What was the point then? He still would have half of his hem hanging down. I thought at that point, it made more sense for him to just keep occupied."

"You're as bad as he is. How's it really going for you, Carl? Are you settling down into retirement?" Mo asked, no longer kidding around.

"If this is retirement, I'd better go back to work to rest! Hey, I helped the ladies freeze green beans and can make a mean potato salad. I heard a recipe today for Hot German Potato salad. I'm anxious to try it. I'll have to ask Nora about it," Kincaid regaled. "Have you ever made it?"

"No, but I've tasted it. It was good. Will you make it when I'm out there? When is the big wedding? Those kids haven't set a date, have they?" Maureen asked.

"Not yet. They are waiting to hear about Ginger and Harrington. I think she could make it down the aisle, but her long distance vision fluctuates or whatever. Her peripheral vision is getting better though. She goes to the eye doctor Tuesday. They'll know more then. I go Tuesday, too. Then I can find out when I can move out and get a place on my own."

"Carl, don't rush it. Will you not, please?" Maureen was very definite. "You could just get yourself in trouble. I know it's selfish but I'd like you to be there at least until after the wedding. Otherwise, we might lose contact."

"Maureen, I'll always let you know how to get in touch with me. But don't worry. I'll be here for the wedding yet, that I already know. The doctors are sure about that. Seems I have this date with a gal for a wedding dance and I'd like to be able to do a slow waltz at least." Kincaid said pointedly.

"Would I know this gal?"

"Might just. She's from Boston. Nice gal, but she talks non-stop!" Kincaid teased.

"Don't know anyone like that! Well, Ian goes to the doctor on Wednesday. Then we'll know more at this end. He's so darned lonesome for Ruthie; I may have to have the Jack Daniels truck make home deliveries!" Mo giggled. "I hope that I do have a date to the dance. I've been dieting. Between starving and my new girdle, I should turn a lot of heads!"

"The dance is upstairs in a hayloft you know!" Kincaid chuckled.

"You mean I have to crawl up a ladder? Why if I fall with all that elastic on my hinder, I'd bounce for six miles!" Maureen laughed.

Kincaid laughed, "Magpie told me there is a regular stairway. That's why I don't know if I can make it up there. He said it's all worked out. That scares the hell out of me! Hard to say what this outfit will come up with! Well, I'd better hang up. He won't take any money for my call and I don't want to be responsible for the foreclosure of his farm!"

"Thanks for calling, Carl. It's good to hear from you."

"Me, too. Good night."

•

Zach came in just as Kincaid said goodbye. "Would you hang this up for me? I hate to bother Magpie."

"No problem. Want some coffee?"

"Sounds good. My cup is here."

Zach peeked in the living room to invite Elton and Nora for coffee, but came back grinning but not saying a word to them. "They are both asleep on the sofa. All cuddled up." He filled their cups and then sat down. "So, what's up?"

"Mo and I were just talking about the wedding. Have you guys set the date yet?"

"After the doctor's appointments," Zach nodded, "It'll be pretty soon though."

"That's what I told Mo. Ian has his appointment on Wednesday. She said he is getting really antsy. I bet it's just killing him," Kincaid said.

"How are you doing? I know this has to be hard for you," then Zach chided, "All these Petunias!"

"It's a pain in the ass most the time but they kind of grow on you. I won't get like them, will I?" Kincaid looked worried.

Zach just raised his eyebrows, "You could do worse, but no. You're too ornery."

"That's a relief. I like those little gophers and all, but I can't see me digging dams and unraveling hems the rest of my life!"

"You never know. If Charlie has anything to say about it, you will." Zach chuckled.

Then Elton popped his head around the door, "Will you check the Pa Bell before you go to bed? Nora and I are going to cash it in. Good night."

After they heard the bedroom door close, Kincaid smiled to Zach, "He's quite the Magpie."

"Yah. I love those people," Zach agreed.

"Well, I wouldn't go that far but they're good folks. Was Nora in a car accident or something? At exertorture, I noticed all the scars and her right arm is really messed up."

"She was mauled by an old sow that went after Pepper when she was a little kid. That's how Pepper got a limp," Zach explained. "She and Elton got married in the hospital so he could adopt the kids, because the doctors thought Nora might not make it. He wanted to adopt the kids anyway to give them a home."

"She's really a neat lady. I can see Magpie adopting those kids. He'd doing something sappy like that. You know, the kids that I've met are pretty decent folks. That Pepper is a good kid and strong! I couldn't believe how much strength she has. For a tiny thing she can really move those old muscles when she does that therapy stuff. How soon are she and Chris going to tie the knot?" Kincaid grinned.

"I don't know. It won't be too long I wouldn't think," Zach was thoughtful. "Both of us couples have many things to work out. Suzy and

I still don't know where we are even going to live! Are we going to take Miriam to live with us? Is Suzy going to quit her job? Am I going to drive back and forth to Bismarck? Our cart is way before our horse."

"Well, at least you have a cart. Better than a lot of folks," Kincaid was thoughtful, then he chided. "I like Suzy. She's much better than you deserve!"

"It's a good thing I don't put too much stock in what you say!" Zach laughed.

12

That night, the new medication worked for Lloyd and he slept through the night. It didn't storm and the different antibiotic was helping Bert. He wasn't coughing quite so much and his fever was down. He actually slept a few hours soundly.

The peace of the restful night was broken about three. Bert started coughing and it did not stop. Kincaid got up with him and started rubbing his back like Zach had shown him. Within minutes, Zach was there beside him helping clear his lungs. Elton and Pepper were both there too, but after a couple minutes, things were coming under control so Zach sent them back to bed.

Zach stayed with Bert about ten minutes after the coughing stopped and readjusted his oxygen. He sat in the rocking chair that Lloyd used when he made his middle of the night visits to Bert. Within a couple minutes, he was almost asleep.

Kincaid put on his bathrobe and told Zach to go to bed. "I can sit here with him. You get some sleep"

"I can stay with him," Zach yawned.

"I know you can, but I don't have surgery tomorrow. Maybe I can convince Charlie to take a nap!" Kincaid grinned.

"Good luck with that," Zach said as he got up and checked Bert's pulse. "Okay, I'll take you up on that. First sign of trouble, you call me. Got it?"

"Got it."

Carl Kincaid sat down in the rocking chair and covered up with one of Katherine's crocheted afghans. He couldn't remember the last time he had actually sat in a rocking chair. Must of have been when he was a kid. He rocked quietly and looked out the sash window.

It was a starry and clear night. The new moon was bright and the big trees in the yard cast long shadows across the grass. The yard looked pretty. The house had gone back to its peaceful quiet. Even the rhythm of Bert's oxygen was relaxing.

Relaxing. That is something that he had not done in years. This place was busy and stuff was always going on, but it was relaxing. Why was that? Forty people had been there for dinner and he was relaxed! Hmm, he'd have to think about that.

It was hard to imagine that people would actually sit around and try to figure out how to get someone in a wheelchair up steps to a dance. Most the folks he knew would think that if you couldn't make it up there on your own steam, you probably didn't need to go. Or that a teenager that would take a book to his father because it was about something his little brother was interested in. He thought back over the conversations at dinner. The men visited about their work and families like most people, but it was different. They didn't belly ache.

Kincaid knew some of the folks he had worked with were like that but he never took enough time to hang out with them. If he'd gone over to their place, then he'd have had to invite them back. He wasn't interested in that. At least, he never knew he was.

Bert stirred and then coughed. Kincaid got up and helped him set up until his lung cleared. After a few minutes, Kincaid propped up his pillow so the man could rest again.

"Thanks," Bert grumped. "You don't need to sit here like a vulture all night. I'll make enough noise before I go, so you won't miss anything."

"I'm pretty certain of that. Hell, you'll have the whole house up!" Kincaid retorted.

Bert was quiet for a while and then he said, "You know, I'll be going soon. I'm not really sad about it. I've been here long enough, but I can't just leave. I need to make sure that things are covered here."

"Covered, like how?" Kincaid asked seriously.

"I listen to Lloyd for hours on end. Mind you, we used to have good conversations, but his mind is really bad sometimes. I hear the same sentence over so many times, I could scream. I know it isn't his fault. I wish you'd known him a few years ago. He was quite the guy. Even you would have liked him."

"I do like him," Kincaid defended himself.

"Yah, but it was different. The only reason that I've hung around this long is because of him and Katherine. They were always so good to Ida and me. I promised Ida I'd help Katherine take care of Lloyd. I thought I could worm out of it when things got tough, but that darn kid of mine keeps reminding me. So, I'm stuck. I thought maybe I could outlast Lloyd, but it doesn't look like it. He'll come wandering in here at night long after I'm gone and he'll need someone to talk to. I figure you could do that."

"Me? Why'd he talk to me?"

"I was figuring about that. I think you need to talk to him and me sometimes. Then he'll get used to you."

"I can't really see me doing that."

"I'd love to be the guy that plays with Charlie and Ginger. You know, when Ken and Katie were that age, Ida and I did stuff with them. Now, I'm useless. I watch how Charlie and Ginger are with you, and that little girl Miriam. You'll have to be their grandpa for me."

Kincaid almost passed out, "What in the hell are you talking about? You must not be getting enough oxygen. They have their Dad and Magpie. They don't need anyone else."

"No, I'm old but I'm not stupid. Everyone needs a lot of people. Have you ever noticed how busy these people are? Elton is busier than a cat in a sandbox. He has two grandbabies on the way and the way he drags people home, he'll have to be building another new addition anytime now. He can use someone to help him, too. Maybe that is why the good Lord sent you to us. It sure as hell isn't because of your pleasant nature," Bert smiled wryly.

Kincaid patted his shoulder, "You aren't getting all mushy now, are you? I'll call Zach."

"Don't. Carl, I'd feel a lot better knowing that I had your word you wouldn't be cutting out on this crew anytime soon. I know you always talk about leaving the petunias and getting back to your whiskey. You could have a shot of whiskey here."

"Bert, I'm moved, really," Kincaid answered with probably more emotion than he had felt in a long time, "But I'm not the person that God would send to do any of His errands. He'd use a Magpie, or even you, but not me."

"Then what the hell are you here for? You dimwit. He already did. And whether you know it or not, you're already tied to these people. I've heard how you talk about Harrington's mom. Why are you so hell bent on pretending that you're this big tough standalone guy? You might be able to pull the wool over a lot of eyes but mostly, no one here believes you. I hope you realize that."

"I think you're delving into my private business," Kincaid didn't really know how to react, but he was feeling very threatened.

"Sorry you feel that way. I sort of figured after you rubbing my back in the moonlight, that we had something going here," Bert laughed and the cough started again.

Kincaid shook his head, "You're a dirty old man! I'd have never figured something like that coming from you. I should let you cough, you old buzzard." Kincaid helped him sit upright.

After he settled down, Bert shook his head weakly, "This is a hell of a way to go, you know. I know that you don't want to talk to me about stuff you've buried for years but look at it this way. Anything you tell me, will be buried again soon!"

"Stop talking like that!"

"It's a fact. And like I said before, if you want to be the Lone Ranger, you sure can. No one is going to stop you. Just remember one thing. He had Tonto. He wasn't really alone. There's nothing wrong with having people that care about you," then Bert grinned, "You could be like me. Nobody thinks that I like them."

Kincaid chuckled, "Bert, we all know you like us. It's just that none of us like you. Hasn't that dawned on you yet?"

"Well, at any rate, I'm going to sleep now. I don't plan on dying tonight so go back to bed. Just think about it for me, will you? I hope you figure it out soon, so I can get my rest."

Then Bert reached over patted Kincaid's hand. "If you decide not to, I guess that's it, but you'd do a good job."

Kincaid crawled back into this bed and pulled the pillow down around his ears. He tried to convince himself that the old man was just addled from his disease. He hated what he said. However, the longer he thought about it, the more he wondered why he was trying to prove that he was a loner. He remembered that night in the Louisiana hospital. Being alone didn't seem so cool then, and it sure as hell wasn't like anyone was envying him.

If he had been a different kind of a person, he might have thought he had some tears in his eyes, but he knew himself well enough to know it was an allergy to some weed that was blooming out in the prairies.

In the morning, Carl was very glad that his old roommate was still sleeping when he went out to the kitchen for breakfast. He was concerned that the old man might get on a roll and just say all that stuff in front of the whole family.

The family was gathering around their beloved coffee pot when he got into the kitchen. Katherine poured him a cup and he went over to the table.

Elton was stirring his coffee and said, "Looks like you'll have sunshine today! I'm sure Charlie is scrubbing up his shovel while we speak! How did Bert sleep the rest of the night? I thought I heard talking in there, but then I decided I must be dreaming."

"No, he coughed once more and we talked a little. Did you hear what we said?" Kincaid was a bit nervous.

"Oh no. I just thought it sounded like when he and Lloyd visit. Boy, Lloyd slept like a rock last night. I have to say, it was good to get a whole night's sleep for a change."

Kincaid frowned, "What do you mean? You were up when Bert coughed."

"Yah, but that's only once. I didn't even have to wake all the way up," Elton grinned.

"You're weird. Do you think I can take the chair outside today?"

"As long as you stay on the concrete. I wouldn't trust the gravel. You might get stuck. I'd think since you guys are so into water diversion, you could fix it up so the yard drains better!" Elton smirked.

"I really don't like you Magpie."

"I know. Oh look, here comes your little buddy now." Elton looked out the window as Ellison's car door opened. He almost bent over in hysterical laughter. "Charlie is carrying his shovel!"

"Lord have mercy!" Kincaid groaned.

13

Pastor Byron and Marly took Bert to his doctor's appointment in the afternoon, while Nora and Grandma kept Miriam and Ginger.

Charlie was already at Schroeders, helping Kincaid. Annie was home from work, so the three planned how to make the water flow to keep Uncle Elton's drive clear of mud puddles. Annie thought they should divert the water into an irrigation system for the garden. A rift emerged in the planning team however when Charlie didn't think they should make the puddles go away. They should just be moved. No one should waste a good puddle.

In the end, Kincaid cast the final vote. The water would be diverted from the driveway to a fine dam that would back up into a big puddle. The overflow from the dam could water the garden.

Charlie was reticent about the plan, but gave in when Annie reminded him about how upset Aunt Nora was when he made a lake under her clothesline. He didn't get a treat for a couple days until the lake dried up and they even had hot fudge sundaes one night. Why, if it hadn't been for Uncle Elton, he wouldn't even got a lick!

After their naps, Ginger and Kincaid worked with Miriam and got her to drive the wheelchair. Within a half an hour, she was doing it on her own. By the time Elton came home, she was wheeling around the house. They all played hide and seek with her and she seemed to enjoy it. It was about the happiest they'd ever seen her.

Elton had come home early that afternoon to meet with the insurance guy. The insurance man came out to look over the new addition on the house and as Elton pointed out, "To raise the rates! He could have done it over the phone, but this way, he gets coffee too!"

The little kids were all in the dining room with Kincaid and Annie. They were making plans for the big lake they would someday build in Uncle Elton's pasture. Miriam was sitting in her wheelchair and Kincaid was in his.

The insurance man knocked at the door and Nora answered it. Mr. Fleischer had brought his wife along because they were going to Minot after Schroeders. Elton invited them in and while they were at the door, Kincaid wheeled into the kitchen.

Elton introduced him to Fleischers. Kincaid was struck by how familiar Mrs. Fleischer looked. She was tall, slender and had wild washed out carrot red hair. Her eyes were almost green and her complexion was pinkish pale. She looked so familiar, even though he was certain he'd never seen her before. He couldn't place her and that bothered him but he refilled his coffee cup and went back into the dining room with the kids. He found himself looking through the door at her several times. Who was she? Who did she look like? It was driving him crazy.

After they had their coffee in the kitchen, Elton and the insurance man walked around the house so the man could look over all the renovations. He was very impressed with the dining room and loved the fireplace.

He was a friendly, jolly guy and he said hello to the kids. They all smiled back and went on with their great plans. Mr. Fleisher joked that if they built a lake, they'd have to be sure to call him to get insurance on it.

Then he went to the kitchen and said to his wife, "Honey, you have to come see this fireplace. You'll just love it."

Nora and Mrs. Fleischer came into the dining room and when she saw the fireplace, she squealed, "Lordie be! This is the kind of fireplace I've always wanted!"

When she said it, Kincaid knew who she reminded him of. Her voice was almost exactly like Naomi's. She looked enough like her that she could have been Miriam's mother's twin.

Apparently Miriam noticed too. Kincaid caught her reaction out of the corner of his eye when she saw Mrs. Fleischer. The little girl turned pale and immediately started to shake. Big tears rolled down her cheeks and she began to whimper.

The mountain of a man reached over and picked the little girl who weighed less than twenty pounds onto his lap. Annie knew she was going into one of her panic attacks and asked Kincaid, "You got it?"

Kincaid nodded. "Yah, I'm going to the nursery. If I have trouble, I'll yell."

In the nursery, he had one hell of a time. The little girl was curling up into the fetal position and no amount of comforting could get her to settle down. Annie stopped by the door and said, "I'll get Dad."

Elton came in and took the little girl from Kincaid's lap. She was holding on to him like a vise grip. She started to really cry and Elton finally got her to relax. She kept saying, "No go. No go."

The men couldn't figure out what she was trying to say but whatever it was, she was very adamant about it. Once she started to cry it only took a couple of minutes before she relaxed a little. Before long, she went back to Kincaid. Elton went out to finish up with the insurance agent.

Kincaid held Miriam until she fell asleep. He put her down on the daybed because he couldn't reach the crib from his wheelchair.

When he came out of the nursery, the women were setting the table for dinner. Ginger asked if Miriam was done being 'frad jelly' and he assured her that she was sleeping.

Elton was putting on his coveralls to go do chores in the kitchen and he asked Kincaid, "What do you think set her off?"

"I know what it was. That insurance guy's wife was damn near the spit and image of her mom, that Naomi," Kincaid said. "When I first saw her, it almost threw me for a loop."

"I never saw the woman," Elton said thoughtfully, "Strikingly similar, huh?"

"Yah. I think it scared Miriam. She's sleeping now but I put her on the daybed. I couldn't reach the crib from this chair. I hate that. She was having such a good day."

"Well, she seemed to settle down pretty fast. It only took her about half an hour. I guess, each time it will get easier, huh?" Nora suggested.

Charlie came running into the kitchen. "Miriam is 'sappeared! I can't find her and Annie and Grandma are looking too! Come quick!"

They all went into the nursery. Charlie was right. No sign of Miriam. Everything else was there, her blanket that she had covered up with, her wheelchair, but Mr. Bear was gone. They looked all over the room and then expanded their search.

Suzy, Kevin and Carrie arrived, they helped. They were all panic stricken. She couldn't walk because of her hip. She'd have to be carried or crawl. Her wheelchair was still by the table, so she wasn't in that. No one could have taken her. They searched the place from one end to the other. Nora and Suzy were crying while they searched and everyone was beside themselves.

Kincaid got felt sick to his stomach and went to his room. How in the hell was he so dumb to lay her down on a regular bed? He should've had someone help him so they could put her in the crib. It was his fault. If anything happened to her, he'd never forgive himself.

He came out of the bathroom and just happened to look toward the corner of the closet where the oxygen tanks were stored. He noticed a little glimpse of pink. It was the sweater that Miriam had been wearing.

He called for the others. Elton and Kevin started moving the oxygen tanks. There was a little path between the back row of oxygen tanks and the wall, about eight inches wide. Kevin crawled back in the corner of the closet and found the little girl. She had squished herself and Mr. Bear against the wall. She was curled up and pressed against it as tightly as possible.

Kevin peeled her away from the wall and she buried her head right in his shoulder, only holding on to Mr. Bear. She was whimpering and mumbling. No one had ever seen her like that.

Elton and Kevin went with her to the nursery and tried to get her to calm down. "What is she saying, Kevin?" Elton asked. "I can't really understand it."

"It sounds like, 'Son, no go'." Kevin shook his head, "Dad, I don't know how to do this. She must have crawled in there. What the hell's wrong? She's shaking like a leaf." He kept patting her back and trying to calm her.

"I think I know," Kincaid said as he came in the room. "I think she thought that woman was her M O T H E R, and she's afraid that she was going to take her. She was terrified."

Elton's face washed with understanding, "That makes sense. Maybe when she wakes up crying about that person it isn't because she is lonesome for her, but afraid that she'll be back to get her! Do you think that is it?"

"That'd be my guess. Shit, if I had to go back to those people, I'd crawl away too. I should have paid more attention. Why didn't I twig on sooner? I should've stayed in the nursery with her. Why didn't I do that?"

Elton patted his friend on the back, "Don't beat yourself up about it, Carl. None of us understood."

Kevin was walking and patting her back, "I think we need to take her in to see the doctor. Her bandage is bleeding. She might've reopened the wound on her hip. Can the others milk tonight? I'll hold her, but we need to get her hip fixed. She won't let go and I don't want to scare her anymore."

"Let me take off my coveralls and get the car," Elton said.

Kevin said, "I don't know how bad this bleeding is."

"Yah, it'll have to be checked. She has a big bruise on her side. She probably did it when she got off the bed. I'll go get the car," Elton said.

By the time they got home from the hospital, everyone was worn out. Zach had her doctors there. They had to give her something to get her to relax enough so they could get her out of Kevin's arms. She had held on to him to tightly, he had gouge marks on his neck.

Nora had dinner waiting for them although the other kids had eaten. Miriam was sleeping in Elton's arms when they came in. Dr. Samuels had been rather certain that Kincaid's observation was probably correct. The little girl had found a safe place and was terrified that she could be taken away. Naomi and Ezekiel had dropped her off at various places over the years; it had probably happened to her before. She knew, once her Mom showed up, she would not be safe. She wasn't old enough to realize that since her parents were dead, they couldn't be back.

The doctors were able to suture the wound without putting her under. She would be okay but it would extend the recovery time. Her nutrition was very improved and she was actually gaining weight. If only they could get her over her fears, she'd do just fine.

14

Byron and Marly returned with Bert. The doctor had reported that the new antibiotic was having a good effect on Bert's lung. The prognosis had not changed however and there was little else to be done. He had refused to go into a hospital, and his family honored his request.

"It'd be foolish and expensive," Bert explained. "And most of all, pointless. I'd almost rather be here with you jugheads, than in some damned hospital with a bunch of strangers."

Elton grinned, "Well thank you Bert. That makes us almost feel good."

"Well then, I'd better rephrase it!" Bert grouched. "Anyway, I need to get some rest. Hell, you hauled me around all day to have some joker tell me I'm gonna croak! I could have told you that this morning and still had my nap!"

Byron laughed and took his Dad to the bedroom to help him get ready for bed. When he was settled in, Byron asked if he could say a prayer.

Bert scowled at him, "If you say Now I Lay Me, I swear I'll find Kincaid's gun!"

"On second thought, you just pray all by yourself!" Then he gave his father a hug, "I love you, Dad."

"You damned well should," the old man took his son's hand, "Byron, I've always been proud of you. I do love you, even though you are a horses' ass."

Byron kissed his Dad, "Gee, I was getting worried. I thought you might be nice there for a minute."

"Seriously Byron, if I don't get up tomorrow, let Marly and your kids know how much I really love them? I never say it, you know. I worry sometimes that they don't know."

"Dad, they do know and I know they all love you, too."

Bert nodded, "Good," and then he turned on his side.

After the Ellison's went home, Miriam's medication was wearing off. She was in a lot more pain than normal and a nervous wreck. She wouldn't let Marly or Ruthie anywhere near her. She only wanted Byron.

She finally fell asleep. She slept only a short time and woke up with a scream. She cried inconsolably. "Dog bite! Dog bite! No go!"

When she woke up enough to realize that Byron was holding her, she held his face in her tiny hands and said, "Uncle" and "Son."

Byron tried everything he could think of, but finally had Marly call Elton.

"I'll be right there. Lloyd seems to be sleeping soundly tonight. See you in a minute," Elton answered the phone.

Within five minutes, he came in. He went right over to her and patted her back. "Hi Miriam," he said softly.

She immediately held out her arms to him and he took her. She cried but seemed to be less agitated than she was with Byron.

"This is a bad one. What are we going to do? Even though I have those pills, I don't want to knock her out again. That can't be good for her," Byron worried.

"Let's just try it this way. I wonder why she is so afraid of Marly now. She was fine with her, and Ruthie and Suzy? My goodness, Suzy is like her mother," Elton said.

As soon as the word came out of his mouth, the little girl started to shake again. The two men looked at each other and Byron nodded, "I think we have our answer."

Elton told the Ellisons to get some rest and he sat down in the rocking chair in their living room to rock the little girl. He hummed and tried to get her calm down.

Frustrated, he finally said, "Miriam, I want to you to know that you never, ever, ever have to go with your mother anymore. Okay? Never. None of us will make you go. You can stay with us forever, if you want. You do not need to go. Okay?'

She quit shaking, but never made any response other than that. Speaking calmly, Elton continued, "You can be with all of us, Son, Zach, Coot, Byron and Ken. We'll all be here. Okay? We won't make you go away anymore, ever again."

She finally quit crying and just hugged on to him as tightly as she could. After a few minutes, she looked at him, "Sharlee?"

Elton grinned with relief, "Certainly, Charlie will be here too. You kids will all be together. This is your home now and no one is going to take you away. Okay? You guys are going to go dig with Coot and be his little gophers. I heard you are planning to dig a big lake in my pasture? Do you think the cows will like that?"

Miriam shrugged.

"I think they might, huh? They might go swimming. Do you think they have swimming suits and beach towels?"

Miriam shrugged.

"I think they have really, really big towels, huh?"

Miriam looked at him and nodded.

"Yah, I agree," Elton continued. "Maybe we can all go swimming there. Would that be fun?"

"If you want to," Miriam said.

"Well, I think we might. Would you like that?"

Miriam asked, "Son?"

"Son could, too. Do you think he'd like it? He's a good swimmer. Are you a good swimmer?"

Miriam shrugged and Elton grinned, "Well, we'll have to learn how then, uh? You and me. I'm not a very good swimmer. Would that be okay?"

Miriam shook her head, "Mr. Bear?"

"Yes, Mr. Bear, too, but he can't get wet, you know. Maybe he can watch over our picnic basket while we swim."

Miriam looked at him, "Chocolate?"

Elton nodded, "We can have chocolate. What else should we have? Green beans?"

Miriam nodded, "Son straw?"

"Yup, we'll have Son bring a straw for our chocolate milk shake. It will be a fun swimming day, huh?"

Miriam nodded.

"I think you might want to shut your little peepers now and go to sleep. I'll hold you right here until you wake up. You don't need to worry. Okay? You better go to sleep for me, otherwise you"ll be too tired in the morning."

"Uncle." Miriam said, and patted his neck with her little hand.

At six the family alarm went off. Elton was still asleep in the rocking chair and Miriam was cuddled up in his lap. Byron woke him and suggested he put the little girl in her bed.

"No, I can't do that. I promised her I'd hold her until she woke up. I think she slept quite a while," Elton yawned.

She started to stir and within a minute, sat up. She looked at Elton and smiled, "Uncle," she said.

Byron held out his arms, "Will you come with me to get some milk or would you like to take a longer sleep in your own bed?"

She held out her arms, "Son."

When he took her, he said, "Son will be over at Uncles. He isn't here Miriam."

"Sharlee, Ginger, Son, Mr. Bear." She tried to explain, nodding her head. Her little black curls bounced as she tried to get her message across.

Byron looked at her and grinned, "Would you like to come over to Uncle Elton's with us to see Son?"

Miriam nodded.

"Okay," Byron smiled. He said to Elton, "It might be better than leaving her here with Marly."

"I'm coming over there, too," Marly said as she came up beside her husband and patted Miriam, "I'm not that person she's so afraid of and I need to assure her of that."

Marly looked at Miriam, "Honey, I will dress you so we can go over to Uncle Elton's to see Son, okay?"

Miriam looked at the men and then back at Marly without expression. It was obvious she didn't want to.

Elton smiled, "If you let Marly dress you, I'll put in your bear tails. Would you like that?"

Miriam hesitated and then said, "If you want to."

By the time they all got over to Schroeder's, Miriam was okay around Marly again. But then there really was not much interaction. Once she saw Kevin, she was in his arms and that was that.

"You should have called me last night," Kevin said when he heard about it. "I'd have come over right away."

Byron patted his back, "I know you would have and if your Dad had been tied up with Lloyd, I would have. But somebody needs to get some rest around this place."

"Okay, but I am a part of this family too, you know." Kevin pointed out. "Sometimes I think you guys don't trust me."

Elton looked at his son, "We do trust you. Believe me. It seemed practical to me last night that since Lloyd was sleeping, you should be home with your wife."

Kevin frowned, "What about your wife? When is the last time you guys got to spend a whole night together without getting up and rummaging around after someone?"

Elton grinned, "I don't know. Was it 1968, Nora?"

"It's not funny Dad. I know you think you are doing me a favor and I appreciate it, but I can help out too."

"Okay, here's the deal. Every other time, you come over. Okay? Let's just hope that we don't have any more times," Byron said. "I know we will though."

When Kincaid came in the room to get his coffee, he asked how things went overnight and they told him, "You know, if you brought her over here, I could help out too."

"We know, but you are watching over Bert," Elton said. "How was he last night?"

"Pretty good. Only coughed a couple times. I think that new medicine is helping," Kincaid said as he watched like an eagle while Elton put cream and sugar in his coffee.

"It just kills you, doesn't it?" Elton noticed Kincaid watching him. "You can put it in your coffee too, if you want. It might sweeten your nature."

"Like hell it would. I'd get diabetes," Kincaid blustered. "So what time are we going to the doctor's today? Miriam and I both have appointments."

Byron smiled "Miriam saw her doctors yesterday, so they both said that she didn't need to come in today. It's just you. Is Elton taking you in, or me? Ginger's appointment is today, too."

"I will," Elton said. "I want to see if they can give him a brain transplant."

The phone rang and it was Zach. He had just talked to Suzy and wanted to check up on Miriam. After he heard all the night's activities, he was depressed. "Suzy and I aren't doing a very good job with her. You guys have done all the work. This isn't working out."

"Zach, you and Suzy have jobs. We're doing just fine and it is really getting better," Elton argued.

"You have jobs too! What are you jabbering about? Ruthie and I just dumped our niece on you guys. We aren't much better than Naomi. It just isn't right!" Zach reiterated.

"I think you're right. You should just quit your jobs and stay home with her all the time. We can watch you. That sounds sensible," Elton said sarcastically. "Don't ever say that again. Hear?"

"Yah, I got it. I'll talk to you when you bring Kincaid in. When is his appointment?" Zach asked flatly.

"At eleven, Kevin is doing the shop today and I'll be home," then he looked at his son, "I'm going to take a nap while he works. Then I'll bring the miserable old cuss into the clinic."

"I'll meet you at the office," Zach said. "And maybe we can have lunch together and we can figure out what to do."

"Then you better have Byron there. He has a dog in this fight too. Here, you talk to him," Elton handed Byron the phone.

"I can't make it in time for Carl's appointment, but I'll meet you guys at the Log House about noon. Okay?" Byron offered.

"Sounds good."

They were all pleased with the visit to the doctors. Kincaid was doing well and the doctor thought he could start walking with the aid of a walker more in the house. He wasn't very happy about his digging, but said he could if he was very careful. He didn't want him to pull on that shoulder very much. When Kincaid asked him if he could dance a waltz in a month, the doctor chuckled. "If the walking goes okay. Baby steps, Mr. Kincaid. Baby steps. Why? Have you got a hot date?"

"What's it to you? Do you think that I couldn't have a hot date?" the agent grouched to his cardiologist.

"No sir. I think that you probably do. I'm glad, but you need to remember not to get too carried away. You get to rambunctious now and you could pay for it down the road."

"Okay. I'll take it cool."

Kincaid loved his burger at the Log House. "By George, that is the best damned burger I've ever eaten. What is so different about it?"

"The meat is never frozen and ground fresh here," Elton explained. "Good stuff. I love their onion rings. Miriam would like this place. She would love their milkshakes."

"That is what I want to talk to you guys about," Zach started in, "Suzy and I feel so guilty. It's like we have dumped her and all her problems on you guys. It isn't fair and it isn't right."

"Are we complaining?" Byron became serious.

"No, but then you wouldn't," Zach answered.

"Well, I sure would," Kincaid retorted. "You just leave that Wee One alone. She's working her way through stuff. It's gonna be a while to get her there, but she even let Annie use a blue colored pencil the other day without curling up. Give her a chance. It hasn't been that long. It has only been a month and a half since Louisiana."

Elton slapped him on the back, "Well said, Kincaid."

Zach looked perplexed, "What are we going to do? We think that Suzy should just quit work and take care of her."

Elton said, "Suzy is a girl."

The other men nodded.

Zach shook his head, "Yah. I know. What has that to do with it?"

"Because Miriam is less afraid of men. If she had her choice, she'd live with Kevin," Byron smiled.

"That's the truth," Elton confirmed. "Look. Leave it the way it is. I kind of promised her that she wouldn't have to leave her home. She has a home now. You kids take this time to get the wedding out of the way. By that time, she'll be much more settled and we'll know what we are dealing with."

"That would be the best idea. Ruthie does okay, but she's a girl too. The only girl she is real comfortable with is Katie," Byron pointed out. "I think that's because she isn't sure if she is big enough to be a mom. She's doing real well with Ginger and Charlie. I'm not so sure it would be a good idea to take her away from them now."

Kincaid concurred, "When we're making out plans for the canals in the yard, she watched those kids like a hawk. She is learning a lot on how to behave, disagree, ask for stuff and that kind of thing from them. The fact that they can say no without getting their teeth knocked out is good for her. I doubt she thought that was possible before. I tell you, if I hear 'if you want to' one more time, I might just go dig her parents up just so I can punch them and bury them again. That kid is so scared of being clobbered for not pleasing everyone, I can't stand it. Now, she even asks for a lick of someone's frosting! She's getting to be a real kid. You just leave her alone."

Byron and Elton both agreed. Then Elton grinned, "Just think, she will be a mixture of Ginger and Charlie." Silence fell over the diners. "Maybe you should move her out!"

15

Marly and Ginger came into the Log House and joined the group.

"Guess what Smitty?" the little girl asked Zach, almost bursting with excitement, "My eye doctor said I can almost see like new. I can be your flower girl in a couple weeks, right Mom?"

Marly smiled, as she scooted in by Byron, "That's right, Honey. He said her peripheral vision is much improved and that the fluctuation in the distance vision has stopped. I know Ginger mentioned that it wasn't 'wobbly' a few days ago. He thinks that the distance may be adequate, so she'll only have to wear glasses to read. She is supposed to come back again in three weeks and he'll give her a prescription for her reading glasses!"

Byron hugged his wife and there were congratulations all around. "Now, Smitty," Ginger turned to Zach, "I can run and play, right? And dig . . . I can dig all over the place! I can't wait to tell Charlie!"

"You can start going up and down stairs again, but you're going to have to go slowly until you get used to it again. Tomorrow I'll look at your hands and see if we can get rid of the elastic braces. I know we can on the left hand but we might have to go slower with the right."

"I can carry the flowers in my good hand. You and Suzy can get married tomorrow if you want."

Zach chuckled, "We need to find out how Harrington is doing. He's going to be my best man. So we kind of need to find out how soon Harrington can be out here. Then we will get married."

Ginger thought, "I can call Badge 11918 and give him the business and make him hurry up."

Her Dad looked at her, "Ginger, think about that. If someone had told you to hurry up and get your eyes well, would you have been able to do it?"

She thought, "No, but . . ."

"How would you have felt if someone kept telling you to hurry up?"

"I would've been crabby about it," she dropped her head. "I guess I shouldn't give him the business, huh?"

"Not the kindest thing to do but you can call him to tell him your good news! And tell him that you're waiting patiently for him to get well."

Ginger made a face, "Okay, Daddy." Then she grinned, "Besides Ruthie always says to him that she can't wait to see him again, so that should make him hurry as fast as he can."

"Yah," Uncle Elton grinned, "That should do it. I'm sure he'll be glad to hear how well you're doing! Zach, how soon can my milkmaid milk by herself?"

"Oh, as soon as we can get that elastic brace off!" Zach smiled.

"Wow! I love you, Smitty! You are the best doctor I know. And I know a lot of doctors, don't I, Mommy?"

"Yes, Honey. You really do," Marly agreed.

"Well, I have some good news! It quit raining, so tonight before chores; Darrell and Kevin are coming over to give Lloyd his car! I can't wait to see the look on his face!" Elton was excited.

"Did you decide how you're going to keep him from driving it?" Byron asked.

"Always Mr. Wet Blanket, aren't you?" Elton gave Byron a dirty look. "At first, we weren't going to put an engine in it but we knew that wouldn't work. So, we're just going to give him the car but not the keys."

"Lloyd will have it hotwired before you can say discombobulated."

Elton looked him in dismay, "Damn. You're right. He will huh? Any brilliant ideas?"

"How about just threatening his life?" Kincaid asked.

"That would be a waste of breath. He won't listen," Elton replied. "I think we'll just have to fix it so it doesn't run. Yea gads, I'll still hear how I don't know how to fix it. That's what I did in the first place and then he took the whole damned engine apart."

"You know, he can't go outside without someone with him now, since you have the place so alarmed up. Hell, I know maximum security prisons that aren't as secure. How would he get out there anyway?" Kincaid pointed out.

"You're right. Maybe we're all too worried," Zach agreed.

"Lloyd is a wily old fox," Elton pointed out. "There isn't much I'd put past him."

Kincaid and Elton finished lunch with their friends and then Elton asked, "Would you mind stopping down to the other station? I'd like to since I'm in town."

"Okay. Which one is this?"

"It is the one we just bought this spring. I used to work here many years ago. My coworker bought it years ago but he had to move down South because his in-laws were sickly. So Glenn offered it to me first. It was a blessing because Keith is moving back. He was going to work for Glenn, until he found out that he had to move. Our family decided to take the plunge and buy it. Keith will run this shop when he gets here."

"What is it Pepper does?" Kincaid asked.

"She helps out with the contracts and business end of things. Kevin pretty much runs the Merton shop. I just sort of hang around and annoy everyone," Elton grinned.

"No you don't. I know how you operate. You're always doing something," Kincaid grunted. "Although most the time, it does include annoying everyone!"

Elton laughed "See? I told you."

They stopped at the station and visited for a while. Elton talked to the assistant manager and went over some financial stuff. When they got back in the car, Elton apologized. "Sorry we got so windy. Is there something you'd like to do before we go back to Merton? Shop or see something?"

"Hmm. I guess I'd like to see where Petunia works. We could hit the library. You know, for Charlie. Although, I think he thought he was coming along."

"We can swing by the hospitals and clinic on the way to the library. We can bring Charlie sometime after we have checked it out. You know, having him in a room that is supposed to be quiet, we need to know what we can do to keep him from being 'figgetty'."

"Yah, might be good idea."

Kincaid was impressed with the size of the clinic and the two hospitals where Zach had privileges. Then they went to the library. They didn't find a lot of information on dirt; someone named Jeannie Frandsen had checked out the maximum on that subject. They looked at each other and grinned.

They had better luck on dams and canals. It was hard to find information simple enough for a little kid and finally gave up. "Hell, he knows most of this stuff already," Kincaid bragged. "If we brought him a little kid's book, he'd be insulted."

Elton agreed. Finally, they decided on three and checked them out. In the car, Kincaid started to laugh. "My God," he said.

"Your God, what?"

"If someone had told me a month ago, I'd be in a library in North Dakota looking for a book on dam construction for a six-year-old, I'd have shot them to put them out of their misery!"

Elton had a good laugh. "You know, that's one of the things I like best! I love how twisted things work out! It's amazing, isn't it? The other thing I like is when I'm ready to throw in the towel; things I never thought of start happening and I get over feeling so frustrated! Life can be fun if we don't put too many restrictions on it."

Kincaid just looked at him blankly, and shook his head. He changed the subject, "Now what?"

"You know, I've been neglecting my girl lately. I should buy her something. I might pick her up a present."

"Is it her birthday?" Kincaid asked.

"No, just to let her know how much I appreciate her," Elton paused. "Hmm, but what?"

"She was telling Katherine the other day that the lining in her summer jacket was worn out," Kincaid suggested.

"Good idea. Do you feel up to going to the store with me? I can get the wheelchair out of the trunk if you like."

"I'd rather walk, but I was on my feet quite a bit at the library. If it isn't too much trouble?"

"Of course not. It'd be easier than having to drag you out of the store by your shirt collar and requires a lot less explaining," Elton had a good laugh.

Kincaid glared at him, "Are you about finished?"

"Just about," Elton chuckled.

Inside the store, they went to the ladies department and looked for jackets. Elton found a lightweight leather one that he was especially fond of. "What do you think?"

"Hmm. Nice but it should have a thing around the neck, you know with a bright color!" Kincaid tried to explain.

"A scarf?" Elton looked at the jacket and nodded, "By George, you're right."

The men asked a clerk who directed them to the scarves. Elton found one for Nora and then kept looking.

"Are you going to get her two?" Kincaid asked.

"No, what are we going to give Katherine. Is her summer coat light blue? I think it is."

"Yah, I think so," then the old FBI agent started looking through the stacks of scarves. "Here's a nice one. Think she would like this?"

"Yes, that would be perfect. Hey, look Kincaid, who does this remind you of?" Elton held out at silk screened scarf with deep red roses on a soft green background.

"Well, I'll be jiggered," Kincaid grinned, "It looks like something Mo would wear. Is that who you were thinking of?"

"Exactly. I think she has a jacket the color of the background. Right?"

"Yah, I believe she does."

"Why don't you get it for her?"

"Why would I want to do that?" Kincaid was puzzled.

"Because it reminds you of her. It can't hurt to butter her up a little. You always butter your hot muffins!"

"Magpie! You're out of your mind! How would I give it to her?"

"Ever heard of Pony Express? Horses leave every day at noon."

"You're such a sap. She'd think I was nuts," Kincaid said as he held the scarf. "It's real nice though."

"Oh, come on. She is a nice lady. Send it to her. I'll even pay the postage!"

"Good grief, you petunias are all whacko," Kincaid was staring at the scarf when the salesclerk came over and asked if she could help them.

Elton handed her the two scarves and Kincaid caressed the one he was holding. "This one, too."

The clerk took them and Kincaid followed her to the cash register. Elton followed behind the wheelchair with a big grin. At the register,

Kincaid insisted that he pay for half of Katherine's scarf and all of Mo's. Elton agreed and asked the clerk if they had gift packages. She said yes and put them in with the other things.

The men left the store all excited about their purchases. Kincaid was very quiet until about half way home. "You know, I really think a lot of Mo," he confided.

Elton answered quietly, "I know."

That was all that was said until they got into to Merton. "I know what we didn't do," Elton said as he pulled up in front of the dime store.

"What was that?" Kincaid asked.

"We should pick up a shovel for you. One that you can use in the wheelchair."

"Don't you have one? I guess it'd have to be short, huh?"

"Let's go look. Hey, want the chair or not?"

"I'll walk as along as we aren't going to be gone long."

In the store, the men found a lightweight, smaller shovel that Kincaid could manage from the wheelchair. Then they saw it. There was a covered sand box about five feet square when assembled with a tent top.

Kincaid's eyes popped out of his head, "That's just what we need. Especially at first. I can have Miriam, Ginger and Charlie in there without having to truck all over the yard. Besides, it'll give Miriam a place to practice.

Before they left the store, they had the car stuffed with the kit for the sand box, sand shovels and some bags of good sand.

Once back in the car, Elton started to laugh. "We'd better get home before we get into more trouble!"

16

It was almost four when they got home. Nora watched their faces as they told about their day and smiled. "Seems like you guys had a great day. Good. You both needed it."

"Oh Honey, I got you something," Elton said as he handed her the package with her jacket.

She opened it and started to tear up. "It's beautiful, Elton. How did you know that my-!" then stopped while a look of realization came over her face. "You told him about my jacket, didn't you, Carl? You're not to be trusted."

Then she gave him a kiss and gave her husband a big hug and kiss. "I love you both."

Kincaid smirked, "I told you to watch out, Magpie!"

"Look what else we got!" Elton handed her the flat little box they had scribbled her name on the top. "Where's Katherine?"

"Right here," Katherine said as she came into the kitchen.

Kincaid took the little box out of the bag and handed it to her. The men both watched as the ladies opened the scarves they had chosen for them. There were more hugs and kisses all around.

"We'll have to send you two to town together again," Nora giggled. "Who's this other box for?"

"Kincaid was going to send it off to Mo," Elton explained, so Carl didn't have to. "Maybe I could ask you guys to get the package ready for us. We aren't good at that."

"Certainly," Katherine agreed. "Elton can take it in to Merton tomorrow. Okay?"

"Sounds good. We went to the library," Elton went on, "Then stopped at the dime store in Merton. Mr. Kincaid put the big purchase on this really snazzy sand box set up! We have to put it together this afternoon. Right after some coffee, okay?"

"Sure, we made some date cake with caramel frosting," Nora said as she got the cups down and Grandma got the cake.

"How are the old guys?" Elton asked.

"Good. Bert is sleeping real well and not coughing. I had to check on him because he was so quiet, I got worred," Nora admitted. "I was so relieved he was sleeping. Lloyd is napping. He was rather depressed and crabby this morning. I wish there was something we could do to make him happier."

Elton beamed, "There is! Darrell and Kevin are bringing the old Ford down before milking tonight. He can go for a ride in it before dinner! That should cheer him up!"

Katherine gave Elton a hug. "It will for a while, but you know what's coming next, don't you?"

"Yah," Elton said, "I know, but I really want to see the sparkle in his eyes again."

After their coffee and cake, the two men went outside to build the sandbox. They put it in the yard, just south of the concrete patio the boys had poured when they put in the walkway for Kincaid's wheelchair. That way, Kincaid and Miriam could get to it even if it was muddy. After it was built, they invited the ladies out to 'ooh' and 'aah' over their work. It did look nice and then Nora suggested, "You know, a nice patio swing would be perfect to my mind; like if I wanted to sit out here and watch the kids."

The guys looked at each other. Then Grandma giggled, "I was thinking a nice picnic table would be handy here, since the boys built this patio and all."

"Okay," Elton raised his eyebrows. "Anything else?"

"A big barbeque. We could put it right over here. Oh look, Elton. It seems there is even a place for one. Imagine that!" Nora said with a grin.

Kincaid shook his head, "Yah, imagine that!"

He and Kincaid started to laugh and Elton guffawed, "I think we've been had!"

"Actually," Elton thought out loud, "We do have a picnic table. It's in the shop. We moved it down there once for something and never moved it back out because we didn't have a patio. I'll get the boys to help me move it. So, my girl wants a swing huh? A cuddling swing?"

"I guess!" Nora smiled. "Anyway, Darrell called. He and Kevin are on their way over and Lloyd is in his chair. I suppose we should get him outside, huh?"

Elton told Lloyd that he had a surprise for him outside. The old man looked at him in surprise, "For me? Why whatever could it be? I don't think it is my birthday, is it?"

They just got down the steps when Kevin drove in with the old Ford and Darrell followed in his car. Kevin waved, honked his horn and stopped in front of the steps.

"Is this what you have been looking for?" Kevin yelled, as Darrell parked his car.

The dear old man got tears in his eyes. "My car! Elton, look! Keith found my car!" he said as he caressed the paint job and fondled the door handle.

"Actually Lloyd, Jerald found it but Kevin and Darrell fixed it up for you," Elton explained. "Would you like Kevin to give you a ride in it?"

The old man grinned and wiped the tears from his eyes, "Can my Katie come with?"

"Sure can," Elton said as he opened the car door.

"I can drive," Lloyd said, "Tell Keith to get over. I'll show him how to drive."

Elton's shoulders fell, "No Lloyd, you can't. Remember, you were going to let Kevin drive because he needs the practice? Besides, you can't see so good anymore. That's why you didn't get your driver's license renewed."

Lloyd looked at Elton in shock. "Oh, I should've done that! Now I can't drive until I get a new one, can I?" Then he looked at Kincaid and whispered to Elton, "You know, these cops will throw me in the clink!"

Elton commiserated, "I know, but you can sit in the car and go for a ride with your lady. Come Katherine, Darrell and Kevin are going to take you two for a ride."

Darrell and Katherine got in the back seat. Elton helped Lloyd get in the front. Once inside, Lloyd patted that dash and smiled, "I love this car."

As they drove out of the yard, Elton put his arm around his wife, "Do you think it made him happy?"

She hugged her sentimental husband, "Yes, I know it did. He loved it."

Kincaid had been watching the whole thing, "Yah, did you see how he patted the dashboard? I hope you realize now someone is going to have to give him a ride in it every so often or he'll be of a mind to take off on his own."

"Yah, but it was worth it to see him happy," Elton justified the venture.

"Whatever, Magpie," Kincaid groaned, "Just don't expect me to be taking him for a ride while you're at work. I suppose that'll be the next thing. Me, Charlie and Lloyd. I can see it all now. I suppose you'll expect that. Do you think that I could drive with my arm? It really shouldn't make any problem, should it? I mean, I'd be well enough. Well, just don't expect me to be doing it."

"Wouldn't dream of it," Elton winked to his wife, "Wouldn't even dream of it."

After the ride, the boys dropped the couple off at the house. Lloyd was thrilled and made Kevin promise to park it in the garage so no one could steal it. Kevin gave his oath and Darrell was sworn to make certain that Kevin kept his word. The boys took off to the garage. Elton went down with them and they moved the cars so Lloyd's was parked in front of another car.

"At least he won't get far if he does get it started!" Elton convinced himself.

"You should've seen him, Dad," Kevin smiled, "He was so happy."

"Yah," Darrell agreed. "He told us over and over how much he paid for it brand new and how many horses are under the hood. He really is proud of it."

"I know. I guess I shouldn't have taken it away from him before. He never got over it. I just hope that we can keep him convinced that he can't drive," Elton shook his head.

"You did the right thing before, and I hope we don't live to regret this. We all know what kind of mind he has. Hell," Kevin chuckled, "He's probably sitting up there in the house right now figuring how to dismantle the Pa Bell."

Darrell laughed, "Wouldn't surprise me a bit. Hey, what are you doing over there?"

Elton was moving a couple of boxes from the top of the picnic table that had been stored in the corner. "The ladies want this up on the patio. I don't know. It looks kind of grungy."

"Of course it does," Kevin said, "It's been sitting down here for at least three years or more. Darrell and I'll help you take it up there, but if I were you, I'd set it on the grass and refinish it. If you sat on the seats, you'd get slivers in your hinder a foot long!"

"Well, I guess it'd only take a little sanding and varnish. Then it'll look good as new," Elton said frowning at it.

"No, Dad," Kevin chuckled, "It'll look like an old scruffy thing that was refurbished. You'd be better off using this for kindling and building one from scratch!"

Elton glared at the table, and then sighed, "Yah, you're right. Since my lady wants a rocker swing thing anyway, I might as well get her a decent table. Huh?"

"You better," Kevin agreed.

"You married men crack me up!" Darrell laughed, "If it was for a bachelor pad, we would think it was good enough!"

"Yah," Elton agreed, "But we wouldn't have a romantic porch swing then, would we? You'll find out soon, it's worth it. Right, Kev?"

"Until they get pregnant, then they can't use a porch swing because they're throwing up from motion sickness!" Kevin joked.

"How is Carrie feeling today?"

"Much better, Dad." Kevin answered, "She took that knockout stuff that Zach gave her for when it gets all out of whack. She is much better today and not even groggy."

"Better keep her groggy," Darrell said, just a serious as could be.

Kevin was puzzled, "Why?"

"If she wakes up all the way, she'll realize what a jerk you are and leave you!"

"Dad? Did you hear that? You have to tell Carrie that she can't talk to him anymore? Okay?" Kevin pleaded.

"What makes you think that she would listen to me? None of you guys ever do, and Carrie just ignores you half the time!" Dad laughed. "Let's get up to the house. Nora and Grandma have some cake to send home with you Darrell."

17

They all had a quiet night. The folks that came to milk never stopped by the house. The girls and Zach were in town for work, so it was just the grandparents, Nora, Elton and Kincaid.

The old fellers both went to bed early. The rest of them were teaching Kincaid how to play whist. Carl and Katherine made a fiercely competitive team and managed to give Elton and Nora a good run for their money. Then they had a piece of pineapple upside down cake with their coffee before they went to bed.

"Your package is ready for Elton to take in tomorrow," Nora said as she handed the package to Kincaid. "We have it already to seal but left it open so that you could write a note in it."

"A note?" Carl was taken back. "I hadn't planned on writing anything on it."

"You need to sign your name or something," Katherine teased, "Or Maureen may think it is from someone she likes."

"Do you think she likes someone?" Kincaid's mind was suddenly flooded with a hundred different scenarios he had never considered. Even though he had never thought about it, he had just imagined that she was just in her house with her two sons and maybe went to the market and church. He never thought that she might even know anyone else.

"Oh Carl, of course she does," Katherine smiled, "She didn't just descend on the planet this spring! From what Harrington said, his family has lived there all their lives. I would guess that she knows many people."

"Oh yah, I know that. I did know that." Kincaid said, suddenly quite nervous, "You know, I think I'd like to go outside for a walk, I mean a drive. Could I bum a cigarette, Elton?"

"What did the doctor say?" Nora raised her eyebrows.

"The doctor said I shouldn't smoke at all, but that as long as I kept it down to one or two a day, I could. I can even have a shot of whiskey, but I don't have any."

"I will tell you what, if you don't mind me tagging along, I'll go with you to the patio. We can have a cigarette and I'll bring you a shot of whiskey. That way, if you pass out, I can wheel you back in."

"Elton," Nora frowned, "You shouldn't encourage him."

"He isn't. I asked the doctor and he said I could as long as I took it easy. I must really want one if I can go sit on the patio with Magpie!" Kincaid joked.

"Okay, but be careful," Nora patted him on the back.

Elton went to the pantry and put a shot of whiskey in a glass with ice cubes. "Want anything else in it, like water or Seven Up?"

"I guess a little water would be okay."

On the patio, Elton sat on one of the folding lawn chairs and put a rusted out tin TV tray between them with an ashtray on it. He handed him a cigarette and set his drink on the tray. "Now, if you get dizzy, you'd better stop. Nora will have my hide if anything happens to you."

"I got that. She's quite the gal," Carl Kincaid took a draw on his cigarette and looked out across the peaceful prairies. In the distance he heard a night owl and the sound of crickets. He took a sip of the whiskey and put the glass down. He had to admit, the combination made him light headed for a second. He leaned back in the wheelchair and looked at the star-filled huge sky.

The two men sat quietly for a while and then Carl said, "Thanks."

Elton looked at him in surprise, "For what?"

"Not saying anything tonight about Mo. I felt pretty stupid about it. I don't know why I said anything about her liking someone. That was stupid!"

Elton looked at him seriously, "I don't think that Katherine thought you meant anything by it, but I know she knows you're sweet on her."

"What did you tell them?"

"Nothing. You don't realize it, but your to whole demeanor changes when it comes to her."

"Bert said the same thing. Damn, I never thought I was so transparent. I have to quit doing that."

"Why?" Elton leaned back and looked up at the stars.

"What do you mean, why? I don't want anyone to know I like her."

"Well you do. What's wrong with that? How about her? She should know."

"Dammit Magpie, you're doing it to me again. I hate it when you start answering me with questions. You should've been in the FBI."

"Nah. That is a good job for Ginger or Pepper, not me!" Elton grinned.

Kincaid laughed, "Yah, you and Petunia should've given me a heads up on that Ginger! Wow! She goes straight to the heart of things and the next thing I know I'm spilling my guts and don't even know why."

"She is psychic too! Man, if you try to cover something up, you're dead meat. That's how she got to Zach. I tell you, that poor guy was wound up tighter than a spring until she got a hold of him."

"Like how? I know he used to throw up all the time," Kincaid nodded.

"Not just that. Every time he would start to relax and enjoy his life a little, he would withdraw again. Almost like Miriam, except not physically. He was always busy with his work. Good place to hide. Hell, he didn't sleep any better than Lloyd."

"All from the crap with his father, huh?"

"Yah. We're all so grateful that he was able to get over it. He used to never smile at all and was all work. Now, he is blossoming." Elton looked across the yard to the horizon.

Carl cleared his throat, "I imagine Suzy had a little to do with that."

Elton chuckled "Yah, she did. He was quite taken with her but he'd have never asked her out because he was so bent out of shape because of his father."

"That man must have been something. He sure messed up his kids. Killed one, drove one totally insane and the other two not far behind. I guess it was dealing with those kinds of people is what turned me off on being close to anyone. It's not worth it. Too many times, they're just messing with you or want something."

Elton turned around to give his attention to Kincaid, "Everyone wants something from you. Don't you know that? What you can't understand is that mostly what people want is to be your friend. Pure and simple. Everyone needs other people, even though they don't admit it. In fact, especially the ones that don't admit it. Hell, who'd you tell a joke to if there wasn't anyone else around?"

"As bad as your jokes are, it'd be better that way!" Kincaid shook his head, "Elton, can I ask you something, between us?"

"Sure. I give you my word, I won't tell a soul without your permission."

"I've been thinking about getting old and dying. You know, all by myself. I'm not sure I like that idea."

"Yah, it isn't an exciting prospect even if you're not alone. I guess in the end, everyone is by themselves when they pass over. But, that's only fair. We're by ourselves when we come into the world."

"So, you think it would be better to die alone than with having a wife that loves you?" Kincaid asked, curiously.

"Well, I don't know which way is better," Elton said thoughtfully. "But living is a lot better when you have someone to share it with."

"What made you decide to go from being a bachelor to a married man with four kids? Why would you cash in all that freedom?" Carl was genuinely curious.

"Is it really freedom, or just being alone? Just because no one gives a damn what you do; doesn't mean you're free. It just means you're alone. I feel freer now than I ever did before. I know it makes no sense. Now, I don't have to figure out everything on my own and I don't have to find something to do to keep from the loneliness closing in. It's really a totally selfish thing on my part." Elton explained.

"Hmm. Never thought of it that way. You're saying like it isn't being free to be able to come home and eat whenever you want; it's because no one gives a damn whether you eat or not." Kincaid raised his eyebrows. "I guess that's about right. I used to brag to the guys at work because I had a bowl of Cheerios for dinner. They'd all say, 'that's so cool.' But the real reason was because I didn't know how to cook a roast beef. I had myself convinced that I liked Cheerios. Now that I have eaten here for even this short time, I'd never say that again. Hell, I'd much rather have to say grace and get to eat a real meal."

"You have to mention that to Byron. Maybe he could use that in one of his sermons. 'The reason you say grace is to get fed better!'" Elton joked.

"It doesn't really matter anyway. I'm too damned old now to find someone to be with. Hell, I got one foot in the grave," Kincaid grumped.

"Not true at all. You have to make up your own mind. Be as brave in your personal life as you were as an agent. Take a risk. If you like someone, let them know. Like write something nice to Mo in that package."

"You don't miss a trick, do you? You knew that threw me for a loop."

"Yah, I saw it because I used to be there myself. You just need to write something simple. You don't need to write a sonnet or anything," Elton explained.

"Oh hell, she wouldn't be interested in me. Like Katherine said, she has tons of friends. What have I got?"

Elton lit another cigarette, "My guess is that she thinks you're an okay guy. I notice things like that. And you do have friends. Like Ginger says, 'I have friends I don't even like.'"

Kincaid chuckled, "And I bet she does! And she probably 'gives them the business'."

"She gives everyone the business!" Elton laughed.

"Are all kids like that?"

"No, but most kids are pretty neat people," Elton smiled, "I like them. It's when they get grown up they get all weird, you know, trying to be pretentious. Like acting like they really are something that they aren't. What's the point? If you make a friend that way, they'll find out soon enough you're full of baloney. So, why bother?"

"You really live like that, don't you?"

"Mostly. I'm too damned lazy to do it any other way." Elton leaned back, and then asked, "So, what're you going to write?"

"Don't have a clue. I thought I'd just sign my name," he looked at Elton. "You're the Magpie, what would you say?"

"I'd probably say, 'I saw this and it reminded me of you.' and then sign my name."

"Hmm. Guess that sounds okay. It isn't too mushy, is it?"

"No, Carl. It's not mushy."

They both turned as Nora came out of the house with a glass of iced tea. "May I join you guys? I promise not to be a buttinsky."

"You're not a buttinsky. Here," Elton said as he got up and offered her his chair. "This chair has all the webbing. The other one is unraveling."

"Thanks, Honey," Nora said as she sat down. "We should all have chairs like Carl."

"I'm hoping to shed this pretty soon."

"Hey, guys," Nora said, "What should we do for Miriam's birthday? It's a week from Sunday and the clan will be here for dinner. Have you got any ideas?"

"I suppose have a birthday cake?" Elton said. "Would she like balloons?"

"Other than chocolate and green beans, do you know anything that she really likes to eat?" Nora asked. "I need some ideas so I can let the other gals know."

"She really snarfed up the macaroni and cheese the other day over at Ellisons," Kincaid offered.

"And drumsticks," Elton suggested. "In the hospital, that was her favorite. So we could have fried chicken and macaroni and green beans!"

"Oh, I know," Nora grinned, "She really liked bananas. I could make glorified rice with bananas. Thanks guys. I'll talk to Marly and Suzy. We can see what else we come up with. We have to let everyone know, no crayons."

18

The next week was filled with activity. The news from Boston was good. Ian would be able to travel in a few weeks. Miriam's birthday party was going to be on Sunday. Tuesday, Keith and Darlene would be arriving from Wisconsin. That weekend was the big anniversary dance for Gilda and Bill. It was also for Elton and Nora. Zach and Suzy had set their wedding date for July 19th. Maureen and Ian would be coming out for a long visit before then, but Father Matthew wouldn't be able to come until July 17th.

Coot and his Gophers were busy. They did their physical therapy in the mornings and the Coot and Charlie dug the canals to drain Elton's yard. They spent the rest of the morning in the garden, weeding and picking vegetables. In the afternoon, Miriam and Ginger came over and they all spent time in the sandbox. Within a week of sandbox duty, they were all doing real digging outside.

Ginger's eyesight was doing very well and she was getting around with ease. She could milk on her own and although it took some adjusting, she was getting used to having only three fingers and a thumb on one hand. Her schooling was going very well, and Jeannie was certain she could rejoin her regular class in the fall.

She had a project for school. She was to build a volcano. Her Dad set up a table in their garage so she could build it out of plaster of Paris. Once Charlie saw it, he was convinced they needed to build a model of Uncle Elton's dam, so they could show him how nice it would be to have that in his pasture. Dad said okay, but he, Jeannie and Kincaid had to oversee the project.

Kincaid was walking almost always in the house and only used the wheelchair if he was very tired or outside. Bert used it in the house and he liked being able to get around. His cough was better and he actually was getting a little color back.

Every day when he got home from work, Elton and Kincaid gave Lloyd a ride in his old Ford. He had asked a few times if Kincaid could give him a ride in the morning, but Zach thought it wouldn't be a good idea until Kincaid could get around better. If they ever got a flat tire or something, they would be in real trouble.

On Thursday evening, Suzy and Zach had asked Elton and Nora out to dinner. Grandma and Kincaid offered to watch over the Grandpas. The younger couple met them in Bismarck at the Riverside Dining Room. After they had ordered, Zach cleared his throat. "We have some things to talk to you about."

"We thought there must be something," Elton smiled. "As much as you like us, we figured the dinner was to soften us up. And no. You aren't building another addition on the house."

Zach became serious. "Well, actually, you're close. We want to live out on the farm. I don't know how to put this without getting mushy, but you're my family. I don't ever want to be far away from you all. You are my Mom and Dad. I love you both. We have the lease on the apartment in town until January. We were thinking though, we'd get a house in Bismarck then. A big one."

"I don't follow you," Nora questioned. "If you don't want to live there, why buy a big house?"

"One that Pepper, Annie, Ken or whoever wanted to stay in town could have a place. Ken will be going to college in the fall, too. You know, the clan pays out a lot of money for rent on places they only use once in a while." Zach pointed out.

Suzy giggled, "This way the house would be used and everyone would have a place to hang their hat. We'd like to buy some of the east pasture by the road from you guys. We'd like to build on the other side of you from Kevin. I want to be able to keep working at the church and it would be the best for Miriam. She needs to be by you all. So, if you would be of a mind to sell us some of the land on the other side of the windrow from the garden, we'd love it. If not, we'll buy from Mom and Dad. It'll be further away, but it will still be closer than Bismarck."

Elton and Nora looked at each other, "How many acres would you want to buy?"

"How many acres does Kevin have around his place?"

"Forty. That is the best for tax purposes." Elton nodded. "You can do like Marty and Kevin do. They fenced off the part south of the back road and rent it to me for pasture. We could do that for you too."

"You mean you'll sell us the land?" Zach was almost bursting with excitement.

"No. We won't. We don't want to get mushy either, but we want to give it to you for a wedding present," Nora took his hand. "You see Zach; you're a son to us and Suzy has always been family. And well, Miriam . . . She is everyone's little sweetheart."

Suzy started shaking her head no. "You guys aren't giving us something like that. Period. Land is too valuable. No way."

"I have money, Elton." Zach agreed. "I can buy it. I want to buy it."

"I could've paid for the addition too, but you did. Just hush up and be good now." Elton said.

"No," Zach said with determination.

Elton studied the young man a bit and then suggested, "How about how we did with Kevin's place and when Nora and I got the place from Engelmanns. We'll get it appraised and you pay the lowest appraised value."

Suzy and Zach looked at each other. "Okay. It's a deal. You won't mind us living right next door to us," Zach got worried. "I mean, there'll be trees between us."

"Couldn't be as bad as having you in the same house!" Elton slapped him on the shoulder. "We'd love it. I can't think of anything more wonderful."

"So, it is settled then," Elton beamed. "I'll call the appraiser Monday. Do you guys have any plans for a house or whatever?"

"We're going to talk to the guy who built the addition," Zach grinned. "We have no idea what we want. So we'll have to do some thinking."

"I've been trying to tie him down with the wedding. If he tells me, 'whatever I want' one more time, I may just get a new fella," Suzy giggled. "He almost sounds like Miriam."

"Bad plan, Zacharias," Elton said. "Makes the ladies real mad when you say that. Just tell them your idea and they'll decide they don't want your input after all!"

Nora whacked her husband's arm, "You're so bad, Elton Gerhardt Schroeder!"

Zach chuckled, "Well actually, Ginger and Suzy planned the whole thing out pretty much in the first twenty minutes. That's how we ended up with Charlie as ring bearer. Yea Gads. Now, I'm worried about Miriam. Do you think her feelings will be hurt if she can't be flower girl too? And if we ask her, will Ginger be put out?"

Nora shook her head no. "Ginger wouldn't be put out but I think that Miriam might not be able to do it. Besides, she's still too 'frad jelly,' as the kids would say. If something scared her, it would be awful."

"Yah, I guess that's right, but it seems like she should be," Suzy said. "I mean, she is like our little girl."

"You kids realize, don't you, that even though you're responsible for her, we all consider her our little girl. I don't think that moving her now would serve any good purpose. If someone has an issue with it, let them. Who the hell cares? She has her own little circle now that she is comfortable in. Let it be, at least for now." Elton observed.

"I agree," Nora said. "I know you kids feel bad, but you really shouldn't. Why not just let her have the same dress as Ginger and be in the pictures? I wouldn't have her go up the aisle, even if she does hold Ginger's hand. It'd be a recipe for disaster, and we want her to have a good time."

Zach and Suzy looked at each other, "I guess it makes sense," Suzy said. "She'll probably find some lap to sit on and be happy as a clam. The only way she would want to be in the front of the church is if Kevin held her!"

"Amen," Elton nodded. "Who are going to be your attendants?"

Suzy grinned, "Greta, Ruthie and Pepper. Then Zach is going to have Harrington, Kevin and Darrell."

"Sounds nice. I get to be the father of the groom, right? Can I wear my new suit?" Elton laughed.

"You and Dad are both going to have a tux and I don't want to hear another word about it! No grumping or whining," Suzy declared.

"Well if that don't beat all. When have I ever whined?"

"Don't even start, Elton," Zach raised his eyebrows. "Don't even start. Hey, how are we going to get Kincaid upstairs for the barn dance?"

"Kevin, Darrell and I got that all worked out. We're going to use the farm hand and scoop him right up to the loft door! It'll work just dandy."

Zach started to laugh, "Oh no! I can hear him yelling already. You'll have to gag him."

"Yah, but if he climbs up the steps, he'll be all done for the night."

"That's true." Zach smiled, "We have something else to tell you."

"Oh?" Nora was surprised, "What could it be?"

"I talked to Grinchboss and we are going to have Miriam baptized on Sunday, second service," Suzy grinned. "Tonight, we asked Kevin and Carrie to be her sponsors and they said yes!"

"That's wonderful. We can celebrate it all at once with her birthday!" Nora beamed. "It's fantastic."

Zach smiled proudly, "And Ruthie will be coming to church with us. She said she wouldn't miss it."

"That'll be nice. I hear that Harrington and Mo are planning on coming out right around the Fourth of July," Elton said. "I guess they'll be staying with us. Harrington called and wanted to know if his invitation still stood!"

"I hope that isn't imposing?" Suzy said. "That will be Mo and Harrington."

Elton gave them a dirty look, "Just where else would they stay? We have more room than the Hilton."

"Yah, but people pay to stay there," Zach pointed out.

"What do you think, Nora? Should we start charging?"

19

The next morning at milking, Kevin could hardly contain himself. "Well, Dad. Did they tell you last night?"

"Yah, they want to build on east of my place," Elton was making him squirm.

"Didn't they tell you anything else?" It was just killing Kevin.

"Oh, yah, something about a baptism?" Elton's eyes just sparkled. He had rarely seen his son so happy.

"Just think Dad, someone actually thinks enough of me to trust me to do that for them! You know, promising to see that someone has a religious upbringing is a pretty serious job. Right? Did you ever imagine that someone would ask me to do that? Do you think I'll do a good job?"

"Kevin, you'll do a fantastic job. You always do the best job you can when you take on a responsibility. I'm very proud of you."

Kevin looked at his stepfather seriously, "Most folks just think I'm a nut."

"You are a nut. You know, a lot of times people act like they have to have a long sourpuss face to be responsible. You and I both know that's baloney. If you can't have fun being alive, there isn't much point in it to my notion," Elton grinned.

"I love you, Dad."

"I love you too, but you still have to clean your side of the barn!"

The canal digging had become a major safety hazard at the farm, although the drainage hadn't improved that much. Elton came home from the parts store in Bismarck with rolls of yellow tape. He made the diggers promise they would cordon off the areas where they were digging. Almost everyone had stepped into a trench of some sort just crossing the yard. The crew appointed Annie as safety man and it became her job to put up the yellow tape.

Saturday morning, right after breakfast, Annie drove the construction crew "Gophers" over to Byron's garage to work on the plastic plaster mixture. The volcano was magnificent, but all white, as was the dam. When they talked about how to color it, Kincaid noticed that Miriam was getting nervous. The group thought about it and decided that it would be a good idea to paint the project right after lunch.

So Jeannie and Annie mixed up some latex paints. There has been only a few times in the history of the human race, that a bigger mess was created by so few in such a short time.

The grand unveiling of the project was to be right before chores. The crew worked, painted and fussed. When the family arrived to see the volcano explode and check out the model of the dam, they were met at the door by Annie.

She was a bit wild-eyed and anxious as she asked them to take a chair. Ken had come over earlier to help them set up the folding chairs and he wasn't talking. He had put up a clothesline with an old blanket as a curtain in front of the chairs, awaiting the grand event. His face was blanched and he was almost expressionless. Everyone looked at him and tried to figure out what was going on.

Then a nervous Jeannie gave a little welcoming presentation before Ken pulled the blanket back. There they were, Coot and his gophers! All four of them were covered in green and pink paint, as was the table, the concrete floor and the wheelchairs! The volcano was pink and purple, with greenish trees. The dam was a color unknown before; obviously a custom mix. There was little doubt that Miriam did the most of the painting on the dam, because her clothes coated in the same custom mix.

Coot had paint on his glasses, Jeannie had some in her hair and Annie had some spilled down the side of her jeans. The kids looked like they had wallowed in it. What exactly had transpired was uncertain.

Then it was time.

Ginger proudly told about how the volcano worked and then pushed the button. The lava bubbled up to the top of the volcano and then the bright purple paint burst out the top and drenched everyone within a four feet radius!

Coot babbled some explanation about the pressure being a bit too high.

Then Charlie filled the dam with darkly tinted blue water. The water came down the 'creek' and filled the 'dam' to the brim and overflowed like it was supposed to. It ran into the drain that Charlie had put in the bottom of the creek. Alas, that had no place to drain. He was in too much of a hurry and didn't hook the drain pipe to the hose that ran outside. Instead, he simply ran the hose into the vat for the 'lava' for the volcano. It filled up and then shot out through the top of the volcano. There was paint water all over the garage for a ten feet! Everyone was laughing so hard, it continued for a couple minutes before Ken had the good sense to turn the water off!

Kincaid was totally mortified as he sat in his wheelchair, with purple paint dripping off his glasses saturated in dark blue water. Finally, he had to laugh. The kids of course, thought it was great. Miriam giggled until she got the hiccoughs again. It was by far, the funniest thing that any of them had seen for some time.

Ken, Darrell, Ruthie and Suzy volunteered to help Jeannie and Annie clean up the garage, while the rest of them went to do chores. Nora and Grandma had made Sloppy Joes with homemade buns for dinner, which everyone thought was appropriate. Pepper took numerous photos and was certain she would have blackmail money coming in for eternity.

The next morning as they took their seats in the pews, they were all cleaned up and looking very neat. There was still a little paint in the hinge on Kincaid's glasses and Jeannie complained that her skin had picked up the blue tint from the water. She said she looked like the walking dead when she woke up in the morning. Her Mom had suggested that she take some iron pills because she looked anemic.

During the service, Byron announced they had a baptism. Zach, Suzy, Kevin and Carrie came forward and Kevin held Miriam throughout the ceremony. She wasn't sure about the water being sprinkled on her but then smiled at Byron when he made the sign of the cross on her forehead. Then she put her arms around Kevin's neck. She behaved very well and they were all proud as punch of her.

Ruthie was impressed with the service. She had sat with Kincaid and commented to him how similar it was to her church. On the way home, she said it was nice to see Marv and Byron doing a service since she worked with them all week. She really enjoyed her visit.

The clan gathered at Schroeder's and everyone brought their portion of the dinner. The fried chicken, macaroni and cheese, green beans and banana glorified rice were a big hit. Miriam sat for her dinner with her high chair wedged between Elton and Byron like she always did.

Then it was time for the birthday cake. Suzy and Carrie brought out the cake and everyone sang Happy Birthday to Miriam. She didn't know what to think. She got very nervous and moved to Byron's lap, but soon started to smile. She loved the little hat and candles. They had to show her how to blow them out. It was obvious she had never seen anything like that before.

Then she opened her presents. She got a racing car from the little boys; Junior, Little Bill, Clark and Charlie. Now she could race with them, too. She got a doll from Uncle Eddie's and clothes for the doll from some of the others. Coot, Ginger and Charlie went together and gave her a dirt shovel, like the other kids had. Byron and Marly gave the entire construction crew hard hats. Charlie and Coot had yellow ones, but Annie, Ginger and Miriam got pink ones.

The Grandpas and Grandma Engelmann got her a pretty dress with matching barrettes for her bear tails. Grandpa Lloyd had insisted that the card be made out to Laura, because that is what he called her.

Then Elton and Nora gave her their present. It was a little rocking cradle for Mr. Bear. Kevin and Carrie gave her the blanket and pillow for it. She was so excited.

Elton was holding her after dinner. She was holding Mr. Bear and getting kind of sleepy. Byron came over and said, "About ready for your nap, Sweetheart?"

She held her arms out to him and he took her. Then she said, "Mr. Bear."

Byron said, "Oh, does Mr. Bear want his nap too?"

She shrugged. Then she said, "Mr. Bear."

Byron tried to figure out what she meant and then she pointed to Kevin. "Son, Mr. Bear."

Kevin came over and she thrust Mr. Bear toward him. "Mr. Bear."

"Honey, we don't know what you mean. Do you want me to do something with Mr. Bear?"

She nodded and pointed to Byron. "Mr. Bear."

"What do you want me to do with Mr. Bear?" Byron was puzzled.

Frustrated, she took a deep breath and then took her bear. With her little finger she made a mark on his forehead. "Mr. Bear."

"Oh, do you want me to bless Mr. Bear?" Byron asked. "Like when we baptized you?"

With a relieved smile, she nodded, "Son, Mr. Bear."

"I'll hold him like I held you, okay?" Kevin grinned as he held the little stuffed bear.

Byron gave him quick sprinkle with water from his drinking glass and Elton wiped it off right away. Then Byron made the sign of the cross on the little bear's forehead. When he was done, she took the bear from Son and held out her arms to him.

Kevin took her and she face broke into a huge smile. "Night, night," she said as he took her for her nap.

20

That evening, the milkers had just returned to the house when the phone rang. It was Maureen for Carl. He self-consciously took the phone and wandered into the living room as far from the kitchen door as he could get. Elton looked at Nora and stifled a giggle. Nora gave him a dirty look and swatted him. No one said anything but everyone tried to give him some privacy.

Annie and Pepper took off for Ellisons. They were going to give the end of the garage one last scrubbing to make certain they had all the remnants of the volcano-dam explosion cleaned up. The Grandpas were already in bed and Grandma Katherine was going to take a relaxing bath.

Nora got Elton and her each a Coke and they went out onto the patio. As she put the colas on the TV tray, Elton opened up the two folding chairs and gave Nora the best one. "You're right. We really need to get something a little nicer for out here. These things are hardly safe. A cuddling swing would be real nice tonight."

"I think they're called gliders," Nora smiled. "I'd hate you to walk in the store and ask for a cuddling swing."

"Don't get fussy lady or you might end up with two milk stools from the barn."

Nora giggled. "Just think Elton, tomorrow Keith and Darlene will be home. All our kids will be back except Andy. Zach and Suzy will be close by. We're so very fortunate."

"Yah, we're at that." Elton lit his cigarette and leaned back on the rickety chair, "That was really sweet when Miriam wanted her bear baptized. Huh?"

"She's a precious little kid. I never saw any one but you laugh as hard as she did when the volcano shot water all over the garage! Poor Carl. He almost died of embarrassment."

Elton laughed, "It's good for him! I thought between Kevin and Zach, we might have to resuscitate somebody. They were so hysterical! I noticed how poor Annie has been drug into the plotting and scheming of the canal builders! Yea gads, that poor girl! Has she heard from Andy when he will get his R&R for sure? She thought it would be in July? I hope they can get to see each other. I know you want to see him too, but I was thinking. If he gets sent to Japan, we can't all afford to go. Then it would be probably nicer if we bought a ticket for Annie to go. If he gets sent to Hawaii, you and I could go too. Would you be disappointed?"

"Yes, I'd be, but you're right. It is more important that they see each other than me," Nora sighed. "I know how I'd feel if I was her."

"Well, let's see how it all works out. We can't make any plans until we hear for sure," Elton gave his wife an embrace. "Maybe I could take my girl some place very romantic later? How would she like that?"

Nora nodded, "I think she'd really like that. I love you, Elton."

"I love you too, Nora," then he looked toward the house, "How do you think Kincaid is doing in there?"

"Be nice to him. You know, he really is a nice person. He is amazing with those kids. I don't know if I'd have the patience he does. Sometimes when they are all jabbering at him, he looks at me and crosses his eyes! I feel so sorry for him," Nora related with a grin.

"He needs it. He has spent too much of his life being lied to and getting conned."

"Well, the kids might not lie to him, but they sure con him." Nora thought, "What is Maureen like?"

"She is like Aunt Gilda, but not quite as boisterous. I can't wait to see those two together. She is a nice lady. You'll like her, Nora."

They heard the back door open and Kincaid wheeled himself down the ramp. He came to join them on the patio with his whiskey. "You aren't necking or something gross like that, are you?"

Elton laughed, "We were going to but you showed up, now we're all out of the mood."

Kincaid put his drink on the table and bummed a cigarette. Elton handed him one and he nodded. He lit it without a word and then looked at the stars. "I have to say, you can see every damned star in the universe. It's pretty, if you like that kind of thing."

"Don't you like it?" Nora asked, innocently.

"Nah. I like the busy streets and honking horns. Human activity. I need to get back to Texas as soon as I can. It gets pretty boring here. I should be well enough pretty soon, you know. I might go right after Petunia's wedding."

Nora and Elton were both taken back. Nora looked at Elton and both knew something had gone wrong that evening. "Carl? Is something wrong?"

"Ah, no. I don't want to wear out my welcome. It's not that I don't appreciate all that you've done for me but this isn't my life. I'm a big city guy with a real life. I know my life might not be what you think it should've been, but it was mine. I was used to it." Carl was defensive.

"I'm sorry if you thought we didn't think your life was important. We certainly didn't mean it that way. Of course, it's important. I feel terrible if you think that we didn't approve or something," Nora apologized.

Carl looked at her and studied what she said for a minute. Then he took a drink of his whiskey. "You didn't. You guys have been great. It wasn't as bad as I thought it would be. But I'm better now and should be getting back on my own. You know?"

Elton was watching him and listening, but never said a word. Nora took Carl's hand and said sincerely, "Whatever you decide Carl, but I'd feel better if you were going home because you were well, and not because we did something to offend you. If it's something that we've done, please let us know. I don't want you to have hard feelings about something. We could try to fix it. However, if and when you're ready to leave, just let us know. We will help you however we can. We think of you as family."

Carl's countenance changed and he almost cried, "Shit. I just don't know what to do with myself anymore. Don't you get it?"

Nora patted his hand, got up and gave him a hug. "Will you do me a favor? You talk to this old Elton Bird, okay? I'll let you guys have some privacy so you can be more comfortable. Goodnight." Nora patted her husband's shoulder and gave him a kiss on the cheek.

Kincaid said, "I'm sorry. I shouldn't be chasing you in."

"No problem," Nora said softly, "There's a hot bubble bath with my name on it."

Elton patted her hand and she went in. He took a swig of his Coke and then changed chairs. "I might fall on my hinder in this thing. I'd best be getting some new chairs pretty soon."

Kincaid nodded and took another swig of his whiskey.

Elton commented, "You took yourself a double shot tonight, huh? Bad day?"

Kincaid said, "The day was fine. It was tonight. Mo called."

"I know. How did that go? Not so good, huh?"

"It went okay I guess," Kincaid said without emotion. "It was okay."

Elton frowned and sat quietly waiting for him to say more so he could understand what was wrong. After a few minutes, it was obvious that Kincaid was not going to offer any more. "So, what did she say?"

Kincaid became extremely interested in Elmer's house and never took his eyes off it while he talked. He said, "She called and told me thanks for the scarf. Said she really liked it and that it was very nice of me to send it and all that. It was pretty sweet. Then I asked her what she had been doing and she told me. She and her brother-in-law, Egan, went to a family reunion in western New Hampshire. I guess they were there all weekend. She said there were about fifty or sixty folks there and they had a wonderful time."

"That sounds nice. Doesn't it?"

"Yah, I guess. Then she said that after Mass this morning, she went to have brunch with the group in the neighborhood. I guess they get together every other month and have brunch at this clubhouse not too far from where they live. She was invited to play bridge with these folks she knows. She 'll do that tomorrow night. She sounded real happy."

"Isn't that good, Kincaid?"

"Yah, real nice. Then she asked what I had been doing. I told her nothing. She said, 'Well, surely you must have done something.' But I said no, nothing. Elton, anything I would have to say would be stupid. What did I do? Nothing like the stuff she does."

"You're a major idiot. You had a busy week. We went to town, the boys gave Lloyd his car back, we had a baptism and a birthday party! You and Katherine almost beat Nora and me in whist. You and the kids built canals and dams all over the yard and you helped make some fine strawberry jam. You and the girls helped build that fantastic volcano and dam thing. How could you possibly say you didn't do anything?" Elton pointed out.

"But Elton, that's all dumb stuff. It is nothing like what she did."

"You think that just because you don't know those people. The people she plays cards with are no different than the ones you do. She'd love to hear about Miriam's baptism and birthday party! I have to admit, the volcano story will go better with pictures!" Elton tried to cheer him up.

"This is stuff that lamebrains do. It's kid stuff, made up stuff, not grownup stuff."

Elton leaned back, "I don't think that's what Maureen thinks at all. It's what you think. You think that everything we do is lame. You're right, Carl. We don't go around shooting each other or arresting anyone. We get the giggles like a bunch of kids and get excited about a birthday party. None of it is fantastic. It is grownup though. I'm sorry that you don't think so. Just because we don't go to bars, get drunk on our asses and pick up loose women, doesn't mean that we don't know how to. Many of us have done it or still do it. We just found something better. I'll give you a bit of information you might want to keep stored in your grownup head. Maureen is just as petunia as we are!"

"Are you mad at me?" Kincaid was surprised.

"Yah, I have to say I am. I don't care if you think I am a sap, but don't include the rest of my family in it. They're all good people and not lamebrains. I hope that you find what you want, Kincaid, and it makes you as happy as your grownup mind can stand! I'm going to bed." Elton stood up and moved the chair back.

Carl Kincaid was flabbergasted. He was shocked that Elton was so adamant. As he started to walk back to the house, Carl said, "Elton, stop."

Elton stopped and stood for a minute before he turned, "Sure, what is it?" He walked back over toward Carl, but didn't sit down.

Carl said, "Could you sit down? You make me nervous."

"Are you just going to tell me how horrible this is for your puffed up macho facade or will you say what's really bothering you?"

"You don't mess around, do you? I'll be straight. Promise. Will you sit down?"

Elton pursed his lips, "Okay, but don't waste my time."

"Damn Elton, I didn't mean to piss you off. I think the world and all of your family. Really, I do. They're the best bunch of folks I've ever met. I don't know how to say this. I mean, I really don't. It has always been important in my job to come from a position of strength, you know? You can't show your soft underbelly because then you're vulnerable."

"You aren't interrogating some serial killers," Elton explained. "When you're talking to your friends, you need to be real. It's impossible for anyone to be a true friend to someone when they don't know where they're coming from. In fact, I think Ginger told you that. A friend has to know your stuff. This isn't a contest about who is toughest. You know, I can be tough about a lot of things but when it comes to my Nora or my family, I'm vulnerable. I don't care who knows it."

Carl sat quietly for a while, "Could I ask you a favor? I really hate to, but could you bring me another whiskey?"

Elton studied his face for a minute, "A single shot, only. No double. Do you want water in it?"

"Yes. Thanks."

Elton returned with the drink. "Okay, what's really eating you?"

"Elton, I'm afraid that Mo has a full life. She doesn't need me. She wouldn't want to move out to the Midwest away from her family and friends. She wouldn't want to live in Texas. I have nothing to offer her. Why would she be interested in me?"

Elton shook his head, "I see, you want her to be friendless, homeless and destitute? Then you could wonder if she really cared about you or just needed you to survive? Man, you are so jumping the gun. Get to know her a little better. Maybe you don't like her as much as you think you do. Maybe she won't like you. Hell, you don't even know how she feels about moving or anything. Just take it easy."

Carl Kincaid nodded and thought quietly. Finally he said, "Do you know how long it has been since I've been with a woman? Or even been out with someone?"

Elton chuckled, "Trust me. That is one area where practice does not make perfect! Just tell a woman that you have been with a different woman every day for the last ten years, and see how far you get!"

"You jackass. I should've talked to Nora," Kincaid groaned.

"She'd be harder on you than I am and I'm not kidding you. She doesn't pull any punches in this department. Just be sincere and honest, with Mo and yourself. Don't come with your carving chisels at least until you guys decide on a stone. Have fun, but Carl, most of all; don't try to be something you are not. You don't have to pretend to Mo that you're a tough guy. We all know better and I doubt very much it would impress her if she thought you were! So, knock it off. She knows you like to have your whiskey but she might not know how good you are with the Gophers. She knows you can be tough, but she might not know how you comfort grumpy old Bert in the middle of the night. That's all you. Whether things work out with Mo or not, you need to start to appreciate yourself."

"That sounds like psycho dribble."

"Not really. If you can say 'hey, I like whiskey and dirty stories, but I also like digging holes with little kids' then you are getting to know yourself. You will be happier with you. Remember, no matter where ever you go, you'll always be there. The one person you can never get away from, so you might as well make peace with him."

"Maybe I could just quit digging holes," Kincaid suggested.

"I have to admit, my yard would be a lot safer," Elton chuckled. "But you do like it. I also know the kids want you to do stuff all the time, but I've heard you tell them no sometimes. You really do enjoy some of it. And you also like to cook! You gripe about it, but you do. However, don't be getting any ideas that you are a better cook than I because I'm better. Hands down."

"Doubt it."

"Wanna bet?"

"I might not be able to beat you right now, but not in a week or two. You're on. I have to have Katherine teach me some recipes," Carl poked.

"Okay, let's have a cook off contest when Mo and Harrington get here." Elton held out his hand and they shook on it. "You're so burned. So, so burned."

"Don't count your prize money yet." Then Carl got serious, "Elton, I'm sorry about tonight. If you keep your mouth shut I'd like to tell you something."

"I give you my word."

"I'm scared to death," Kincaid said, his voice cracking. "I'm afraid of dying, afraid of living, afraid of being with people and afraid of being alone. Have you ever been like that?"

"For years, Carl. I lived like that for years. It takes a while but you'll get over it. Hey, I know I'm just a lamebrain Magpie, but if you need someone to bounce things off, I'm here."

"Oh Lord! Ginger says that is what married people do!"

"I know. I've heard her say that but I think she's really referring to is that there are a few people that you need to be close enough to, so you can turn to them when things go to hell. I don't know how I survived before I ran into Byron."

"Yah, but you have Byron. You'd never turn to me."

"Carl, I have a lot of people that I depend on. You're one of them. I have turned to everyone in the clan at one time or another, for one thing or another. Of course, mostly I depend on Nora, but there are things that she wouldn't begin to be able to help me with. Just like there are things that I can't help her with. You worry too much. Just relax. Take this time to just kick back. There will still be a Texas bar willing to serve you if you decide on that. I can promise you."

"I'm sorry. I hope you aren't mad at me about being so ornery earlier," Carl apologized. "I didn't mean to insult your family. I really think they're fine folks."

"No big deal. Sorry I got so hot. You know, some days I get bent out of shape too. Usually if I get too far out there, Katherine will call Byron. Then he comes over and gives me hell. It isn't pretty."

"I want to see it," Carl laughed.

"Patience my friend."

21

That night, even though he had more to drink than ever since being shot, Kincaid couldn't sleep. It had been very upsetting. He didn't like how he felt when he talked to Maureen. He hated himself for how he insulted Nora. She was one of the nicest people he'd ever met. The only woman he ever thought was nicer was his Cecilia, and maybe Maureen. Then she was so darned sweet about it when he acted like he did. It wasn't so much what he said, but the sarcastic way that he said it. She was only being kind and he was flat out rude. And he knew he was, all the while he was doing it. Why did he do that? It was like he was aching for a fight.

Magpie had every reason to be upset with him. He was so sarcastic. Elton actually should've punched him in the mouth. He had to admit that he was very taken back that Elton got as angry as he did. It wasn't like him. He usually just let stuff go. It did surprise him but then Elton was always surprising him. That was a certainty. And yet, as irritated as Elton was about everything, he did stick around to talk to him. He didn't seem to hold a grudge, but Kincaid also knew that he better never pull that again. Even though Magpie was not the type of guy he'd ever pick for a friend, he'd always been more than decent to him.

Bert coughed and Kincaid watched until he settled down and turned over to go back to sleep. After checking his oxygen was in properly, Kincaid's interest turned to watching Elmer through the window. That dumb dog was still digging in that gopher hole. 'Stupid dog. Determined though, I'll give him that.'

He thought about what Elton said. Carl always thought he knew himself. He knew he wasn't a sentimental, mushy person. He never had time for that and had done okay most of his life without it. He felt better when all he had to worry about was winding up the next case. Now, he worried about if he hurt someone's feelings or if a kid was going to cry. He worried about how to talk to a lady. Hell, it would be easier to just go back to Texas. He could pay some hooker a few bucks and not have to talk at all! He could probably get his little one bedroom apartment back, walk down to the corner bar every night and get his whiskey. He wouldn't have to talk to a damned soul if he didn't want to. Then he knew he wouldn't hurt anyone's feelings.

Kincaid turned over and wondered why his pillow was so darned lumpy and uncomfortable tonight. He just couldn't get it adjusted right. For some reason, he was reminded of Miriam, when she tried to get Mr. Bear stuffed under her shirt so she could hold him and dig too. No matter how she readjusted it, her shirt was so tight she could hardly breathe.

The Wee One was doing okay. Once she got the hang of the sand shovel, it took her no time to graduate to the big shovel. The only thing holding her back was her hip. She could only dig where the dirt was loosened up. Kincaid would either find her a soft spot or go dig it up the night before, so she could dig there the next day. She didn't seem to know that was what he was doing, but he knew that Charlie and Ginger had twigged on. They always directed her to the 'predug' area. They were nice kids. Miriam would be too someday.

But Magpie was wrong. Mo would've politely listened to him talk about the stuff he did, but it wasn't any big deal. Hell, what he did didn't matter one way or the other in the great scheme of things. She had a real family and was a lifetime member of her church and neighborhood. It wasn't like him. He knew his landlord as well as anyone, and his bartender. Bob would see him sit down and bring him his two whiskeys. He would give him the money and Bob would nod. Most the time, they never said a word.

It sounded like she and this Egan, her late husband's brother, got along pretty well. They went to the reunion and visited with all their in-laws and relatives they had known for years. Mo had a real history with those folks. He had nothing like that. The guys he knew the best were a few old FBI derelicts and they could hold their convention in a broom closet. All they could even talk about was the cases they had worked on together. Yah, she wouldn't be interested in that.

He probably knew these North Dakota folks as well as anyone. They were only polite to him because of Miriam. He figured they somehow thought they were beholding to him for trying to keep her from getting shot. Kincaid figured Zach was only nice to him because Miriam was his niece. Father Matthew was a priest, Ruthie had been a nun and Byron was a preacher. Those kinds of people have to be nice to everyone. And of course, Magpie was just that way. Who knew what made that guy tick!

Bert started to cough again and Kincaid got up with him and helped him sit up. "You're coughing pretty good again tonight, huh?"

"Yah, damn stuff," the old man hacked.

After about fifteen minutes, Kincaid got his lungs cleared somewhat and raised the bed. Bert of course, griped that it was too high and that no one could sleep that way.

Carl just smiled, "You really are a miserable old goat, aren't you?"

"Yup." Bert leaned back on the pillow, "Kincaid, did you decide?"

"Decide what, Bert?"

Bert shook his head, "You damn fool. If you're going to be my backup!"

"Hell, Bert," Carl answered, "I don't think I'm going to stay here much longer. As soon as I'm well enough, I'm going to go back to Texas. I don't belong here."

Bert took his hand, "You do, but too stubborn to admit it. I really wish I could give you time to change your mind. I don't think I'll be able to. I was counting on you."

Carl answered seriously, "Bert, it's not a very good idea for you to count on me. I'm not good at this domestic stuff. Never have been."

"No damned reason why you can't start! Who do you think that you are that you get to worm out of it? I can tell you, you won't get out of it, ever. If you don't bite the bullet this time, the good Lord will put you in another situation just like it. Count on it."

"I think He has better things to do than to worry about me."

"I sure as hell would, but not Him. He'll keep throwing it in front of you until you are smart enough to do it. It probably won't help me much though. You aren't the guy I'd have picked either but I asked God to help me out. Next thing I know; Elton dragged you in here, and into my room no less! I thought 'what the hell?' But after I watched you, I figure you'd do a good job. I was really hoping you would come around to my thinking before I had to check out."

"You aren't ready to check out yet, Bert. You're cough isn't so bad now. It is much better than it was there for a while."

"Well, I'll hold on a while longer to give you another chance to get your shit together. Something's eating at you. What is it, a woman?"

Kincaid looked at him, "You nosey old goat. What is it to you?"

"Well, there aren't too many reasons people do stuff, after you rinse off all the bullshit. Usually its money, sex or covering something up to do with money or sex."

Carl chuckled, "I've plenty of money and there is no woman in my life."

"Ah, that's it then," the old man smirked. "Should have figured it."

"Figured what?"

"No woman. You need one, unless you are one of those homo fellers. Then you need a guy. Everybody needs somebody. Don't figure why. Guess it's the way we're cut out. You know, some creatures go off and live alone but some live in herds. Humans are the herding variety." Then he started to cough hard again.

After they got the cough calmed, Carl asked Bert, "So how did you know that you and Ida would have a good marriage?"

"Who the hell said we knew?" Bert groused. "We didn't know. Every day we just got up and did the best we could. We decided to throw in together. Back when we got married; nobody ever asked or cared if we're happy or not. You could be happy or miserable. That was up to you. I guess Ida and I both just figured we'd just as soon be happy."

Carl chuckled, "You're something else. So what do you think I should do?"

"I think you should tell me that you'll be here. Not necessarily in my room, but here for Lloyd and the kids. The rest of them can make it okay, but you know. Elton tries to be there for everyone but he could use some help. He can't do it all by himself. He gets tired. I know sometimes he and Byron get together and have a good bellyaching session. Other than that, he rarely complains. It's unnatural, I tell you. I think you could be a good help to him if you weren't so damned self-centered."

"I'm not self-centered," Carl retorted.

"Yes, you are and you know it. Don't need to argue with you. If you believed you were supposed to be on your own, you'd have already left. You can't fool old Shep!" Bert started coughing again.

"You better keep still you old buzzard," Kincaid said as he helped him set up, rubbed and patted his back. "Do you think I should call Annie?"

"Nope. I'm okay. I want to go to sleep now. I'm so damned tired. I can't ever remember being this tired," Carl leaned back. "I suppose you think you're going to leave after the wedding, huh?"

"How did you know that?"

"Because you want to stay for the good stuff. Have a couple dances and see that Mo lady. Then you think you can go skipping away all happy and leave the rest of us all sitting in it. Typical selfish attitude. It's too bad. You'd have been good at it. I guess I'm not very good at persuading you. I'm going to try to get some rest. I am so tired."

"Yah, you need to get some good sleep. You quit talking and settle down. I'll be here if you need me."

Carl sat in the rocking chair and waited until the old man went to sleep. It made him feel bad that he couldn't promise him to be his back up. It would be okay if it was for just a while but this was like an open-ended deal. No, Bert was an old man and didn't realize that he still had a life to live.

That old goat grumped, griped and moaned all the time. He never gave up and kept his teeth clenched on a gripe like a cocklebur in dog hair. No doubt God would have His hand's full when that old dude came home. He could about imagine the list of complaints Bert would have about Heaven in an hour or two!

After about a half an hour, Carl checked his roommate and then went back to his bed. He turned over and fell asleep.

The door opened to the room and Lloyd shuffled in and went to the rocking chair. He started talking to Bert about some battle in World War II. He talked for a little while as Kincaid listened to him. Bert never answered.

After a few minutes, Lloyd raised his voice, "Bert, you dead? Well, I'll be damned! The old goat just plain up and died! What the hell am I going to tell Elton? He'll be so mad at me."

Lloyd tried to stand up out of the rocking chair and couldn't do it. Kincaid got up and went to him. He put his arm on his shoulder and scared the poor fellow half to death.

"It's okay, Lloyd. I'll check to see how Bert is. You just sit, okay?"

Carl was getting worried himself. Bert was hard of hearing, but even he should have heard that. With the oxygen machine on, it was hard to tell if he was breathing or not. He touched his face and he didn't feel cold. He didn't want to risk turning off the oxygen to see if he was breathing on his own.

Lloyd was getting nervous, "Was it something I said? Did I do something wrong?"

"No you didn't, Lloyd. You didn't do anything wrong. You're good to him. I'm going to get someone to help us, okay? You just stay sitting here, okay?"

"I didn't mean to kill him. You know that, don't you?" the elderly man worried.

"You didn't kill him. Lloyd, you're fine. Don't worry," Kincaid went out into the hall. He knocked on Elton and Nora's bedroom door. "Excuse me. I need some help."

Elton opened the door and Kincaid just said, "It's Bert."

Elton followed him to the room and Nora was right behind him putting on her robe as she followed. When they got to the room, Kincaid turned on the light. Annie and Pepper were coming down the steps.

Annie checked his pulse. "It's very weak but he's still with us. You might want to call Byron."

Bert opened his eyes, "Annie, you can go with Andy now. I don't think Lloyd will mind. It is better for you to have a younger guy. We're too damned old. Andy needs a good wife. He'll be lucky to have you."

"Thank you Grandpa Bert," Annie fought back the tears. "You know you'll always be my favorite fellows."

Kincaid walked with Lloyd back to his room but there was no way he was going to stay there. Katherine went with them to the kitchen and made coffee. Elton called Ellison's. It was only minutes before they drove in.

Byron and Marly went in to Bert. Lloyd was apologizing all over the place. Elton was trying to calm him down. Annie sent Pepper out to call Zach. He said he would leave town right away.

The kids took turns going in with their parents to tell their Grandpa goodbye. Ken took it real hard. After he told his grandpa goodbye, he and Pepper went for a walk. Charlie came out of the room, ran straight to Kincaid and crawled up in his lap. "My Grandpa is going to leave us. We won't see him no more. I don't like that."

"I know," Carl said, "I don't like that either."

The little boy crawled up into Carl's arms and cried onto his shoulder. Kevin and Carrie had come over. Kevin helped Lloyd get dressed and went with the frail man so he could tell his dearest friend goodbye. When Kevin brought him back into the kitchen, he said, "Mom and Dad, Bert wants to see you."

Kevin helped Lloyd get his coffee and then he sat down at the table. Then the young man started to cry. Kincaid, without thinking, reached over and patted his back. "It'll be okay Kevin. Is there anything I can do to help?"

Kevin turned around and put his head on the FBI agent's other shoulder and gave him a hug. "Thanks, but I'll be okay. I'm so glad you were with there with him. He thinks a lot of you." Then he grinned, "As much as he can think of anyone."

The men both laughed softly. The door opened and Zach came in. He looked around and said, "Is he gone?"

"Not yet," Kevin said. "Marly, Byron, Dad and Mom are with him now."

Zach nodded and went to his room to check him. Annie stayed to help him. Before long, Annie emerged. She shook her head. "It won't be long, but Bert's still awake."

Katherine went in and they talked a while and when she came out, she said to Kincaid, "Bert said for you to come. He hoped you had enough time to stew. I don't know what he meant."

Carl shook his head, "I do, the old goat."

He went into the room. It was just him and his roommate. Kincaid looked out their bedroom window. It was still dark out. Elmer's head was resting between his front paws and he was watching by the gopher hole apparently waiting for his second wind.

"I got your message. I'm here," Kincaid said as he put his hand on Bert's shoulder. "I thought I told you my answer. You don't give up easy, do you?"

"Nope. You know, this stinks. I was hoping to just sleep through it. But no, I have to wake up so I can enjoy every damned minute of it," the dying man grumped.

Kincaid smiled at him and shook his head, "You're so hard to please."

"Well? Are you going to give in to me or not?" the dying man demanded.

"Well, I was thinking. I'll try. I can't promise. Is that good enough?"

"Hell no, but I guess it's honest. Carl, I'm glad I had time to get to know you. You know, you and I, we have to keep these folks from going too soft on us. That'll be your job now. I know you can handle it. I feel so much better knowing I left them in good hands. Now, don't let me down."

"I won't Bert. I'll try not to anyway," Carl's was trying to keep from crying.

"Now, get the hell out of here. I'd like to have my room to myself at least once before I croak. Then you can spread your stuff out all over it. You probably better send Byron in. Otherwise, he'll get all weird. Now, let me get my rest."

Carl gave him a hug and just plain cried. "I'll probably even miss you, you old goat."

"I know you will," Bert smiled weakly. Then he squeezed the agent's hand tightly and nodded.

Marly and Byron went back in and were with him when he slipped into his final rest about an hour later. When he was gone, they came into the kitchen and told everyone. Lloyd looked at Elton and said, "I think he went to find Ida. Don't you think so, Elton?"

Elton patted his hand, "Yah, Lloyd. I think so."

22

It was just turning daylight when funeral home came out to pick up Bert and take him to Bismarck. The men went down to do the milking early and then everyone had to leave for their work. Everyone had been notified and Pastor Marvin stopped by on the way to the church and of course, would do Bert's service. They decided to have the funeral on Thursday morning. The Ellisons want to make certain that Annie and Marty could be there without having to take off work. They'd both been so good to him. Chris would be able to switch things around so he could make it home for the funeral. Darlene and Keith were scheduled to arrive Tuesday.

At breakfast, the family divided up what they needed to do. Elton told Ken he didn't have to go to the garage, but he wanted to work. He didn't know what good he would be just 'bawling around,' as he put it. Even though Nora offered to have the reception at their place, Marly said it would be better to have the church ladies circle's do it, so no one would be offended.

When they talked about the service, they discussed the flowers and the music. Ginger got all bent out of shape.

"Daddy! This time I know that Grandpa Bert didn't like Mrs. Meyer's squeal singing either! He and I talked about that! Don't let her sing 'sprano!"

Byron looked at her and smiled, "I know Honey, he told me that too. We'll have the choir. Then you won't have to plug your ears."

"Okay Daddy. That will be nicer. Grandpa wouldn't like it otherwise."

They decided to have Marty, Kevin, Keith, Chris, Zach and Darrell be his pall bearers. Danny, Kevin and Elton were going to dig the grave, but Ken insisted that he help. Then of course, Ginger and Charlie wanted to also.

"I don't think so kids," Byron said. "You are good diggers, but that is a big, big job."

"Daddy," Charlie said as he crawled up in his Dad's lap. "We'll only dig on the top and I promise we'll be so good, we can't stand it. I think Grandpa would want us to help. Kincaid will make us mind."

Byron looked at Elton, "What do you think? Could they help?"

Elton shrugged, "I don't see why not, especially if Kincaid comes along to keep an eye on them. What do you think, Carl?"

Kincaid had big hopes of staying beneath the radar. He thought about it, "Yah, I imagine the old goat would probably appreciate it. When are we going to do it?"

"Tomorrow or Wednesday," Kevin answered.

"Okay, I'll work with them for the next two days. Can we do it on Wednesday? You kids can't be quite so sloppy. Okay, Gophers?"

Ginger and Charlie both nodded and then Kincaid said, "It is decided then. Charlie and Ginger will help."

Then they heard Miriam say, "Uncle."

Elton turned to where she had been watching the whole thing from her high chair. "What's the matter, Honey?"

He took her into his arms and she took his face in her hands, nodding her head yes as definitely as she could. "Coot, Ginger, Sharlee, Mr. Bear."

"What Honey?"

"Gopher." Then she patted herself, "Gopher. Son, Uncle." She patted herself again and nodded yes.

"Do you want to help too?" Uncle Elton asked.

"I know that's what she wants," Kevin smiled.

"Why not?" Byron said. "We will do it Wednesday. You can help, too. We'll have the men and then Coot and the Gophers. That'll be real nice of you all. I think Dad would get a kick out of it."

'Yah, I am sure he would,' Kincaid groaned to himself. He could just imagine that old buzzard smirking that he had snared Kincaid into it!

Pepper helped the crew with some abbreviated physical therapy. Elton and Byron went for a long walk out to the pasture. Lloyd had been moved to his recliner, but he was restless. After 'exertorture,' Kincaid pulled up beside him and said, "Hey, what do you say we go take our naps?"

"I was waiting to talk to Bert. He will never get things straightened out about Iwo Jima. I don't know how many times I have tried to tell him. Do you think I made him mad and now he doesn't want to talk to me? Is that why he isn't here?" Lloyd worried.

"No, not at all Lloyd. He had to go. He loved talking to you. I know that for a fact. You know what? He told me that you would tell me about Iwo Jima because I never could understand it. We were fighting the Germans there, right?"

Lloyd shook his head, "Don't any of you people know anything? It was the Japanese."

Carl spent the next hour hearing every detail of the battle Iwo Jima. Finally, Katherine came to put Lloyd down for his nap. She patted Carl's arm, "Mighty kind of you."

"It was nothing." Then he wheeled off to the kitchen to talk Nora out of a cup of coffee.

As he came into the kitchen, Elton and Byron came in from their walk. Byron looked tired but rather calm. It was hard to tell by looking at them who was taking it harder. They both were. No question about that. Kincaid wondered if he would ever have a good friend like those two were. 'Nah, probably not.'

Then much to his surprise, Byron said, "Hey, Carl. Can I have a minute with you after we have our coffee?"

Kincaid was shocked, "Sure I guess. What did I do?"

Byron smiled, "Just good stuff. Don't get all worried."

After coffee, Byron and Carl went to the corner of the big dining room. "Carl, when I talked to Dad before he died, he told me. He said you were going to be his back up man."

"What the hell did he go tell you that for?" Kincaid snapped with a frown.

"He told me why. He wanted me to keep bugging you, the way I bugged him," Byron laughed. "My Dad was a lot of things, but mild mannered was not one of them."

"He was a miserable old goat! That's what he was! I just agreed to keep him quiet."

"I know, he just said you'd try to squirm out of it. At any rate, I talked to Elton."

"Did you go blab it to Magpie? Now why did you go do that?" Kincaid was thinking about getting mad. "You guys never leave anything alone."

"No, I didn't tell Elton that. We were talking about Dad's passing. Elton told me how many times at night you'd get up and help him breathe and stuff. And how you talked to him. I just want you to know how much we appreciate it. You know Dad was not an easy person to buffalo. He wouldn't have even let you talk to him if he didn't think a lot of you. I just want to thank you from the bottom of my heart. I know before Lloyd got sick, Dad would have turned to him. I'm glad that you were there for him."

Kincaid didn't know what to do. "Ah, you're welcome, but it was really no big deal. Hell, I was there anyway. I liked the old buzzard. He was a feisty old grump and ornery as hell. I'm going to miss him." Then tears betrayed his self-control.

Byron put his arm around him, "Yah, that he was. Well, I didn't want to make you upset. I just wanted to thank you. You mean so much to all of us. You need to know that. Anyway, Elton and I are going to take Dad's hospital bed down so you have more room in there. That rocking chair takes up a lot of room."

"Byron, leave it there. Lloyd uses that chair to talk politics in the middle of the night. He'll miss it if it isn't there," Kincaid said quietly.

"But who will he talk to?"

Kincaid couldn't believe his own ears when he heard his voice say sincerely, "Me."

Byron patted his hand, "Sure, we'll leave it."

Nora came in the dining room, "Carl, could we ask you to go pick us some leaf lettuce and cucumbers for salad this noon?"

Kincaid wiped his eyes, "No problem. Come on Gophers. Miriam can ride on my lap. Charlie, you need to carry the bowl. It's your turn today. There might be a few fresh tomatoes if you're interested, but the radishes are getting kind of woody."

Miriam held out her arms and he put her on his lap and the gang headed out the door. Grandma Katherine looked at Nora as they watched them cross to the garden and started to cry. "He was sitting in there listening to Lloyd."

Nora took her in her arms. "I know. I heard them."

After lunch, Ellisons went home and Lloyd went to bed. He was worn out. Everyone was. The celebration for the arrival of Keith and Darlene had been put on hold. Nora had contacted the Red Cross to see if it was possible for Andy to get an emergency leave. They wouldn't do it, since Bert was not his biological grandfather.

After dishes were done, they all took a short nap. Kincaid didn't like his room nearly as well without Bert there. There was more room but it wasn't the same. In fact, he almost hated it. It seemed so empty and quiet.

"Honey, I was wondering if I should go to town. I want to get some lawn furniture. I don't want anyone falling through those stupid chairs," Elton asked his wife. We're going to have folks around and it could be dangerous."

"Sure, good idea," Nora agreed.

Kincaid had been in the doorway and overheard the last of the conversation. "I'm glad on both counts."

"Which counts?" Nora asked.

"That your son'll be home and that Magpie's going to get some lawn furniture. Hey, mind if I ride along? I'd like to get out of the house," Kincaid interjected.

"Sure, I'm taking the pickup though. It might not be as easy to get in and out of, but we can get more stuff in it," Elton grinned.

"You guys managed to get enough in the station wagon when you went to town the last time," Nora pointed out.

"That we did," Elton hugged her, "That we did. Just think what we can do today! Hey, anything you need from town?"

Before long the two men were on their way to town. They drove several miles without talking and then Elton asked, "How you doing? I want to thank you for being there with Bert last night. I'm sure it meant a lot to him."

"Thanks." Kincaid answered. "You had to go blab to the preacher that Bert and I used to visit. Magpie! He thanked me."

"He should know how much did for his father. It's only right."

"I can't believe you said anything to Byron after I was such an ass last night. You were right to get mad at me. You should've kicked me in the rear. I'm surprised you didn't kick me out."

"Ah, that sounds too much like work," Elton said, "We all get our heads on backwards sometimes. Anyway, do you think I should get a grill today?"

"No," Kincaid said. "I want to get it. Sort of a thank you gift."

"You don't need to get me a gift." Elton pointed out.

"Not for you. For Nora and Katherine. I figure I had better butter up the girls so they can help me beat you in the cooking contest. Hey! I have an idea. Instead of real cooking, let's have a grilling contest. You haven't done that much, have you?"

"Well, no I haven't," Elton admitted.

"That would be a more level playing field then."

"I guess. If you say so, but I'll still win," the mechanic boasted.

"Yah, yah Magpie. Just keep telling yourself that!" the FBI agent chortled.

The men went to the home improvement store. They looked over everything in their outdoor department and were confused. They ended up buying a couple extra-long picnic tables with attached benches, a child-sized picnic table with attached benches, a big grill that had a table on one end, a couple rocking chairs, a glider and some chairs with a short coffee table between them. Elton found chairs like the one that had blown away from Kevin's back yard during the storm and got a couple of them, too. They'd drop them off at his place.

"Good grief man, you could have a picnic for half the county with all this stuff," Kincaid grumped. "You'll have to expand the patio! How damned many people do you think you're going to feed?" As soon as he said it, he grinned. "Forget I asked."

On the way home, Kincaid asked, "How's Byron doing?"

"Pretty well. We all knew it was coming for a long time, but it still hard when it's here. Byron handles that stuff better than I do, though. He feels guilty that he should have been with his Dad more."

"Ah, he was a good son. Bert wanted it this way. There was nothing he loved more than talking to Lloyd. I bet those two were a real pair when they were younger," Kincaid observed.

"Yah, they whittled through at least a forest of trees and gabbed all the while. Argued politics I should say."

"Which party did who belong to?" Kincaid asked the obvious question.

"No one knows. One day they would argue one side and the next day the other. They probably voted the same. Wouldn't surprise me a bit!"

23

At home, they went out to the patio with their tools and assembled all the patio furniture. They spent their time reading instructions and squabbling about what went where. Darrell came over and started to help. Before long, Marty showed up. They had themselves quite a time and ended up getting the giggles and messing things up more than once. Marty was convinced he should bring one of the fire trucks and the newest ambulance when they first lit the propane cooker. “We might have a disaster of Biblical proportions!”

Kevin and Carrie showed up when they were almost finished. “Hey Dad,” Carrie said as she kissed her father-in-law, “Thanks for the chairs. You didn’t have to get them for us.”

“I wanted to. Carl and I had a great time at the store,” Elton grinned. “Didn’t we? We can shop with the best of them!”

Nora had come out to admire their work and agreed. “Yah, the Bismarck Chamber of Commerce will probably pave a road in a straight line to our place if they keep it up!”

“We aren’t that bad!” Carl defended himself. “It’s all Elton.”

“Yah, well, what’s the story with all these cooking utensils and this mammoth grill you bought?” Nora asked.

“This is the story,” Kincaid announced. “Magpie and I have a contest. When Harringtons get here, we’re going to have a grill cooking contest! I know I’ll win but I am going to let him sweat it out for a while.”

Nora giggled, “What are the rules for this contest you have going?”

Kevin spoke up, “I want to know what the prize is?”

The two men looked at each other with a new realization, "Well," Elton admitted, "We haven't got around to that yet."

Everyone else was in hysterics. "You crazy idiots! Most people need to know what they're doing!" Kevin laughed.

"Well," Kincaid retorted indignantly. "We don't."

Darrell cracked up, "Obviously! Yea gads, you two are the nuttiest boneheads I've ever met. Have either of you ever grilled before?"

Elton sat down, "No, but it can't be that hard. I don't think it's so funny. We're just having a contest."

Carrie put her arm around her father-in-law and tried to comfort him, "We got that. So, do you want us to set the rules and stuff for the contest?"

Elton looked at Kincaid, "I don't think so, do you?"

Kincaid was thinking, "No, we don't need them, do we? We'll just have our contest by ourselves."

"It'll be a tie," Marty chuckled, "You will each vote for yourself! I can tell you that already. Do either of you have any idea of what you are talking about?"

Kincaid blustered, "We don't need any ideas!"

Darrell laughed so hard, he was in pain and could hardly breathe. "Well, this should be good. I can't wait. Are you grilling steaks, chicken or burgers?"

The guys looked at each other.

"Are you both cooking the same thing?" Nora asked. "And what about the rest of the food? A meal isn't just one thing."

Elton looked at Kincaid, "We'll talk it over and get back to you. Won't we?"

Kincaid nodded in agreement. "Or we might not tell you about it at all."

"So this is going to be at Zach's wedding?" Kevin cracked up.

Darrell laughed, wiping the tears from his eyes, "Maybe it will be his wedding dinner!"

Marty was sitting on the concrete now, holding his stomach, "I can see it all now! In this corner, we have Elton's burnt hamburgers and in this corner, we have Kincaid's blackened chicken legs! Oh, and by the way, there is no wedding cake because it got stuck to the grill!"

Elton put his arm around Kincaid, "Ignore them. They haven't had a good idea since Hoover was president!"

That evening, Marty helped with chores and stayed for dinner. After dinner, he, Kincaid and Elton visited with Lloyd until it was time for him to go to bed. They were trying, rather unsuccessfully, to keep him mind off Bert. After about every other sentence, he went back to asking where Bert was and when he would be back. They were all relieved when it was time to give him his sleeping pill so he could go settle down. After he was asleep, Marty left for home.

Katherine was worn out. She had a terribly emotional day. Bert and Ida had been their dearest friends and now they were both gone. In fact, the most of her contemporaries were gone now, or so confused she couldn't talk to them. It was almost like their brains had passed on and just their bodies were left behind. She knew that it wouldn't be long before they would be planning Lloyd's funeral, or hers.

Everyone knew that Lloyd wasn't going to get over his asking for Bert, any more than he did asking about his car. It was tiring for Katherine. She tried to be patient, knowing he couldn't help it. She still loved him but it was painful. He was still her loving husband; that had never changed. He had never gotten mean toward her or the family, ever. That made it easier to take however she was also aware that it was just how Alzheimer's affected one person or another. Some kind folks became horrible, and vice versa. She thanked God every day that she didn't have to face that. It was hurtful enough to have him not remember who she was most the time.

Katherine was very grateful for Nora. Katherine had never had a daughter, but she knew that she'd have been hard put to have one better than Nora. They had fun together and confided in each other. They got on each other's nerves rarely and when they did, they talked it out right away. It never lasted more than a couple minutes. She was certainly blessed.

Nora gave her a hug, "You are so important to our family. I can never explain how much you mean to Elton and me."

"I love you all, too. I'm just depressed."

"I understand. It won't be the same without Bert," Nora hugged her.

Annie and Nora were hemming Katherine's skirt that she was going to wear for Zach's wedding, when Kincaid and Elton went out to the patio with Kincaid's whiskey and Elton's coke. Elton sat in one of the wooden patio chairs with the cushion. He leaned back and sighed, "This is so much nicer than that wobbly, threadbare chair."

"I think I'll sit in one. I can just use the wheelchair to go back inside, huh?" Kincaid said as he got up and moved to one of the new chairs. "Yah, now this is the life."

They each had a cigarette and leaned back to enjoy the night. After a few minutes, Kincaid said, "What time do you expect your kids from Wisconsin tomorrow?"

"They thought about noon. They drove part of the way last night, because they didn't want to get in here in the dark. I think they stayed in La Crosse tonight."

"Am I going to be in the way when they get here? That is a lot of folks."

"No. That's why we built the addition. We have enough room for everyone. No problem. We will have room for Maureen and Harrington here, too. Don't worry. We'd move you out to bunk in with Elmer, if need be," Elton grinned.

"So, Marty is your real brother's son, right?"

"Yes, he is engaged to Greta, Suzy's sister. I don't know what we would do without him. He is always helping out with baths for the old guys and stuff. Not many young men would bother, but he does. He is a fine fellow," Elton said.

"He is real good with them too. I have to say, the young folks in the clan are all pretty amazing people. How did that happen?"

Elton grinned, "Lots of skinnings! We have been lucky but we've had a few go off the reservation on us. They all know what is expected but they also know that if they don't live up to the standards, they won't be shoved out the door. No matter how far off track they get, they can always come back. It's their clan too."

"But none of them drink or carry on, at least that I've seen," Kincaid pointed out. "I think that makes a difference. If they did, you'd have more trouble."

"Oh Carl, they all have had their scrapes and some pretty good ones at that! You'd be surprised. A person needs to know that you have a place to land when you are all done messing up everything and hurting everybody. That doesn't mean that you won't have to make things right, but you'll have a place to work from. If you don't have that, it is kind of hard to start over again. It seems we all have to do it."

"Have you or Byron ever just kicked someone out?" Kincaid questioned.

"You can't kick someone out of a family. If they're family, they are family. Good, bad or indifferent. Family is something you can pull yourself away from, but they are still family. So, you might as well get used to it. Sometimes, they make you so proud you could just bust and you honestly can't believe they're so great! Then again, sometimes they're so stupid and impossible, you can't believe that either! I have to say, I was ready to get a new bunch the way those guys carried on about our grilling contest. Bet they don't know how to grill either!"

Kincaid chuckled, "Yah, they wouldn't do any better than us. I know that."

Nora came up behind them with her iced tea, "If you really believe that you should open your contest up to the whole clan."

"That would be fun," Annie grinned as she pulled up a chair. "It's really nice to be able to sit out here."

"Did you girls get your sewing done?" Elton asked.

"All done. Are you guys hungry for a treat or are you good for tonight?" Nora asked.

"I'm good," Kincaid answered, "You know, Magpie, Nora might have an idea there."

"How would we do that? We don't even know how we are going to do our contest." Elton thought aloud.

Annie ran into the house and came back with a paper and pencil. "Well, let's figure it out. That is, unless you guys want to keep this down to a grudge match between you two."

The men looked at each other.

"No. We'll take second and first place. No question about it. Of course, I'll be first," Kincaid boasted.

"Don't polish your tail feathers yet, Mr. FBI" Elton poked. "Have you got any ideas, girls?"

"Well, first, we need to know when Harringtons are going to be here," Nora suggested. "Do you think that Harringtons could be here by then?"

"I need to talk to Mo again, but I think so. Ian's doing pretty well," Kincaid said, "But Ruthie would probably know more about it."

Annie giggled, "If Ruthie and Ian had their way, he'd be out here already. He is going bonkers out there with nothing to do and she is so lonesome for him, it is ridiculous. Honestly, they are worse than Andy and I!"

Elton patted her knee, "I have to say, Annie, I have been very proud of how both you and Andy have handled everything."

Annie gave him a hug, "Thanks Dad. That means a lot."

Kincaid watched and thought to himself that kind of thing was a big part of it too. He figured that maybe acknowledging someone's attempts to do the right thing was just as valuable as skinning them when they didn't.

Carl leaned back in his chair. "So, July first. We'll have time to practice then."

"What're you going to cook? Just meat or the whole meal? Are you going to work alone or have helpers?" Nora asked.

"I have no idea," Elton thought. Then he burst into a grin, "I know, let's do it up proud!"

"How do you do it up proud?" Nora shook her head.

"Well, we can have a pie contest, and a hot roll contest," Elton started.

Kincaid interrupted, "And a potato salad contest."

Annie giggled, "And a bean contest. Then we would have all the food. Can anyone enter anything or as many foods as they want?"

"To make it fair," Nora giggled, "We should ban Katherine from the rolls, Marly from the pies and Lucy from the beans. They'll win for certain."

"I know," Kincaid said, "We can have them be the judges for those categories. Then they can't enter; but since they're the best, the contest will be judged by experts."

"Good idea," Annie said. "We need a potato salad judge. Who would that be?"

Elton said, "You know, we should have a regular salad contest too. Elsie makes a mean coleslaw."

"Good idea," Nora agreed, "We can have Julia be the Potato Salad Judge. No one in the county makes better potato salad."

Elton got excited, "Oh, and we need a pickle contest and I'll be the judge. I can't make them, but I'm a connoisseur."

"Good idea," Annie smiled, "Well, I'm an excellent judge of lemonade. I can spot a powdered lemonade at fifty paces."

"Okay, but what about the meat? What kind?" Nora asked.

"I say any kind you want to cook, huh, Kincaid?" Elton offered. "It's up to the griller."

"We won't have a big enough grill," Kincaid pointed out. "How can we do that?"

"Let's find out who wants to enter and then we can borrow enough grills. You know those little round things with briquettes aren't too bad for cooking. We need to know how many we'll need. I doubt that anyone will even want to challenge us!" Elton boasted.

"You might be surprised," Nora giggled. "Are you going to allow teams for the cooking or single cooks only?"

"Hmm. I think that if you feel you need a team to beat us, we should give you the opportunity!" Kincaid blustered. "What do you think, Magpie?"

"I agree. But who is going to be the judge?" Elton got serious.

"I know," Nora explained, "We can have the meat judged by everyone. Like a secret ballot thing. Then you guys won't know who to butter up and connive!"

"What are you trying to say there, woman?" Elton got defensive.

"That neither of you are not one bit above bribery," Nora said flatly. "Admit it."

Elton chuckled, "Well, I'll be jiggered. I think she has my number."

"I think that a secret ballot vote on the meat would be good and fair," Kincaid nodded, "So what have we got there Annie?"

She read back all their ideas and they thought about it. The only change they made was to include another category called "Side Dishes" for anything else that someone wanted to bring. Jeannie would be the judge of that because every clan meal, she brought a different fantastic side dish.

Annie said she would type up the contest directions and rules so they could be handed out on Sunday at the clan dinner. She would mail Harringtons a copy. It would be fun. Then she got very quiet. "You know what, though?"

"What? Nora asked.

"What are the prizes?" Annie asked.

"Hmm." Elton laughed, "Leftovers!"

After he got whacked by everyone, he and Kincaid decided to get the prizes together. The seven smaller contests would have $15 cash prizes and the meat contest would be worth $50. They were confident that they would win it, so it wasn't a problem.

24

Grandpa Lloyd slept quietly all night, for which they were all grateful. It was cloudy in the morning and rather windy. The phone was awake before the family.

The first phone call was from Darlene. She called at about five to say they were just leaving La Crosse. They no more than hung up when Harrington called. Ruthie had told him the night before about Bert and he wanted to express his condolences to the family. He spoke a few minutes and said he'd call Zach in town.

Then it was Elton's turn to talk. He invited Harrington and his mother out so they would be there before July first. Harrington chuckled, "I'd love to be there and that's a blasted fact! I'll talk to my doctor today and see if I can make it. That's only two weeks away! I don't know if I can make it, but it isn't like I'm doing anything here. I want to see Ruthie and you all! Elton, can I tell you something in confidence?"

"Certainly, Ian."

"Mom won't let on, but she's anxious to see Carl. Don't say anything."

"I won't and the feeling is very mutual. Same rules, got it?" Elton answered cryptically.

"Got it. So, does that mean that you want us to stay for the whole time until Zach gets married, or to come out twice? Cause we can do it either way, we just need to get the tickets."

"I'd just as soon you stayed but I understand that it might be difficult for you. I miss you guys."

"How could you miss us with all the folks that you have around there?" Harrington laughed.

"Easy. You've met some of these folks! You should understand!" Elton chuckled. "So, I hope the doc says you can make it for the world's best grilling contest. Of course, you'll vote for me! Huh?"

"I don't know. I might enter myself. I'm not too bad on the grill," Harrington chided, "You and Coot had better plan your concession speeches for when you hand me the prize!"

"What do Easterners know about grilling?"

"About as much as you and Kincaid, and that's a blasted fact! I know that Mom will plan on taking the bean contest by storm. Man, you guys made a big mistake there! Hey, I will throw a twenty in the pot for prize money."

"No need to do that!" Elton said. "This is for fun. Coot and I just want to prove a point."

"No, put me down for twenty. It'll give me a stake in it and put my name and Mom's on the list for entries! Thanks so much for inviting us. I'm going to start packing as soon as I hang up," Harrington laughed. "I can't wait and that's a blasted fact!"

While they were filling their thermos, Marly called and asked if they could watch the kids so she and Byron could go to town to make funeral arrangements. Nora said of course, and besides, Coot wanted to practice with his Gophers.

Marly also mentioned that since Andy wasn't going to be there, Ken would do an Old Testament reading for Bert. They were going to have Danny do the New Testament reading. Katie was trying to find a nice poem to read for her Grandpa. There were wondering if someone could help her with that. Annie said she would love to and that she had some Native American readings that she might be interested in.

Chores went quickly and Kevin told his Dad to stay home from work. "Ken and I can handle it and you should be home when Keith and Darlene show up. Okay? We'll do fine, won't we, Ken?"

"Yah, we will," Ken answered. "I want to be busy. I don't like just thinking around."

Elton looked at Ken, "You might need to spend some time doing that, you know, Ken. It sort of has to be done."

Kevin gave his Dad a nod and whispered, "I got it."

Elton smiled back and patted his son's shoulder. He really loved his goofy kid. His second oldest son was becoming a fine upstanding young man.

After breakfast, Marty came over and gave Lloyd his bath. Then he hung out with him and talked about World War I. Elton went out to grind some feed for the livestock. Coot went out with the little kids.

Annie and Katie disappeared into her room to look over some things for her to read. After about an hour, the girls came down and asked for Grandma and Nora's opinion. They had found a Lakota prayer that they liked and had figured out how they wanted her to say it.

"This is taken from a Lakota prayer.

May the Great Spirit watch over you, and may you be at peace.

Great Spirit, you take the sun from us and cradle it in your arms, then you bring darkness onto us so that we may sleep. When you bring the darkness to my friend here, do so without the nightmare that he has had for so long. Let your moon shine on my friend in a gentle manner as he looks at the stars. Let us remember that those stars are the spirits of my friends shining on them and those friends are at peace."

"What do you think?" Katie asked. "Is it silly?"

Grandma hugged her and Nora said, "Not at all, Katie. It's wonderful. I love it. Thank you Annie for helping her. It's really nice and I'm sure that Pastor Olson will think it is good. Why don't you call him and read it to him?"

Katie thought a minute, "Annie, could I ask you to go over to the church with me? I would rather talk to him in person. Pastor Olson had mentioned a poem that he knew that Grandpa like too."

"Sure, I'll get the car."

Outside, there was a lot of commotion going on. The Gophers had descended on the area that Coot had plotted out. There was dirt flying all over and Elton could tell when he returned from grinding feed that things were more than a bit out of control. He wandered over to the excavation. "How's it going?"

Kincaid rolled his eyes, "Just ducky. Give me a rope and a tall tree!"

Elton chuckled, "Can't help you there. What's up, kids? Your Dad will have your hide if you go after it this way. You'll have dirt spread all over the cemetery. Here, let Coot and I help you. Charlie, come here. You need to stick the shovel in carefully and slowly. Just get a half a shovel of dirt. You need to keep a straight edge all around. You have to put the dirt on a tarp, so that it can all be put back in to cover the casket."

Charlie looked at him blankly, "What is a gasket?"

Elton explained, "That is the box that Grandpa is in. It is called a casket. And you need to keep all the dirt really neat so that we can cover the casket up to the top."

"Why?" Ginger asked, "Wouldn't it be easier to just bury him close to the top?"

Elton shook his head, "No, it has to be deep."

"Why?" Charlie asked, "So he can't get back out?"

Elton was getting frustrated, "He won't get back out. That isn't why."

"Then why?" Ginger asked.

"So animals can't dig him up." Elton mumbled. He didn't look at Kincaid because he knew that he had already lost control of this conversation.

Kincaid raised his eyebrows and shrugged back at him like 'you got yourself into this.'

"What animal? Elmer is the only one that lives by here that would dig him up," Ginger pointed out. "You could just keep him on his leash, Uncle Elton. Then he won't dig up Grandpa."

"We're going to do it this way," Elton answered bluntly.

Charlie thought a minute, "Maybe it would be better if we put Grandpa in the basement and then Elmer wouldn't dig him up."

"Look kids," Elton was wondering how much booze Coot had left in his bottle. "It's a tradition. It might not make sense but this is the way that we do it. Either you do it this way, or you can't help. Okay?"

Charlie shrugged, "Okay, but I still think it is pretty dumb to set a gasket outside where Elmer can get it. I wouldn't do that."

Elton muttered, "I'm sure you wouldn't, Charlie."

It took a little while but finally the men got the bigger kids to dig a little more carefully. Miriam dug such little shovels full that it didn't matter. Then they all went to the house. They were all the way up to the doorstep before Elton looked at Coot. They both started to chuckle.

Nora told the kids to get washed up and asked the men to go out to pick some fresh leaf lettuce for lunch. Once outside, Kincaid couldn't help it.

"Congratulations Elton," Kincaid cracked up in laughter, "You handled that lesson in grave digging better than anyone could've wanted!"

Elton gave him a dirty look, "Just hush up. You didn't seem to be doing much better."

Kincaid laughed, "No, I sure didn't. We never got past whether it was better to dig fast or good. Charlie was digging and throwing his dirt on where Ginger was trying to dig neatly, but slower than molasses. It was going to break out into bloody murder until you showed up! Miriam even called them goats.

Elton shook his head, "What an outfit! Some days I wonder how far away I could run?'

"Ah, you'd miss it," Kincaid said, apparently oblivious to what he had said.

As they were heading back toward the house, a car and a pickup with Wisconsin plates turned into the drive. Elton waved, put the lettuce on the steps and went over to open the car door for his daughter-in-law. There were hugs all around. Elton introduced Kincaid and the kids both greeted him warmly.

"We have heard such good things about you. We're glad to meet you," Darlene said.

"Well, thanks. The same here." Kincaid smiled back.

"Where do you want to put your stuff?" Elton asked.

"We tried to divide it up. The things in the pickup can stay there until we get our own place, but the car stuff we kind of need," Keith answered.

"I can drive your pickup to the machine shed if you want to go in and tell your Mom hi," Elton said.

"Thanks Dad. Come Darlene, we can leave this in the car for now, huh?"

"Sure. Are you coming, Mr. Kincaid?"

"Just call me Kincaid," Kincaid answered, "I have to take the lettuce in to the ladies."

"See you got your wheel chair all souped up?" Keith laughed.

"Kevin did it for me," Carl explained. "He did a fine job, don't you think?"

Keith bent down and looked it over. "I think he did a great job. He's good at that sort of thing. What is all this sticky bluish stuff all over the back of the engine casing?"

"Ah, it's from the volcano," Kincaid answered matter-of-factly and offered no further explanation. His hope was that he would forget it.

Keith gave him an odd look and then said, "Oh."

25

The girls returned after talking to Pastor Olson. He suggested since Annie was definitely one of Bert's favorite people, that she read the Native American prayer and that Katie read one of his favorite poems, Death Be Not Proud by John Donne. Pastor Olson knew that Bert always liked it, especially the 'modernized' version. After reading it, the girls decided it would be an excellent idea.

Elton and Keith unpacked the car that afternoon and by dinner time, the young couple's things were all put away. Darlene had put things in drawers, closets and 'nesting' as Elton called it.

Before chores, they got a phone call from Boston. Harrington said the doctor said he could travel but put many restrictions on his activities. They booked their tickets and would be out on June 19th to return July 20th. He wanted to check with Elton it that would really be okay before he confirmed the tickets because it seemed like a very long time for them to put them up.

Elton watched Kincaid's expression and knew he was excited. Between the happiness of Ruthie and Kincaid that the visit would bring, twice as much time would be not too long. He looked at Nora. She was watching Kincaid and smiling. He knew it was okay with her. He assured them it would be perfect.

That evening, Kevin, Carrie and the Ellisons joined the family for dinner after chores. Elton and Kevin had a chance to talk in private. Kevin told Elton that he and Ken had a long talk that afternoon while they were fixing a carburetor. The talk seemed to do Ken good and he was in much better spirits. Elton patted his son on the back, "You are a heck of a guy, Kev. You make me proud."

Kev stopped what he was doing and looked at his stepdad. "Thanks," he mumbled and went to the restroom for a minute.

After the others went home and Lloyd went to bed, the family went out to relax on the patio. "After blowing and blustering all day, it turned out to be a beautiful evening," Nora said as she put the pitcher of iced tea on the picnic table.

Grandma and Nora sat in the rocking chairs. Darlene and Keith sat together in the cuddling swing and Kincaid was sitting in one of the larger chairs by the coffee table with his whiskey. Elton looked around and grumped. "Well, if that don't beat all! I set up the cuddling swing and end up sitting next to this ornery cuss! See if I ever get conned like that again!"

Nora giggled, "Oh, you will."

"Humph," Elton gave her a dirty look and then smiled, "I imagine I will. So, what are the plans for tomorrow?"

Kincaid asked, "What time are we going to dig the grave?"

"In the morning," Elton suggested. "There's visitation at the funeral home tomorrow afternoon."

"I can help with the grave, too," Keith said. Keith was a bit shorter than Kevin and his hair was darker, but other than that, looked just like him. "How about right after breakfast? That should a good time for everyone."

"We have to get the kids rounded up," Kincaid pointed out. "I hope it goes better than the practice session this morning! Magpie almost lost grips with reality!"

"You were no help, I might add," Elton retorted. "None whatsoever."

"What happened?" Keith asked innocently.

Kincaid took great glee in explaining what happened and everyone was in stitches about it. Elton didn't think it was as funny as they did.

"Miriam's a sweet little thing. She's so small for her age. I can't imagine what her life must have been like," Darlene said. "Did you notice how she watches everything and everyone's reactions?"

"She is downright relaxed now compared to how she was! She was so jumpy and everything scared her. She hasn't had a curling up thing for a few days now," Elton replied.

"Curling up thing?" Darlene asked.

"The doctor says is it to make yourself a smaller target, you know. She goes into the fetal position," Elton explained.

"And when she does that, it is only Kevin, Byron and Dad that can get her out of it. Even Zach usually can't," Nora explained.

"If you ever encountered her mother or father, you'd understand. I think Zach's father must have been a real piece of work," Kincaid shook his head.

"Anyone that can make his own child put his hand in a gunny sack with a rattlesnake, tells me about all I need to know about him," Elton shook his head.

They all sat lost in thought for a minute and then Katherine said, "But Miriam is doing well now and gaining weight. I think before long, she will be digging away with the rest of the Gophers."

"I shudder to think what those three will be able to accomplish when the girls are both well," Kincaid made a face. "I couldn't believe the disaster with the volcano."

"What about this volcano business and how did your wheelchair get blue sticky stuff all over it?" Keith laughed.

"Aha! Now I get to tell the story!" Elton crowed. He proceeded to tell the entire story with a great flourish. Nora had to run in and get the Polaroids of the disaster. Everyone had a great laugh.

"You must really like kids, huh, Kincaid?" Darlene asked. Darlene was a happy girl with a huge smile. She wore her dark hair in a shag. Her petite figure was just beginning to show signs of her pregnancy.

"Not really," Carl groaned and gave Elton the 'keep your mouth shut' look. "Never been much of a kid person."

"Well," Grandma Katherine smiled as she got up, "One would never know it. I have to say good night to you all. I'm so glad you kids are home again."

Everyone told her good night and she went in. Dad got everyone another Coke except Carl who wanted his second whiskey. When Elton returned with the drinks, Nora shared the news from the latest letter they had received from Andy. He had said that he had been on sick call.

"Andy is sick?" Darlene was instantly worried. "What does he have? Is he okay?"

"The letter I got yesterday said that he was laid up a few days with some foot rot or something. He was going back on patrol. So, I think he is okay now. They wouldn't be sending him out again if he wasn't well," Nora said, trying to assure herself.

Keith and his father exchanged a glance, "Well Mom, their idea of well and our idea of well are different, but I'm sure he must be okay."

"I don't like the way you say that, Keith," Nora said. "Don't treat me like I live in a marshmallow. I want to know the truth. You guys both know how angry that makes me. I was hoping against hope that he'd be able to come home for Bert's funeral."

"Honey," Elton said, "The Army needs soldiers and they look at your son as a soldier, not as your son. What you think is reasonable, they don't. But they don't want to send someone out on patrol that they have to carry back. I'm sure that Andy is tough enough to handle whatever they think they need."

"Elton Schroeder! You sound like a politician!" Nora frowned. "Anyway, I know he wasn't on sick call yesterday when I got in touch with the Red Cross and he wasn't dead or wounded then. He was out on a patrol though, so, I'm not going to worry. What you hear now, how does it compare with when you were there five years ago?" Nora asked.

"Mom, it's a lot worse now and it wasn't nice then. Anyway, let just take it as it comes, huh?" Keith nodded.

"Yah, good idea," Mom hesitated and then abruptly changed the subject. "And so, two weeks, the Harringtons will be here! Gee, Carl, you are going to have to practice dancing at that anniversary party on Saturday!"

"Are you all still doing that, what with Bert's passing and all?" Kincaid asked.

Katherine smiled, "Of course. First off, Bert would've wanted us to and second of all, we've put if off before. You know, you can't stop and wring your hands every time something goes amiss. You need to keep on with life."

"Hmm, never heard anyone but Magpie say that before," Kincaid shook his head. "I know that Bert wouldn't have wanted everyone to sit around and moan about him being gone. He wanted to go himself for a long time."

"Ever since Ida passed away," Nora confirmed. "He gave up then, but we all badgered him into hanging on."

They all sat quietly and then Kincaid chuckled, “That old goat. He gave me more hell than anyone I’ve encountered in the last twenty years! He relished it!”

“Yah,” Elton agreed. “There was little the man loved more than giving someone grief.”

26

The next morning after chores, Elton, Keith and Kincaid arrived at Ellisons. The kids were waiting with their shovels. Byron was holding Miriam, but even she was holding her shovel. As they got out of the car and Keith got the wheelchair set up, Kincaid looked at Elton. "Lord have mercy!"

The assembled group went to the cemetery. Darrell, Danny and Kevin had put out the tarp for the dirt. The kids were surprisingly quiet. Byron apparently had given them a lecture before Schroeders arrived. They were so subdued that Elton wondered if they were indeed the same children.

Keith helped Kincaid get set up at the end of the gravesite so he could keep an eye on the Gophers. Byron brought Miriam over and asked Kincaid where he wanted her. Kincaid said, "Set her down here, in front of me."

So it began. Charlie was within two feet of Uncle Elton and Ginger was on the opposite side by her Uncle Darrell. The digging began. It went very neatly and quietly at first. Everyone was impressed, especially Kincaid. Even Miriam was digging neatly and very well. After a few minutes, there was a universal sigh of relief.

It continued for few minutes until Charlie hit a rock with the end of his shovel. His eyes got as big as saucers and he jumped about two feet straight up into the air. He yelled, "I hit a gasket! Somebody's getting out!"

Ginger screamed. He took off like gangbusters with Ginger close on his heels. Miriam got scared and started to cry, so Kevin picked her up. Elton and Kincaid looked at each other and started to laugh. They laughed so hard they couldn't even talk. It wasn't polite, or respectful, but they couldn't help it.

Within minutes, Marly came down to the cemetery. "What did you guys do? Charlie is hiding under his bed and I can't get him to come out! Ginger is in her room praying like crazy!"

By now, they were all just dying of laughter and trying to pull themselves together. "I'll come in and talk to them," Byron gasped, trying to keep from choking.

"Charlie didn't even put his shovel down," Marly related, "He went under his bed shovel so fast that I hardly knew what happened. He's smack against the wall and I can't even reach him."

Byron headed for the house and the guys finished digging the grave. Miriam just watched quietly from the safety of Kevin's arms and never said a word. After they finished, some of them had to go do their own work, but Elton, Keith and Kincaid went to the house.

Pastor Marvin had stopped by and he was talking to Ginger, who was much calmer now. Byron was halfway under Charlie's bed, trying to calm his son down.

"What on earth happened?" Marly asked as Pastor Marvin came out of Ginger's room.

He grinned and took a cup of coffee, "Seems that all their Dad's talk of doing it correctly, being respectful of the dead and that, scared the little tikes. I don't know what you told them Elton, but they thought that is what they had dug up some dead person's *gasket* and they would get out and come after them."

Kincaid was in misery with the giggles, "Way to go, Magpie! You scared the bejesus out of them."

"Not just him. Byron gave them a stern talk this morning about being respectful of the people who were buried in the cemetery," Marly explained. "You know how they are. I thought he was laying it on a little thick but he never said they would get out and chase them."

"We can thank Elton for that!" Kincaid tattled.

"No, you can't. Charlie asked if we had to bury them so deep so they wouldn't get out. I never said anything like that." Elton tried to explain himself. "I only said they had to be buried deep so nothing could dig them up!"

"What?" Keith said in shock! "You said what?"

Marly shook her head, "I think it'll be a long time before those little rats will want to be digging again. They're quite the Gophers."

Miriam looked at everyone from her seat on Kincaid's lap, patted her chest and said, "Gopher."

"Yes, Honey," Marly hugged her, "You guys are quite the gophers."

That afternoon, the Englemann clan assembled at the funeral home to pay their last respects. Charlie held his father's hand as tight as humanly possible and he stayed within two inches of him all the while. Even though his Daddy had assured him that he dead weren't about to come chasing him around, he was taking no chances.

Miriam stayed in Kincaid's lap until he started to walk up to the casket. Then she went to Kevin, as he walked beside Kincaid. She looked at Grandpa Bert and said, "Goat." She made a snoring noise.

"That's right, Miriam," Kevin answered softly, "Grandpa Bert is taking a good rest now."

Kincaid had never been one to go to funerals, and if he did, stayed as much out of the emotional end of it as possible. He hadn't known Bert that long and figured he'd walk up, nod and walk away. It didn't quite work out that way.

He looked down at his roommate. The elderly man looked more peaceful than Kincaid had ever seen him. The makeup had given him more color and he actually looked younger. Kincaid reached to touch his hand.

Bert's hand of course, felt like plastic and it was obvious to Kincaid that this was just the shell of the man he had been. Tears came to his eyes when he thought about their talks in the middle of the night while he rubbed his boney back. He thought of how they used to argue and how Bert was always trying to get him into trouble.

Once Carl started to cry, he couldn't stop even though he told himself how stupid he was being. He was at a loss what to do but couldn't seem to move away from his friend.

The next thing he was aware of was Elton taking his arm. He turned him around and gave him a hug. Normally, Kincaid would have been mortified, but this time he was glad that he had someone to hold on to. Byron came over and patted his shoulder, "You're a good friend to him. My Dad told me that he was glad that you were sent to us, even if you were the most stubborn, miserable, cantankerous old cuss he had ever met."

Kincaid looked at him and groaned, "Sounds like him. Thanks. I felt the exact same way about him, you know."

"Yah," Elton patted his shoulder, "We know. Want to sit down now?"

"I think I better."

That evening was very quiet at the Schroeder home, except for the kids arriving home. Pepper and Zach got home about seven and Chris drove in about nine. Annie and Marty got back at ten-thirty

They sat on the patio and visited a little. Carl had his whiskey. Zach was introduced to Keith and they had a beer together. While the family visited quietly, Carl was still reflecting on the afternoon.

He had never had a reaction like that in so many years he could hardly remember. It was almost frightening to a man who had prided himself on his self-control. He knew these petunias were rubbing off on him. The worst part is that he wasn't sure if he cared that they were.

The clan met downstairs in the church hall before the morning service. It was quiet, but not really sad. Everyone had known for a long time that this was something that Bert had looked forward to. Even though none of them wanted him to leave them, they all knew how long he had struggled and put up with the oxygen for them. They had to appreciate that.

The family followed Bert's casket down the aisle behind Pastor Marvin. Carl was surprised that he was included, as was all the clan, as family. He left his wheelchair at the back of the church and walked in with Annie.

Lloyd and Katherine sat with Elton and Nora. Miriam sat on Elton's lap throughout the service.

The kids all did a great job with their readings, even Ken who was very nervous. His voice only cracked a few times while he did the reading.

Katie held back her tears while read the poem, the modernized version of *Death Be Not Proud by John Donne*, but there wasn't a dry eye in the place.

> "Death be not proud, though some have called you
> Mighty and dreadful, for, you are not so,
> For, those, whom you think that you overthrow,

Die not, poor death, nor yet can you kill me.
From rest and sleep, which you picture with
Much pleasure, then from you, much more must flow,
And soon our best men with you do go,
Rest of their bones, and souls deliver.
You are slave to fate, chance, kings and desperate men,
And do with poison, war, and sickness dwell,
And poppy, or charms can make us sleep as well,
And better then by your stroke; why do you swell then?
One short sleep past, we wake eternally,
And death shall be no more; then death, you shall die."

The choir and congregation sang *Rock of Ages,* Bert's favorite hymn, as he was went down the carpeted aisle for the last time. At the end of the aisle, Annie helped Kincaid back into this wheelchair and then Jerald Oxenfelter helped him take it through the cemetery. Kincaid was beginning to understand why Magpie always spoke so highly of Jerald. He was one of those quiet people, who was always there with a reliable helping hand and never asked for any fanfare. He was the epitome of a clanner.

Outside the brick church, the pallbearers carried Bert's dark oak casket to his gravesite, next to his Ida. The pallbearers did a good job and Kincaid watched the young men as they lowered Bert's casket into the grave. These were some fine young men. Carl wondered how many men that age he had arrested and thrown into jail. He questioned if maybe he had been wrong all along. Maybe those guys were really the petunias and these guys were the tough ones.

Pastor Olson had Annie step forward and read the Lakota prayer. After Pastor Marvin said the final words, every one of the clan came to the graveside and placed a single rose on his casket. It was beautiful.

When Kincaid put the rose Marly had given him on the casket, he said tearfully, "Good bye my dear friend. You old goat."

Elton handed Miriam to Carl because they were having some problems with Lloyd. He took Lloyd's arm and they walked off to the side and talked quietly. Elton had a way of getting Lloyd calmed down. It wasn't so much what he did, but the fact that Lloyd trusted him.

After the burial, some of the men closed the grave while the others went inside to the church hall for a lunch. Pastor Marvin Olson led grace.

He had given a nice sermon. Carl had to say that both of these preachers could give good sermons. He was impressed.

Charlie came over and asked Kincaid if he could sit by him while he ate his lunch.

"Sure, Agent Ellison," Kincaid grinned. "I thought maybe you were mad at me after yesterday."

"Nah. I wasn't mad. I just didn't want you to remember how dumb I was."

"Oh, I forgot about that already. Are you feeling better now?"

"Yah. Daddy explained it all to me. You know, Agent Kincaid," Charlie observed. "A guy can have a good talk under the bed. You should try it sometime."

Kincaid smiled, "I think I prefer sitting up."

"Yah but, under the bed, it is dark so people can't see if you feel really dumb."

"I'll keep that in mind. Thank you for telling me Charlie."

"That's okay."

That night while Carl lay in his bed watching Elmer through the window, he thought about the day. He had to admit that he really liked being here. He felt a part of this family and they treated him like he belonged.

He watched Elmer as he dug relentlessly after that stupid gopher. "Even their dog is stubborn. I imagine Magpie trained him that way!"

Then he looked over where Bert's bed used to be, "Damn dog is as stubborn as you, Bert. I doubt either one of you ever will get all you want, but I have to give you this. You got a hell of a lot closer than I'd have ever thought."

He turned over and tried to go to sleep. He missed the coughing and the grumping. He missed his grouchy roommate.

27

Friday was a quiet day until Nora, Darlene and Katherine decided that it was time for Kincaid's dance lessons. He really wanted to be able to dance with Mo at Zach's wedding, but did not relish the ladies ganging up while teaching him. When Marly drove in with Ginger, Charlie and Miriam, he thought maybe he could escape outside to go digging. But alas, that was not to be. It turned out to only mean that Ginger was going to dance with him, too. Kincaid was extremely grateful that Miriam had to take her nap.

At first he thought Charlie would be his way out, but that failed when the ladies decided that he was old enough to learn how to dance better, too. He and Charlie exchanged a lot of cross-eyed looks and stepped on a lot of feet, but in the end, they both had their lessons.

Lloyd intently watched the whole process from his chair and finally decreed, "If that ain't the damnedest mess I ever did see."

Then he stood up and in the end, sort of danced with Katherine once and Nora once. Then he sat down and smirked to Kincaid, "Now I showed you how it's done kid; get with it."

Kincaid's stamina certainly wasn't what it used to be, but he did manage to dance slowly. He did the steps okay but had to be able to stand up and not collapse.

"I'll sit it out and watch you guys," Kincaid explained.

"You'll have to mostly but if you do the slow dances, you'll be able to dance tomorrow night. If you're careful, Elton and boys got it worked out how to get you to the loft without you having to climb the stairs. Then you can use your wheelchair and save your energy for the dancing," Nora stated.

"I see. Am I going to like how they get me upstairs, or do I need to be thinking about getting appendicitis by tomorrow night?" Kincaid asked.

"You're going to the dance; appendicitis or not, buddy," Marly said. "So you might as well make up your mind to it. And no. You probably won't like how we're going to get you up there. That's why we aren't telling you. We don't want to have to listen to you whine about it."

"Lord have mercy," Carl mumbled.

"You seem to say that a lot for a non-religious man," Katherine giggled.

"If it wasn't for the fact I need you to teach me how to make that Hot German Potato Salad, I wouldn't even be civil to you, Miss Katherine," the man advised.

"Oh, are you entering that contest too?" Marly asked. "I sort of thought that you were just going to do the grilling."

"No, I'm not entering the contest. I was just going to learn how to make it."

"I'll only teach you if you enter it in the contest, Carl," Katherine instructed. "We can be teammates in the potato salad contest, if you'd like?"

"Can't you just teach me?"

"Not going to do that. Either sign up or hush up," the little lady decreed.

"Whoever said that women are the fairer of the species never met you guys," Carl grumbled. "Oh alright. I'll do it, but I won't have time to do that much that day, because I'll be grilling."

"What are you going to cook? Hot dogs?" Marly giggled.

"Downright insulting, ma'am." Carl acted offended. "I'm going to make something extraordinary."

"Like what?" Marly asked.

"I'm not certain yet," he mumbled. "I think I'd better go sit down now. I've had it."

"You don't have any idea, do you?" Marly chided.

"None of your business, little miss. What are you signed up for? You can't enter the pie contest, but what are you signed up for?"

"I am going to enter my hot chili pepper pickles," Marly stated. "They are so hot; they'll make Elton's eyes bleed!"

"Cruel. You're all a bunch of spiders." Carl grumped.

"We don't like spiders, do we Kincaid?" Charlie asked his mentor, sitting down beside him and mimicking his movements.

"Not much. We'll let these gals get away with it though because it's your Mom and all. Okay, partner?"

"Okay," the little guy shook his hand.

Ginger ran over to Kincaid, "But what about me? I'm not a spider, am I? I squish them when I see them."

"No, you're a Gopher. You and Miriam. You're good guys," Kincaid assured the little tomboy.

Ginger was relieved. "Good. Then will you dance with me at the dance?"

"Sure Ginger. I'd love to." Kincaid answered. "But I really do need to take a nap now. Okay guys?"

"Okay, Agent," Charlie said. "Ginger is going to help me do the Chicken Man chores now. We'll do pretty much a good job."

At dinner that evening, it was just family, which was always a weird term to use around the Schroeder household. It could mean anything from four to forty people. Kincaid was going to ask someone someday how they differentiated but then decided that they probably didn't know either.

Zach was home and Suzy came over. Chris was there, so Pepper was happy. Kevin and Carrie joined the family for dinner, and of course, Keith and Darlene were now back as live-ins.

Everyone was making a special effort to talk to Lloyd who talked about Bert incessantly. He wanted everyone to go search for him and was convinced that he was lost somewhere. They would get him convinced that he was okay and had gone to be with Ida. He would nod, agree it was good and five minutes later, start all over again.

Over dinner, the conversation turned to the upcoming dance the following evening. Nora told how well the dance lessons went with Kincaid. Kincaid would've been willing to forego the praise; when the usual, expected harassing began. Even Lloyd put his twenty cents worth in; giving a unique critique of Carl's dancing skills. Carl wondered how someone who could forget what his wife looked like, but still relate to an eager audience every misstep he had taken earlier that morning!

He endured the criticism as long as could be required of any human, before he finally told Lloyd to mind his own business. Within two sentences, the guys were arguing about who could dance better, and Lloyd wasn't about to back down. He knew he was a better dancer than Kincaid.

"I went to dances before you were born, you Whippersnapper! You don't begin to know the first thing about it," Lloyd said flatly. "The only thing you know is what I showed you today."

"I do to know how to dance," Kincaid blustered. "I used to dance years ago. Now I can't do it so well because of my injury."

"Did you injure your head?" Lloyd asked with a laugh. "Elton, you should see this guy! He dances like a mule."

"I guess you would know how a mule dances," Kincaid shook his head. "You dance just like one."

"Do not," Lloyd stated. "Just ask my Katherine."

"She would lie just to shut you up. I won't ask her."

"Elton, tell him he can't dance."

Elton shook his head, "No way. I am staying out of this one. You're on your own."

"Well, if that don't beat all!" Lloyd said, "Nora girl, you tell him."

"Tell who what, Lloyd?" Nora asked. "You have to be nice. Carl is recuperating and can't dance a jig like you do. He has to get well first."

"Really?" Lloyd said. "I didn't know that. I'm sorry. What do you have?"

"I got shot," Kincaid answered.

Lloyd studied him for a minute, "Doesn't surprise me, the way you act! Seems to me that you didn't learn much from it though."

Kincaid frowned at him, "What is that supposed to mean?"

"If I got shot for being ornery, I'd try to be nicer," Lloyd declared.

"I wasn't shot for being ornery," Kincaid glared at him.

"What did you do? Cut in on another guy's woman? I keep telling Elton, that catting around will bring no good. Hear this Elton? He got shot for catting around."

"How did I get into this?" Elton was defensive. "I'm not catting around."

"I didn't get shot for catting around, Lloyd," Carl tried to explain. "I was an FBI agent. I got shot in the line of duty."

Lloyd cracked up in laughter, "Yah. That's a line alright! Okay, have it your way. But you should get a good woman and settle down. This tall kid and my relative here, they are settled down. You tell him boys. All you need to do is buy a cow."

"What?" Carl gasped. "Buy a cow?"

"Yes, Grandpa makes all us boys buy a cow before we can get married. Right, Grandpa?" Keith grinned. "You know, Chris doesn't have one yet."

Chris looked at Keith, "Thanks a lot, big mouth. Now I'll hear about it."

Grandpa looked at Chris is disgust. "Bert is right about you, too damned tall to be trusted. You better get a cow before you hitch up with this girl that you threw water on."

"Okay, Grandpa," Chris smiled as he took Pepper's hand. "I'll do that."

"And pretty soon, too. I see how you look at each other. You better go to the sales ring this weekend to my notion. You need to be making an honest woman of her," Grandpa was on a roll.

"Lloyd," Nora patted his hand, "You better keep out of their business."

"Like hell. It's my business. They're my relatives, right Elton?"

"Yes Lloyd. They surely are."

"Well, Elton. You better take him to the sales ring tomorrow to get a cow. Okay?"

"If we have time, we'll do that, Lloyd," Elton placated his old friend.

"Don't be blowing smoke. I'll check up on you," Lloyd stared at Chris.

"I know, Grandpa. I know you will."

"Okay then. I'm tired now, so you better take care of it. Okay Elton?"

"I will Lloyd. I surely will."

After the dishes were done and the grandparents were in bed, Nora, Elton and Kincaid went out to the patio. Keith and Darlene had gone over to Kevin and Carrie's place to look at the crib that they had bought. Suzy and Zach had gone for a walk, as did Chris and Pepper.

Kincaid lit his cigarette and took a drink of his whiskey. "You have quite the outfit here, Magpie."

"Oh? Good or bad?" Elton asked.

"Good, but crazier than hell. Do I have to buy a cow?"

"Are you planning on getting married?" Nora giggled. "Those old guys really did tell all the young men that. Didn't they, Elton?"

"Yah, why do you think we have a barn full?" Elton chuckled. "Guess to them that means that you were an adult and responsible."

"Good grief," Kincaid leaned back. "Lloyd was pretty sharp tonight, huh?"

"Yah, but very confused. I bet he'll be up tonight," Elton said sadly. "He really misses his friend."

"You know, don't tell a soul," Kincaid said quietly, "I miss the grump, too. It's so quiet in my room at night, I almost hate it."

28

As they had feared, Lloyd was up most of the night. First he went to visit Bert in Kincaid's room. Carl talked to him about an hour and he went to back to bed. Then about an hour later, Zach came in the house and found Grandpa Lloyd going through the pantry. He had just started 'cooking' and Zach was lucky enough to catch him before he did anything major and was able to talk him in to going back to bed.

Then about three-thirty, the Pa Bell went off. Elton ran out to the kitchen to find the old man half way out the door. Keith was right behind him. Those two had their hands full for the next hour talking him into not going to search for Bert. It was almost five o'clock, before the family got some rest. Pepper's alarm went off at six.

As everyone gathered in the kitchen around their beloved coffee pot, the prevailing thought was they should forget the dance that night and just sleep. Holloways had volunteered to come out and visit with Lloyd and Katherine so the others could go to the dance. Kincaid told them that wouldn't be necessary as he would happily stay home. His plan was vetoed instantly. There was no way the rest of them were going to let him worm out of going to the dance.

"We got it all figured out how to get you to the loft! You can't stay home," Kevin decreed when he heard it.

"That's why I want to stay home," Carl griped.

That evening, Carl reluctantly got into the car for the ride over to the dance and grumbled, "Now I know how a prisoner must feel on the way to the gallows."

"Ah, it won't be so bad," Elton grinned.

"Honestly Carl," Nora tried to assure him, "It has been done before, more than once. It is easier than trying to carry someone up the steps."

"I think I'd honestly just as soon stay home. I won't know anyone here, I can't dance and I already know I am going to hate the whole thing."

"Yah, yah, yah," Elton chuckled. "It also has a lot of the things you like. Women, whiskey and food. Besides, you'll know a lot of the people there. As much as I'd love to embarrass the pants off you, Nora won't let me. So, relax."

At Heinrich's yard, Elton drove behind the barn instead of parking in the front. When they stopped, there was Darrell, Kevin and Dick Heinrich. Dick had his tractor and farm hand all ready. Kevin opened the car door and Carl wanted for all the world to just die, right there on the spot.

Since Carl Kincaid had shown up at this place, he had been put through more humiliating turmoil than in the last forty years of his life! Granted his life was never in jeopardy, but he had died a million deaths. He had to go to exercise class with a bunch of girls, help peel potatoes, dig in a sandbox with toddlers, get covered in volcano goop, argue politics with demented people—and no one could even begin to guess what Magpie and his minions had drummed up now!

Dick had the scoop bucket of the farmhand lowered to the ground. Darrell put a tarp in the bottom of the bucket and Elton placed the collapsed wheelchair in it. Kevin helped Carl get into the bucket.

If he had his gun, he would have shot them all and himself to boot. They were all grinning like a bunch of jackasses, but didn't laugh until Dick started to raise the bucket. Carl had to admit, he was scared to death! What if he fell out? Who was at the top? How would he get out of the darned thing? Would everyone be watching the spectacle?

Darrell seemed to read his mind and assured him that Keith was going to be at the top of the loft door to help him out. It was somewhat calming, but then he heard Kevin say, "Darn. We forgot to have him go to the bathroom first. Kincaid," he shouted, "The outhouse is down here. If you have to go, you'll have to get one of us guys to help you."

Carl made a mental note to buy a one way plane ticket as soon as he could get to town. Maybe he could bum a ride into Bismarck with someone in the morning. It didn't matter where the ticket was to, just so it was to someplace far, far away!

At the loft door, Zach, Keith and Chris were waiting. Kincaid had to admit they were very nice. They smirked to each other more than once, but for the most part, did their best not to humiliate him. It really didn't matter. He was humiliated enough already. Few other folks paid any attention to his grand entrance for which he was extremely grateful.

Marly came over as soon as the boys got the wheelchair set up and were closing the haymow door. She smiled, "See, it wasn't so bad, was it? I'll show you where we're sitting and then where the food and drinks are. I can introduce you to some folks, too, but I really think you know most everyone."

"Thanks," Kincaid muttered. "I really don't need to meet anyone. I'm surprised that no one was staring when I was being unloaded like a stack of hay."

"We've done it before," Marly knelt down beside the chair. "These people are just folks. We know that things happen and sometimes we have to make little concessions for each other. It's no big deal. Someday, you might be helping load one of them into the farmhand. Okay?"

"But Katherine doesn't come to the dances when her arthritis is bad because she can't make the steps," Carl pointed out.

"Carl, that is because she doesn't want to leave Lloyd. She has said that he would stay with her if it was the other way around," Marly explained.

"Why doesn't she just say so?"

"She has told us that, but she doesn't want Lloyd to overhear. You know him. He would insist that he take her then."

"Oh, I guess that's true."

"Here we are," Marly said as she pointed out the buffet tables and then the bar table. "I'd suggest you fill you plate and get your drink before we sit down. I can help you."

"Good night!!! How much food did you women bring? Are you feeding an army?" Carl looked over the massive spread of food of every variety.

Marly looked around the room, and giggled, "Maybe not the whole Army, but at least a regiment or two. We might want to check out some recipes for our contest. You know, Gilda's June berry pies are over here. They're the best."

"I have heard Magpie rave about them. I should try one, huh? Wow! What kind of casserole is that?"

"We call them hot dishes. I don't know. Do you want to try some?" Marly said as she put some on his plate.

The dance was a lot more fun than Carl had in at least thirty years. He sat with the clan and danced a few of the slow dances. He only danced with the clan ladies because they were very understanding to his situation. He danced with Ginger as he had promised and she was so happy. Charlie danced with the clan ladies also and before the evening was over, even danced with Maddie Lynn Olson, Pastor Olson's daughter.

Carl was amazed that there were folks there of every age. There were little kids and old folks. Everyone mixed together and danced with each other. Byron and Marly brought Miriam and she spent a lot of time sitting on Carl's lap. That was good for both of them. But she also got to dance with the clan men while they held her in their arms. She loved to dance with Kevin and he, of course, was her favorite partner. He carried her in a polka before he put her down to sleep with Charlie in the coatroom.

Carl had heard of barn dances but had never been to one. It was fun and happy. He was amazed that the teenagers took part in everything since teenagers usually don't want to be around adults and vice versa. Ken Ellison was obviously sweet on Becky Oxenfelter and they danced together a lot. Rod Anderson was dancing with one of the Swenson girls.

He enjoyed watching his new friends dance with each other. He almost died of laughter when Byron and Elton danced the *Beer Barrel Polka* with each other. It was a tradition and everyone in the neighborhood expected it. He had to admit that Magpie was a good dancer. He questioned if some of the moves were actually part of the dance but no one seemed to care. It was good fun.

Bill Heinrich and his band played for the dance as they always did. Carl was almost sad when they played *Good Night Irene* to signal the dance was over. He would've been more sad except that he really had to go to the bathroom.

Once the scoop of the farmhand hit the ground, Darrell helped him make a beeline to the outhouse. The old wooden outhouse was by far, the most elegant bathroom Kincaid had ever seen!

On the way home, he babbled, "I think that Mo will like a barn dance. Don't you? She'd love the buffet! Do you think that she'll know how to dance all the dances? And she'll be able to make the stairs. I'll be able to then huh? But if I can't, I don't think that she'd be embarrassed if I had to go in the bucket, do you? It was really nice of the boys to help me—"

"Down! Sit! Stay!" Elton grinned. "Who put a nickel in you? You're wound up tighter than a three day clock!"

"I have never gone to anything like that in my life! And you know what? I did know a lot of folks there from church. And of course the clan! Do you think that Mo will think that I have friends?"

Nora turned to Carl, "I'm certain of it because you do have a lot of friends. People like you."

Elton chuckled, "They just don't know you very well!"

"Hush up Magpie."

"Okay Coot," Elton laughed.

"Hey, only Mo and the Gophers call me that."

Nora grinned, "To your face."

Carl gave Nora a disgusted look, "You are as bad as that husband of yours!"

29

The next morning had a rather dreary beginning. It was blowing and raining outside. Even Elmer was not out, apparently deciding the gophers could take over the north forty if they wished.

When Kincaid woke and looked around his room, he was immediately depressed. He missed hearing Bert's oxygen machine and his grumping. The old geezer had really thrown a monkey wrench into his plans and took great glee in doing so. However, Kincaid had to admit that he really did like some of his new life Bert had thrust on him.

The dance the night before was like nothing he had ever taken part in before in his life. First of all, he had a lot of friends there. He couldn't remember a time since high school when he had so many friends. Granted, he hadn't known these people long, but they had shared a lot already. Tragedy, death, fun and happiness. The whole enchilada. They had included him in all of it.

There were even Kincaid stories in the clan now. Mostly Kincaid and the Gopher stories! There wasn't one of these clanners that he didn't feel he could ask a favor of, tell a story to or pick a light-hearted argument with. He was as comfortable talking about cooking as he was irrigation. He could talk with the grownups, teens or little kids. He could give them guff and they'd give it right back to him. Yah, all in all, Kincaid figured that Bert had done him a favor of sorts.

He turned over and watched the water from the downpour of the old house swirl its way down to toward the drive. He thought, "It's going to run right into the yard, and the Gophers and I are going to hear about how we messed up Magpie's yard again! Yea Gads!"

Then he sat right up and got out of bed. Before Pepper's alarm went off, Kincaid was in the kitchen, drinking the coffee he had made and drawing out water diversion plans. When her alarm went off, he looked at the clock and wondered how soon he could call over to Ellisons and tell Charlie his plans. This would be such a cool project!

When Elton came into the kitchen and saw Kincaid pouring over his plans, he started to chuckle. "As I live and breathe! What are you doing up this early, man?"

"I got this idea to divert the water from the house drain this way," Carl answered not looking up from his drawing.

Elton stifled his grin and filled his coffee cup. "Just a minute, I have to get my caffeine fix. What time did you get up?"

"Don't know," Kincaid said, studying this drawing, "A while ago. Charlie will be so excited. See, we've been just trenching stuff. That's why you have had the canals all over the yard. But I was thinking, if I picked up some drain pipe, we could run it under the road and over to the garden. The kids never laid pipe before. Think they would like that?"

Elton looked at the extensive plans. "I imagine they would. But Carl, you'll have to buy the pipe."

"So? I got more money than brains. How much can a little pipe cost? Besides, I think that it would be a good thing for them to learn how to do. Don't you?"

Elton could see that his friend was excited about the project and really anxious to do it. "Why yes, Carl. I think that might be a very good thing for them to learn. You know, if you talked to Darrell, he could tell you where to get the pipe. He uses it for his place. In fact, he might have some to donate to the cause."

Kincaid looked up for the first time, "No. I'll pay for it. He is a young man and starting to build his own family. He doesn't need to be paying for any of this."

Elton smiled, "Suit yourself, but you know he might have some older or bent stuff you could use. You should talk to him."

"I'll do that," Kincaid grinned. "He will be at dinner today, huh?"

"Who will be?" Nora asked as she and Keith came in the kitchen. "Wow! Who made coffee? I know Elton didn't have time."

"I did. Hope I did it right. I've been up a while," Kincaid answered as he started to become self-conscious about what he was doing. He began folding up the drawings.

"Hey," Keith said after he filled his cup, "Can I see them? That is, if they aren't private."

Kincaid looked at him reluctantly, "No, they aren't private, but they aren't good. They're just something that I put together for the Gophers. You know, kid stuff."

Keith was impressed, "Man, these are good. I have seen plans that engineers drew that weren't much better. I'd be glad to help out with the project, if you like."

"Well," Kincaid beamed, "I'd like that. You know however, you'll have to be on Charlie's probation for a while. He's pretty strict about that. He even had Annie on probation. He almost fired her when she wanted to drain one of his favorite puddles. He can be a tough task master!"

"How did you handle that?" Elton laughed.

"Well, I told him that we could compromise. Man, that was a bad plan. We ended up wasting the next hour explaining what a compromise was. Finally, we had convinced him it was a good thing to do. So he got the idea to talk to his mom about compromising about his bed time."

Nora laughed, "I bet your name was Mud at their house! How did you get around that?

Kincaid got a big belly laugh, "I just told him that his Dad would explain it all to him. I bet Ellison could have killed me!"

Keith laughed, "Remind to me never let you babysit for our baby!"

"Ah that's too bad," Kincaid refilling his coffee cup, "We may need recruits before long. You know, school will be cutting into the digging time!"

"Good grief, Carl," Nora smiled, "You're getting worse than Charlie."

Grandma Katherine came out and took her cup. She gave Carl a hug and kiss good morning. "You ready to help me make baking powder biscuits this morning for breakfast? I have to get the buns ready for lunch too, so I figured I could show you how to do the biscuits."

"I suppose," Kincaid smiled, "Do I have a choice?"

"Nope," she giggled. "Not if you want to eat. Hey, how are we coming with the signups for the cooking contest? I bet we'll have a lot more signups today after Sunday dinner."

"Hmm," Nora thought, "We have Mo signed up for beans. I guess she is going to do Boston Baked Beans; Grilling is Elton, Kincaid and Harrington; Suzy signed up with a June berry pie; Marly for Hot Chili Pickles and three have signed up for lemonade! Becky, Katie and Eve."

Just then Zach joined the group in the kitchen, "I am signing up for the grilling. And I am putting a $20 the pot, like Harrington did."

"Good idea, I will too," Keith said, "No point in these old boys paying all the prize money, since they aren't going to win any of it back!"

"Whaddyah mean?" Elton was taken back. "It's in the bag. I'll win first and FBI here wins second."

"Oh yah?" Keith blustered, "Well, my grilling will have something to say about that!"

"What do you know about grilling?" his Dad asked. "Everything you know about cooking, you learned from me!"

Nora piped up, "I don't think so, Mr. Windy! What about me?"

Elton gave his wife a panicked look, "Well, Honey, you know what I mean."

"What do you mean?" Nora questioned him with squinted eyes. "Just for that, the gloves are off. I am signing up for grilling too."

"Girls can't do that!" Kincaid blurted out.

"Why not?" Darlene said as she entered the fray. "You're such male chauvinists! Mom can out cook you with one eye closed and the stove turned off!"

"Oh yah?" Elton smirked. "I was cooking before she was born!"

Katherine just cracked up, "I wouldn't want to go down that path if I was you, oh Ancient One! By the way boys, there's nothing in the rules that says that girls can't sign up for grilling."

"Oh brother, Magpie," Kincaid muttered glumly, "We've been had."

Pepper came in the kitchen, "Well, I hope we can because Chris and I are going to be a team in grilling. So there. Barbeque chicken will win in a clean sweep."

"Well, my Wisconsin Brats will take your catsup on chicken," Keith teased.

"Dad, make him stop!" Pepper whined, "Are you going to let him say that?"

Elton studied the situation, "I believe I am."

Pepper turned to her Mom, "Mom?"

"You're on your own. I'll beat the pants off all of you with my Marinated Spare Ribs."

"Oh," Darlene jumped in, "And I'm signing up for sauerkraut buns, to go with Keith's Brats. We're so going to wipe up in those categories."

"Well, I might as well tell you, I know I'll get a ribbon in potato salad, because I'm entered twice," Grandma admitted. "Once as Kincaid's partner in Hot German Potato Salad and again as Charlie's partner in Mustard Potato Salad."

"Isn't that a conflict of interest?" Kincaid was suspicious.

"It doesn't say no in the rules," Katherine defended herself. "Besides, you and I had already decided to be a team before Charlie asked me to help him. I couldn't very well tell him no."

They all agreed that she couldn't. Then Darlene frowned, "What are we going to do for ribbons? I don't suppose you two thought about that, did you?"

Elton and Kincaid looked at each other and shrugged. Then Elton answered, "No, but you can buy your own with your winnings."

"What about second and third places?" Darlene asked.

"You guys are getting way too complicated," Elton sat down. "It was going to be a simple contest between Kincaid and me. Now look!"

"This way, we can all have fun. Darlene, you and I will worry about the ribbons," Pepper giggled. "Okay? We'll draft Annie. We know it's way over these guy's heads!"

Before long, all the milkers gathered in the kitchen. Chris, Ellisons and Kevin and Carrie. Everyone was babbling about the contest and bragging.

"Well, I can tell you right now, Marv and I are going to win the grilling contest," Pastor Byron boasted. "We have the Big Guy on our side."

"You always told me, Uncle Byron, that God doesn't take sides in this kind of stuff," Pepper emphasized.

Byron got a devilish grin, "In this case, He does."

Kevin punched his arm and said, "I don't think so. And if He does, then you and Pastor Marv only get to compete in the best grace contest."

"No fair! I think Grandpa Lloyd won that a long time ago with his prayer about his car," Keith grinned.

"I think you're right there, Kid," Elton laughed. "Let's go milk those old cows."

"Oh, put me down for my Kosher Dills," Carrie said. "And Kev and I want to put in a $20 toward the prize money."

"My goodness," Nora said, "You're all putting in so much."

"That's good," Carrie giggled, "Since we're all going to win. I think Jenny's going to sign up for pie."

"Wow!" Elton clapped Kincaid on the back, "At least we'll eat good!"

Miriam spied her Son and Kevin relented. He took her to the barn, even though it was raining. She loved him so that she would probably have waded through a raging river to go with him. Everyone grinned at how those two got along. Carrie giggled, "I think Kevin is learning to be a Daddy. He'll be broke in for our own baby."

Miriam looked at Carrie with surprise, "Baby? Gopher's baby?"

Everyone was flabbergasted. Carrie was pleased, "Yes, little one. You, me and Son are going to have a baby! Won't that be fun?"

Miriam looked at Carrie and nodded. Then she took her bear out of her shirt, "Mr. Bear?"

"Oh yes, and Mr. Bear."

Miriam shook her head no and pointed to Byron and wiggled her finger on Mr. Bears head. "Gopher's baby?"

Kevin burst into a huge grin, "That's right Miriam. When our baby comes, we will have Pastor Byron baptize it like he did you. Won't that be nice?"

Miriam nodded and got a big grin. Then she stuffed Mr. Bear into her shirt again and tucked herself into Kevin's chest for the trip to the barn.

After they left the house, Nora turned to Katherine, "She is quite the little girl, isn't she?"

"She really is. I was worried for a minute that she might be jealous of the new baby, but I guess she'll be okay with it."

Kincaid observed, "Yah, now that it's a figment. When it's a real, live baby that Kevin is holding, things might change."

30

Lloyd was very insistent that Keith drive him and Katherine to church in his Ford. Keith and Darlene did and everyone had to admit that Lloyd was probably the happiest man alive when they drove out of the yard. Elton watched them as they turned onto the main road and was lost in thought.

Nora came up beside him and took his hand, but he never took his eyes off the car. Then he reached out, pulled her closer to him and gave her a hug. "I love it when he's happy."

Nora nodded, "I know you do. Come on honey, we have to get this crew off to church."

Kincaid watched them from the kitchen table. He was so envious of their relationship and their family. Even though now he had a much better understanding of what effort it took to have a good relationship, he still felt it must be worth it all. Not for him, but for other folks.

He figured that that Mo and her husband had the kind of relationship that Elton and Nora had. He made a face. She'd never settle for him, he knew nothing about being like that. That depressed him, even though he wasn't sure what he really wanted in the way of a relationship with Mo. His face must have been a puzzle, because Nora came over to him and put her hand on his shoulder, "Are you alright, Carl?"

He jumped because he had been so lost in thought that he didn't see her come in. "Oh yah, I'm fine. Guess I got up too early this morning. I'm running out of caffeine. Hope Ellison can keep me awake!"

"I think Pastor Olson is preaching this week," Pepper said as she bounced into the kitchen. "So, are you ready for Harringtons to arrive, Kincaid? They'll be here by next week at this time! Aren't you excited?"

"Yah, it'll be nice to see them again," Carl said, playing down how he really felt. "I bet Ruthie is going nutty, huh?"

Pepper grinned, "Pretty much. I thought I was bad about Chris but I think I'm better than her."

"Don't be breaking your arm with the pats on the back, honey," Nora laughed. "You guys are about a horse a piece."

"What is the longest that you and Dad have been apart, Mom?" Pepper asked.

Kincaid was curious too, he wondered how much 'testing' their marriage had withstood.

"Well, let me think. We were sort of apart during the pig accident and you kids were with Dad while I was in the hospital. That turned out to be a long stretch. But other than that, no major distances. I would think probably three weeks or so. You know with helping folks out here or there and stuff like that. We try not to be apart, but if things come up, then that's the way it has to be. Dad always says we were apart for the first fifty years of his life and he doesn't want to waste any more time!" Mom smiled. "Why do you ask?"

"Oh I was just wondering how you handled it." Pepper grinned.

"Well, it was always different for us. We had all you kids, so it wasn't like we were dating just the two of us. You know, we have only been alone together for the month or so after you were a BJC and Andy was in basic training. Then the Grandparents moved in. So, what is that? Maybe a little over a month! My goodness. I've never figured that out before," Mom giggled. "Hmm, maybe if we were alone, we wouldn't like each other."

"Oh, I think you would, don't you Kincaid?" Pepper smiled.

"Yah that'd be my guess. You're both pretty weird. Doesn't it ever drive you crazy, not being alone?" Carl asked.

"No. I really don't know how that'd even be. But late last fall, when we're alone together, it didn't seem any different," Mom explained. "We've always had a lot of people around. It was just quieter."

"Well, I hope someday Chris and I can be together alone," Pepper said. "This is for the birds."

Kincaid laughed, "Women. Men don't worry about that stuff."

"Oh yah!" Pepper blurted out. "You're so, so wrong! I know they do! They might not say so, but they do! Why do men always think it's so cool to pretend like they don't have feelings? We all know they do. They just look like boneheads when they try to cover them up."

"What's that supposed to mean?" Kincaid asked, "You saying I act like a bonehead?"

"No. I'm not saying that, but if they shoe fits, wear it!" Pepper giggled. "Are you riding with Chris and I or Mom and Dad?"

"I might just stay home," Carl snapped.

Pepper turned ashen and she knelt down next to his chair, "I'm so sorry Mr. Kincaid. I didn't mean to be impertinent. I got carried away. Please forgive me."

Carl was taken back, "Ah, not to worry. You're fine. We're just kidding around. But, you're right somewhat. I guess men do try to pretend like we're unfeeling. I always thought that women liked that. You know, the John Wayne type."

Pepper smiled, "I have to admit, most girls like other men to be like John Wayne and their man to act like John Wayne in public. But personally, they want to know their feelings. You know, you can't have a relationship very easily if you don't understand how the other person feels about things. That's part of the recipe for a good relationship."

Carl patted her hand, "Thanks Pepper. I'll remember that. You're the first person who ever explained it that way. I appreciate it."

"Hey," Elton chuckled as he came in the kitchen with Nora's jacket, "You ready to go or are you busy flirting with my daughter?"

"Yah, I'm ready to go. Pepper and I were just exchanging recipes," he winked at Pepper. "I'm ready to meet my Gophers."

"You might want to refrain from telling them the new water diversion plans until after church. It's hard enough to get Charles to sit still," Nora suggested.

"I have never heard him called Charles before," Kincaid shook his head. "He sure doesn't act like a Charles, does he?"

Elton cracked up, "Not hardly. I'll bring the car up. You two wait by the steps."

Charlie had waited at the back of the church as patiently as he could for Kincaid to sit down and then asked very politely if he could sit by him. He grinned when Kincaid said, "I was saving this place for you."

Carl watched as Miriam came in with Zach and Suzy but went immediately to Kevin when she saw him. Ginger sat with Uncle Darrell and Jeannie. Kincaid smiled to himself. His little Gophers all had minds of their own. He reached down and patted Charlie's head. Charlie looked up at him in surprise and then just gave him a big smile before he went back to folding an extra offering envelope into a tiny wad. Kincaid grinned.

After church, they hurried home to get dinner on the table before the clan started to arrive. Everyone was wet from the rain, but in good humor. It was a fun day and the kids were very excited when they heard Kincaid's plans for the piping. Darrell volunteered to help out where he could and Ginger was elated.

Charlie said it would be okay if he and Keith were each a Project Man, but they had to be on 'promotion'. The men accepted the positions with seriousness duties of that caliber required. Charlie told them they wouldn't get their hard hat until they passed 'promotion.'

By dessert, the talk turned to the cooking contest. Things became competitive and boastful within seconds. Nora read the list of signups for each category and then things really got out of hand. Pride and bravado took over the scene in no time. Everyone was certain they could take at least second place in their favorite category.

Miriam watched as all the kids entered the contests, and soon was very quiet. When Ginger announced that she would enter the lemonade contest, Miriam turned her little face into Kevin's shoulder. She started to whimper.

Kevin left the table with her but couldn't get her to look at him. Elton joined him and together they tried to figure out the problem. It wasn't until Carrie came to the kitchen to see if she could help, that they figured it out. Carrie patted her head, "Maybe she wants to enter the contest too?"

Miriam looked at Carrie and then patted her own chest, nodding all the while, "Sharlee, Ginger, Mr. Bear, Gopher."

"Would you like to enter the contest with me?" Carrie asked.

Miriam smiled shyly, "If you want to."

"Okay then. What should we make? Green Bean Salad or Chocolate Pie?"

Miriam nodded happily, "Green Beans. Chocolate. Gopher, Mr. Bear, Cawwie."

Carrie gave the little girl a hug, "Okay, Miriam. You got it."

Carrie's eyes filled with tears as he hugged her young husband, "Kev, I think she likes me. She called me Cawwie."

Kevin kissed his wife, "Well, why shouldn't she? You're the best, Carrie."

"That's right. She has good taste, Carrie," Elton said as he gave his daughter-in-law a hug. "Let's go get you signed up."

That evening after chores, the family sat around the table in the kitchen to relax. It was still raining outside, so they couldn't go out to the patio. Kincaid was fussing because there was nowhere to have his cigarette. "You know, Magpie, you should have a screened in porch for rainy days. Or a cover on the patio."

"We just turned the screened-in porch into the dining room!" Elton explained. "You guys never leave the house alone."

Elton looked at the boys, "So what are you cooking, Zacharias?"

"Actually, Harrington and I joined forces and we'll be a team."

"Elton and I are going to do it alone," Kincaid blustered. "Right Magpie? We don't need this team stuff."

"I know, but Nora is on her own, too," Elton pointed out. "I'm worried. She might just cream us both."

Kincaid squinted at him, "Magpie, are you thinking about hooking up with her? That wouldn't be fair, you know. Not fair at all."

"No," Elton said, sheepishly.

Nora raised her eyebrows, "Elton. Tell the truth."

"Well, ah you see," stammered, "I kind of asked her and she told me no."

"You dirty scoundrel! What a low life!" Kincaid crowed with an accusatory point of the finger. "You sneaking coyote!"

"Yah, I would've decided not to, I'm sure. I'd have done the right thing," Elton tried to reassure him.

"You're such a liar, Dad," Keith chuckled. "No one believes you, so give it up."

"Yah. You're right," Elton's mind scrambled to change the subject, "What about that Miriam?"

"That was really something! She's getting to be a regular kid, huh?" Zach almost burst with joy. "It was amazing! There was a time when I wondered if she'd ever be like a regular kid. But look!!!"

Nora gave him a hug, "I know. She is doing so well. It is amazing! I'm glad that she is letting Carrie in her life, especially since she thinks so much of Kevin."

Zach became crestfallen, "I wish she liked me as much as she likes him. I mean she should like me. Right? I mean, I'm her guardian."

"Listen, Zach," Elton got serious, "Everyone has their favorite people, but that doesn't take away from how they feel about anyone else. She adores Kevin and he adores her. Ginger would rather be with her Uncle Darrell than anyone on earth. That is the way it goes. Ginger also loves her Daddy and you. Don't ever doubt that. There's just something about Kevin that Miriam feels comfortable with and that's a good thing. So, don't start getting all paranoid. Who knows? Kevin's kid might just think you are the coolest thing ever."

"Thanks. But Suzy and I have spent so little time with her," Zach said.

Keith turned to him, "How else would you do it? Her being with Ginger and Charlie, I think, is the best thing in the world for her. That is why she thinks she should join the contest, dig Bert's grave, be a Gopher and all that. She identifies with the kids. You don't happen to have a house full of them yet."

Zach laughed, "We don't even have a house yet. Oh, by the way, I'll be signing the papers with the contractor tomorrow. Our house should be done by our wedding, if all goes well."

"Have you made any plans for your honeymoon yet?" Kincaid asked.

"Not yet. Harringtons will still be here for the wedding and we don't want to leave while they're here. The house is scheduled to be finished that week." Zach explained. "I have to do some work in this year. Man, I was gone so much with all that garbage with my family that I need to get back to my work. The honeymoon can wait."

31

Kincaid lay in his bed and thought it all over. It would only be a few days before Mo and Harrington showed up. He had to get his act together. He needed to make up his mind about what he wanted out of life before Mo arrived. Why? He didn't know. He just thought that he did.

Hell, realistically, he didn't even know what he was going to cook on the grilling contest, let alone what he wanted out of life! He chuckled to himself. He was a fool. Was he really under the misguided impression he could have a life like Magpie? The kind of life that he had always made fun of! It was everything he said that he didn't like. So homey, cuddly and cream puff it made him sick. He never wanted that. It was all Bert's fault. Bert told him that he should want it.

He looked out the window, "You old Goat! You're just swindling me. I'll never have what Magpie has. Mo doesn't care about me and this family will do just honky-dory without me. You just told me all this to make yourself feel better so you could leave in good conscience."

He knew when he said it, it wasn't true. Bert never said that. First, Bert never cared what Kincaid wanted. Bert wanted what Bert wanted. Bert only told him to be there for Lloyd, the little kids and help out Elton. He never cared if he got married or even got laid for that matter. He was very single minded.

Kincaid was delighted that Miriam had come out of her shell so much. He loved that little kid. He had to admit, he enjoyed being with the kids. All of them. He was really surprised that when Keith even teased that he wouldn't let Kincaid babysit for their new baby, it shattered him. He knew

Keith was only joking about it; but somehow, Kincaid has automatically assumed that Keith and Kevin's children, as well as baby Matthew, would all become his Gophers. He actually was looking forward to it.

He turned over in his bed. 'My God. I'm losing my mind. It must've happened when I got shot. Messed up the blood supply to my brain. Yah that must be it. I don't even think that Magpie thinks like this. Dammit, I need to get out of here. I think I'll ask someone to drive me to Merton tomorrow and I'll look for a place to rent. I promised Mo I'd be around here. That is close enough. I got to get out of here. This is driving me insane.'

Kincaid turned over and hit his pillow. He felt like he was being torn apart. Everything that he had ever believed in was shaken. Well, not really everything. At one time when Cecelia was alive, he just assumed this was what his life would be. It would be like what Elton and Nora have. When she died, it all changed. He had even quit thinking about it.

In fact, if he wanted to blame someone, it would have to be that Petunia. Why couldn't Zach have just left the business with his father alone? The man never cared about him in his life. There was no reason for Zach to delve into his death. And if that wasn't bad enough, why didn't Zach just leave the old FBI agent alone in that hospital in Louisiana? He didn't know him from hole in the ground. He could've even stopped by and said hi, but went on his way. No one would've expected more. It would've been easier all the way around.

Carl couldn't sleep but he didn't want to think anymore. He hated this whole darned thing. He wished he had someone to talk to. He even considered waking up Zach. He had always said he could anytime. Nah, Petunia had surgery in the morning so he would be leaving early in the morning to get there. He needed his sleep. He supposed he could talk to Magpie, but then, that guy never had enough sleep. While he was thinking about it, the door opened and Lloyd shuffled in.

Lloyd sat down in the rocking chair and said, "You awake, FBI guy?"

"Yah," Kincaid answered as he turned over to face the older fellow. "How you doing?"

"Where is Bert? Is he in the can?"

"No, I'm sorry Lloyd. He is gone. Remember, he went to be with Ida," Kincaid answered softly.

"Hmm. Figured he would do that one day. You know, he missed her a lot."

"Yes, he did."

"Yah. I'd miss my Katherine too, but I think she's still here. She is, isn't she?"

"Yes Lloyd," Carl smiled, "She is here."

"Sometimes I get mixed up and forget. I know sometimes it makes her sad. I can see it, but I can't fix it. You know Carl, I know my brain isn't good anymore. I hate it. I sometimes worry about it. Folks don't know it but I can see it in their faces when I am saying things I'm not thinking or can't remember what I'm thinking. And sometimes, I want to remember someone's name and I say a name. It isn't right and when I hear it, I know it isn't, but I can't get it right. I hate that."

"Sounds awful," Kincaid agreed while trying to think of how horrible that would feel.

"Yah, but sometimes it doesn't bother. Sometimes I wonder where I am, or even who I am. I never used to be this way. I'm so glad that Katherine is not gone though. She has been a good wife. One of the finest people you ever could meet. And Elton. He is always there for me. He tries to be a good guy. Don't you think so?"

"Yes Lloyd, he's a great guy."

"Even if he messes it up, I know he tries his best. You know, he loves me, even when I can't remember stuff or when I wreck stuff. That is really good of him. Some guys would get mad."

"Yah, Lloyd. but I think you're always good to him, too."

"I don't know. I hope so. I have a headache tonight. It kind of hurts so bad, it makes me sorta dizzy. Do you think I should tell Katherine? Or my relative, that tall guy?"

"You mean Zach?" Carl asked, as he climbed out of bed, "I can call him for you, okay? If it's bothering you, you should talk to him. You stay put right here and I'll go get him. Okay? Promise you'll stay put."

"I promise."

Carl patted his friends shoulder and went out into hall. He hated to yell but he couldn't make it up the stairs. He didn't think he could wake Petunia unless he woke up every one in the house also. He didn't want to disturb everyone. Finally, he decided to talk to Elton. He went and knocked on his bedroom door. A minute later, a disheveled Elton opened the door. "Huh?"

"Could you come with me? It's Lloyd."

Before the words were pronounced, Elton was half way down the hall. He burst into Kincaid's room. "What is it? Is he okay?"

"He said he had a headache and thought he should talk to Zach," Carl explained.

Lloyd was still sitting in the rocker, "Hi. You aren't my tall relative. FBI is mixed up."

Elton was visibly relieved and assured Lloyd he was going to go get Zach. He nearly ran by Kincaid on his way upstairs to get Zach.

When the men returned seconds later, Lloyd smiled at them. "Are we going to have coffee?"

"Not now. Elton tells me you have a headache? Is that right?" Zach asked.

"Yah. I told FBI. It hurts in my eyes, kind of and I can't hear so good because I can hear my heart beating in my head too loud," Lloyd explained.

Pepper came in the room and Zach asked where the stethoscope was. She found it and the blood pressure cuff and handed it to him. Zach listened to his heart and lungs and checked his blood pressure.

"I think you should take an aspirin for your headache, Lloyd," Zach said. Nora was up now and went to the bathroom to get the aspirin bottle. By now, Katherine had joined them.

"Well, if that don't beat all," Lloyd said, "I just was going to have some coffee."

"I think that might not be a good idea right now, with your blood pressure the way it is. Hey Pep, are Bert's prescriptions still in the medicine cabinet?"

"Yes," she answered.

"I'll check and see what he has left in there. Hopefully, we can get Lloyd's blood pressure down without having to take him in."

"Is he okay?" Pepper asked quietly.

"His blood pressure is dangerously high right now. There's a limit to what we can do," Zach said.

"I'll go get him something to drink. There is some nectar in the fridge; can he have that?" Pepper asked.

"We can try it. Good idea, Pep," Zach said read Bert's pill bottles.

About twenty minutes later, the aspirin and Bert's medication were bringing Lloyd's blood pressure down to normal. Elton was able to convince Lloyd to go back to bed and get some sleep. Once he was in bed, the rest of the family went to the kitchen.

"What happened tonight?" Zach asked.

"He was very restless," Katherine said. "He was tossing and turning but he does that sometimes. Then I fell asleep."

Carl told what he knew. "He came in to my room a bit before I got Elton. He was very lucid and talked quite sensibly. He told me that he had figured that Bert would go to Ida soon. He told me how lucky he was to have his Katherine. Then he explained how hard it was to say the wrong name, know it was wrong and not be able to remember the correct one. He told me how much he thinks of Elton and how good he was to him. Then he said he had a terrible headache and asked if I thought he should see his relative."

Zach listened carefully, "Yah, he had very high blood pressure. That could explain the span of clarity, too."

"But Zach," Katherine said, "He normally doesn't have high blood pressure. He never has. It is usually low."

"I know," Zach said, "It could have been a fluke or something triggered it. At any rate, it is back in the safe range again. You know, there has been a lot going on and he has been quite upset about Bert's passing. He'll probably sleep soundly the rest of the night. I think we should all go do the same. You did the right thing, Carl, and acted fast. He could have had a stroke. Thanks Carl."

"Yes, thank you," Katherine said as she gave him a hug. "You are a dear man."

Everyone else went off to bed, but Pepper followed Carl back into his room to put the pills and stethoscope away. He was sitting on the edge of his bed when she came out of the bathroom. She turned the rocking chair around and began to move it back to its place.

"You okay?" she asked the man.

"Yah. I'm really glad he didn't die on us. Gee, just a week after Bert. I'd never let anyone in my room again," Carl said quietly.

"I thought of that, too," Pepper said as she patted him on the shoulder. "I hope you know how important you are to our family. Please don't ever leave us. We need you, you know."

He looked at her in shock, "Ah, well, I don't think you do. You guys are pretty self-sufficient."

"Not really. We only are that way when we have each other. You are an important part of this crazy group and we all love you for it," Pepper continued. "I know I blab out of school all the time but I wanted you to know. I can't wait to meet this Maureen. She is one lucky lady to have someone like you interested in her."

"Oh, I'm interested in her but she probably couldn't be bothered with me. She has a great life and a large family. I have nothing. She's just being nice to me. I'm an old dude."

Pepper looked at him incredulously, "So you aren't twenty anymore, but neither is she. She probably wouldn't be interested in a teenager."

"I'm too old to be getting interested in anyone anyway." Kincaid announced.

"Hmm, I didn't know there was an age limit on it. Besides if you wait, will you be younger? Don't think it works quite that way," she questioned him.

"You really are your Mom's daughter, aren't you?"

"Yup and I learned a lot being Magpie's kid too," she giggled. "You know, Dad wasn't a kid when he met Mom. It's never too late. Everyone deserves as much happiness as they can get in this world, as long as they don't hurt someone else to get it."

"Well, that might be true at your age."

"Oh, where does it say you can be happy until you're thirty and then you have to cash it in and be miserable the rest of your life?"

"No, I don't think that. But I do think that if you are too late getting started, you may have missed your chance."

"Dad and Aunt Gilda both say that as long as you are alive, you still have a chance."

Kincaid grinned, "I can just about hear them saying it. Well maybe, but Mo isn't interested in me. Why do you say that she might be?"

"She calls you every so often. What do you think that means?"

"She's a nice lady," Carl explained. "Pepper, I have nothing to offer."

Pepper smiled, "You have your heart to offer and a fine one at that. That is a huge gift and never to be sneezed at. She should count herself as lucky. Now, don't go getting a big head and an inflated ego or anything. You and Dad both do that. First you both think you aren't good enough. But then if you do think you're good enough, you automatically think you're the best! Goodnight, Mr. Kincaid."

She patted his shoulder and he gave her a quick hug. "Thanks Pepper. You're a great kid."

Carl put his head back on his pillow. It felt pretty darned good and he was tired. He couldn't get over it. He had wanted someone to talk to that night and ended up talking to an eighteen-year-old girl. The last person in the world he would have ever thought to talk to. Seemed that sort of thing was happening to him a lot these days. At any rate, he was glad Lloyd was okay and very glad that Pepper had talked to him. He fell right to sleep.

32

The next morning early, the phone rang at the same time that Pepper's alarm went off. Kincaid heard Nora rush to the kitchen and in a few seconds there was a knock on his door. "Carl, the phone is for you."

Carl hurried out to the kitchen, wondering who on earth would be calling him, "Hello?"

"Hi there, you old Coot! I'd say I'm sorry I woke you but that would be a bald-faced lie. I was sitting here for the last half an hour waiting for it to be six o'clock out there," Maureen greeted him.

"Is everything okay?" Kincaid sat down as he had walked out instead of taking his chair.

"Everything's fine, I guess," Mo said, apprehensively. "But I was sitting here, rattling the old rosary and getting myself into a fluster. I don't know what I'm doing. Ian said I should talk to you. Now that I am, I don't know what to even say."

"Motor Mouth not knowing what to say? That must be serious," then he thought of what Pepper had said about knowing each other's feelings and decided to be more serious. "What's troubling you, Maureen?"

"Well, I don't know exactly what to say about whatever it is! I think I'm just anxious about coming out there, seeing you, all those people and all that. You must think I'm being really an airhead, huh?"

"Not at all. What's making you nervous? The trip?" Carl was at a loss.

"Not that. I've flown all over, and besides I can't let my boy be gallivanting all over by himself, you know. Doctors won't let him travel alone yet. What do I do when I get there? I don't know those people and will be staying at their house!"

"Mo, Mo. These're the easiest people in the world to be around. They invited you and I know they looking forward to meeting you. They even put up with me, so why couldn't they put up with you?"

"You're easier to get along with than me," Maureen answered reluctantly.

Kincaid burst out laughing, "I hardly think so! I'm impossible. They'll all love you in no time. Besides, you do know a lot of us. There's Byron, Zach, Suzy, Ruthie and Elton. Wait until you see how well Miriam is doing! I'm so proud of her. She is getting to be like a real kid. You'll love that. Things will be fine. I promise."

"Hmm, okay. I'll never keep everyone straight. From what Ian says, there is a clan or something. How will I ever manage that?"

"Listen Mo, if I can figure it out; you can, too. You have a big family of your own."

"But you're a professional investigator. I'm just a homebody mom person.

"All those things you mentioned take a lot more brains than my job ever did. I can assure you of that! I know what it is like now that I'm around Nora and Katherine so much. And the Gophers."

"Gophers? You have rodents?" Mo was surprised.

Kincaid laughed, "Yah, I do. Charlie, Ginger and Miriam are my Gophers, because they love to dig all the time. We spend a lot of time every day doing that. I suppose you think that is pretty dumb, huh?"

"Not at all. Do you like it?" Maureen asked curiously. "I mean you always say that you don't like kids."

"I guess I shouldn't have said it because I was never around them enough to know what they're like. Don't tell anyone but they aren't too bad. I can't wait to show you the Polaroids of our science project volcano and dam! What a mess! It was crazy."

"Sounds like fun," Maureen said almost sadly.

Kincaid was very taken back. "What on earth is wrong, Mo? What's bothering you? I've never heard you like this."

"I don't know." Maureen was almost in tears, "You're so adjusted and happy there. It is great; but I'm just, can I say it- scared to death?"

"Of what? What on earth would you be afraid of? You're such a confident, fun person. I can't imagine you feeling that way," Carl was in shock at the mere thought that Mo would be nervous about anything.

"Well, I guess I had you snookered, then," Mo answered softly. "Carl, I feel like I pushed myself on to you as far as the wedding dance and all that stuff. I acted like I had the right to do that and I didn't. Maybe you don't want to take me to the dance. I want you to know that you needn't feel like you have to. Maybe there's someone else that you want to take. I'm so sorry. I got carried away with myself."

"Mo. There's no one else I'd rather take to the dance than you. You're the main reason that I've been trying to get my sea legs back. I want to see you again, and if you weren't coming out here, I'd be dreaming up an excuse to come see you. I miss you and our talks. Okay?" he couldn't believe that he was saying those things.

"Really?"

"Honestly. I've been afraid that you'd think I was too dependent on you! We make a great pair, huh? I'm looking forward to seeing you and don't even start imagining that you might stay home. That'd kill me. Got it?" Carl said emphatically.

"Got it. You sure? I mean . . ."

"Hush. Zip up your motor mouth. It'll be just fine. Count on that. Okay? I'll make up a list of the whole clan, sort of a clan map, and mail it to you."

"It won't get here in time."

"Oh, yah. You're right. I'll keep it here. I'll probably need help with it anyway. And then we can both use it to keep everyone straight. How does that sound? And I want to show you all the things here. Mo, thanks for talking to me. I'm glad that Ian told you to call me."

"Thanks. You won't hang up and laugh at me, will you?"

"Maureen Harrington, you're a dingbat. There is no way. I really appreciate it that you called. Okay. Now, go pack your exertorture suit and get on that plane. Okay?"

"Okay. Coot." Maureen finally giggled.

"That's my girl. See you in a couple days. Magpie is going to have to take me to the barber so I look presentable. Thank you for calling. Bye Maureen."

"Bye, Carl."

It wasn't until Carl hung up the phone that he realized that almost his entire conversation was within complete earshot of the whole family. When he noticed them, he turned beet red. They were all nice enough to not acknowledge it. Before they left the house for milking, Pepper gave him a hug and a kiss on the cheek. "Good work!"

The older man looked at her and grinned, "Couldn't have done it without the recipe!"

Pepper giggled and ran out to catch up with the rest of the milkers. Zach was just getting ready to leave for the hospital. He took Kincaid's shoulder, "If you get the Clan Map done, I could use a copy too!"

Carl just nodded. He felt a little foolish, but then he was getting used to feeling that way. He had felt that way a lot since he had come to the farm. Kincaid went back to his room to get dressed. Then he'd have to go back out there and face the ladies.

Darlene, Grandma and Nora had all heard the conversation too. Hell, the most sincere, emotional conversation that he had in forty years and he did it right smack in the middle of a family convention! Good grief. He hated what he had become. Damn that Bert. He could imagine the smirk on the old guy's face.

Then he looked at himself in the mirror and shrugged. "Not much I can do about it now except put on my tutu and kick up my leg! What was it Ginger said? Be a high kicker?"

Thankfully, the ladies did not bring it up. While he was cutting up potatoes, Nora asked him if he'd thought of what kind of meat he was going to make for the grilling contest.

"Haven't even thought of it yet. Maybe I'll talk to Mo about it when she gets here," he said without thinking and then he blushed slightly. "Look, you all heard everything. I know. I feel like an ass. Okay?"

"You shouldn't," Darlene offered, "I thought you were very sweet. I'll be happy to help you with the Clan Map. We can do it right after breakfast, if you want. I imagine we're a very confusing bunch to most folks. It was very thoughtful of you to suggest it. Is she nervous about meeting us all?"

"She says she is, but I can't imagine it. Although, Nora made me a list of folks when I got here. It really helped. But Mo has a million friends and could make friends with anyone. I was surprised she feels that way. She seems so confident all the time," Kincaid explained.

"We all act like that more often than is true," Katherine smiled, "She must have confidence in you to feel she could talk to you."

"I have no idea why. She even thinks I am easier to get along with than her! Can you imagine?" Carl laughed.

Darlene teased, "She must be dreadfully misguided! Maybe she just doesn't know you well enough yet! We'll keep quiet about it and let you spring it on her later!"

Kincaid gave her a dirty look, "My deepest thanks."

After dishes were done, Darlene took out her pencils and paper and motioned Carl over to the dining room. "Let's get this out of the way. You know, I've never seen it written all out before either. It might be kind of fun to see."

"Or just more confusing."

After working on it, they called Nora and Katherine in to look over their work. They both really liked it and made a few observations and corrections here and there. "You know, it's a lot more confusing than I ever think of it being," Nora smiled.

ENGELMANN CLAN MAP

Lloyd and Katherine Engelmann

Pastor Byron and Marly (Jessup Petfarken) Ellison
Ken (Petfarken) Ellison
Katie Ellison
Ginger Ellison
Charlie Ellison

Elton and Nora (Spanner Grainger) Schroeder
Keith (Spanner) and Darlene (Olson) Schroeder
Kevin (Spanner) and Carrie (Jessup) Schroeder
Andy (Grainger) Schroeder—fiancée Annie (Packineau) Grover
Victoria (Grainger) Schroeder—fiancé Christopher Holloway

Pastor Marvin and Glenda (Owens) Olson
Clark Olson
Maddie Lynn Olson

Doug and Julia (Heinrich) Anderson
Rodney Anderson
Little Bill Anderson

Jerald and Elsie (Gertz) Oxenfelter
Rebecca Oxenfelter
Junior Oxenfelter

Eddie and Lucy Schroeder
Marty Schroeder—fiancée Greta Heinrich
Danny and Jenny (Jessup) Schroeder and baby son; Matthew
Megan Elizabeth Schroeder—fiancé Dick Heinrich
Darrell Jessup—fiancée Jeannie Frandsen

Eve Jessup—fiancé Mervin (Chatterbox) Olson

Zacharias Jeffries—fiancée Suzy Heinrich; niece Miriam Carla Jeffries

Ian Harrington—Ruth Jeffries

Maureen Harrington (mother of Ian and Father Matthew)

* Keith and Kevin are Nora's brothers; all cousins to siblings Julia, Greta, Dick and Suzy

* Darlene is cousin to siblings Pastor Marv and Mervin (Chatterbox) Olson

* Marly's siblings are Carrie, Jenny, Darrell and Eve.

*Elsie was the widow of the cousin of Elton and Eddie, who are brothers.

*Zach's niece is Miriam and his half-sister is Ruth

33

After Darlene and Kincaid finished the Clan Map and breakfast, she gave him a ride into Merton to the barbershop. They stopped at Ellison's for exertorture classes. The kids were all jazzed about their contests. After exertorture, they got their choice of Ken's Strawberry Lemonade, Ginger's Raspberry Lemonade and Katie's Tart and Sweet Lemonade. Kincaid had a half a glass of each and raved about them all. He had to admit he was very glad the decision was not up to him.

When they got back into the car, Kincaid was certain that he heard the liquids splash inside his belly. "The kids are all so excited about it. Yea Gads, how is anyone going to keep from hurting anyone's feelings with this competition?"

Darlene laughed, "With honesty and all colors of ribbons for every possible excuse for a prize! Now, you and Elton, no one will worry about! You are supposedly the grownups! Even if you win, you'll be insulted. Count on it."

"Harrumph. You all treat us like we're big babies," Carl grumbled.

"Go figure!" Darlene giggled. "Have you any ideas of what kind of meat you are going to cook?"

"Just between you and me, Darlene, I was thinking I should call this guy from the San Antonio office. He used to bring in his barbeque pork ribs. They were pretty good, but I don't know if I'd know how to cook them. Maybe he could give me a pointer or two. What do you think?"

"Sounds like a good idea. If you call him right away, you'd have a chance to practice it before the contest. Then you would know more about how to do it on Judgment Day!"

"You think so? Will Magpie try to copy me?"

"No. He talks a big game, but he wouldn't want to steal your thunder. Besides, he's going to have to practice his, too. So, you'll both know what the other guy is cooking and will probably have even tasted it. Now, you won't get a peek even at Nora's because she won't need to practice; or Keith's, because he has done it so many times. He is going to buy a grill this weekend to cook his on."

"He has cooked it a lot, huh?" Kincaid probed.

"Yes, but don't panic. We used to cook our combo, his brats and my sauerkraut buns at cookouts back in Wisconsin. That's the only reason I am entering the bun contest, because we always served them together," Darlene giggled. "You'll need to practice your sauce the most, however. That's the secret of ribs from what I hear."

"I wonder how Keith's morning is at the new shop. He and Magpie left early this morning for Bismarck. Is he excited?" Kincaid asked.

"Yes, he has worked with his Dad and brothers before, so he has a good idea of how things will be. He loves working with them. You know, he was about six when he real Dad died. Then he lived with Nora and Evan, her first husband. Evan was nice; but his family, the Graingers, was something less than desirable. He just loves Elton. Of course, he thinks the world and all of Nora. She just took care of those boys, Kevin and him, without any thought, no matter what. He feels he got the best of the crop in the parents department."

"He's a fine young man. I'm really impressed with all Magpies' kids," Carl observed. "I haven't meant Andy, but if he is like the rest of them, he must be a good guy."

"He really is. He is like Darrell. They could be twins," Darlene smiled.

"How many kids are in your family?"

"I have two older brothers. Dave and Don. My Dad died of a heart attack about a year ago, but Mom is still good," Darlene turned into the yard, "Well Good Lookin', we are home now. It looks like Charlie is knee deep in his Potato Salad. When are you and Katherine going to practice your Hot German Potato Salad?"

"Tomorrow. I want to make it once before Mo gets here. They'll be in tomorrow night. Zach is bringing them out after work."

"Carl, it isn't any of my business, but I hope things go well for you and her. Well, anyway with that snazzy haircut, you'll have to beat the women off with a stick. You did very well without the wheelchair this morning."

"Thanks Darlene," Carl said sincerely. "Everyone has been so great to me, I just can't believe it."

Darlene laughed, "And given you a lot of grief too, from what I hear! At least it looks like it won't be raining anymore for a while, so you and your Gophers can get back after the canals and all."

Indeed, the kitchen was covered in varying degrees of potato salad. Grandma decided since they were already in over their heads, they would do the Hot German Potato Salad at the same time. Charlie had insisted that after everyone tasted his potato salad at lunch, he take the rest home for his family's supper. He even conned Uncle Elton into taking a sample of his potato salad to Aunt Julia so she would know what it looked like ahead of time. Nothing like softening up the judge!

Everyone had to admit that he and Grandma did a fine job with the Mustard Potato Salad and that they possibly had a winner on their hands. Charlie was happy, but a little concerned that Grandma was going to help Kincaid in the afternoon with his. "I don't think you should get to practice if you are over six years old. Do you, Coot?"

"Sorry Charlie, but I do. I have to practice my grilling."

The little guy was crestfallen but then smiled, "Oh well. I will win you anyway. Won't I? My potato salad is better. Mine has boiled eggs in it and yours doesn't. It is sure a good thing that I'm a Chicken Man, right? Then I can use eggs."

"It really is, Charlie," Uncle Elton agreed.

"Oh, Magpie," Kincaid said, "I used your phone this morning to call San Antonio. I owe you some bucks for that."

"Don't worry about it," Elton replied.

"When you know why I made the call, you might change your mind."

"What do you mean?"

"I called to get the winning grilling recipe. I will be making San Antonio Barbequed Pork Ribs. Got the recipe from a co-worker who is fourth generation Texan," Carl said with great bravado.

Elton laughed, "If you could get him to mail you the sauce, you'd have a fighting chance!"

"Hot Shot, what are you making? I haven't heard you announce it yet," Carl poked.

"I decided to keep it a secret," Elton answered smugly.

"You just haven't figured it out yet, that's all!" Kincaid laughed.

Elton shook his head, "You know, if I didn't know better, I'd think you are making fun of me."

Lloyd had been very quiet all morning, but perked up when he heard that. "You folks leave my Elton alone. He can't help it. He has a good heart even if he can't fix a car worth a damn. You'll make me mad if you don't be nice to him. Say you're sorry."

Everyone got quiet but no one said they were sorry. Lloyd looked around, "I said say you're sorry. I mean it. I take you to the wood shed."

Charlie's eyes got huge, "I'm sorry. Uncle Elton."

Lloyd smiled at him and then Miriam said, "Gopher sowwy."

Lloyd said, "See, little Laura even said she was sorry. Good girl, Laura."

"Laura good," Miriam nodded.

Then everyone said they were sorry and Lloyd was happy. Then he said, "Elton, if you want to cook something, I'll help you. I can cook real good. Right Katherine?"

"Yes you can Lloyd. You just haven't done it for a long time. But this is a contest between Elton and Carl."

"Can't I cook too? Why can't I cook? I can cook, can't I? It is my house! Right Elton?" The older man was getting frustrated.

"Yes, Lloyd it is your home. I'll help you, okay? We'll do it together. You can help me. Just don't do it alone. Deal?" Elton was thinking as fast as he could.

"Okay. You and me, like always, the two of us. We help each other out. Right Elton? Just us guys." Lloyd was dead serious. "Does Byron have someone to help him? I wouldn't want him to feel bad."

"Marv is helping him. That was nice of you to think of him, Lloyd." Elton got the coffee pot.

After dessert and Lloyd was taking his nap, Elton said, "Lord above! How are we going to do this? He sounds determined. I just hope he doesn't start cooking while we're asleep. Aye! Aye! Aye! This could be a tragedy."

"Maybe he'll forget," Katherine offered, albeit not very convincingly.

"Yah right and I'm a professional basketball player!" Elton sputtered.

That evening, Carrie picked up Miriam on her way home from the bank where she worked. She wasn't going to help milk, but planned to practice her recipes with Miriam. She had baked the pie crusts the night before.

Miriam was very excited about going to Son's house, but was disappointed when he put on his milk clothes to leave for the farm. She wanted to go along and the young couple thought they might have to rethink the whole idea. However, when Kevin said that she would be back to eat her Chocolate and Green Beans; she decided it was okay although she wasn't very happy about it.

She and Carrie waved goodbye at the door and Miriam had huge tears in her eyes. Carrie tried to ignore them and showed her the aprons they were going to wear. Carrie had made aprons the night before for a surprise. They were identical, except that Carrie's was bigger. Miriam stared at them for a time, watched carefully while Carrie put one on and then broke into a big smile when Carrie put the little one on her.

Miriam patted her apron and then said, "Cawwie, Gopher, Apurn." Then she picked up Mr. Bear, and said, "Apurn?"

"Hmm. Let me see," Carrie carried her and Mr. Bear into her sewing room. She went through the material and found a scrap of the material she had used for their aprons. She fashioned an apron for Mr. Bear! "Will that be okay, until I make him a better one tomorrow?"

Miriam gave Carrie a big hug. "Cawwie, might fine indeed. Mr. Bear apurn."

By the time Kevin got back, their chocolate cream pies were cooling in the fridge and the green bean salad was ready to taste. Carrie and Miriam had made the filling. Miriam did some of the stirring and a lot of tasting of the whipped cream. They had a mess in the kitchen and even Mr. Bear managed to get chocolate on his apron. Kevin came in the house and started to laugh. "You guys must have been busy!"

Carrie gave Kevin a kiss and grinned, "The hamburgers are almost done. We were very busy, weren't we Miriam?"

Miriam nodded very seriously, "Cawwie, Mr. Bear and Gopher busy. Son lick?'

He had hung up his coat, washed his hands and then took the little girl, "It looks like you and Mr. Bear did a lot of licking, huh? Is the pie pretty good?"

Miriam nodded. Kevin smiled, "I see Mr. Bear has an apron too."

"Cawwie fix."

"She is a great fixer, isn't she?" Kevin asked with pride.

"Cawwie good fix. Mr. Bear lick! Gopher Ooops!"

"What is she telling me?" Kevin chuckled, looking to his wife for clarification.

"Oh, that Mr. Bear got chocolate on his apron when the filling went Ooops, like Miriam did when the whipped cream got on her little face. Right?" She winked to the little girl.

Miriam turned to Kevin, "Cawwie lick Ooops!" Then she pointed to Carrie's apron where there was a spill.

"Aha! Sounds like you left part of the story out, Carrie," Kevin chided.

"That I did," Carrie giggled, "But Miriam told on me, right? You little rat!"

Miriam giggled and proudly patted her chest, "Rat!"

Later when the young couple took a very tired Miriam back to Ellisons after supper, everyone worn out.

"How did it go?" Byron asked.

"Really well," Carrie said. "We had a good time, didn't we, Miriam?"

Miriam nodded from Kevin's arms, "Cawwie good. Ooops! Rat Ooops!"

Marly shook her head questioningly, "What?"

Carrie giggled, "It's a long story, but we spill alot when we lick, don't we Miriam?"

"Mr. Bear Ooops!"

"And so does Mr. Bear. Well, you better go to Marly now and have a good sleep. We'll see you tomorrow. Thank you for coming over," Carrie said.

Miriam gave Son a hug and then gave Carrie a kiss.

"I'm honored," Carrie said emotionally as she hugged the tiny girl.

Kevin and Carrie were both so excited about how well the evening had gone that they had to stop over to Elton and Nora's on the way home. The family except for Lloyd was sitting out on the patio, swatting mosquitoes.

"Darned things, the minute the wind goes down, they start descending on a person," Elton groaned. "What brings you over?"

"We had to tell you about Miriam!" Kevin said.

"Everything okay?" Everyone gasped at once.

"Of course," Kevin grinned, "My Carrie and her had a great time. Tell them, Carrie."

Carrie told them all the adventures of the evening. Everyone was very happy to hear how well it all went. "She is really a neat little kid. I'm so relieved that she didn't cry or curl up. I was so worried."

Nora hugged her daughter-in-law, "Oh Carrie, you're great with kids. I knew you'd do just fine. I'm so glad you two hit it off."

"I thought tomorrow I'd sew Mr. Bear a real apron. This piece of material he has on will unravel. I think she likes me, Nora."

"Of course she does," Nora smiled.

Elton got up and gave her a hug.

34

Carl woke up when Lloyd came in his room about two-thirty. They talked about World War I for about forty-five minutes and then Lloyd went back to bed. Once he heard Lloyd's door close, Kincaid tried to go back to sleep.

Carl couldn't get comfortable. He worried about all sorts of things. He couldn't remember how Maureen looked. He knew she had very dark auburn hair, sparkling hazel eyes, a dimpled smile and a creamy complexion with peach colored cheeks. He thought she was beautiful. She was short and had a round figure. She was perky, bubbly and the only time that he had ever heard her down was this morning when she called because she was worried.

He wondered what her husband had been like. Ian and Matthew were both good guys and he liked them. Ian was short, but Matt was about five eleven. From that, Carl deduced that her husband must have been tall. He bet he was a real good-looking guy. She wouldn't be interested in an ordinary person like him. He had himself convinced of that.

Sure, the ladies here all told him that she was, but they didn't know her. Maureen was the kind of person that would call just to be friendly. She'd worry about getting along with folks. That was like her. She was a genuine sweetheart.

He was glad that Miriam was doing so well. He knew that Mo would be pleased by that. If anyone ever deserved to be loved, it was that little girl. He wondered what in the hell scared her so much about crayons. His mind thought of all sorts of horrid scenarios and finally, he gave up. There was nothing they could do about it, except maybe sometime convince Miriam that whatever it was that happened, wasn't the usual. They had to do that before she went to school. He wouldn't have her curling up in school. That would be intolerable.

Kincaid chuckled about Charlie trying his best to con Aunt Julia with his potato salad. He sure hoped that he didn't run and jump on Mo. He'd knock her over for certain. He knew that Charlie would have her by the hand and in the kitchen before the car door went shut. Oh Lordie, and give her a tour of the chicken coop and the digging operations, no doubt. He'd probably insist that she go digging with them. He wondered if he would put her on 'promotion'. After thinking about it, he decided that Charlie would probably put God himself on 'promotion'.

Ginger would have her interrogated fully within an hour. He wondered if he should plant some questions in Ginger's mind so she could find out for him. He smiled to himself, 'Not necessary. I'm sure she'll think of everything and some besides. Knowing her, she would probably tell Mo that I wanted to know!'

He hoped that he didn't act too stupid around her and that the family didn't put him in an embarrassing situation with her. Eventually he convinced himself, 'Nah, they wouldn't, if they could help it.' Carl had come to trust them all, with the exception of Lloyd and Charlie. And they were after all, Lloyd and Charlie.

What on earth would they do if Lloyd persisted in his plan to cook in the contest? He had only mentioned it a couple times tonight, but how he managed to fit it into World War I trench warfare, Carl still wasn't certain. At any rate, he had not forgotten it. Kincaid shuttered to think what the old fellow could do with an open grill. Poor Elton.

Finally he went to sleep, but before he did, the old FBI agent actually had a little talk with the good Lord. It had been a long time since he had said a prayer. He wasn't much of a praying man. It was more like a talk than a prayer. Like Ginger would say, like having a cup of coffee with God.

Pepper's alarm brought everyone into the glaring morning with great unwelcome jolt. They were all worn out, except Lloyd, who was still sleeping. Carl pulled on his clothes and wandered out to the kitchen to meet up with the rest of the family around their coffee pot.

It was funny. This morning, they all stood there, silently, cups in hand staring at the coffee pot. It was a few minutes before they all realized what they were all doing and started to laugh.

"Man, we need to get more sleep around this joint," Magpie laughed. "I wonder if the Harrington's had to get up early this morning. They might already be on their plane. I bet Ruthie didn't sleep at all!"

"Probably not," Nora grinned. "Marly told me yesterday that Ruthie has about worn herself to a frazzle, stewing about everything she could possibly dream up in her head. She almost had herself convinced that Ian didn't really want to see her!"

Elton burst out laughing, "Well, I'd bet the farm that isn't the case! They are pretty much done for. Both of them. What do you think, Kincaid?"

Carl looked like he had been caught with his hand in the cookie jar, "About what?"

"Badge 11918 and Ruthie! Where is your head this morning?"

"Oh, those two? Yah, their goose is cooked. From what Mo and Zach say, it is pretty much a done deal. In fact, even Father Matthew mentioned it. Oh my," Carl gasped.

"Oh my what?" Elton asked.

"Mo will probably want to go to the Catholic Church, huh? With Ruthie and Ian. I never thought of that. Oh well, I guess it doesn't make any difference," Carl mumbled to himself.

"You could go there too, if you wanted," Darlene assured him. "Or you can each go to your own church and meet afterwards."

"I've enough trouble going with you guys. Besides, who'd sit with Charlie?"

Pepper started to laugh. "Yah, who indeed! Who else would sit there and let him unravel his jacket!!"

"Will I never hear the end of that?" Carl asked.

Pepper studied the situation a minute and then grinned, "Nah."

"Figured," he grumbled. "Oh Magpie, Lloyd came visiting last night. He hasn't forgotten about helping you cook. If you want to call off the contest, I'd understand."

Keith poured his coffee, "I thought about that last night. Grandpa Lloyd and a hot grill is not a healthy combination."

"Yah, I thought about it too," Elton shrugged. "Maybe he'll forget."

"We can only hope, Dad," Keith said. "But like you always say, it's a good idea to have a contingency plan."

"I know. I'm thinking about it, but we can't call off the contest now. Everyone is too involved. My goodness. Nora was telling me about the sign ups. We are going to have enough food for the county. We better limit the amounts of each, huh?"

"Nora and I already told everyone," Grandma said.

"Zach told me that Ian and Mo have a whole cooler of frozen halibut steaks and stuff they are flying out extra cargo. He wanted to make sure that Zach has some extra ice to ice it down again when they got here!" Elton said, "I checked the deep freeze in the shop and made room for their stuff. Hey, Carl. Don't be buying any meat, unless it's something we don't have. Okay?"

"That hardly seems fair. Not only will I beat the pants off you but with your own groceries!" Kincaid shook his head.

"Well, don't clear off the shelf for your trophy yet," Magpie laughed. "Well, if I stay in the house much longer, I might just wander back to my little beddie-bye."

"Good grief, Dad," Pepper laughed, "You're such a big baby."

Grandma told Kincaid that he was making the biscuits for breakfast, while she did some other things. He looked at her in astonishment. "All by myself?"

"Why yes." Grandma smiled, "You know how. You'll do just fine. I have to get this dough set for tonight. I want to impress your lady friend and her boy with steamed biscuits when they get here. You know how. Oh, by the way, your German potato salad was very good. We might want to cut back on the vinegar a tad, but other than that, it was very good. What did you think, Nora?"

"I agree. It was okay the way it was, but I like it with a little less vinegar," Nora smiled. "So I am making sausage, gravy and hash browns to go with your eggs and biscuits."

"My eggs?" Carl raised his eyebrows. "Yea gads, the next thing you guys will have Carrie fit me with an apron too!"

Nora laughed, "Good idea! I might mention it to her."

Carl's face was flooded with horror, "You wouldn't."

Nora giggled, "Not unless you cause me trouble."

"Extortion, I tell you. Flat out extortion. This country has laws, you know."

"Yah, yah. Just get to work. You know how the milkers are when they get up here. If we don't have food for them, we'll be in deep trouble," Nora pointed out.

"You know, until I was here, I never realized what it was like to cook meals three times a day. I always just figured they just appeared. I mean, I knew they didn't. But, well, you know," Kincaid rambled.

Grandma patted his shoulder, "Yah, we know. Oh, by the way, Suzy called me last night while you guys were on the patio. Pastor Olson will be dropping the kids off here this morning. You'll have two more Gophers. I forgot to tell you. Glenda has to go see the doctor, so I was thinking about that. Sorry. I hope it is okay."

"It is fine," Carl was actually somewhat pleased. "I hope she's okay. Anything serious?"

"Don't know. That is why she's going to the doctor. Her back has been giving her a lot of trouble, but she thinks it's her kidneys."

Kincaid nodded, "I think Darrell is coming over after he feeds cattle this morning. We're going to start on the pipe project. He has some old pipe that he said we should use for this, rather than buy new. I wanted to pay him for it but he said it would just sit around and rust otherwise. You know, he'll need his money to start his home and all. How do you think I should handle it?"

"I'd just keep my ears open and find out something he needs. Then I'd buy it for him as a 'whatever' gift," Nora suggested.

"What is a whatever gift?" Carl was baffled.

"That is when you give someone something for whatever reason you want," Nora giggled.

"You guys. You don't even speak English," Carl grumped as he started to roll out the biscuits. "Look pretty good, don't they?"

"Yes, they do," Grandma nodded. "Mighty fine."

"Nora, I was thinking about entering my Watermelon Pickles. I have several jars that I brought back from Wisconsin. I'll have to go to the shop and dig them out of the pickup. I think I remember where they're packed. If they are too hard to get to, Keith said I could enter next year," Darlene said. "I was wondering if you would go down there with me."

"Sure, in fact Annie can come too, unless the Gopher Brigade is going to need her this morning," Nora questioned Carl.

"I think we can spare our surveyor for a while. Sounds like it is an important task. I have never tasted Watermelon Pickles, but I have Cactus Pickles."

"I guess folks pickle darned near anything," Grandma giggled.

The morning was fun. The Olson kids, Clark and Maddie Lynn, joined the Gophers and Carl was very grateful that Annie helped him out. He was trying to be as much without the wheelchair as possible, but didn't want to get too tired out before Harringtons arrived. Annie just plunked him in it and told him to take it cool. End of story.

Annie, Darlene and Nora had gone to the shop just as Darrell arrived. He was great with the kids. Kincaid never ceased to be amazed with the young men of the clan. Even though they were hard working and strong, none of them ever hesitated to take the time to be nice to a kid. Carl had learned to appreciate that. He knew now how much patience it took sometimes. Especially, when they were helping you do something that you could do alone in half the time with a fourth the explanation.

Darrell had loaded up the pipe and brought it over. The kids were very impressed when he backed it up to the side of the yard to unload it. One would have imagined they were taking delivery on four trainloads of construction material. They just beamed. They all stood there, with their little shovels and were careful to stay behind the imaginary line that Carl had given them. He and Miriam were in the wheelchairs, but the rest of the kids all stood with both hands on their shovels. When the ladies came back from the shop, Carl motioned for them to come over. "Could you take a Polaroid of my crew?"

Nora nodded and ran to the house. She got a couple good shots of them while the pipe was being unloaded. Carl was ecstatic. It crossed his mind to send one of the Polaroids to the FBI office in San Antonio. The guys would be flabbergasted!

By noon, the pipe was laid from the downspout by the house to the road. Glenda came to pick up the kids and shared lunch with them. Her kids were excited about their adventures that morning and wanted to know if they could get shovels of their own.

"We'll have to see. But until then, you'll have to borrow, okay? It looks like you had a lot of fun, huh? Did Mr. Kincaid take good care of you?"

Clark's deep brown eyes got very big, "You call him Agent Kincaid. That is how the BFI says it. And he didn't even have to arrest us. We were good, right Agent?"

"Yes you were," Kincaid grinned. "I might even have to get you some hard hats of your own."

"Only after they are done with 'promotion'," Charlie pointed out. "Uncle Darrell should get his first. He is the bestest helper. You can dig pretty fast. Did you know that?"

"I suppose I can. I never timed it, though. Did I pass 'promotion'?" Darrell asked.

"Hmm. I think so, but Agent and I have to talk it over in private. In case we have to say bad stuff about you, we don't want you to cry if you hear it," Charlie explained.

Darrell patted his head, "That is very thoughtful, Charlie. Well, thanks for the lunch you guys. I really need to get home now. I have to try to fix my grill. Kevin and I are going to make Cornish Game Hen for the contest. This morning, I knocked the doggone thing over and smashed the lid on it. I'm trying to fix it but I don't know if I can. Looks like I sprung it. Anyway, see you later."

"Thanks, Darrell. I owe you one," Carl said.

"You don't owe me a thing," Darrell grinned. "I'm anxious to see how it works out."

"I need to take off too. Come on Kiddlewinks. We have taken up enough of their time. Thanks so much for the lunch and the babysitting," Glenda said as she got up.

"Let us know how the tests come out. Okay?" Nora asked, "I hope it is nothing."

"The doctor said it was likely just a kidney infection. So I'm hoping," Glenda smiled. "Maybe he'll say I need a long tropical vacation!"

"You wish," Darlene giggled, "They never seem to say that."

After everyone settled for their naps and Annie left for the Fire Hall, Kincaid asked Nora and Darlene, "Do you guys know what kind of grill Darrell has?"

"No, but I can sure find out. Why?" Darlene asked.

"I want to get him one."

"You do? Why?" Darlene asked.

"It's a whatever gift, right Nora?" Kincaid needed back up on this.

"Yes, that's it," Nora answered seriously.

"Oh," Darlene smiled. "Tell you what, if I bring the car up, could I interest you in riding into Merton with me to the bank? I want to get some cash and we could ask Carrie. She'd know."

"Sounds good," Carl was pleased. "Need anything from town, Nora?"

"No, I think we're fine. You guys have fun."

After stopping at the bank, Darlene and Carl learned the kind of grill that Darrell had. They went to the Merton Hardware store where he had bought it and got another one. They took it over to his place.

He was down at his shop when they drove into the yard. Carl had never been to his place before. It was west of his parent's place, which was just over the hill. He had a small two-bedroom house, a large barn and a shop. He was in the shop banging on his smashed grill.

Darrell looked up from his task and had a curious look on his face. Then he waved and welcomed them. "What's up? This is a surprise. Welcome to my humble abode."

"Nice place you have here," Carl was truly impressed. For a young man only twenty, he had an impressive place. "Your barn is huge. I can't believe this is all yours."

"Well, mine and the banks," Darrell answered modestly. "Want a tour?"

"Actually, we came to bring you something. Then we can think about a tour," Darlene said. "Can you come help me? I can't get it out of the trunk and Kincaid shouldn't be lifting it."

Darrell had a puzzled look, "How did you get it in there then?"

"The guy at the hardware store put it in for us," Darlene answered.

"What did you get?" Darrell asked as he went to the trunk and looked in. "I thought that you already bought a grill, Kincaid. Is it yours, Darlene?"

"Keith has one. This is for you," Carl smiled. "It is a whatever gift."

"What are you talking about? Why are you giving me a present?"

"Not me, Carl."

"And because I want to. I asked Nora and she said it is a whatever present. It is for whatever you want it to be for," Kincaid grinned.

"You're nuts." Then he stood straight and looked at Carl, "Is this for that old bent up pipe? You lame brain. You don't need to get me anything for that junk. I told you no."

"I want to. You not only gave me the stuff, you loaded it up, unloaded it and helped dig it in. I really appreciate it. So take it before I get mad."

Darrell shook his head, "Don't want you to get mad. Thanks. You really didn't have to do this."

"I know. Darlene was nice enough to help me. Now get your junk out of her trunk so I can get a tour of that barn before I keel over."

They unloaded the grill and Darrell showed him the barn, although Carl didn't walk very far. "How many goats and cows do you milk?" Kincaid asked.

"Thirty goats and twenty cows," Darrell smiled. "I will be milking more goats next spring."

"Wow! That must keep you busy."

"It really isn't a big deal. I suppose I should get a real job before I get married, huh?" Darrell looked at Kincaid as if he wanted his approval.

"You know Darrell, there are a lot of guys twice your age that don't have as much going for them. You work at Eddie's Cheese Factory a couple days a week too, don't you? How much more do you think you should do?"

"I don't know. It doesn't seem like much. I just fiddle around."

"You do a fine job. A lot of folks couldn't begin to do half this much. Well, Darlene," Carl smiled, "You had better take me home before I conk out on you guys. I should get a nap before our company comes tonight."

"Oh, that's right. Harrington will be in. He's a nice guy," Darrell said. "I like him. Thanks so much for the gift. I'll put it together right away. I appreciate it. Thanks again."

35

Carl was ready to take a nap by the time he got home. Even though he was nervous about Harringtons' arrival, he was more worried he'd get too tired and be wheelchair bound. He didn't have time for a very long nap but extracted a promise from the ladies they would wake him in half an hour. Now he hoped he would be able to get to sleep.

He thought about Darrell being not quite twenty-one yet and already owning a farm. When he was twenty, he had a souped up car and the clothes on his back. He was in college, but Darrell had gone to BJC too and graduated with his AA. Apparently, he had plans to do other things, but after his heart went bad on him and he was laid up for the best part of the year, he decided this would be his life.

Darrell was a great guy and everyone loved him, but he felt that he was a failure. He didn't finish four years of college and the military wouldn't take him. He ran his dairy and worked at the cheese factory. It was quite a feat, but he never thought so.

Carl really liked him. If he had ever had a kid, he would have wanted him to be like Darrell or Kevin. And if he had a daughter, he would want her to be like Pepper or Darlene. Oh heck, any of Magpie's kids would be just fine with him. Then he fell asleep.

There was a knock at the door and Grandma woke Carl. "I didn't want you to oversleep. Zach just called and is on the way to the airport to pick them up. Best be getting beautiful," she teased.

"What about you? Did you get beautiful?" Carl groaned as he sat up.

"Already am," Grandma joked. "I'm more worried about getting the table set for dinner. If you were any kind of guy, you'd be helping me."

"Slave driver," Carl grumped. "I'll be there in a jiff."

Elton came home early and started the chores before anyone else got there. As the rest showed up, they dashed down to help out. By six thirty, the chores were finished and everyone was getting cleaned up for dinner.

The dinner smelled great and the table was all set. Ruthie had arrived. She was a basket case and Kincaid could commiserate. He knew just the turmoil that she was going through. Now he appreciated Pepper and Annie. He caught himself thinking about it and shook his head. 'Lord above! I've turned into a glorified creampuff."

Even Ellison's kids were anxious for the travelers to arrive and when Zach's car finally pulled into the yard, Ginger and Charlie was outside before anyone could tell them to slow down. Ruthie was right on their heels.

Ginger gave Ian a hug before he got out of the car and then whispered to him, "Say it!"

He grinned, "Badge 11918."

Ginger clapped her hands and kissed his cheek. "I couldn't wait for you to come out to see us! Are you all well now?"

Harrington smiled, "Just about. I see you are doing well. I couldn't wait to get back to see you."

Charlie was right behind his sister, "Harrington, do you still have your secret project ring?"

"I do," Harrington answered with great seriousness and reached into his pocket to retrieve his key chain. "Here it is."

Charlie gave him a hug, "Good, I was afraid you'd lose it."

"No way," Harrington said, "It's very important. Do you still have yours?"

Charlie reached in his pants pocket and pulled out his plastic soda pop cap ring that was caked in dirt and pocket lint. "Right here. Oh, Harrington. I kept my eyes on her for you. Ruthie cried sometimes, but not too much. I think she's all better now."

"Thank you, Charlie. Where is she?" Harrington got out of the car. Ruthie came running into his arms. They embraced and were soon lost in an impassioned kiss.

Charlie got out of their way and shook his head to Zach, "Harrington must like girl germs. Ick."

Zach laughed, "Someday, you will too Charlie."

"Not me, ever."

Darrell kindly walked down the ramp with him, so Carl could walk out instead of wheel out. Kincaid really appreciated that. Seeing the welcoming crowd around the car, Darrell asked Carl if he wanted him to clear a path, but Kincaid just chuckled, "We'd get trampled!"

Suzy had bounced out and opened the door for Maureen. She helped her out of the car and then began to introduce her. Mo remembered Byron and Elton and greeted their wives with a big smile.

Miriam seemed to remember her, but wasn't certain. Mo asked Miriam if she could give her a hug. Miriam looked at Kevin, who was carrying her, and then nodded. Miriam brushed her cheek against Mo's, smiled and then quickly turned to hide her face in Kevin's shoulder.

Kevin grinned and shook Maureen's hand. "Hi, I'm Kevin. One of Elton's kids. This is my wife, Carrie."

Carrie shook Maureen's hand and Miriam turned to watch all the introductions. She looked at Mo and pointed to Grandma Katherine, "Chocolate."

Grandma Katherine giggled, "She calls me Chocolate and my husband Laura. I'm Katherine and this is Lloyd. We're so happy to meet you. We all love your son and have heard such wonderful things about you."

"I have heard great things about you too! In a few days, we can get together and compare reality with all the hype!" Maureen laughed.

"I look forward to it," Katherine said, making up her mind that she liked this lady. She could see why Kincaid was so taken with her. "Oh, back here is someone you might want to see. This is Darrell Jessup and see who he has with him!"

Maureen greeted Darrell, "You're the one that took my Ian horseback riding, is that right? He loved it. Thank you so much."

"Boston is a good rider! I'm glad to meet you," Darrell grinned. "I'll take you riding when you have time."

"Me? On a horse? You'd need a Clydesdale, young man!"

Darrell chuckled, "Oh, I think the horses will manage!"

Kincaid was trying to move, but couldn't. He just stood there like a dope. He looked at her and could barely swallow. She was even more fantastic than he had remembered. Maureen smiled at him, put her arms around him and gave him a big hug. "How is the Old Coot?"

He hugged her back and mumbled, "Pretty good, and you?"

"Why, my butt is numb up to my eyebrows! That's a long plane ride! It's good to see you standing on your own two feet! You going horseback riding with me when this fine looking fellow takes me out?"

"I suppose I could, if Zach says I can. And if Darrell gives me a broken down old bag of glue."

"I could arrange that!" Darrell laughed, "Or get you a cushioned pony cart with fluffy pillows!"

"Watch it, there," Kincaid warned. "I still have my gun."

"Glad to see your kindly nature is still in place," Maureen teased. "I can't believe I actually missed you!"

Kincaid just beamed, "There is no accounting for what some folks do!"

Then Harrington came over to Kincaid and gave him a hug. Kincaid had to mask his shock. Even though he had his big grin, Harrington looked very frail and quite tired. "Well, you must have missed us too! It looks like you even put on a clean shirt!"

"They made me," Kincaid gave his friend a hug. Kincaid was taken back that Ian's right arm was extremely weak and barely moved, but his left one was still strong.

After a few more greetings and hugs, Kevin and Zach brought their bags in while Keith and Elton took the halibut to the shop freezer. Darrell gave Kincaid his arm while they walked into the house.

As Carl had suspected, Ginger immediately began her interrogation of Maureen. She asked her about how many kids she had, their names and if they had kids. She checked out if she threw up at church, was Catlick or went to their church. Ginger also told her that Uncle Elton did his skinning on Tuesdays, so that is the only day that Maureen had to listen to him.

Carl watched Maureen's face as Ginger babbled on. She was smiling like crazy. "You're quite the cookie, aren't you?" Mo asked with a giggle.

"No. I'm a little girl. Kincaid and Uncle Elton call me Gopher, but I'm really a little girl. I wrecked my hands and face, but Smitty helped them grow back. He's a pretty good doctor. Did you know that he and Suzy are going to have a wedding? And I get to be the flower girl! And you know what? Charlie is the ring carrier kid, but I hope he doesn't lose the ring. He can be 'buncitons. Sometimes Coot says that he'll give him ten to life. Do you know what that means?"

Charlie overheard that and came right over to defend himself. "I won't lose the ring. Mommy is going to sew it on the pillow."

"Charlie, you unsewed your jacket in church when you sat by Coot. Mom went to her wit's end. Mrs. Harrington, you know that Mom won't let Charlie and Smitty sit together in church anymore because they giggle." Ginger rattled on, "She only lets Coot sit by him because he's his extra legs."

"Oh, I'm glad to know that," Maureen smiled. "Everyone needs good legs."

"Do you need good legs?" Charlie asked, eagerly. "I can be your Goer and Getter Guy too. Kincaid is better so he doesn't need me to get stuff so much anymore. I'll have time. I am Uncle Elton's Chicken Man. Agent Kincaid and I are Weeders in the garden. Are you a good weeder? Have you seen the chicken coop yet? I can take you out there if you want."

Kincaid felt he'd better intervene, "Charlie, Mrs. Harrington had to a long day today. I think she would like to relax tonight, okay? Maybe we can take her to the chicken coop tomorrow?"

"Okay," Charlie said as he climbed up on Carl's lap and made himself at home. Charlie watched Maureen for a bit and then turned to Kincaid, and whispered very loudly, "Is she frad jelly like Miriam?"

"No Charlie. She isn't fragile. She is just tired out. She didn't get much sleep last night and had a very long day. That's all."

Charlie was relieved, "Oh good. Then she can help us dig tomorrow after she sleeps, huh?"

"We'll see. Now, best you get washed up for dinner, Gophers."

The kids looked at him, nodded and ran off to wash up. Kincaid looked at Maureen and apologized, "I hope they didn't drive you wacky. They can do that."

"No, they're good kids, Carl," she reached over and patted his hand, "I can tell they think a lot of you."

Carl shrugged, "Ah, they like everybody. Well, we had better get to the table before Magpie eats it all."

At the table, miraculously, Maureen was seated next to Kincaid. Carl smiled to himself, 'These ladies are as subtle as a sledge hammer.'

He had to admit he was glad he got to sit by her though. He looked over to Ruthie, sitting by her Ian. They both looked happy. When everyone held hands to say grace, Ruthie just picked up Ian's weak hand in hers without a flinch. He looked at her and she smiled back.

'Yah,' Kincaid thought, 'Their goose is so cooked!'

Miriam had her chair wedged between Kevin and Carrie tonight. She was a good mood and exceptionally talkative. She had her milkshake and her favorite vegetable, green beans. Then she said, "Cawwie, Gopher, green beans, Ooops!"

"What did you say, Honey?" Nora asked.

Miriam got a little self-conscious and looked to Carrie for support. "She's telling about when we practiced our green bean salad for the contest and we spilled. Didn't we? We went Ooops!" Carrie explained.

Miriam giggled, looked at Elton and said, "Mighty fine indeed."

Elton looked at her and chuckled. "You're on a roll tonight. I think you had fun at Son's and Carrie's last night. Didn't you?"

Miriam nodded, "Mr. Bear apurn."

"I heard that Carrie made matching aprons for you two and Mr. Bear. Oh, Carrie," Nora got a devilish grin, "I want to put an order in for an apron for Kincaid."

Carl could have passed out, "You old bat. You said you'd keep quiet about it if I made the biscuits and gravy."

""Oh my, I forgot. You did make them, didn't you?" Nora teased.

"You know, Magpie," Carl was serious, "When I first met Nora, I wondered how you could ever find a woman as kind, gentle and beautiful as her. Now that I know her better, I almost think she is lucky she got you!"

"I've been trying to tell you that. No one listens to me," Elton stated.

"You baked biscuits?" Turning to Carl, Maureen was impressed. "How did they turn out?"

"Well, what do you think? I did a great job," Carl blustered.

"They were okay, Carl. I wouldn't exactly say they were barn burners or anything!" Elton started in. "No one would pay money for them."

"Well, I haven't tasted yours, so I think mine are better. It is easy to talk when you don't have to prove yourself," Kincaid pointed out.

Miriam shook her head and smiled to Kevin said, "Goats."

Everyone laughed, even Carl and Elton.

"Is this how the grilling contest hatched?" Harrington asked. "I bet you two were bragging your pants off, huh?"

"Kind of," Elton grinned. "Kincaid is so windy. He scrambled one egg and now he thinks he is the Galloping Gourmet. I have been cooking since I was five years old."

"Just because it took you longer to learn, doesn't make you better!" Kincaid retorted. "We'll see how this goes. You aren't even entered in anything but the meat. I am."

"Sorry Kincaid," Elton was unimpressed, "Entering the potato salad contest with Katherine as your partner shouldn't even count. She'll do all the work! We all know that!"

"She will not. She's the real bossy type," Carl defended himself. "Tell them Katherine, how you make me do all the work."

She smiled at him like butter wouldn't melt in her mouth. "Me? Bossy? Sweet little old me?"

"Oh good grief. You guys are impossible," Kincaid was flustered.

Charlie listened to it, "I'm going to win the potato salad contest. I hope you don't cry, Agent."

"No, Charlie," Kincaid groaned, "I won't cry."

Maureen asked, "How many are entered in the potato salad competition?"

Nora got the list, "Julia is the judge and there are five entries."

"My, it sounds like I'll have to buy an outfit from Tent and Awning so I can taste it all!" Maureen laughed. "Ian brought enough halibut to feed the entire state."

"We need some to practice on, Mom," Harrington pointed out. "Zach and I have to try it a couple times."

"You guys need to use the grill some night?" Elton asked.

"No, we're going to use the one at my apartment. I'll bring it out for the contest," Zach offered. "What are you going to use for grills for the contest?"

"We'll buy as many as we need," Lloyd volunteered, "Right Elton? He and I will do that. You can use ours, right Elton? Elton and I are good partners, aren't we?"

"Yes Lloyd," Elton assured him. "We surely are."

36

That evening after dishes, some of the family went out to the patio. Carl had his whiskey while he and Elton enjoyed their cigarettes. Zach and Suzy took Keith, Darlene, Ruthie and Harrington over to the place where the construction crew had started to dig their basement earlier that day.

Nora and Mo sat at the picnic table and the men sat in the armchairs to relax. "I hope your trip wasn't too miserable. How many layovers did you have?"

Mo smiled, "The flights were good, just long. We had a layover in Chicago and in Minneapolis. Oh, by the way, Matthew says to tell you hello. He's feeling sorry for himself because he can't be here. He is looking forward to coming out."

"We really enjoy him," Elton said. "If your other kids are anything like these two, you did a fine job with them."

"Thank you. Some days I don't even mind having folks know I'm related to them. Most the time, I prefer going by an assumed name!"

Nora giggled, "I know the feeling. How many kids do you have?"

"Eight. Three boys, then three girls and then Ian and Matthew," Maureen explained. "That's enough. When Sean passed away fifteen years ago, I thought it was eight too many! But you know, they kind of held me together. You hear some widows say that they have nothing to live for anymore. I was so busy that I hoped I'd survive!"

"I thought four was a lot!" Nora grinned, "Did you hear that Elton? Eight!"

"I'm certain that you had it all under control," Elton assured Mo. "From what I know of you, they were in good hands."

Maureen looked at him, "Wow! You're being so nice that it sends shivers down my spine! I'd better go lock up my wallet. You okay?"

"I'm just fine," Elton grinned. "Or as Miriam would say, mighty fine indeed."

"I hoped she would forget that," Carl groaned. "The poor kid will have to go to speech therapy before school if she keeps hanging around you."

"And what about you? You have Ginger asking everyone how you can give Charlie ten to life! What were you thinking?" Elton chortled.

"You should have seen him! That little spitfire was supposed to be picking peas and instead, he was pulling up the plants and then picking the pea shells off! Yea gads!" Kincaid shook his head. "So I showed him the right way and two seconds later, he was replanting the pea plants he had pulled up! That's when I said it. He knew exactly what I meant. I told him I'd send him to jail for ten years to life, but Ginger didn't hear it all. You know how nosey she is. She asked him but he's not telling to drive her bugs. Now he thinks it's funny that she is asking everyone what it means."

"You do have a time, Kincaid." Elton laughed, "You and your Gophers."

"Yah well, tell Maureen what you said about digging up Grandpa Bert's gasket! Smarty pants! Scared the kids half to death!"

"I did not say that! They did," Elton defended himself. "Don't be spreading a tale when you know I never told them that!"

Nora explained it all to Maureen and she got the giggles. "I don't think either one of them is a worry to Captain Kangaroo!"

"Well, I never," Elton mumbled. "I'm going to get another soda pop. You guys want anything?"

"My other whiskey, please," Kincaid handed his glass to Elton. The ladies nodded and Elton went inside. "What do you think of the patio furniture? Magpie and I bought it one day when we were in town!"

"Maureen, I tell you," Nora recounted their adventures, "These two guys with an empty vehicle is dangerous business!"

Maureen laughed, "Sounds like it. It's usually the girls that get in trouble for being avid shoppers."

Elton returned with all the drinks. After he passed them out, he sat down by his Nora at the table. Carl looked at him seriously and said, "Magpie, I think we're going to have a problem with Lloyd and the contest. He is determined he's going to help you cook, you know."

"I'm afraid so," Elton lit another cigarette. "I'm hoping it works out. He's so damned stubborn. Maybe he will forget, huh? We can hope."

Nora patted his hand, "I think Keith is right, Elton. We need to think of a backup plan. He'll get carried away and I would rather not have him clean out the pantry again."

Elton took her hand in his. "I know."

Kincaid got up from the armchair and sat down next to Mo across from Elton. "I'll help you keep an eye on him. I think we might as well just accept he's going to do it."

Elton was thoughtful, "I know. That old fox is probably in his bed right now figuring how he's going to remodel the grill!"

The kids came back from their walk over to Zach's land. Keith and Darlene said goodnight and went in. Zach and Suzy said good night and then went off alone to tell each other good night before Suzy went home. Ruthie sat down with the older folks and Harrington went in the house.

"He okay?" Nora asked. "I hope this isn't too much for him."

"No, he said he had to go get something. He says he feels fine," Ruthie smiled.

"His doctor told him not to get overtired," Maureen explained. "But I don't think that sending him to his room now would accomplish much. He has been looking forward to getting here so much. Ruthie, I'm going to ask you to try to get him to shut it down early tonight though."

"Sure, I will," Ruthie patted Maureen's hand. "I don't want him to get sick again."

Harrington returned with a small package in gold foil wrap. One look at it and Ruthie broke into a big smile. "You remembered!"

"I wouldn't dare forget and that's a blasted fact!" Harrington grinned as he took her hand. "Come, let's go check out the airplane."

"Ian," Maureen reminded, "Take it easy tonight. I don't want to drag your limp and bleeding body back to the house. You know what the doctor said."

"Don't worry, Mom," the young man gave his Mom a kiss on the top of the head, "I remember."

Harrington and Ruthie went down to the shop to see the progress on the airplane. At least that is the excuse they gave. Elton watched as they walked off hand in hand. "Is that an engagement ring in that box? She seems pretty calm about it."

"No, it's a box of some fancy caramels," Maureen explained. "Ian about had a conniption until he got them for her."

"Oh yes," Nora nodded, "She does love caramel. How's Ian doing?"

"Some days good, some days not so much," Mo stopped and shook her head. "He gets so frustrated that his arm won't do what he wants it to do. He is improving, but not as fast as he wants."

"I was surprised that it's so weak," Carl admitted. "I just thought it would move slower, but not be so weak. I guess I don't understand how it works."

"Neither do I, but the doctors are confident that if he keeps up with his therapy, he will regain a lot of the strength and movement. But it will never be like before." Mo pursed her lips. "I'm so glad that he's had Ruthie to lean on. Without her, he'd have been really depressed about it all. He is bad enough as it is."

"I imagine it would be hard," Elton agreed.

"The thought of having to give up the job is horrible," Carl related, speaking as much for himself as for Ian, "It just makes me sick sometimes to think that I'll never be an agent again. I feel so worthless."

"You shouldn't, you know," Nora pointed out. "You do a lot around here. Lloyd and the Gophers rely on you. And even though he would never admit it, so does the Old Elton Bird."

"Do not," Elton retorted. "Him? He is more of a torment than a help!"

"You're just damn lucky I even talk to you half the time," Kincaid groused. "You know, I spend half my day straightening out the stuff you tell the kids."

"Yea gads," Nora laughed, "You guys are almost as bad as the Grandpas."

The older couples visited a bit more and then Nora took her husband's hand, "Come on, Gas Jockey. You have to get up early tomorrow. Let's hit the sack."

Elton winked at his guests, "She can't wait to get me alone!"

"Dream on, buddy," Nora laughed. "Good night you two. Oh, Maureen, you don't need to get up with the mob unless you feel like it. This is your vacation."

"Thank you Nora and thanks for the wonderful dinner," Maureen smiled. "I'm about to cash it in pretty soon myself."

"Good night," Carl said to the Schroeders but he didn't get up.

He panicked. He wanted to talk to Maureen alone, but what would he say to her? What was he going to do? What if she wanted to go in and was just being polite to him? Should he have said, 'I'm going in, too?' Yea gads. Instead he just sat there. Maybe she was thinking she had to sit there to help him go in and she really wanted to go in, but would never say so. In his turmoil, Carl continued to sit there, not thinking of a word to say. After an eternal minute, he lit another cigarette. Then, like an idiot, he asked her if she wanted one. As soon as he did it, he could have kicked himself. He knew she didn't smoke.

"No thank you, Carl," she looked at the huge sky, "I can't believe all the stars. I don't think I've ever seen such a big sky."

"Yes, if you lean back in the chair you can really see them." He could have knocked himself in the head. What sort of a stupid sentence was that? You could see just as many stars from where she was as if she was leaning back in a chair. He just felt himself melting into idiocy.

She saw a shooting star. "Do you know much about stars and constellations?"

"Nope. Never did. I always thought folks were just imagining they could see stuff up there. I can't tell one star from another. Can you?"

"No. Never saw this much sky before. You seem to really like it here. Do you?"

"I don't know. I didn't think I did, but I am afraid I might," Carl was trying to be as honest as he could be, thinking of what Pepper and Darlene had told him.

"Why afraid?" Maureen was almost as to the point as Ginger.

"Oh, you know. It's so different from what my life was," Kincaid answered. The cotton in his mouth was spreading inside his brain. He knew he wasn't cut out for this personal conversation stuff. He hated it.

"I suppose you want to get back to all your Texan friends and stuff, huh?" Maureen probed.

"No more than a handful of folks who even knew who I was," Kincaid explained. "It never bothered me before, but now that I've been here . . . . I mean, these people have real family and friends. It's really something. You know? Well, of course you'd know. I'm sure that is the way that your life is out in Boston."

"Not really," Maureen smiled. "My life is mostly kids and grandkids. A few neighbors and mostly Sean's family. My family tends not to be long-livers."

"I didn't know having a long liver was good without bacon and onions," Kincaid smiled.

"They're turning you into a real chef, huh? I'm anxious to try some of your specialties," Mo giggled.

"I just peel potatoes mostly. The ladies tell me what to do. Honestly, Magpie is right about that. Don't tell him I told you, okay?" Kincaid looked directly at her for the first time since they were alone.

He froze again. He wasn't sure what to do. He knew what he wanted to do but then thought that Mo would think he was a lecherous old fool. He cleared his throat, "I suppose you want to go to bed, huh?" he blurted out.

As soon as the words were out of his mouth, he could feel himself turn beet red.

Maureen smiled at his embarrassment, "Well, yes. I guess I do. It has been a long day and I need my beauty sleep. We should go in. You're doing very well, Carl. I'm glad you've made so much progr—"

He leaned over and gave her a kiss on the mouth. It was a short, nice kiss, but probably more than he should have done. Abruptly, he stood up. "We'd better go in, before I act even stupider," he grumbled.

Maureen took his arm and looked straight at him, "Do you think giving me a kiss was stupid? Because you wish you hadn't?"

"No way. I mean, I wanted to kiss your right away. I didn't know if you'd belt me. Would you have?"

"If I wanted to belt you, I would have!" Mo shook her head. "You should know that."

Carl looked at her and laughed, "Yes Motor Mouth. I know you. I'm so glad you're here. I really missed you."

Maureen took his arm and they walked in together. After putting their things in the sink, they went to the hall. Carl gave her a nice kiss on the cheek by her bedroom door and then went to his room.

Kincaid looked out the window from his bed and watched Elmer. 'I don't think I have any better chance with Mo than you do with that damned gopher. I should just forget about it. I can't begin to talk like these folks do. And I'm not even sure that I want to. What would there be to gain? Yea gads, she lives half way across the country and I don't even have a real home. I could probably never be a husband to her.'

Then for the first time in an extremely long time, he cried. He just turned into his pillow and had a very long cry.

37

The morning light began filtering through the window as Kincaid opened his eyes. The first thing he noticed was Elmer, asleep in his front paws at the edge of the gopher hole. Kincaid made a face, 'Stupid dog.'

He was already dressed by the time Pepper's alarm clock went off. He wondered if she had an exceptionally loud clock on purpose, or was it was just that everyone was subconsciously listening for it. No one else even had an alarm clock. That dumb clock went off when she wasn't home. That figured, for this weird outfit.

He walked out to the kitchen to find Grandma Katherine making the coffee. "You're up before breakfast this morning. Looking for a worm?"

Kincaid looked at her and frowned, "Huh? No. Just woke up. That Elmer goes after that same gopher hole all the time. Think he knows he'll never get the gopher? By now he should have figured it out, you'd think."

Grandma laughed. "Hope springs eternal. Ah heck, Carl. It gives him something to do better than chasing porcupines!"

Carl nodded somberly, "He could just sleep."

"What's the fun in that?" the tiny lady said as she started to take down the cups.

"Let me," Kincaid reached for them, "I can reach them easier than you. What are you, even five foot?"

"No, used to be 4'11', but I've shrunk. How tall are you?"

"Around six foot," Kincaid mumbled.

"That just makes it harder to tie your shoes, to my notion," Elton joked as he entered the kitchen. "Coffee done yet?"

"Not quite. Still perking," Grandma answered. "I heard Lloyd talking in his sleep last night. He was taking the meat out of the fire. Don't know if that is a good sign."

Elton shook his head, "Probably not. Yea gads. It's getting so dealing with him is as bad as it was talking around Miriam. She was really a jabberbox last night, wasn't she? I've never seen her like that ever."

"That was really something," Carl agreed. "She wanted to tell about her stuff too. Being with the kids is good for her."

"Yah, I think so," Elton smiled at the FBI agent, "And being with you."

Carl almost smiled. It pleased him but he wished that Elton hadn't said that. After last night, he had pretty much decided to just take off. Leave the farm permanently and soon.

He couldn't live like they did, he knew that. Even if he wanted to, which he wasn't sure that he did; he'd never have what they had. It was just too much for him. He couldn't deal with it. He'd do just fine with his two whiskeys and a burger.

Katherine frowned at him, "I don't think you got enough sleep last night. You seem to be like that TV show, *Lost in Space.* Something bothering you?"

"No," Kincaid lied, "I'm okay. I woke up too early."

Elton and Grandma exchanged a look and both raised their eyebrows. Elton thought a minute and then said, "Hey, want to go to town with me today? I'm going in to the Bismarck shop to check the hydraulic lift. Keith wanted me to look at it. You can get out of the house."

"I might just. This morning?" Carl asked, hoping the answer would be yes.

"I'll be home for lunch and then go in. You got something planned for today?"

"No," he sat down at the table and put his head in his hands. "Nothing."

Elton looked at Katherine again and he mouthed, 'What?'

She shook her head. Elton poured their two cups and took Carl's over to him. "You okay, Man?"

"Yah, I just got too tired yesterday and not enough sleep last night."

The phone rang and Katherine answered it. "Okay, I'll let them know. Take care you two."

She hung up and told Elton, "Kevin and Carrie are going to give it a miss this morning. Carrie was upchucking again last night. Neither of them got much sleep."

"That's okay," Keith said as he and his mom came into the kitchen. "There are enough of us, right Dad?" Keith noticed Kincaid and added, "You don't need to come down either if you don't feel like it."

"No, I will," Elton didn't want to draw any more attention to Kincaid than necessary.

"What's for breakfast?" Zach asked as he bounced into the room. He stopped short when he saw Kincaid and filled his cup. He caught Elton's eye and then pointed his head toward Carl.

Elton shrugged and put his boots on. Nora opened the door when Ellison's came in. Byron was carrying Miriam and Ruthie was with the other kids. Miriam looked around and noticed that Kevin wasn't there.

"Son?"

Grandma took her little hand, "No Son this morning. He had to stay home with Carrie. Her tummy hurts."

Miriam's eyes got huge, "Dog bite?"

"No, no dog bite," Katherine tried to explain quickly. "Just a tummy ache."

Miriam started to shake and Byron began to rub her back. "It is okay, Miriam. Really. No dog bite. Honest. No dog bite." Miriam started to panic, "Now listen Miriam. Everything is okay. Carrie and Son are fine."

The little girl was having none of it and beginning to whimper.

Grandma went to the phone and then turned to Byron, "Miriam, Kevin wants to talk to you."

Byron held the phone to Miriam's ear. "Hi Miriam. This is Kevin. We are just sleepy this morning. Carrie ate too much chocolate last night and got a tummy ache. No dog bite. We're fine."

Miriam looked at the phone and then put her ear back to the earpiece. "Son, Cawwie, mighty fine indeed?"

"Yes, Honey, we are mighty fine indeed. Are you with Byron?"

"Bywon."

"Okay, can you be a good girl or should I come over?"

Miriam nodded to the phone but Byron spoke into it. "She is nodding yes. Thanks Kevin, but we'll be okay. Right Miriam? We'll be mighty fine indeed."

Miriam nodded.

"Okay, night, night. I'll see you later, Miriam." Kevin hung up.

Miriam said "Night, night." Then she looked at Byron and made the snoring noise.

Byron grinned, "Okay? Is everything okay now?"

"Okay," the little girl said reluctantly.

Kincaid had been watching the whole thing from the table. Finally, he said, "Bring the Gopher here. You can help me while they do chores? Okay, Miriam?"

"Okay Coot," Miriam said as she held out her hands to him.

"So," Kincaid asked the women, "What should we cook this morning?"

Miriam pulled Mr. Bear out of her shirt and looked at Kincaid. He added, "And Mr. Bear too."

"You guys can peel these boiled potatoes for us, okay?" Nora said as she set the bowl down on the table.

"We can do that, can't we Gopher?" Kincaid asked.

"Okay," Miriam answered.

During this time, Maureen, Harrington and Pepper joined the gang in the kitchen. Everyone was getting their cups filled and the thermos was ready.

"You feel up to coming with?" Elton asked Harrington. "You can stay in if you want."

"And miss out? I don't think so," Harrington grinned and took Ruthie's hand. "Besides, I'm going to supervise today."

Elton slapped his back, "We can always use a good supervisor."

Maureen asked the ladies how she could help, and they asked her if she wanted to make the eggs or fry the ham. She chose the ham and soon was slicing slabs off a large picnic to fry. Kincaid worked on the potatoes and only spoke to Miriam, who was not much in the way of help. When she finished slicing the ham, Maureen took some of the potatoes and started to help. Carl gave her a quick glance and then looked away as fast as he could.

Nora noticed that Maureen was more than a little taken back. "Carl," Nora said, "Would you like me to take Miriam and then you could help Mo?"

Carl bit his lip, answered sarcastically, "Maybe it would be better if Gopher and I just didn't help with breakfast this morning. We'll go look at a book, okay Miriam?"

Miriam nodded and they went off to the bedroom. Nora didn't know what to say and felt bad for Mo. She tried to excuse Carl by saying, "He is concerned about her. He is very good with her."

Maureen didn't look up, but only said, "He seems to be."

Nora and Grandma exchanged questioning glances and changed the subject to the contest. Maureen had seemed very chipper when she first came into the kitchen, but was quite withdrawn now. Nora and Darlene tried their best to be cheerful, but it wasn't working.

Katherine finished what she was doing and took off her apron. "I'm going to check on Kincaid. He hasn't been himself since he woke up. I might need to bat him upside the head."

Nora nodded, but Maureen never acknowledged the comment.

In the nursery, Kincaid was turning the pages of a book for Miriam and she was looking at it. "Might be nice if you read it to her. She can't read, you know!" Grandma pulled up her chair. "So, what's eating you? And don't give me this not enough sleep routine."

"There's nothing eating me."

"Liar."

Miriam looked up and repeated, "Liar."

"Now look what you did?" Carl said, trying to keep his voice soft, but his look conveyed to Katherine that he was very angry.

"I'm sorry," Katherine apologized, "I shouldn't have said that. Look, I know I might not be the person that you want to talk to about what's bugging you, but I know it's something. I've been around a long time and have seen a lot. This has all the earmarks of being a matter of the heart. Am I right?"

Carl gave her a dirty look.

"I'll take that as a yes," she continued. "Now, I wouldn't presume to tell you how to live,"

Kincaid gave her a sardonic laugh, but she went on. "I mean, I can't tell you who you should care about but I can tell you that you shouldn't hurt someone's feelings."

Carl looked at her for the first time, and seemed genuinely surprised, "Whose feelings did I hurt?"

"Maureen's," Katherine answered immediately. "Whatever you're thinking, you were barely civil to her. It was obvious. She's embarrassed and my guess is that she has no idea what you're thinking. If you want to be mad at someone, the least you can do is tell them why."

Carl straightened up the book, "I'm not mad at her." He turned the page and then said, "Not at all."

"Okay, then why are you trying to hurt her?"

"You really are a badger, aren't you?" he looked at the elderly lady.

"I guess, but that doesn't change the state of your situation one bit. Does it?"

"Huh?"

"Carl, you shouldn't go around hurting folks for no reason. If you aren't upset with her, you should be nice and talk to her alone. Simple as that."

"It isn't simple," Carl looked at her almost in a panic. "You don't even begin to understand."

"Try me."

"I just can't deal with this right now," Carl fussed with Miriam.

Katherine sat for a minute and then took Miriam. "I'm going to take Miss Miriam out for her milkshake and then you and I are having a talk. So you can either plan on telling me the truth or figure out a good lie that I'll believe."

With that, Katherine and Miriam left the room. Kincaid sat there, staring at the door.

He thought to himself, 'Lady, how can I tell you what's bugging me, when I don't even know myself.'

A few minutes later, she returned. "I told the gals that you weren't feeling well. I think they believe it."

Carl nodded. "You can sit here forever, but I've nothing to tell you. I don't know why or how I feel. So there. Does that make you feel better?"

"Why would that make me feel better? You crazy man. What do you think that this could be about?" the lady patted his hand kindly.

He turned to her and almost burst into tears. "My life is nothing. The only life I have is one that Zach set up for me because I was a lonely, sick, old man. I can't begin to imagine that someone like Maureen would even vaguely be interested in me. This is just stupid. The only family I have is a borrowed one. I don't have one shred of real life."

Katherine drew the large man into her arms and gave him a good motherly hug. "I thought so. You silly rabbit. I swear, the bigger the man: the softer the head. Now you listen to your old Grandma. You have a life and a family. You have as much of a family as the rest of us. I know that Maureen is interested in you. Although, you don't have so much of her heart yet that you can continue to act like a jackass and get away with it."

"You cut to the quick, don't you?"

"Too old to mess around and in the long run, you might as well just get it out there in the first place. She's sweet on you, but you have to treat her with respect. No more garbage like this morning. It isn't her fault that you're coming out of a crisis. Don't punish her for it."

"I didn't mean to—I didn't think that's what I'm doing. I bet she even thinks I'm a bigger sap now, huh? But I-, I don't-, I mean-."

"Oh be quiet or I'll have to smack you on sheer principle. Do me a favor. Even if you don't think that she could possibly care about you, will you just pretend she might? For a few days, at least? Just try it and see how you feel. Will you do that for me?"

"Don't know what that will accomplish, but I guess. What're you swindling now?" he squinted at her.

"Sometimes you just need to act like you aren't spastic about something, to find out if you really are or not. By the time you figure it out, you're either over it or you don't care anymore. So it is better."

Carl made a face, "My God, now I know why Elton's so messed up!"

"Truthfully, I got messed up listening to him!" Katherine laughed. "Now, why don't you go take a shower and start this day over? And when you get time, will you apologize to Mo for being rude this morning?"

"Yes Ma. I will," Carl said sarcastically. Then he squeezed her hand, "Thanks Katherine."

38

Kincaid had just finished his shower and was getting ready to leave his room, when there was a knock. "Who is it?"

"It's Zach. May I come in?"

"Yah," Kincaid said as he buttoned his shirt.

"Hear you are a bit under the weather today, huh?" Zach asked. "Maybe I should listen to the old ticker."

"I'm fine, really," Kincaid answered, "Unless you have a cure for crabbiness."

"Oh how I wish I did. Too much excitement?" Zach studied his friend.

Just then, Carl got a dizzy spell and reached to the dresser to steady himself. Zach helped him sit down. "Look Dude! That isn't orneriness. Carl, tell me how you feel. And don't cover anything up."

Carl was frightened by his weakness. It was totally unexpected. "Honestly Zach, I thought I was having a crisis of some kind."

Zach raised his eyebrow, "You are."

Zach listened to his chest and then took his blood pressure. "How long have you felt this way?"

"Since yesterday, but mostly last night. Zach, between you and me?" the man's look penetrated the importance of the request, "Okay?"

"Of course."

"I cried last night. First time since Cecelia died. I think I'm cracking up. This morning, I could hardly stand being awake. What the hell's wrong with me?"

"Could be that you tried to do too much yesterday. I hear you dug in pipe, were in Merton, over at Darrell's, not in your wheelchair and then last night Harringtons came in. That is a lot for your system. You've been rather sedate, you know." Zach emphasized as he pulled up a chair, "Physically and emotionally. Give yourself a break. You can't ramrod yourself into being like you were. It just won't work."

Carl nodded, "I know, but I really didn't do too much yesterday. Well, maybe I did. I was very tired before dinner. Shit, won't I ever be able to do anything without feeling like this?"

"Yes, you will, but you will have to build up to it slowly."

"Can't you give me a pill?"

"I wish. It just takes time and exertorture."

"I don't think I could do that today," Kincaid said seriously.

"I agree, not a good idea. I'll let Pepper know. In fact, a couple days, but then you need to keep exercising and working on it. If not, it'll just get worse," Zach was unbending in his comment.

"I know. Zach, why do I feel so worthless?"

"Because you're physically very tired. I think that it might be that you wanted to do more now that Harringtons are here and have realized that you aren't going to be magically well just because you want to be. That is part of the depression."

"Man, I could hardly sit at the table this morning and I was so awful to Mo that Katherine gave me hell about it. I was just plain rude," he looked to Zach. "Is that part of it?"

Zach thought a minute, "Probably. Doctor-Patient, okay? Tell me the truth? How do you feel about her?"

"What's that got to do with anything?"

"Just answer me," Zach repeated in a no nonsense tone.

"I don't know. I really don't." Carl groaned, "Well, I might be pretty damned serious about her. By the time I left the hospital in Shreveport, we were pretty close. But I have nothing to offer and not even my health. I can't even walk up a damn slope without help. I might as well cash it in."

"Does she know how you feel?"

"I don't know. I kissed her last night and she didn't belt me," then he smiled at Zach, and then sat quietly a minute. He cleared his throat and then asked barely above a whisper, "Do you think that I'll be able to get frisky again? Or is my circulation too bad? I'm scared to death. I mean, not that she'd even consider it, but if she did, you know?"

"From what I know about your condition, you should be able to. We can make an appointment to see your cardiologist." Kincaid started to shake his head no. Zach patted his knee, "Want me to just ask him?"

"Could you? I know that's cowardice, but I'd rather die," Kincaid almost begged. "Because if I can't ever, I'll just go away. I'd rather not even see her. I want to have a relationship with her and I think I could even do all the stuff the women have been telling me—you know; honesty, feelings and all that crap, but if I can't even be a man, forget it."

"I think it's a lot brighter than what you think, Carl." Zach reassured his friend. "I have to go in this afternoon anyway. Do you want me to call the cardiologist today? Or what?"

"That'd be fine. I just need to know. You know, I'd hate being all cream puffy for nothing!"

"Oh, you're such a jackass!" Zach laughed. "I think you'll be fine, but I'll call the doctor this afternoon. Until then just be a cream puffy, because it's a lot more pleasant for everyone that way."

"Oh, Magpie asked me if I'd ride to town with him this afternoon. I suppose I can't go."

"You can, but I want you to take it easy this morning. Just visit with Lloyd or something. And when you get to town, don't be shopping all over . . . Wheelchair only today! Hear?"

"I hear. This is just another big dump, huh?" Carl needed reassurance.

"Pretty much. I think you're too worried about Harringtons' arrival and all this frisky business. Your health has taken quite a set back and you can't bounce back as quickly as you want. It may take time, but you'll be okay. So, try to take it easy. Remember, worrying is as bad on your heart and health as almost anything else. Let's go out there and eat before they clear the table."

Carl sat in the wheelchair. Before they went out the door, he grabbed Zach's hand. "Thanks."

Zach opened the door, "No problem."

Byron took the kids home after chores, since he knew that Kincaid wasn't feeling well. Carl felt bad about it because he knew they wanted to dig in more of the pipe. "They're going to be so disappointed," he mumbled.

"Why don't you call them after a bit and let them know you're feeling better?" Pepper suggested. "They'll like that. They don't want you to be sick."

"I'll do that," Kincaid nodded. "They might be glad to have a break from me."

"Doubt that," Darlene giggled, "You're their Job Supervisor. Who else draws out plans for water diversion for them?"

Keith grinned, "That's right. Like Mom said, you're the head of the Gopher Brigade. Besides you need to rest up, so you can come in and check out my shop this afternoon. Are you still coming in with Dad?"

"Zach said I can, but Magpie, we can't go shopping in a lot of stores!" Carl smiled for the first time.

"Hallelujah!" Nora giggled. "I can relax then!"

"Don't get to comfortable there, Lady," Elton teased, "There are always drive thru shopping places! 'Sides, that's what wheelchairs are for!"

"Yea gads."

After breakfast, Pepper took Harrington off to do his physical therapy. He grinned at Kincaid, "This shouldn't be too hard. She is just a little bit of a thing."

Carl made a face, "Just keep telling yourself that. We'll talk after you recuperate."

"Oh, that bad, huh?"

"Yup, and that's a blasted fact," Kincaid laughed.

Pepper shook her head, "Oh come on! Men are such big babies."

The ladies did up the dishes and Zach gave Grandpa Lloyd his bath before he went over to check on Carrie. Carl did a few things here and there, but mostly just felt in the way. He knew he needed to apologize to Mo, but that wasn't his favorite thing. When they finished drying the dishes, Carl cleared his throat and asked her. "Could I interest you in having a soda with me on the patio?"

"I should help the ladies put things away here," she smiled, but Carl got the message. He was going to have to work a little harder than that.

"That's okay," Nora said. "We're almost done."

Maureen shrugged, "I guess I've been fired. Okay, need help down the ramp?"

"No, I can make it by myself," he went to the refrigerator, "Seven Up?"

"Okay," she hung up her dishtowel and went to the door. She opened it for him and waited until he got to there. Then she followed him outside.

He stopped by the swing, "I need to talk to you."

"I would think so," Maureen said as she sat at the picnic table. "You weren't very nice. If you have a bone to pick with me, just say so. Don't embarrass me in front of everyone."

Carl was taken back. She was more of a no nonsense person than he had imagined and he knew that she didn't put up with much foolishness. "I'm sorry. I didn't feel good and I took it out on you. I don't have any bone to pick with you. I really didn't mean to embarrass you or anything. I just wanted to be well when you were here and I'm not. I got so frustrated that it made me mad at you."

"Coot, why didn't you just say so? You could've told me that last night. You don't need to be doing a jig for me. I don't expect that. You and Ian are a pair. Both beating yourselves up because you are not instantly well. All the Saints and Angels! Why do men have to be so macho?"

Carl chuckled, "Don't hold back there Mo."

"I was there when you almost croaked a few times, remember? Don't think you're going to impress me by throwing your ticker into spasm. But if you plan on making me the cat you kick when things don't go right for you, save yourself the energy. I've lived like that once and don't plan on doing it again. Thank you very much."

Kincaid was glad he was in his chair or he would have passed out. What did she mean by that? Should he ask her? Was it Sean? He figured he was not back in her good graces enough to go there. So he simply reached out his hand to hers. "I'm sorry. I won't do that again."

Maureen smiled, "Okay. If something is eating you; just tell me, but not in front of everyone."

"I will, but honestly Maureen, I wasn't sure just what was bothering me."

"Okay," she smiled. "Let's not waste the rest of the day over it. So, you're going to town with Elton this afternoon, huh?"

"If you don't want me to, I'll stay home," Kincaid offered sincerely.

"Not at all. Nora and I are going over to meet this Aunt Gilda. We are going to see Suzy's wedding dress. Don't imagine that would be up your alley."

"Not really. You'll like Gilda. She is a lot like you, but I like you better," he grinned.

"Oh brother," Mo teased, "You aren't going to win me over with faint praise, but I have to say, I like hearing it anyway."

Without a thought, he leaned over and gave her a kiss on the cheek. "Okay. I really am glad you came out. I was looking forward to it more than you know."

"I wouldn't have missed it, although I have to admit, a few hours ago I was wondering if it was worth my legs swelling up into tree stumps!"

"Huh?"

"On the airplane," Maureen giggled.

"Oh, by the way, Darlene and I made the Englemann Clan Map for you. Darlene We can go in and I can show it to you."

"Okay, sounds like a good idea. I think I must have met almost everyone last night, huh?" Maureen was hopeful.

Kincaid smiled, "No. You didn't."

"Lord have mercy!" Maureen laughed, "No wonder they invented birth control."

Inside, Carl went to get the Map and then he and all the ladies gathered around the table to look it over. Harrington and Pepper came out of the living room and joined them.

"You're right, Kincaid," Harrington moaned, "She is a tough little gal. Poor Chris, he won't be able to get away with a thing."

Pepper laughed, "That's right and that's the way it should be."

"Men should be in charge," Harrington pointed out.

The women all looked at him, Kincaid shook his head, "So very, very stupid, Harrington. That's one of those things we can think, but never say."

"Well, that comment wasn't very smart either!" Darlene poked, "No wonder it takes the FBI so long to get anything done. I bet women could do it faster."

Kincaid nodded, "I might have to agree. Ginger would make one heck of an interrogator!"

Harrington added, "I think that the Wee One will be a lot like her and Charlie. They have been real good for Miriam. She is really attached to Kevin, isn't she?"

Nora took out some paper, and said, "Yes. He's her special buddy. That is good. Everyone needs one. I'm going to write a grocery list to send with Elton. If you guys can think of anything you need or want, speak now or forever hold your peace. Think about what you'll need for the contest."

Darlene asked Carl, "Do you have your recipe from your friend? I can check it over for you, if you'd like. You'll need enough ingredients to make a couple practice runs."

Kincaid and Darlene went off to his bedroom to retrieve the recipe. Nora giggled, "My goodness, we are going to have eaten so much of this so often before the contest that we will probably be sick of all of it."

"Not my sauce," Kincaid boasted as he and Darlene gave the list of ingredients for he would need. "This should be a winner, right Darlene?"

"Yes, second place. Right after Keith's Bratwurst."

"Oh, I forgot," Carl said. "You'd probably want him to win, huh?"

39

On the way to town, Carl and Elton engaged in their usual banter without getting serious about much of anything. Carl wondered if Zach had said something to him or if he just seemed to know that Carl didn't want to go into anything about this morning. Elton was like that, almost clairvoyant sometimes.

There was a lot of talk about the contest. "You know, Kincaid, our little contest got out of control." Elton grinned. "Good grief, now everyone thinks they're a chef, even Miriam!"

Kincaid chuckled, "That's no lie. There'll be so much food; we'll never be able to eat it all. Your group always goes overboard."

"My group? What do you mean? You're as much in this group as anyone else," Elton blustered. "In fact, you're worse than a lot of them."

"How do you figure?" Carl asked, watching the farmers from the pickup window while they were cultivating their cornfields. It was a great sunny day and the rains had kept everything green.

"Who is up before dawn figuring how to get pipe for a downspout?" Elton laughed. "It sure wasn't me."

"That's different," Carl smiled. "I just knew the Gophers would like it. And besides, you might actually get some drainage for your yard. Sort of pay back for all the ruts we dug in it."

"I appreciate that," Elton nodded. "It was wrecking the suspension in my car every time I drove in. You guys should really take a whack at Preacher Man's yard."

Carl laughed, "I thought of that myself! I mean, after all, most of the Gophers are his! But then I figured he'd get all preachery and want us to fill them in."

"Yah, he probably would. Notice how quickly he and Marvin invoked God's aid in the contest! What a dirty deal! Guess it never dawned on them that God might prefer our cooking!" The men had a big belly laugh.

Elton slowed down as they followed a stack mover down the highway. It was loaded with a huge stack, from the abundant alfalfa crops.

"Oh, Nora gave me this enormous list of stuff to pick up. I want to pay something toward the cost of all this. It isn't right that you pay for all of it," Carl offered.

"Don't worry about it. Nora will use whatever's left or Lloyd will stir it into the flour during his wanderings some night. You know, I was thinking maybe I should lock up the pantry. Think that would help?"

Carl thought a bit, "Elton, you can't lock up everything. Good grief, you'd have to be a locksmith to cook breakfast! We just have to keep an eye on Lloyd. I'm glad that Katherine can sleep through most of it."

Elton drove slowly for a while until he could pass the creeping stack mover, "I want to thank you for all the time that you spend talking to Lloyd at night. It really helps. I know I don't know every time he is up, but I know it is a lot. I have to admit, I was getting worn out."

"Can see where that could happen," Kincaid said. "He's a kind soul."

"He really is," Elton agreed. "He gave me a second chance when few others would have. Whenever I doubted I could do right by Nora and the kids, he said I could. Actually, he said he would box my ears if I didn't, but the message was the same."

Carl listened carefully, and then grinned, "Did he make you buy a cow?"

"You know, he didn't right away. I suppose because Nora and I got married sooner than we had planned and then adopted the kids right away. It wasn't until it was all done about two months and I was up one night rocking Pepper, that I wondered what in the hell I had gotten myself into."

"Did you ever regret it? You were a bachelor for a long time," Kincaid asked seriously.

"Nope. Never did. You know, I never really enjoyed being a bachelor that much. I would leave work, go to the bar and get hammered. Sometimes pick up some barfly and get laid. Wake up with a hangover and wonder where my money went. That isn't much to look forward to every day."

Carl nodded, knowing full well what Elton meant. "It must have been a heck of a change though?"

Elton laughed, "Maybe if it had happened the regular way, but with all the hospital stuff, everything got clouded by that. By the time every one was on the mend, a few months had passed. I was married before I knew I was, you know?"

"Hmm." Carl said thoughtfully. "I know when Cecelia was alive, I never imagined being with anyone else. Didn't even want to. The car wreck took care of that."

"That must've been horrible. I can't imagine how you lived through that. I don't know if I'd have been able to," Elton said sympathetically.

"Ah, you could. I did and you're much more that way then I am."

"I wasn't always, Carl, and still am not. Hell, not long ago when Pepper's real uncle Ned tried to rape her, I only wanted to kill him. I couldn't think of anything else. Good thing the boys stopped me," Elton admitted. "And then of course, Katherine got her old dial finger out and called Preacher Man right away. Man, I got more than one lecture over that! I hated to see his car drive up."

"I never knew anything about that. But then, I guess that's not for publication, huh?" Kincaid was amazed. "How long ago did this happen?"

"Oh, early this spring, before Ginger's deal with the spot remover. I had to keep Preacher Man from going nuts over that adventure. See, we don't really have it together better than anyone else. We just try keep an eye on the other guy. When one of us starts to wig out, the other guy drags him back to reality."

Kincaid was lost in thought for a while, "So, is Pepper's uncle in jail? Was he a clanner?"

"No and no. I wanted to have him arrested, but Pepper was terrified of the trial. You know how messy they can get. Ned doesn't live here, so he wouldn't have cared; but Pepper would've had to face all the gossip. We decided not to press charges. Ned's dad promised to put him in therapy. I still wanted to beat the hell out of him. My damn hand gave out on me.'

"Oh, that's how you got the cast that you kept trying to saw off?" Kincaid smiled at his friend; trying to put all this new information into the biography he was building. "You're quite the Magpie."

"Now you know, I don't have it together," Elton said flatly.

"I think you do. I only have my whiskey."

"I used to try that, but hell, it doesn't give such good advice! At least the brand I drank didn't!" Elton laughed.

Kincaid chuckled and then fell back into deep thought. Finally he asked, "Do you think there comes a time when a person shouldn't think about getting married and settling down?"

"Don't know. As long as you are alive, there's time to make a change. In some ways, it is harder when you are older and in some ways a lot easier. I mean, at our age, we are pretty set in our ways, but we don't have the unrealistic notions that young folks do. Then again, we have to be careful to not be too cynical. I imagine in your line of work, it could be difficult."

"I guess, but even I know that not everyone is a deceitful conniver. I probably think a lot more about it than you do, but then you're too far the other way."

"Sometimes, but I'm not as understanding and forgiving as Byron. I'm sure glad he is that way. I'd still be roaming the bars of Bismarck if he hadn't come in for gas that day."

"Doubt it. I think you were always a Petunia. You just didn't have yourself convinced yet," Kincaid observed.

"So, what do you have yourself convinced that you are, Kincaid?" he asked pointedly.

"Not a Petunia, but I have to admit," Carl's voice became very quiet, "I am a lot more cream puff than I used to be."

"Not so bad, is it?" Elton grinned.

"Sometimes. I actually enjoy it sometimes, just sometimes! Yea gads! It about drives me crazy some days. You know, I went from no one to a houseful. I'd never been around kids in my life! With the wheelchair now, sometimes the kids think I'm a lap on wheels!"

Elton burst out in laughter. "You should tell them to back off when they get to be too much."

"Like you do? I hear you say that all the time!" Carl raised his eyebrows.

"I guess that's true. My notion is this is your fate. We can either fight it or give in to it. I figure, giving in to it is a lot easier." Elton changed the subject, "I have to say, I was quite taken back that Harrington was as bad as he was. I should've known better,"

"Me too. Poor kid. I bet it is just killing him. He was a good detective. Now, what the hell will he do? We can't all sit around and entertain little kids."

"Carl, don't put down what you do. Miriam isn't like any other kid and neither is Ginger. Although, she's getting back to her old self again. Not everyone would take the time or the patience to help them. You're good at it."

"Thanks," Carl said sincerely, "But sometimes, I'd just like to go cuss out some scuzzbelly out and kick the crap out of them. Know what I mean?"

Elton laughed, "Sadly, I really do. Probably wouldn't be a good thing with the kids, huh? Hey, what do you say we hit a cowboy bar and break some bottles over heads?"

The men stopped in the gas station and Keith and Kincaid shared a Coke while Elton looked at the hydraulic lift. After he did, he joined them. "I think you might as well get some new hoses. In fact, I would get them for both the car bays. These are pretty ratty."

"Okay. That's what I was thinking," Keith agreed. "Just wanted a second opinion. I'll do that today. So, Carl, are you ready to come work for me?"

"Only if I can arrest someone!" Kincaid laughed.

"As much as you can with the Gophers," Keith grinned.

"But they don't know that. I gave Charlie ten to life the other day and he thinks I can really do it!"

Keith had a good laugh. "He probably needs it!"

Kincaid didn't even grump when Elton set his wheelchair up at the Warehouse Market. Simply the looks of the outside of the store made Carl tired. "Are we going through that whole place?"

Elton laughed, "As much as we can, unless you poop out on me. Since Nora limited our shopping today to one store! I say we show her how much stuff we can buy at one store! She'll wish she'd let us go to the Hardware Store!!"

"I got the list and you better get a cart or two! There's a lot of stuff on it."

It took them over two hours to make it through the whole market. They bought spices, sauces, candy, anything that either of them thought looked good and even a few things that neither of them had ever seen before, simply because they had never seen it before! Mostly, it just had to be on the shelf. After going through the grocery area, they got to the 'seasonal' aisle.

There was an entire section that apparently Nora didn't know was there, with patio things. They bought Tiki torches, plastic plates with matching napkins and each got a big straw hat with leaf fringe on it to go with their garishly colored flowered Hawaiian shirts.

After they took a deep breath, they decided they were selfish. So they took another run at it.

This time, they bought Lloyd a hat like theirs and got Katherine, Nora and Mo each a muumuu. They got a beautiful, artificial flower lei for Katie and the little kids each got a coconut shaped cup with an attached straw. Then they felt bad for the older kids and bought two huge boxes of tropical candies. They also bought a case of fresh pineapple, just because it was there. When they got to the check out, they almost passed out. They had spent a fortune, but convinced themselves it was worth it while they both emptied their wallets.

When everything was finally packed into the back of the pickup, Elton said, "I'm having the kids unload this when I get home. We should seriously consider Shoppers Anonymous, Kincaid. I think that Nora will probably flatten my hat with a frying pan when she sees all this."

"Will she really be mad?" Kincaid was concerned.

"Nah, but that won't stop her from giving me the business!"

40

They were correct. They were in big trouble. Had they not come in the house wearing their stupid straw hats and grinning like a pair of chimpanzees; it probably wouldn't have generated quite so much fervor! Even Grandpa Lloyd thought they were crazy.

No way on God's green earth would Lloyd even put the straw hat on his head! Instead he gave it to Charlie who had come over to do the Chicken Man Chores. Even though it was about six sizes too big, he loved it. He wore it to the coop. The poor little kid could hardly see where he was going because it kept falling over his eyes, but he wore it anyway!

Zach, Darlene and Ian helped bring the things in from the pickup. They ended up loading up Andy's old red wagon to bring the stuff in. Every trip, Nora would shake her head. Maureen just giggled and Grandma offered to write up their last will and testaments.

Finally it was all in, except the Tiki torches that were left on the patio. Before they had their coffee, the guys decided it would be wise to hand out the gifts. Maybe that would alleviate the trouble they were in.

After they handed the candies to Zach, Darlene and Ian, they were in good graces with them. Everyone was in agreement that Katie would love the lei and the little kids would like their cups. The muumuus might have gone over better, if their own Hawaiian shirts had not fallen out of the same bag.

Nora looked at Elton in disgust, "I don't ever want to hear you whine again about wearing your suit. You hear? And you better wear this crazy thing!"

Elton gave his wife a kiss, "Yes ma'am. Do you like your muumuu?"

Nora looked it over, "It's very nice. I love the sunset colors, but really Elton. Where am I going to wear it?"

"Right here," Elton was shocked that was even a question. "Look, Katherine and Mo got ones too. You guys can all wear them."

Katherine held hers up. It was several shades of blue flowers. "It is beautiful, but Elton! How tall do you think I am? I will have to cut enough off the bottom to make another one!"

He grinned, "Kincaid and I talked about that! We figured you could make muumuus for the little Gophers girls. They didn't have any kids ones or we would have bought them."

Nora rolled her eyes, "I'm sure you would've."

Mo took hers out of the bag, "It is beautiful. All the deep reds and maroons. Thank you Elton."

"You are welcome, but actually it is from Kincaid. He and I went together to get Katherine's because we both love her. Then I got Nora hers and he got you yours. See?" Elton could feel himself going over the cliff. He didn't dare look at Kincaid. He didn't need to. He could feel his laser eyes burning holes through his flesh.

Maureen smiled and gave Kincaid a big hug and a kiss on the cheek, "Thank you, you old Coot. That was very sweet."

Carl beamed and then Elton felt it might be safe to look his way. Carl just raised his eyebrows to say, 'You just barely skated by that one, Buddy.'

Then the attention turned to all the groceries still waiting to be put away. Nora asked, "What on earth were you thinking when you bought all this pineapple?"

"For the cooking contest," Elton answered numbly.

"Dad, they are very nice, but they won't last for two weeks," Darlene pointed out.

"We thought about that, didn't we Magpie?" Kincaid tried to justify their purchase. "Do you remember what we decided?"

"Ah," Elton was thinking as fast as he could. "We started to decide but then thought you girls would have the best ideas. Wasn't that it, Kincaid?"

Zach burst out laughing and looked at Harrington, "I hope we never get that bad."

After things were put away, Carl went to his room to rest a bit before dinner, while the other guys got ready to do chores. There was a knock at the door and it was Zach. "I thought you would want to know, I spoke with your cardiologist. He said that you should be fine, but you need to be careful at first. Your heart isn't up to par yet, but it is getting better. We can talk more about it later. I just thought you'd want to know,"

"Thanks, I really appreciate you finding out for me. A huge relief."

"I can imagine. It is not a question that comes up in my pediatric practice a lot!" Zach grinned. "Well, I better go help with the milking. We can talk in more detail later. Okay?"

"Okay."

Carl turned over on his bed, flooded with relief. It was really nice of Zach to find out for him and such a relief to know that he'd be okay. A huge ton of worry had been lifted off his shoulders. It had turned out to be a pretty good day after all. He felt a lot better.

Dinner was a lot of fun and afterwards, there were a couple tables of Whist. Carl and Mo clobbered Zach and Suzy, while Elton and Nora whipped Ian and Ruthie. Ruthie complained, claiming that cards had not been a requirement at the convent. After Coot and Elton finished harassing her with Bingo stories, Ruthie backed off. But she was still certain that Father Matthew would back her up if asked.

Ian decided that rather than play another hand, they would go for a walk back down to the shop and check out the airplane.

"I sure hope you two are working on it! Seems to me there is a lot of looking and not much work getting done," Elton chided.

"We'll work on it tomorrow," Zach announced, "That is if you two go down there instead of running around Bismarck with your wallets open. By the way, tomorrow night Ian and I are practicing our recipe for the contest at my apartment. So we won't be here for dinner, Nora. Or our girls either."

"Thanks for telling me. I guess Keith and Darlene are going to the movies with some of their friends and Kevin and Carrie are going over to Darrell's place to practice their recipes. Pepper is going to Holloways' after work to practice Mrs. Holloway's barbeque sauce that she and Chris are using for their chicken." Nora added thoughtfully, "You know, there are so many entries, I think I may withdraw my Marinated Spare Ribs. We are going to have way too much meat!"

Elton's eyes lit up like a Christmas tree. Nora noticed and frowned, "Oh no Gas Jockey, don't even think about it. I won't be your partner, so don't ever bother to butter me up."

"Not fair, you know," Elton pouted. "Darlene has been helping Kincaid with his sauce. I don't hardly think that is right."

"Oh honey, you'll live," Nora giggled. "Did you guys hear all the entries? There are so many without my ribs! We can have them some other time. I think this will be more than enough," Nora suggested.

"But your ribs are good, Nora," Elton said.

"I don't care about a ribbon, though. You do. I'd hate to win the prize you covet and then have to listen to you whine about it all winter," Nora jabbed.

"You know Lady, I could take your muumuu back. They have a return counter at that store," Elton teased.

"Hmm," Zach considered, "I wasn't aware there was another fish entry. Darlene and Glenda, huh? Looks like we have our work cut out for us, Harrington. Those gals know their way around a kitchen."

Ian grinned, "But do they know their way around a grill?"

Kincaid laughed, "We'll see. No need for you to get all competitive with the girls, because I'm going to win anyway."

"When are you going to practice?" Mo asked.

Kincaid turned white, "Ah, I don't know. Whenever Nora says I can, I guess."

"Why don't you guys practice all your stuff tomorrow since all us kids will be out of your hair. Annie is at the Fire Hall. It will be almost boring around here," Suzy giggled.

"Just why, little girl," Elton huffed and puffed, "Do you think that we'd be bored when it is just us? We have plenty of wind in our sails yet!"

Zack cracked up, "Yup, wind as in hot air! Okay then. Tomorrow we'll work on the plane and then after chores, leave you old sailors to do your thing. How does that sound?"

"I don't even like you," Elton snorted to Zach. "You can be downright obnoxious."

Zach and Suzy walked over to check out what their contractor had done that day, while Harrington and Ruthie went to the shop. Kincaid, Mo, Elton and Nora went to the patio for the guys to have their evening cigarette.

Elton sat on the glider and then drew Nora to sit with him, "This is the first time that I have sat in this cuddling swing. Ever since we got it, some kid has gotten here first. Those brats! Actually thinking we'd be bored without their company!"

Nora patted his knee. "Calm down, they just don't get it."

Kincaid and Mo had taken seats on the two rocking chairs. Kincaid looked around, "Where are we going to put the Tiki torches?"

"We'll have to figure that out," Elton replied. "Not tonight though, I think that shopping tired me out."

"I actually feel pretty good tonight," Kincaid grinned. "A wheelchair is the only way to go to Warehouse Market."

"You have that right," Elton agreed. "So are we really going to practice our entries tomorrow night? The kids might have a good idea there, since they won't be sneaking around taking notes."

"We could," Nora said, "What do you think Maureen?"

"I guess so. What are all our entries?"

"Let's see, besides the meat, your baked beans, my dinner rolls, and Carl and Katherine's Hot German potato salad. Then for dessert we will have Katherine's sour cream raisin pie and your cranberry apple pie, Mo. How does that sound?" Nora asked.

"Sounds great to me," Elton crowed. "How many steaks should I plan on? And how many ribs should Kincaid cook up?"

"There'll only be six of us, so maybe three steaks and three pounds of ribs?" Nora suggested. "What do you think Mo?"

"I think it sounds good. I could make my pie some other time," Mo offered.

Elton immediately responded, "No. We need some for dessert and then another pie before bed. Two pies sound about right!"

"I swear this guy has a tape worm!" Kincaid groaned. "He eats steady."

The two couples had a nice visit and then Nora and Elton decided to go in. "This cuddling swing is giving me ideas," he laughed.

Nora crossed her eyes, "You don't need a swing to get ideas!"

"Get out of here. You two are making me sick," Kincaid groused. "Good night!"

After they went in, Kincaid and Maureen sat and rocked quietly for a bit. Then he chuckled, "Hey, want to try out the cuddling swing?"

"Is that really what folks around here call it?" Mo asked innocently.

"No, just Magpie. Let's see if it lives up to the reputation," he moved over to the swing and Mo joined him.

"It is nice," Mo smiled as she leaned back on the cushioning. "It is as comfortable as the rocking chair."

Carl put his arm over her shoulder, "I hope you have forgotten what a jackass I was this morning."

Mo smiled, "I can't forget if you continue to remind me to forget it."

"Well, I really feel bad about it. I had a lot on my mind. I wanted to impress you and I was mad first at myself because I couldn't and then at you because I couldn't."

Maureen watched his face with a small smile, "You don't need to impress me. Let's forget it, okay? We're too old to waste time dwelling on something."

Carl grinned, "That's my girl."

Then he leaned back for a bit and looked off into the yard. He asked softly, "You are, you know? Or do you have guy in Boston?"

"No, there's no guy in Boston, but I didn't know you wanted me to be your girl. Are you my guy?"

"Hmm. I could be convinced."

"Maybe I need to be convinced," Mo teased. "That sounded a little male chauvinist."

"More than a little," Kincaid agreed with a chuckle. "Darlene would have my head on a chopping block!"

"Well I guess we need some equal convincing?" Maureen suggested.

They kissed each other and it quickly turned into a passionate embrace. They backed away. They were both surprised at their passion for each other.

Kincaid took her hand, "We'd better be careful. We're playing with dynamite."

Maureen agreed, "And Suzy thinks we would be bored!"

Carl cleared his throat and leaned back again, "Did you have a good day? How do you and Nora get along?"

"We get along great. Katherine is a real firecracker! I think she is almost more women's lib than Darlene! We had a ball. I like them all. And then we went over to Gilda's. She is a riot, but you should have warned me. I didn't know she learned her hugs from Killer Kowalski! I almost had to call Zachie in to wrap my ribs! Have you seen Suzy's wedding dress? It is fantastic."

"No, I haven't. I heard them talk about it, but I don't understand most of that stuff. I have to say, I've learned more about girl stuff this last while than I ever knew in my whole life. Sometimes, it is a relief to go digging with the Gophers."

Maureen smiled, "I bet. How are you dealing with the changes, Carl? I imagine it has been hard for you. No job and all. I know it has been beastly for Ian. He tries to cover it up, but it's still killing him."

"I'm doing okay. I mean, I have my ups and downs, like this morning. I don't know how long I can tolerate it, but things are okay. Some of it, I really like, in fact." Carl tightened his arm around Maureen. "I know I'm going to have to decide what I'm going to do pretty soon, but not yet. These guys all said I should just take it easy until it is time. That there's no rush. Does that make sense to you?"

"Yes, it does. I'm glad you're taking their advice," then her eyes glinted with laughter, "But I'd wager the Oldsmobile that you fought it all the way!"

Kincaid laughed, "You got me there. I hate almost all of it, especially that exertorture. Hey, how did Ian's physical therapy go today?"

"Good," Mo leaned her head on his shoulder. "You know Carl, he just can't get his strength back like he wants."

"Or as fast as he wants, would be my guess," Carl observed. "I know the feeling. Mo, has he made any plans as far as a job or getting married? Or is it too soon?"

She sighed, "He wants to be married already and have a good job like he had. But there is a lot to work out on both fronts. I don't know how he'll handle it."

"Maybe he and I'll talk about it. Not that I have any answers, but at least he'll know I understand the questions," Kincaid offered.

"That'd be very nice. I don't believe anyone can give him a good answer right now; because it's such a turmoil," Mo thought aloud.

"Yah. That's so right."

The couple leaned back with Mo cuddled in the crook of his arm and watched the starry sky. Finally, they heard Suzy and Zach telling each other goodnight at Suzy's car. After she left, Zach came toward the house. He told them good night and went in.

"Elton always says his front yard reminds him of Peyton Place!" Kincaid laughed.

"I think he's right about that," Maureen agreed. "Well, we'd better get on in ourselves. Sounds like tomorrow is going to be a busy one."

"Before I came here, I thought I'd be bored out of my mind every minute. As it is, I hardly have a spare second!" Carl laughed.

He gave her another long kiss and then they went in. At her bedroom door, he kissed her on the check and said, "Good night, my girl."

"Good night, Carl," Maureen replied.

41

Pepper's alarm jarred Kincaid out of the most restful sleep he had had in years. Maybe he was just really tired but he thought it was more than that. He really cared about Maureen and was thrilled that she seemed to feel the same. How much or for how long? It was too soon to tell. But it was more than he could've hoped for.

He took his shower and got dressed. He stared at his wheelchair for a few seconds and then decided to just sit down and hush up about it. Maureen didn't seem to be of a nature to go through yesterday's rigmarole on a regular basis. He wanted this to be a good day.

As soon as they gathered around the trusty old coffeepot, Nora reminded everyone to get their meat out of the freezer for their cooking that evening. Elton volunteered to bring up some ribs for Kincaid when he got his steaks. After extracting a promise that he wouldn't replace them with lizard ribs or something, Carl thanked him.

"Gee, I can't understand why no one appreciates how nice I am?" Elton looked for sympathy.

"Sorry Dad, you need to ask a different crowd to get the answers you want," Pepper tormented. "We all know you way too well."

"Cut to the quick! See that?" Elton feigned pain and everyone ignored him. Then he laughed, "Hey, take some pineapple to Holloways. You grab some for Preacher Man, and anyone else you can think of. Okay?"

"Yes Dad," Kevin chuckled. "We will. You just wait until you get your smackers on our Cornish Game Hens, right Carrie?"

"They're really good," Carrie smiled. "I have to say, I am impressed. Miriam and I are going to practice the chocolate cream pie one more time.

I got Mr. Bear's apron finished last night. You guys should've seen her. She was really funny with him. She'd poke her finger in the whipped cream and then hold it to his mouth and say Ooops! Then she licked it herself and giggled until she got the hiccoughs. She can really giggle."

"You seem to have found her funny bone, Carrie. The other night at dinner, she was almost an extrovert!" Keith grinned. "I bet that is her real personality, huh? Really outgoing?"

"Might be. Or else she learned it from Ginger and Charlie! Speaking of which, here they come. Prepare yourself Kincaid. Whirlwind has his shovel and is wearing the huge straw hat! You're going to have fun today!" Kevin laughed as he opened the door for the Ellisons. "Where is my Miriam?"

"She is getting her bear tails in and was a little pokey. Marly is going to bring her over when they are done," Byron explained. "How's the crew this morning?"

"Why we are just a galaxy of little sunshines surrounding your planet, Pastor Ellison," Maureen patted him on the back.

"Boy! Sounds like you guys had enough sleep last night," Byron grinned. "Say, Marly and I wanted to ask Elton, Nora, Kincaid and Mo out to dinner tomorrow night. The rest of you'll have to divide up the kids, if that is okay?"

Carrie smiled, "We were going to have Jeannie and Darrell over for pizza, so sure. We can take the kids. No problem."

"Suzy, Ruthie, Ian and I will stay with the Grandparents here," Zach suggested. "We want to practice Whist anyway because we think you guys cheat."

Byron smiled, "We're thinking either the Riverside or the Cattlemen's? Your choice."

"Might be easier for Kincaid to get in and out of the Cattlemen's, huh?" Elton pointed out.

"Maybe I don't need the chair?" Kincaid asked hopefully.

He was greeted with a unanimous no!

"Okay, Okay. No need to get all huffy!"

Byron nodded. "Okay, the Cattlemen's at six-thirty?"

"Wow!" Zach groaned, "You leaving us poor children with all the chores?"

"Why, I believe that is the plan, young man. It builds character," Byron laughed.

"I don't know if they can take two nights without us," Pepper teased.

"We'll tough it out, Babe," Elton poked. "Trust me."

Before he went to the shop, Elton mixed up his marinade. He started with soy sauce and Sake. Then it became a dump, taste and dump some more process. He had lemon and a whole myriad of spices in the sauce. Then he set it aside in the fridge so he could put his steaks in the marinade before cooking.

Carl and Harrington went outside with the Gophers. The kids were very excited about digging the pipe in across the drive way. Carl took the front with Ginger and Miriam while Harrington and Charlie filled in after the pipe was laid. It was quite the process but by noon, the project was completed across the road.

Charlie had serious problems keeping his humungous hat on his head until Harrington told him to run in house and ask for a shoestring or yarn. He came out with one and the men fashioned a tie around it. Charlie was elated, oblivious to how the purple yarn looked jammed through the holes in the loosely woven reeds of the hat. When it was tied under his chin, the top had a crease across his head. It crammed the whole shebang down over his ears.

Ginger just looked and rolled her eyes, but never said anything. Miriam however, started to giggle. Charlie gave her a dirty look. "When you're over being frad jelly, I'm going to so whop you!"

"Charles?" Kincaid questioned, "What did you say?"

"I'm sorry, Agent. Maybe I won't whop her. I'll give her ten to life," Charlie announced.

Kincaid looked at Harrington and they both tried to conceal their laughter. Meanwhile, Miriam patted her chest and said with pride, "Ten to life!"

Harrington shook his head, "You're going to have explaining to do."

Carl agreed and told Harrington, "I might want to go to church with you guys this Sunday."

Charlie heard that and went into a tailspin. "You can't go the Catlik church. You are the sitter-by-me guy. I'll have to sit by Mom if you don't come. She doesn't let me get figgetty. I'll be done for."

Kincaid pulled the little guy into a hug, "I won't leave you. I'll sit beside you in church like always. Okay? You can count on that."

"Okay. Otherwise, I might have to go to the Catlik place to so I can sit by you there. Ginger told me that they clean up messes at the Catlik church."

"No Charlie, they have Masses," Harrington started to explain.

"I know, that's what I said." Charlie hopped off Kincaid's lap and started patting down the last of the dirt. "I hope we have jelly sandwiches for lunch. I'm hungry, aren't you?"

Miriam and Ginger nodded yes. Carl and Ian glanced at each other and smiled.

"What do you think, Ian? I suppose you want at least a dozen, huh?" Carl poked.

Crossing his eyes, he grimaced, "At least."

After lunch the kids all went home, Ian took a long nap. After a short rest, Carl started his sauce. He had simmered his ribs in spiced marinade in the morning while they were digging outside. The sauce was done in no time, because he and Darlene had made the spicy part and chilled it before. Now all he had left to do was add the tomato paste and then put the sauce over the ribs before he put them on the grill that evening.

He and Darlene had done a lot of tasting and thought it was pretty good. Maybe a bit on the hot side, but Kincaid liked it that way. However, now when he tasted the sauce, it was so hot he could hardly swallow it. As he was guzzling gallons of water, it came back to him what his coworker had said. 'The longer it sits, the hotter it gets.'

He looked at the pan of sauce through his watering eyes and panicked. He kept opening tomato paste, but there wasn't enough. In order to dilute this down to edible, he'd require at least a 50 gallon drum of tomato paste. Darlene had gone over to her Mom's and he didn't know what to do.

He couldn't ask Nora, because she had threatened both him and Elton with heinous death if they even started. Grandma was taking a nap. Should he ask Mo? Would Elton think that was cheating? Would she think he was cheating?

He couldn't stand it and finally asked Nora for Darlene's mom's phone number. He wasn't sure if he saw her giggle; but at that point, it didn't matter. He got the phone number. He put in his emergency call to Darlene.

Mo and Nora sat in the living room and tried to contain their laughter. He knew it. He could hear them. He decided they better keep their mouth shut. If they'd said one thing to him, he wouldn't be held responsible for the outcome.

Darlene was very shocked to receive a call from Kincaid, let alone an emergency one. He tried to whisper as quietly as he could and still be heard over the phone. He was almost certain that he heard Nora and Mo giggling in the other room, hanging on his every word. Darlene couldn't make out the situation and finally offered to come home. "Will that be okay?"

"Bless you Darlene. You're an angel. I love you with all my heart!" the old FBI agent blurted out.

Darlene was very gracious and didn't even crack a smile when she got in the kitchen. Kincaid huddled with her where he met her in the mud room, so the ladies wouldn't hear and told her his dilemma. She listened to the whole thing and patted his shoulder. "We can fix it. Don't worry."

They went into the kitchen and Darlene dumped three fourths of the sauce down the sink. They refilled it with the tomato paste she had brought from her mother's house. It was a lot better, but still very hot. Darlene suggested they add molasses and a brown sugar. They messed with it until they got it about right.

"Add a little more tomato paste tonight before you put it on the meat and you should be okay. I'll stop in Merton and pick up more tomato paste. Okay? It really is pretty good, Kincaid." Darlene reassured him.

Carl Kincaid decided then and there that he had just encountered the most wonderful angel in the world! "Thank you so much, Darlene. Tell your Mom thanks, too. I was really panicked. You better pick up a case of paste, huh? I'll never be able to repay you!"

Darlene gave him a hug, "Ah, you'd have figured it out once you calmed down. It's good. You are just fine."

"I love you."

Then she giggled, "And I love you too. Now, get to work on your potato salad. I'm not helping you with that."

"I think I need a break after this!"

"I think you need to start on your potato salad. I'll stop at the Piggly Wiggly in Merton and go over to Mom's."

"Here's some cash for the tomato sauce. Be sure to thank your Mom and replace hers. She's a saint!"

By the time Grandma woke up from her nap, Kincaid had the potatoes and onions all diced for the salad. All that was left was the last minute details before supper. Carl went to take a rest. As he wheeled through the living room, he thought he might've heard a couple snickers, but after a filthy glare; he chose to ignore the women.

He went in his room and closed the door. He would've locked it, but that would've been silly. He had lost all sense of dignity. He needed a break from the obvious merriment that his cooking had brought to the women. Women that he used to admire! Now, he knew their true colors and it wasn't pretty.

He got out of his chair and stretched out on his bed. When he put his arm by his head, he felt something wet and sticky. He looked at his arm. It was covered in barbeque sauce. "I have to get out of here!" he moaned to himself.

42

After chores, the six prepared for their tastings. It was a beautiful evening, so the ladies decided to eat out on the patio. Kincaid assured them that the Tiki torches had something in them that would keep away the mosquitoes. He and Elton were anxious to test them out.

The girls worked hard that morning to get their muumuus shortened. None of them wanted them floor length for around the house. There was plenty of material left over so they could make a short muumuu for Miriam, Ginger and Maddie Lynn. They offered to make one for Katie, but she thought she would rather have just a top. Charlie thought he should have a shirt like Coot and Uncle Elton, so the ladies promised they would make him one. It would be his Chicken Man uniform. Miriam wanted a shirt for Mr. Bear too.

While the ladies fussed with the table, the men placed the torches and then started the grill. They brought Lloyd out and got him comfortable in a rocking chair. He seemed content to sit there and said nothing about wanting to help cook. The ladies thought it was mostly because he didn't want to stand anywhere near the guys while wearing their Hawaiian shirts and straw hats. Every so often, he'd look at them and roll his eyes.

The food smelled delicious. Elton had placed his rib steaks in the marinade about twenty minutes before cooking and Kincaid put the last of the tomato paste into his sauce. It was diluted enough now to be not so hot. Then he smothered one side of his ribs and placed them over the hot coals. They smelled wonderful.

After a few minutes, he turned them over and then smothered the other side. Elton put his steaks on the other end of the grill. Now, Lloyd was interested. The aroma from the meat was mouthwatering and he decided he should put something on the grill too.

There wasn't anything for him to put on, so Nora ran to the house and got a piece of boiled chicken and brought it out to him.

He smelled it and curled up his nose. Then he placed it in Elton's marinade for a bit and kept poking it with the fork. Finally, he took it out and put it on the grill and slobbered some of Kincaid's sauce on top of it. He grinned and was proud as a peacock.

When the men took their meat off and put it on the platters, Lloyd also took his off. He put it on a plate with the announcement, "Now, this is how it's supposed to be!"

They all clapped and he sat down. Elton cut each of his steaks in half and gave everyone a half. Kincaid divided up his ribs into six portions, and then Lloyd took the knife. He cut his piece of chicken into several smaller pieces and put them all on his own plate. When the ladies asked if they were going to get to taste it, he reluctantly gave them each a tiny piece but saved the rest for himself.

After grace, there was a lot of tasting and raving. Of course, Nora's dinner rolls were fluffy and delicious. She always made great rolls. Everyone agreed that Maureen's baked beans were the best they'd ever tasted. Katherine and Carl's Hot German potato salad was perfect. The amount of vinegar was just right.

Then they tasted the steaks. Everyone took a bite and chewed. They were thoughtful and then began to nod. Yes, they were wonderful. It was an interesting mixture of sweet and spicy. They were done to perfection. Even Carl had to say they were very good.

They each took a bite of the tender ribs. They were mouthwatering. They weren't too spicy, although they packed a bit of a punch. The molasses really added something to them. Carl was happy with them.

Then Lloyd said, "Taste my hamburger. It's the best. You haven't tasted my hamburger yet."

"You're right, Lloyd. We were saving the best until last!" Elton said as he took a piece of chicken from Lloyd's plate and popped it into his mouth. He couldn't believe it. It was wonderful. It was by far, the best chicken barbeque he had ever tasted. "Wow! That's really fantastic!"

Lloyd gloated, "Told you so."

The rest tasted it and all had to agree. It really was the best. Lloyd's super chicken had won the contest that evening, hands down, even though he thought it was hamburger.

They finished their meal with Katherine's sour cream raisin pie. It was always great. After the table was cleared and fresh coffee poured, they decided to taste the Mo's cranberry apple. It was very wonderful combination of sweet and tart, and great with vanilla ice cream. They had eaten everything! It was amazing.

The chef's all relaxed and complimented themselves. They didn't need a contest. They were certain they were the best.

Later, after dishes were finished and the grandparents had gone to bed, the others went out to the patio. The men lit the Tiki torches which did seem to keep the mosquitoes away. However, they emitted an odor that would keep away most of God's creatures. It finally got so strong that their eyes were watering, so they had to be snuffed out.

"I think that Aaron and his wife had something like that, except they were like candles in little buckets," Mo shared. "After they were lit, we all started to get sick and went in the house."

"Is Aaron one of your kids?" Elton asked.

Mo smiled, "He is the oldest. He's going to be forty in a couple months! Can you believe that? That makes me old, huh?"

Elton laughed, "I prefer to think of it as 'not dead'!"

Maureen giggled. "I like that!"

"So, tell us about your family," Nora was interested. "Aaron is married?"

"Yes, he and his wife, Theresa have three kids. Liddy, Pete and Joey. The next is Patrick. He and his wife Margie have two, Lonnie and Lorraine. Then it's James and his wife Vivian. They have five kids, Jimmy, Bobby, Mack, Bill and Linda. Thank goodness they finally had a girl, or they'd still be at it! Then there are my girls; Colleen and her husband Frank have two kids, Frankie and Molly. Next, Nancy and her husband John. They have three, Tony, Tammy and John Junior, but everyone calls him Turk."

"Turk?" Kincaid was shocked, "How did he get to be Turk in a bunch of Irishmen?"

"It's a horrible story. He weighed over ten pounds when he was born. His Uncle Pat thought he looked like a Thanksgiving turkey. He has been called Turk ever since! He's about Charlie's age. I'm afraid if those two every met, the world would never be the same!" Maureen laughed. "The last girl is Abby. She and Allen got married a year ago last spring and are expecting in November. So, that's the rest of my crew."

"Sound like a fine family. Do they all live near you?" Nora asked.

"All in Boston, except for Abby. She and Allen live in Maryland. He works in the shipyards and she works for an insurance company there. The rest are all nearby, in fact within a few blocks of me. It's nice, but it can also be bit much some days. All the saints above! I go through more peanut butter and jelly now than when I my kids were home!"

"So, how old is the oldest grandchild?" Nora asked. Kincaid was glad that Nora was being the inquisitor, so he didn't have to ask the questions.

"Liddy, Lorraine and Lonnie were all born the same month. Liddy is Aaron's and Lorraine and Lonnie are Pat's twins. We call Lorraine Rain, most of the time. Those kids all graduated from high school this year. Liddy and Lonnie are going to college, but Rain doesn't know what she wants to do. That girl has the wanderlust. I have to admit, she's one of my favorites. She has always been full of the devil and quite the tomboy. There was never a tree too high or a creek too wide! She can get in and out of more pickles in ten minutes than most folks do in a lifetime. Not that she is bad, she is just like, ah say a larger Charlie!"

Everyone groaned and laughed. "Yea gads!"

"Sound like quite a group," Elton agreed. "What do your boys do?"

"Aaron, Pat and James are all in the Boston PD, as is Nancy's John. And Colleen didn't get too far from the family business because her Frank is an attorney with the public defender's office. I guess that is why Ian became a police man. This family doesn't know any better. Except for Matt."

"My family is almost all mechanics," Nora said. "I guess if you are around it all the time, it comes naturally. How did Matthew escape?"

"He was just barely thirteen when his daddy was killed in the line of duty. It was hardest on him and Ian because they were the youngest. Abby was in college and had just left home, so it wasn't as life changing. I think that is why Mattie hated law enforcement so. Now with Ian, it went the other way. It made him more determined to be a good cop to honor his daddy. I guess you can cook whatever you want out from the eggs in your basket, huh?"

Nora smiled, "I guess so. Has Ian got any ideas on what he is going to do now?"

Mo looked down, "Nothing, unless he and Ruthie have come up with something. I know he wants to get married, but he won't until he finds a job. He is too proud to do that. I just don't know how it will all work out. How is Ruthie doing?"

"Pretty good," Nora nodded. "She seems to be enjoying her work at the church although she still feels ambiguous about it not being the Catholic church. I think she still feels hurt that they encouraged her to leave the convent."

"Well, good night!" Kincaid burst out, "She wouldn't have stayed with it anyway. She and Ian were generating so much electricity. A guy almost has to be grounded to be around them! They'd have hooked up anyway."

Maureen nodded, "That's what Matthew said! He said if ever two people were connected, it was them."

Elton lit another cigarette, "So does Matthew have any ideas on what Ian should do?"

"No. He's been wracking his brain, but can't come up with a thing. You know, my Mattie is thinking about making a leap too."

"Matt, getting married?" Elton tried to keep from choking. "Leaving the church?"

"No, leaving Boston. He wants to stretch his legs as he puts it. Evil of me to say, being a Catholic and all, and the good Lord knows I have no shortage of grandkids, but I wish he'd get married. But it is not my affair. Each person has to do their own thing, even if they do it wrong!" Mo giggled.

"And your way is right?" Kincaid chuckled.

"Most of the time," Maureen smiled. "I make tiny errors from time to time, just to keep humble."

Kincaid and Elton exchanged a glance and both chuckled. Maureen saw it and reprimanded them, "Watch it there! Or you'll be getting your undies starched!"

"So, what do you do, Maureen? To keep yourself busy?" Nora asked.

"I babysit. I've raised so many kids, I feel like I'm one of them. Don't get me wrong, I love my grandchildren, but Father Murphy's Gold! There're so many. First my eight and then fifteen grandbabies. I shudder to think how many great grandbabies the kids will be dragging in! Don't tell the Pope but I feed all the girls in my family Grandma's Special Punch. Fruit juices laced with birth control pills!"

Elton nearly choked to death and Kincaid almost spit his whiskey clear across the table! He turned to Mo, "You wicked woman!"

"Yah, I feel so much remorse," Maureen smirked, and then continued, "It's nice when folks ask you how your kids and grandkids are, but really? Why don't they ever ask how you are? Like, hello? I'm a person! Did you notice?"

Nora agreed, "I know. It is easy to get your identity lost in the shuffle."

"Do you feel that way too, honey?" Elton asked with concern. "I never thought that women minded that?"

"Well, a little of it is nice, but would you like to always have people ask you about their cars?" Nora pointed out.

Elton gave his wife a quizzical look, "Nora, they do! Hell, within a few minutes of conversation, I hear about everyone's engine knocks. I know more about people's cars than I do them!"

"I'm sorry honey, I guess I never thought of that. People do tell you that, don't they?" Then Nora turned to Kincaid, "What do people ask you?'

Kincaid looked down, "How is the therapy coming?"

"I'm so sorry, Carl," Nora patted his hand. "That was unthinking of me. I meant before you were shot?"

"Nobody wants to talk to an FBI agent about what they've been doing," Carl responded. "I guess they're know you'll catch them in some villainous crime."

Mo took his hand, "So, what are we all really saying? What do we want people to ask about? I guess we are just being stupid. No one is going to say, "Hello, have you found complete fulfillment? Not exactly the thing you'd hear in a receiving line!"

They all thought a minute and started to chuckle. Soon, they were all in fits of hysteria at the prospect.

After Nora and Elton went in, Carl and Maureen sat on the swing. She was tucked under his arm and they were both relaxing. Carl broke the silence, "It was a nice tonight, don't you think?"

"Yes, it was. Very nice. I really feel comfortable with Nora and Elton."

"I like them too, but I especially like it when I'm with you," he looked at her. "I mean that. You make me feel like a real person. Like maybe you'd ask me how I really am and mean it."

Maureen cuddled a little closer to him, "And I like feeling like I'm not just someone's mom or grandma."

"Maureen, I'm honored that you give me the time of day. I could care less if you have twenty kids."

"Do you ever miss not having a family?" Mo turned a looked at him.

"For a while after Cecelia died. Then I got involved in work and put that in the back of my brain. It wasn't until the shooting, that it came back. Now, I feel like I was wrong. I missed the most important part of my life."

Maureen kissed his cheek, "Well, it isn't over until the fat lady sings."

Kincaid laughed, "Yah, but I heard her tuning up a couple times recently. I think I had best be taking heed. What do you think I should do?"

Maureen sat straight up and looked him in the eye, "I'm not on that committee, Buster. You have to decide that. No one else can do it for you. You need to decide which carrots you want to pull from your garden. Then I'd be happy to help you stew them. Deal?"

"What if you play a part in my decision?"

"Still not going to say," she leaned back into his arm. "Why? What is bothering you?"

"I guess, I just wonder if you'd ever leave Boston?"

Maureen thought a while, "I don't know. I guess it would depend on many things. To where, with whom, why? All that. But I'm not tied to the geography."

"What about your family? You'd miss them if you were gone from them."

"I know. Carl, they have their lives too. We all have to follow our own paths. After Sean was killed, I wanted to run so far away. I would've, but I had nowhere to go. His family was great support and I love them to death. I mean, really, they're the kindest people in the world. The kids and I needed them.

"But, to them and most of the neighborhood, I'm still Maureen, Sean Harrington's widow. Might as well be his wife. I mean, they all treat me like I still am. But he's gone. I know I sound ungrateful and I do understand how they feel. Most of the time, I appreciate the fact that they remember him, but sometimes I just want to scream, 'Dammit I'm Maureen Margaret Finn Harrington. I'm me alone, not one of a couple!' Looking at Sean's picture just doesn't cut it sometimes." She stopped short and got up. "I'm sorry. I don't want to talk about this. It's embarrassing. Forget it, please. I'm going in."

Carl grabbed her hand and pulled her back to sit down. "No. You aren't going in. I'm not embarrassed and you shouldn't be either. I'm glad you told me. Mo, you can tell me anything. Alright? Ginger says that if you want to be good friends, you need to know the other guy's stuff. I want to know your stuff and I want you to know mine. You're more than just my friend. You're my girl. Remember?"

She didn't say anything and then he put his other arm around her and gave her a kiss. She didn't respond at all. He kissed her again.

"I feel ridiculous now," Mo started to cry. "You must think I'm some kind of an ungrateful, selfish person."

Kincaid caressed her back, "I honestly understand how you feel. I do. I don't think that you're ridiculous. Unless folks have been through it, they really don't get it. I'm sure that I don't understand how folks feel about a lot of things, but I do understand this. When you love someone and they die, you really want everyone to think well of them and know that you miss them. But life isn't meant to be one big long mourning thing. It just doesn't work that way. I remember thinking; it was a lot easier for Cecelia than it was for me. How selfish is that? Sometimes I honestly hated her for being the one that got to die and leave me to face every day, picking up pieces of half a life and keep going. I can't imagine what it would be like to have kids to deal with too. So, for what it's worth, you aren't ridiculous to me. Okay?"

Mo didn't say anything, but gave him a tender kiss which he returned. Within minutes, they were almost overtaken by desire. "We had better stop this before the kids drive in. If they saw all this carrying on, they'd be damaged for life!"

Carl stopped, "Yah, it might teach them a thing or two."

Maureen giggled, "I don't know Coot, I think they do alright in this department?"

Carl laughed. "Yah, you're probably right about that. Let's go in before I can't stop. I want you Maureen, but on Elton's cuddling swing? I don't know about that!"

Maureen laughed, "I think your spicy sauce went to our heads. Let's call it a night."

From his bed, Kincaid watched Elmer digging his heart out. He wondered if Elmer ever thought about what he would do if he caught that gopher!

43

The next morning, Zach took him aside for a long talk. After he gave him the bad news that he'd have to resume exertorture the next day, they discussed his heart and what he could expect from it. He'd have to keep on his medication, diet and exercise. He had to keep his cigarette consumption down. Zach preferred that he quit, but knew that was wishing for the moon.

"So, how are things in the romance department?" Zach asked as professionally as possible.

"Good. Last night, Maureen and I were . . . Well let's just say, I know things were in working condition. Know what I mean?" Carl didn't want to have this conversation, but on the other hand, knew he had to. "Does that mean it'll okay?"

"Yah, but take it easy. You know how you almost passed out from walking around too much. I don't want you to have a stroke or heart attack. That's not very romantic. Take it cool. I mean it. It will take time to regain your stamina and endurance."

"I know." Then he looked at his young friend, "Zach, I think that Maureen and I might really have something worthwhile."

Kincaid was more sincere and without any bluster than Zach had ever seen him. "You know when I was in the hospital, she sat with me a lot. We talked about more things than I think I've ever talked to anyone about. All kinds of stuff. When I came up here, I missed it. I didn't think I would. I didn't realize it was her I missed until she called. Now that she's here, I don't want to take any chances of losing her."

"Sounds like you're very serious about her. Are you thinking about getting married?" Zach tried to conceal his surprise. He knew they had hit it off, but had no idea how much.

"Yah, I actually am, but good grief," Kincaid shook his head. "I have no home and no job. What the hell am I thinking?"

"You sound like Harrington. You're a bit luckier, I think. You can retire. You have your pension and all that. You don't need a job. Hell, Kincaid. You have devoted almost twenty-four hours a day to that job for your whole life. Now, you need to take some time for you. You earned it."

"Do you think that folks would think I'm a being a bum?" He was mostly trying to decide that himself.

"Not at all. Have you thought about where you would like to live and all that?"

"I was worried that Mo would want to be in Boston, but I think she'd be okay with settling someplace else, too. You and I know though, she'll need to go home to see her kids a lot, from wherever we live." Kincaid sighed, "Listen to me. I act like she said yes already and I haven't even asked her to marry me."

Zach smiled, "Oh, I think you guys have talked to each other enough to know. Some things don't have to be said. Sometimes you just know."

"So, you don't think I'm out of my mind?" Kincaid waited for Zach's reaction.

"Yah, I do. Then again, I always thought you were!" Zach snickered. "But do I think this is crazy? Seriously, not at all."

"What do you think that her kids would say?" Kincaid worried.

"I suppose they'd all have their opinions, but I know that Matthew and I were working out your dowry in Shreveport!" Zach chuckled.

"You're kidding! Why on earth . . . what made you even think that?" Carl gasped.

"The way you were together. It was obvious," Zach grinned. "You guys just seemed to click. I know that Harrington thinks you guys should just get hitched. He says his mom hasn't been this happy in years. She never dated or anything since his dad died."

"I don't figure that out. She's an attractive lady," Kincaid pointed out. "Why not?"

"From what Harrington said his Dad's family, more or less took over her life. He figured that she couldn't have squeaked a smile at a guy if her life depended on it."

"Sounds sort of like what she said, but she made Sean's family sound nicer."

"Harrington said once she became friendly with a fellow from town. Sean's family made no bones about that was not the way that she should treat his Dad's memory. He'd been gone eight years by then!"

"Yah, I guess that explains why she feels the way she does. Maybe that's why she said she would consider moving, huh?" Kincaid considered.

"Could be. So, what're you going to do?" Zach asked, with a wink. "Buy house with a picket fence? You know, you could use the back side of my lot. On the other side of Elton's garden, close to your Weeder job! There's plenty of room. I'd love to have you as my neighbor."

Carl stared at Zach in shock, "Damn. I didn't expect that. Did you seriously think about that? I was thinking of going to Texas."

"What in hell have you got in Texas? You moron! Your family is here! Hers is in Boston. And you want to go to Texas! I think you have rocks in your head!"

"Calm down, Petunia. Just settle down. I'd like to be around this family but we both know it isn't mine. You just let me share yours." He spoke vehemently.

"You're so full of it. You just waltz out there and try to tell that to Charlie, or Miriam! What're you going to do about Miriam? And Magpie? And what about Lloyd? You're just making me mad now."

Carl studied Zach's face, "Do you really think these people give a damn? Or they even think I am part of the clan?"

Zach patted his back, "Yes I do. I really do. So don't ever ask me again. And you know what? Even if they don't think so, I think of you as my family. Ruthie and I didn't name that little girl Miriam Carla for nothing. That has to mean something. I mean, what more do you want? What else could we do for you? I guess if that isn't good enough, then you should leave."

"Oh for heaven's sake," Carl thought a bit. Then he grinned, "I guess I couldn't very well take off on the Wee One, could I? I'll have to talk to Mo. Don't say anything to anyone, including Harrington, yet, okay? I really need to talk to my girl."

"You got my word" Zach patted his shoulder and turned to leave. Then he looked back, "Tomorrow, exertorture!"

Carl Kincaid spent the day sorting through things in his mind. Zach was right. There was no reason to think that he should go to Texas. If not Boston, then Merton would make the most sense. After learning more about Sean's family, he didn't think Boston would be that good for his Mo. She had the right to be herself. But maybe Maureen wouldn't be happy in North Dakota. He'd have to talk to her about that. He would want what would be the best for her.

He knew he had the money to get a house. He could easily retire. His pension was very good and he had never spent a cent on anything but whiskey in his whole life. He would have to talk to Maureen about a house though. Maybe she didn't want to live in the country. Maybe she didn't want to live between Zach and Elton. Maybe she didn't even want to babysit for Miriam. He didn't want her to have to trade one set of grandchildren for another. That wouldn't be fair. Yah, he definitely needed to talk to Maureen.

That afternoon, most of the gang went down to work on the airplane. Pepper was very adept at putting the tiny pieces together. Harrington knew what and how to do it probably better than anyone, but was very frustrated with his bum arm. Pepper helped him out and seemed to be able to encourage him without him being aware of it. Nora and Maureen polished, shined and applied the decals. Mostly they all just chatted and goofed off. There was so much giggling and joking around, they were all surprised that by four o'clock, they were almost done with it. Suzy and Ruthie arrived after work at the church and checked it out. Zach and Elton thought they might be ready for the maiden flight after Sunday dinner tomorrow.

Zach thought that when his contractor got finished with his house, he'd have him build a real airplane hangar with runway. His garage would be attached to his house but they really needed a place large enough for this most necessary work. They all thought it was an excellent idea.

Kincaid took a short rest. He was genuinely tired. It was important to him to not poop out that night. He was determined he'd be able to dance at least the one time that Zach had allowed. He slept about half an hour and then got ready to go to dinner with Ellisons.

Dinner at the Cattlemen's Club was a ball. They had a wonderful meal and a great visit. They then adjourned to the bar and dance area for after dinner drinks and a little dancing. Carl and Mo watched as the other couples got up to dance. He felt uncomfortable. "Zach said I could dance one slow dance tonight, if I took it easy. I'm sorry. You're welcome to dance all you want but could you save one dance for me? I'm just no good anymore."

"Of course, a girl always saves a special dance for her guy. You old Coot! I don't need to dance at all. I love sitting her with you. I don't want you to get sick," Maureen patted his hand. "I've had a tremendous time. I feel like I've known these folks forever."

"They're like that, aren't they?" Kincaid watched them while they danced. "You know, Zach told me that I am a clanner. Can you believe that?"

Mo studied his face, "Carl, I don't know what a clanner is, but I know that these folks consider you one of them. Is that what you mean?"

"I guess. I never really thought about what a clanner was, huh? I guess that's what it is. You know, we just try to watch out for each other," Kincaid shook his head. "I guess it is no big thing, huh?"

"Carl, a lot of folks say it. The difference is that these guys really live it," Maureen took his hand. "And in this day and age, that's a big thing. And you are right in the middle of it all!"

"I don't think I'm at all. I don't even begin to know how these guys do it. It seems to come naturally to them. You're the same way, you know. Maureen," he squeezed her hand, "I need to talk to you about some serious stuff. Not right now, but soon. Okay?"

Maureen patted his hand, "Sure."

When the song was over, the band played a waltz. Carl took her hand and got up from the wheelchair. "Okay, Maureen. You need to hold on to me and no fancy stuff! Don't be expecting me to throw you in the air or anything!"

"Lord have mercy, I hope not. Why that would mess up my hairdo!"

"Your hair looks great. I won't mess it up."

"Great Balls of Fire! I have so much hairspray in it, it feels like helmet!"

"You nut!" Kincaid laughed. "Stifle your motor mouth and dance."

During the dance they held each other very close. Kincaid said that it was in case he felt weak, but they fooled no one. They had a very nice dance and when it was over, before they went to sit down, Carl kissed her cheek. "I love you, Motor Mouth."

She gave him a funny smile and said, "And I love you too, you old Coot."

44

Lloyd wandered in and visited with Kincaid for over an hour during the night. He was all wound up about the Treaty of Versailles. Kincaid had to admit that he learned quite a bit, even though it might not be correct. It was about four when Carl walked Lloyd back to his room.

Sunday morning began as controlled confusion, but soon degenerated into just flat out chaos. It was blowing and threatening rain outside. The cattle had gone back out to the far end of the pasture, so Keith and Kevin went out to bring them back. That put everything behind schedule.

The Ellisons didn't come over, as was usual for Sunday. Ruthie called to say that she would pick up Ian and Maureen for Mass at nine. They decided that after Mass, they would also go to Byron's service. Carrie wasn't feeling well again and Zach went over to see her. Pepper did a quick physical therapy with Coot and Harrington.

Zach brought Carrie back to the farm with him, so she could rest at the farmhouse. The medicine was starting to help, but it made her very tired. She would nap at the house with the grandparents, in case Katherine needed help with Lloyd who was quite confused.

Carl helped Grandma make breakfast, which was simply scrambled eggs and sausage with homemade bread toast, while Mo and Nora got the roast beef in for dinner. Darlene set the tables and helped get everyone else organized, pressing a few shirts and helping fix hair. Carl had insisted that he didn't need the wheelchair for church and Zach reluctantly agreed.

However, by the time they entered Trinity Lutheran Church and shook Byron's hand, one would have thought the family had just stepped out of a peaceful morning depicted on a Currier and Ives canvas.

As soon as Carl came through the door, Charlie was right there. He took his hand and they walked down the aisle to 'their seat'. Kincaid told him that they needed to be certain to keep room for Harrington, Ruthie and Mo. He wanted them to sit with them. Charlie thought it was silly because they could sit any place, but finally gave in.

"As long as you sit right by side of me, okay?" the little boy asked.

"You got it, Champ."

Charlie grinned and made himself comfortable. He produced several pieces of straw from his right suit pocket and Kincaid frowned, "What is that for?"

Charlie shrugged.

"You might want to put them away until after church, huh?" the older man suggested.

Charlie looked at him, "I'm going to weave them for you. I heard this story and I want to do it for you."

"That's nice Charlie, but maybe not in church."

"Or maybe?" the little guy raised his eyebrows. "To keep not being figgetty."

Then Maureen, Harrington and Ruthie came in. Charlie and Carl got out and let the others in first. They sat back down, Charlie by the aisle, then Kincaid, Maureen, Ruthie and Harrington.

All was quiet and Maureen took Kincaid's hand and gave it a squeeze. He smiled back at her. He whispered to her, "How was Mass?"

"Nice," she whispered back.

He noticed Charlie out of the corner of his eye. The little guy had produced about two hands full of straw out of his clothes.

Kincaid tapped his shoulder, "What you doing? I thought you were going to put that away?"

"Ah, no," Charlie started to explain. "I decided not to."

Kincaid's eyes became huge, "Away, now!"

Charlie made a face of dread and quickly tried to jam the straw into the pockets of his suit jacket as the whole congregation rose for the opening hymn. Some of it missed his pockets and fell on the floor. He stooped down to pick it up and cracked his head on the back of the pew in front of him.

Carl bent down to see if he was okay and helped him pick up the straw from the floor. He handed it to Charlie who was busily jamming it into his suit. He couldn't get it in so it fell on the pew. Carl ended up putting some in his own suit pockets. This was all during the first hymn!

Each time they stood up or sat down during the liturgy, more straw got spread further. Kincaid looked at the kid in wonder. How in the hell could he pack that much straw in his suit? Carl hadn't noticed any before the service started. Where was it coming from? But mostly, what could he do with it now?

By the time the sermon started, Kincaid was worn out. Kincaid was wondering if he could get a defense attorney that would defend him for clobbering a small lad during a church service? Surely, there had to be one somewhere!

When they settled in for the sermon, Carl grabbed the kid's hands and held them. He glared at Charlie and seethed, "Don't even breathe."

Charlie knew he was in trouble, so he nodded. Kincaid relaxed and let go of his hands. He started to listen to the sermon. In a minute, Charlie let out with a huge gasp, trying to get his air. The little kid grabbed his neck like he was being choked and his face was all red. Byron noticed something was up from the pulpit and gave Kincaid a worried look.

Carl patted Charlie's back like he thought he was choking and then whispered loudly, "Charles Elton Ellison!"

Charlie started to giggle and Kincaid frowned at him. Then the kid sat real still, looking straight ahead. Kincaid looked back to the pulpit. Byron was trying to keep his place in his sermon, had to stop, cough and restart. Then he looked at the other side of the church.

Within seconds, Marly quietly slid in next to Charlie. He turned pure white and sat very still. She was in no mood to mess with him. Kincaid started to apologize, but she glared at him. Now he knew what the kids meant about the red fire from her eyes. Yes, the lady was truly at her wits end. He turned his attention back the sermon, which had become only background noise by now.

He wondered how many times he had wanted to die since he came to North Dakota. He knew it was often, at least daily or more. He knew that everyone in the place knew that he couldn't even watch a little kid for couple minutes without messing it up. The Texas desert was looking better all the time.

Carl didn't look at Maureen, Harrington or Ruthie. He knew Ruthie would understand, but she was sitting beyond Maureen. He decided he might quit going to church altogether. He knew Lutherans didn't excommunicate or ban folks from their church, but he was rather certain they would be looking through the fine print to see if it could be justified in this case.

The straw didn't all make it back into anybody's pockets. There was some in the pew, on the floor, in the hymnal and even in the collection plate as it was passed by. Marly saw it and shot Kincaid a stony glare that would bring the most hardened felon to his knees.

When they stood for the last hymn, Marly had a death grip on Charlie. Maureen patted Kincaid's arm and they shared the hymnal. That was the only part of the service that he really could say he paid attention to.

When church was over and the folks started filing out, Kincaid tried to scoot the crunched up straw under the pew, so the others didn't have to walk over it. It was extremely slippery on the hardwood.

Marly and Charlie were half way to the house in a heartbeat. Kincaid wasn't certain, but he figured Charlie would be rather quiet the rest of the day or maybe the entire week.

He stepped out of the pew and let Maureen out ahead of him. Then he put his arm around her waist and they walked to the door. He had hoped he could say goodbye to Pastor Marvin and maybe skip Byron. He engineered it so that Maureen was on Byron's side of the door.

His plan worked very well, until the folks ahead of him apparently thought they had something very important to talk to Pastor Marvin about. They just settled in, and there was no graceful way that Kincaid could not shake Byron's hand and keep the crowd flowing.

Maureen had shook Byron's hand and said she really enjoyed his sermon. He gave her a quick hug, thanked her and then reached out to Kincaid. Carl took his hand but didn't look at him.

Byron pulled him close and gave him a quick pat on the shoulder. "Tough day, huh?"

Carl just mumbled, "I'm so sorry."

Byron looked at him with compassion, "I don't think you are the one that needs to apologize."

In the car on the way home, it was very quiet until Ruthie said, "I think that Charlie is going to have his ears pinned back when Marly gets him home. What was with him?"

"Oh God, you guys!" Kincaid let go with his frustration, "I don't how on earth that kid got all the straw stuffed in his suit! What the hell possessed him to do that? He has never done that before! Where did he get the straw?"

Harrington was just killing himself with laughter. "I'd bet real money that he won't do it again in this lifetime! What did he think he was he going to do with it?"

Kincaid shook his head, "Weave it. Can you believe that? He told me he was going to weave it. Yea gads."

"Poor Byron," Ruthie said, "I could see that he was about dying up there. Did anyone hear his sermon?"

"A little," Harrington chuckled. "I think it might have been good. Now I understand why priests aren't supposed to marry!"

Dinner was fun for everyone but Charlie. He wasn't allowed to race cars or sit by Kincaid. He had to stay by his parents or take a nap. In the kitchen, Marly apologized to Carl.

"I'm so sorry that little brat did that. I have no idea what goes through his head half the time," Marly tried to explain. "Where did he get the straw?"

"Out of his pockets!" Carl explained. "I saw a little handful first and told him to put it away. The next time I looked, he had a bread pan full! I have no idea where it came from."

"Well, he is in deep trouble now. His Dad grounded him. He has to stay home and in the house until Wednesday. He was going to make it longer, but I had to beg for mercy! I hate it when the kids are grounded. They drive me nutty," Marly admitted. "Now he is all worried that he will lose his Chicken Man job with Uncle Elton. Byron told him that was up to Uncle Elton and he'd have to talk to him today. He's scared to death."

"Poor kid," Kincaid said, knowing how much that job meant to Charlie.

"You say that now! I bet you wanted to tan his hide a while ago!" Marly pointed out.

"No, I was thinking more along the lines of clobbering him!" Carl admitted. "But he really meant no harm."

"Mr. Defender, can you explain to me what he was trying to do?" Marly asked.

"Ah, he told me he wanted to weave," Carl almost whispered. He knew it sounded extremely lame.

"Weave? Nora, where's the bottle? I need a stiff drink! My son thinks he is going to weave." Just like that she stopped and her eyes widened with realization. She covered her mouth with both her hands. "I know that this is about. I read the kids the story of *Rumpelstiltskin*! I bet he was going to make you some gold. Now I get it. But still, he shouldn't have done it in church."

Byron was listening, "That was nice of him, but he should do his weaving in the barn."

Uncle Elton grinned, "Oh now Dad, don't get so particular. I think it's kind of sweet of him."

"Of course you would," Byron groaned. "You can sit by him in church next week."

"Well, I wouldn't get all that carried away, but I'll go talk to him. He can keep his job as Chicken Man. I guess it is up to Kincaid if he's still a Weeder and Gopher."

"Of course," Kincaid beamed, "I never had anyone want to make me gold before."

45

At dinner, Annie made an announcement. "I have something to share with you guys that shouldn't be of any surprise. I waited until I talked to my father, so now it's official. Andy wrote and asked me to marry him while he is on R&R. Dad and I talked about it and he gave his blessing. I wrote to Andy yesterday and told him I'd be honored to be his wife."

Everyone cheered and hugged everyone else. It was very exciting news. "Well, how am I going to be his best man?" Darrell asked with a grin.

"Guess you will have to come to his R&R! We really want you to be there," Annie said.

"When is it?" Darrell asked.

"He hasn't heard yet. He said he'd get a message to me when he finds out when and where. I really hope you can make it. We can talk later, but Andy and I really want you there."

"If it's Hawaii, plan on it. Otherwise, it will have to be just you and him. Hmm. Imagine that!" he gave her a hug. "I think it's wonderful, Annie."

"Dad and I couldn't be happier!" Nora embraced the young girl. "Have you any idea how soon it'll be?"

"None. I'm trying to get things organized at work so I can take off. They were very nice about it and said they'd let me know on Tuesday when I get back."

"How long will he have leave?" Keith asked.

"One week, that's it. But he is almost half way through his tour there. So, he'll be home after the holidays," Annie smiled. "If all goes well."

"It will," Uncle Eddie stated positively, "I just know it. It'll be just fine. Sorry I'm going to miss the shindig. Say, when he gets home though, we can plan a real big deal, huh?"

"That sounds wonderful," Byron said. "Once you guys find out where he'll get sent for leave, let me know. I can help you line up a church."

"Andy says he'd really love to have you all at his wedding, but he just wants to get married. He hopes you all understand," Annie apologized.

"Of course we do," Uncle Jerald said. "I'm so glad that you kids are getting married. Tell him I said so. Oh heck, I'll write him myself. You can have someone take pictures! I think it's fantastic."

"Gee," Pepper giggled, "I guess this means we don't have to buy a wedding present!"

"Dad, make her stop! She's so cheap!" Kevin whined. "Tell her to be nice!"

"I'm too happy right now to ruin it trying to get Pepper to be nice!" Elton beamed. "I'm anxious to see the planning the women are going to do for this!!"

"Don't worry your little brain about it. We'll have plans," Nora grinned.

"Oh yes," Elton chuckled. "I'm sure of that! Well, we must get together with your father and your brother, and soon."

Miriam looked at Annie, "And soon."

Annie grinned, "Yes, pumpkin, we'll do it very soon."

That night as the two couples sat on the patio to contemplate the events of the day, it was very peaceful. Crickets and hoot owls could be heard in the far distance. The sky was again bright and filled with the entire galaxy of shining stars.

"I really enjoy these night skies," Maureen said as she sat next to Carl in the cuddling swing. "Back home there are so many trees, you can only see a little bit of sky at a time. Here, you can see the whole thing."

"Yah, no one would ever accuse us of having so many trees we block the view!" Elton teased. "Are Zach and Ian still down at the shop? They were so excited about the maiden flight today! That plane is really cool. They're going through the catalog to pick out the next plane. We may end up with an entire air force. Too bad the girls went home early."

"They said they had some things to get ready for Bible School tomorrow. No Gophers for you all week, Coot! I think that Byron forgot about Bible school when he grounded Charlie. So the little guy will get to go out of the house anyway!" Nora giggled. "He told Elton that he stuffed the straw inside his shirt! That must have really itched!"

"Poor little guy," Elton related, "He told me the he wanted to make Coot happy and he was going to surprise everyone with the gold. He didn't know it was just a fairy tale or that he'd get into so much trouble. Boy, was he relieved to find out that he still had his Chicken Man job."

"Yah, when I talked to him," Carl explained, "He gave me a big hug and said he was sorry. I said just don't bring straw to church anymore. He said that he wasn't sorry for that because God didn't care about straw. He knew that because He put it in his baby's bed. He was sad that he couldn't make gold. How can you be upset with a little guy like that?"

"You can't," Maureen agreed, "But you still can't let him take straw to church. What was with the choking thing he did? Is he allergic to the straw?"

Kincaid shook his head, "No. That was my fault. I was so exasperated that I told him to sit there and don't even breathe!"

Everyone laughed.

"Yea gads! Kids really keep you hopping," Nora grinned. "And what about that Andy? He wrote that he was thinking of getting married on leave, but he never said for sure. I guess it makes sense that he would ask Annie before telling his mom. I'm so happy for them but I have to be honest. I really wanted to see him and their wedding."

"Well, why can't you?" Kincaid asked. "Can't you guys be there too?"

"We talked about it. If it is Hawaii, we're going over to see him but if it is someplace else, it'd be better to help Annie pay for her trip," Nora explained.

"I guess," Kincaid said. "Makes sense. Do you think that Darrell will go?"

Elton lit his cigarette, "He and I talked a bit this afternoon. He said he will if it is in Hawaii, but otherwise, he couldn't afford to go either."

Maureen shook her head, "You guys! Let's just keep hoping that he gets sent to Hawaii! You should go, all of you."

"Well, that's true," Nora agreed, "But we have the grandparents, the shops, chores and all that."

"Oh for crying out loud!" Kincaid blurted out. "You just plan on going and I'll be here for them. Keith and Kevin take care of the chores and the shops. You guys just go. If I had a kid over there, I'd want to see him. If money is an issue, I'll pay for your tickets."

Elton looked at him in shock, "What! Have you lost your mind? Why would you do that for us?"

"Why did you take me in?" Carl glared.

"Hmm, because no one else would have you," Elton chuckled. "Really, thanks, we can get the money but we have to keep an eye on things."

"I can keep an eye on things," Carl proposed. "Who's going to help Darrell milk?"

"His brothers, Sammy and Joey and probably Danny Schroeder. Those kids all help each other out as much as they can." Elton finished his Coke, "Anyone else ready for seconds? I'll go get them."

Everyone nodded they were and Elton went in to get the drinks. Maureen was thoughtful and waited until Elton returned before she spoke, "I was thinking, I'd be very willing, in fact I'd like to, come back out here and help Kincaid while you're gone. I don't know most of what you all do, but I think I could bandage a knee or make a salad."

Nora's mouth fell open, "Really? You would do that for us? Why Maureen, that's so nice of you! Elton, did you hear?"

"Yes," Elton said as set the sodas down and hugged Mo. "I think that's wonderful. Thank you so much. Let's just keep that in mind until we hear from Andy when and where. Okay? But we'll really consider it."

"You guys!" Kincaid puffed, "I volunteer and you say no. Mo volunteers and you think it's wonderful! Jiminy Christmas, you act like I couldn't handle anything."

"On the contrary, Kincaid," Elton smirked. "We know you could handle everything else, but who would handle you?"

"You know what, Magpie?" Carl blustered, "You two deserve each other!"

Nora took Elton's hand and smiled sweetly, "We think so."

"Good grief, Mo," Carl grumbled, "A guy can't even insult these two!"

"Now calm down, you old Coot," Maureen took his hand in hers, "I agree with them completely."

"Anyway, I think I'll just go over and stay at Darrell's house. He is nicer than any of you guys!" Carl retorted.

"I hope he can make it. You know, he and Jeannie were waiting for Andy to get back so he could be their best man when they got married.

This kind of throws a monkey wrench in that," Nora pointed out. "He'd never say so though, but it's kind of a pickle."

"Darrell is really a great guy," Carl nodded. "You know, he doesn't realize all that he does. He thinks that everything that he does is unimportant."

"I know someone else like that," Elton looked directly at Carl. "But you're right. He was all set to go on to more college and then he had that heart thing."

"What sort of heart thing was it? It must've been serious but no one ever says what it was." Kincaid asked.

"A major vessel to his heart got a kink in it and he had a heart attack. He was just barely eighteen. Thank God he survived, but he had a couple surgeries and he was really under the weather for a while," Nora told the couple. "He was left with some heart damage. He was always such a happy-go-lucky kid, but he went into a depression after that. He finished junior college, but never went on to anything further. His Dad needed help then, so he stayed home and helped him."

"It'd seem that he should go to college and get job that would be less physical than taking care all those animals," Maureen suggested.

"We tried to tell him that, but he just seemed to lose interest in everything." Elton leaned back in the rocker. "He said he always loved his goats, which he really did, and that was good enough. Eddie got him interested in the cheese factory. That was real good. He works there a few days a week. Eddie says he is very knowledgeable and knows all the cultures and stuff. He was going to ask him to come to town and work full time with him, with an eye on someday taking it over eventually. Then Albert Frandsen put his land up for sale."

Carl frowned, "I don't follow."

"Well," Elton continued, "Frandsen, Jeannie's dad, owned all the land north of the road here and up to Jessups, Darrell's folks. George Jessup had rented the pasture land for years, but didn't have the money to buy it when it was for sale. So, Darrell and his Dad bought it together. Once Darrell was involved in the land, he had to make a bigger income, so he started milking even more goats. The whole thing just got away from him. Now he is stuck."

"He has a nice little house," Carl observed, "And a huge barn. I think that's really something for a kid his age."

"Ever been in the house? It was an old sheepherder's cabin that he moved on to the place. It has one regular bedroom, and an overgrown closet he calls a second bedroom and he then added the bathroom. The rest is one room, kitchen and living area. It is okay for one person, but not for a family." Elton said. "Now that his Dad is slowing down with his chemotherapy, he needs to retire and is thinking about selling his share of the pasture. Darrell doesn't know just what he's going to do. He knows his Dad can't keep up at the pace he was going. That's why Darrell took over milking most of his cows, but the kid can't afford to buy the pasture land straight out. We'll all help him out as much as we can or he will allow. It is a bit of a mess right now, but whatever happens, I'm sure that Darrell will do fine. "

Carl smiled at Elton, "I think that you're right. Whatever happens, will be for the best."

Nora gave Carl a funny look and he smiled at her.

46

Lloyd stopped by during the night and talked to Carl for about half an hour. He was very concerned about Andy in Iwo Jima. Finally, Carl was able to calm him down enough to get him to return to bed.

Then he was wide awake. He thought about Andy. He had never met the kid, but everything he had heard about him was good. Carl thought the world and all of Annie, Jeannie and Darrell. He certainly hoped that Andy got sent to Hawaii, for all their sakes.

The man turned over and looked out the window. There was faithful Elmer at his post by the gopher hole. The dog was sleeping and suddenly sat straight up. He instantly started digging like crazy and then stopped. He put his head down by the hole as if listening. After a minute or two, he stretched out and put his head between his front legs to go back to sleep. He certainly was vigilant.

Kincaid wondered what he should do about Maureen. How was he going to ask her to marry him? Even if he was more settled about what he wanted; it'd all change in a heartbeat if it wasn't what Mo wanted. Everything he wanted depended on her.

However, he finally had things that he cared about. It was time to start acting on some of it. He couldn't keep lingering between decisions. Either use the pot or let someone else in the bathroom.

Zach was one great guy. That was really something that he'd ask him to build on his lot. But he wasn't certain that would be good to live in his backyard. If he married Mo, then what about Harrington? And her other kids?

He wondered how Darrell was going to get married with nothing more than his sheepherder's cabin. Although, he knew Jeannie well enough to know that she would make do with almost anything. She had her teaching job which would help out.

It was all moot, if George Jessup couldn't keep on farming and wanted to retire. He could help out Darrell some, but he wouldn't be able to hold on to all that land. It would be horrible if Darrell lost it all before he got started. He needed an investor.

Investments. Now that was something that he needed to think about himself. He had all this money stashed in a fund in Texas. He hadn't looked at it in years, but had put well over half of his paycheck put into it every payday. He had better check into it if he was going to be getting a house for his Maureen and he needed a car.

He wondered what kind of a house she wanted. They had never even talked about that. He would do that very soon. Probably he should be trying to find out where she wanted to live, or if she wanted to marry him.

He turned over in his bed and pounded his pillow down. After fluffing it back up, he nestled into it. Yah, that was better. He started to fall asleep.

Just as he was about to doze off, he sat straight up in bed. He knew! Not everything, but he knew some of what he wanted to do! He turned his clock. It was only quarter to four. He could hardly wait for morning so he could begin doing what he knew in his heart that he wanted to do. Now that he knew, he was impatient!

When they gathered around the coffee pot, Carl asked Zach what his plans were for the day.

"Well, I guess that Harrington is going to the shop with Dad. I'm going to hang out here and meet with the contractor about the house. Then I have to go to the bank. I need to be back here about three. Is there something I could help you with?"

"I need to go to a bank. I have some things that I need to get done. I want to close my account in Texas and transfer it up here. A person should never be too far away from his money. Should I just go to the Merton bank?" Carl asked the group.

Carrie smiled, "Merton is a branch office. If you want to transfer funds and all that, I'd suggest that you go to the main bank in Bismarck.

If you open an account there, you can still do all your regular banking here."

"Thanks. If Zach would be so kind?" Carl asked.

"Sure. I'll be going in about ten or so," Zach smiled.

After the men went outside, Carl asked for Darrell's phone number. Nora gave it to him and asked him quietly and curiously, "What are you up to, Mr. Kincaid?"

"I'm not sure yet." Kincaid answered honestly. Then he went to the phone.

"Good morning, Darrell," Carl grinned, "Did I wake you up?"

"Oh, hello Kincaid. No, I was just heading out to milk. What's up?" he answered, obviously very puzzled.

"Are you going to be home? I mean, can I come visit you?"

Darrell couldn't conceal his surprise, "Something wrong? Want me to come over?"

"Calm down. Nothing is wrong. I just want to see you."

"Sure, come on over. If I'm not at the house, I'll be at the barn. Want me to come get you?"

"No, thanks. I think I can get a ride." Carl hung up and asked Darlene. "Could you give me a ride over to Darrell's?"

"Sure, when?"

"Now would be good."

"Before breakfast?" Darlene giggled. "Wow! It must be important."

Carl grinned, "I was planning on grabbing a caramel roll before I left the house."

Nora shook her head no, "Not a good idea. If you are going over to Darrell's, you had better take him one, too!"

"Okay, you talked me into it." Kincaid grinned.

"Are you taking your wheelchair?" Darlene asked.

"I really don't want to. What do you think?"

"Oh, take it along. Then you have it if you need it."

When Darlene dropped him off at Darrell's barn, she asked, "What are you up to?"

"Don't know for certain yet. Thanks for the ride and let Zach know that I'll be home in time to go to Bismarck."

"If you need a ride, call me," Darlene offered.

"Thanks. You're an angel."

Darlene giggled, "I bet you say that to all the girls."

Carl parked the wheelchair beside the barn door and went inside. "Hello? Darrell?"

"Hi, I'll be right there in a second." Darrell yelled from the back.

Carl waited until the young man showed up. "Nora sent some caramel rolls."

Darrell grinned, "Wow! I am hungry! What brings you over here before sun up? Want the wheelchair in?"

"I was curious about your operation. I'd like to see it, if you don't mind. Do you think I can get around in the chair?"

"I used to," Darrell nodded. "Where did you park it? I'll go get it."

Darrell showed him the whole set up. There were ten cow milking stations and ten goat stations. The milk machines were all inline, so the milk traveled from the animal directly to the refrigerated tanks. It stayed there until the truck from the Cheese Factory came out and collected it.

Carl visited with Darrell as he moved the animals in and out of the milking stations until the milking was done. Then he cleaned everything and invited the old FBI agent to the house so he could make some fresh coffee to eat with their caramel rolls.

Inside Darrell's house, Carl could understand what Elton meant. It was neat, well-kept and clean, but very old. There was a modern bathroom and running water, but it was added on.

Darrell put the cups on the table and poured the coffee. "So, this is killing me. I love your company, but what's this about?"

"Ah, well. I'm not sure really. I need to talk to you. I have something that I think I might want to do, but I don't want to blab it to Magpie. Last night, he was telling me that your Dad needs to slow down and wants to retire. Is that right?"

"It is. Dad had cancer surgery last year. He's doing okay, but it really knocked him back. He just can't keep doing like he used to. You know? I feel bad for him. I took over milking his cows. It just tires him out. You know, Dad and I are partners in the land and the milking. He needs to have me buy him out. I went to PCA."

Carl interrupted, "What is PCA?"

"It is a farm credit place, Production Credit Association," Darrell explained. "I could swing the loan, but they want me to expand the barn and upgrade the cattle. See, they won't give a loan unless everything is all modern. I guess the old-fashioned way isn't good enough. They want you to go to ultramodern milking parlors, even though mine is—they want more stations. Problem is; it costs a fortune. Then by the time you pay for it, you have sold your soul to the devil. They won't give the loan unless you do. One guy I know bought this place that had eleven wooden granaries that were about thirty five years old. They were solid and secure. No leaks, excellent condition. The only way he could get the loan for the farm, was to tear them down and then replace them with steel bins. Well, he did, but it added a pile onto the loan. His wife has taken a job in town to help pay the bills. Those old bins were perfectly good. I doubt that the grain would have cared! It's frustrating."

Carl listened carefully, "How much money are you talking about?

"Like what do you mean? For the whole section of pasture?"

"How big is a section?" Carl felt himself getting in way over his head. Obviously, he knew nothing about any of this.

"A section is 640 acres. Dad and I have 640 acres of pasture. The 400 acres of cropland I have is my own. My brother Sam is buying the home place and Dad's cropland. He works at the power plant in Stanton, so he can't milk. In fact, I rent his cropland. He has some great hay land that I rent!" Darrell explained. "Why all the questions?"

"I don't mean to be nosey, really." Carl got very serious, "But here's the deal. Not for publication, okay?"

"Sure, I'll keep my mouth shut," Darrell promised.

"I want to get married."

Darrell broke into a great grin, "That's fantastic! Coot! Good for you! When is the happy day?"

"Ah, I haven't asked her yet. See, that's part of the problem. I mean, I think she'll say yes, I think. But, I have no home or anything like that. I was worried that she would want to live in Boston but she said no. She'd move. Then I thought about going back to Texas." Carl knew he was rambling.

"Texas? What on earth do you want down there? You belong up here!" Darrell gasped. "You can't leave us. Every clan needs its own FBI agent!"

Carl was very pleased at Darrell's reaction. It made him feel that he was making the right decisions. "I know. Zach gave me hell. Zach said I could build on the back of his lot, by Elton's. But, you know, that might not work so good for Maureen and her family. You know?"

"I think it'd be okay but I can see where it might not be good being in everyone's pocket."

"But I want to be near," Carl began to explain.

Darrell smiled, "Oh, I see. You were wondering about buying some of the pasture land for you to build your house. I'd love to do that, but it's to up to my Dad."

"Kind of what I was thinking. Mostly though, oh hell. Here's the deal. I have money invested a Texas investment thing. I want get that out. I need to reinvest it. I was thinking, I would like to invest in you."

"Me?" Darrell frowned, "How could you invest in me?"

"I'm wondering if I could buy out your Dad's share and we be partners. I'd be a really silent partner and no help at all. But we could be partners. However, I'd like to buy the land across the road from Schroeders, to build a house for me and Maureen. I want you to know though, even if Mo says no to having a house there, I'd still like to be your partner."

Darrell sat back in his chair trying to take it all in. "Man, that is a lot of money. It would be about $250,000 for Dad's share of the pasture. You can't do that. That's a lot of money."

"Darrell, right now it's sitting in some investment account being handled by some sleazy fellas in polyester suits. I don't know what they're doing with it and I'm just an account number. I want to be a part of something real. Something tangible. I want to be able to pick up the phone and say, 'How is the south forty?'" he gave a silly chuckle, "I always heard that on some TV show!"

They started to laugh. "Seriously Darrell, I don't mean to push my way into anything. If you don't want me involved, I'd sure get it. I mean, I know nothing about anything about any of this. I feel like I'm horning in. Maybe you wouldn't want me to be your partner."

Darrell just sat, spellbound. His mind was trying to grasp what this man was saying. After a few minutes, he got up and brought the coffee pot back. "That isn't it at all. It's awfully generous of you. I mean, like you don't know if I'm a good farmer or dairyman. Maybe I wouldn't be a good partner. I have no problems with having you for my partner, but you might not want me for yours. Kincaid, why me?"

"I know you have a good character and you are a decent hard working person. The rest is all details."

Darrell studied his face, "So, what would you want from it? I mean, what would you get for it?"

"A share of the profits, milk and the feeling that I belonged somewhere and maybe matter a little bit."

Darrell stared at him in total amazement. "You're nuts."

"I know. Okay, we can make this as big of a partnership or as small of a one as you want. I could just buy a piece of property or I could build by Zach. I have just about convinced myself that I'll be the head of the Gopher Brigade in my old age. That's okay. But I want to have a real involvement too. I thought this might work out. You don't need to answer right away. Think on it. It's a big step. I'm going in with Zach to the bank today, so I can get my money out of Texas. Then I'll know more of where I stand. Okay?"

Darrell barely nodded, lost in thought.

Carl smiled, "Anyway, I need to bum a ride home. Zach is going to town at ten. Or I need to call for a ride."

Darrell smiled, "No you don't. If you're thinking about investing, don't you want to look at the land at least? It's only a little after eight. I can give you a ride around and then take you home. Okay?"

Darrell drove all around the green rolling pasture, the acres of cropland now bearing corn, barley, oats, wheat and alfalfa. They drove until they came out on the road by his father's place. "That's the grand tour."

"Impressive. I think it is impressive." Carl was taken with how Darrell explained the fields and pastures; what was good soil, what wasn't, all the things that were bad about Carl's plan as well as all the good things. Kincaid knew he was being totally honest.

"It isn't much," Darrell responded. "It is just a farm."

"Stop that. Most people live their whole lives and never some close to having a piece of dirt they can call their own. It isn't just a farm. It's your home. It is where you and Jeannie are planning on raising your family."

"Yah, that could be a pickle. I know she'd never say so, but I really need to get a better house than this shed for her. I was thinking about getting a double wide trailer," Darrell said.

"Well, if I buy the land for my house, then you could build too, huh? I think Elton said something about forty acres to be a farmer for taxes or something. Would I need to buy forty acres?"

"Not if you're a partner in a whole farm! You'd be a farmer!" Darrell chuckled. "A real one."

"Hmm. You know, Zach said if I was going to build, I should talk to his contractor. Maybe our partnership could get a deal if we built two houses. Yours and mine!" Carl laughed.

"Might just, but I have some serious thinking to do. I really appreciate that you would even consider this, but I don't want to let you down. I was hoping God would show me what He wanted me to do by the time Andy got home after Christmas. Now he is getting married sooner, so it kind of blew my plan."

Carl looked at the young man, "You know, I'm not a religious sort, but maybe He did. Maybe you and Jeannie should go over to Hawaii and get married there too! Your idea might have been good, but God has a different time line!"

Without a word, Darrell got out to the pickup and opened the gate to the pasture. He drove the pickup through and then got out and closed the gate. Now they were driving inside the pasture.

Carl looked at him, "Where you taking me?"

"Out to the land you are talking about homesteading on!" Darrell laughed. "I'm worried about all this. It is too much like the answer to my every prayer. It scares me."

"I do understand. Why if Maureen says she'll marry me, I'd probably die."

"Hmm. Hardly worth buying a wedding ring then, huh?" Darrell laughed.

47

The news at the bank was good for Kincaid. All the money he had stuffed away for years and all the interest had compounded and earned, netted him well over $600,000. He opened a checking account and a couple savings accounts at the bank. When he was filling out the papers, he asked Zach to be the cosigner on all his accounts, in the event that something should happen to him. Zach nodded and signed the papers without a thought. After all, he had done it before for the man.

When they were back in Zach's car, Kincaid thanked him. Zach smiled, "No problem. I hope you're planning on reinvesting that money somewhere rather than just leaving it there."

"I am. I'm working on it," Kincaid smiled.

"So, you decided to stay in these parts?" His eyes watched for an answer.

"Yah. I guess I will. It's the closest thing to a home I have," Carl smiled. "You knew that, didn't you?"

"Not really. It was your choice to make but I knew it was here if you wanted it," he grinned. "Did you pop the question to Maureen yet?"

"No. I don't know if I should buy a ring like they do on TV or if I should ask her first and then we both go looking for the ring. What do you think?"

"Unless you already know what she wants, I'd ask her first. Then she can decide which one she likes. That is what we did. Of course, that doesn't make it right," Zach shrugged.

"How're you doing with the wedding? I mean, how do you feel about it?"

"You know, it seems like the natural thing to do. I have no qualms at all. I just wish the house was done but it's coming along," Zach said. "I still feel bad about Miriam. I don't think she has any desire to come home with us."

"Sorry to say, I agree with you. But give her time," Carl said thoughtfully. "I think when the kids start school again this fall, it won't be as much fun for her at Ellisons. She loves those kids and they're good for her."

"She does okay with the clan," Zach grinned. "Actually, she is becoming a real little character. She talks almost as much as Chatterbox."

Carl nodded, "So, how's Harrington doing? Think he'll pop the question soon?"

"I know he and Ruthie have talked about it. They plan on getting married," Zach related as he pulled onto the highway. "He's trying to find his niche. And in a way, so is she. The longer she works at the church, the less she worries about the nun business."

"Good for her," Kincaid agreed. "I haven't had a good talk with Harrington yet. I was hoping to soon."

"So, if I may ask, what was the deal with Darrell this morning?" Zach asked curiously. "That took me by surprise."

"Oh, nothing yet. We're talking about something though. What do you think of him?"

"He is real solid guy and he can be a lot of fun. Why do you ask?" Zach probed.

"Nosey, aren't you?" Kincaid teased. "Well, keep your mouth shut, but I'm thinking about going into partnership with him in his farm. It was my idea. He's thinking on it. I don't know if he will or not."

"Does he need a partner?"

"Yah, his Dad is not up to par since his cancer bout last year and needs to retire. I thought I might as well put my money some place with someone I know rather than a faceless company. I suppose you think I'm crazy, huh?" Carl watched for Zach's reaction.

"Not at all. I did hear about his Dad. I just never realized that he might want an investor or I would've done it. You know Carl, Ruthie and I got a pile of money from all that business with my dad," Zach continued. "Harrington wouldn't need to work a day in his life, but it would kill him if he didn't. I wish he would just forget it and get married."

"Zach, you and Ruthie both work. Why do you think it would be any different for him? He needs to feel worthwhile. He'll find something. I'm pretty sure of that," Carl pointed out. "He just wants to feel valuable."

Zach gave him a long look and then Kincaid said, "You better watch the road there. Oh, I just realized. I have to get a driver's license again. Yea gads. I might just go back to Texas."

When they got to Merton, they decided to stop in at Elton's station to see what was going on. When they got inside, they asked for a Coke.

Harrington took them into Elton's office and Elton yelled he'd be there in a minute. Rod and Ken were watching the pumps.

"Where's Kevin?" Zach asked as he took the Coke from Harrington.

Harrington looked rather solemn, "We got a call from Byron. Seems everyone overlooked the fact that there would be crayons at Bible school!"

"Oh dear God," both men gasped.

"This morning Miriam did well, but this afternoon, the poor teacher pulled out the crayons for the kids, and she screamed "Dog Bite!" Then she panicked and curled up into that damned ball thing she does. Byron was right there and took her home. He couldn't get her to come out of it. Marly called here and Kevin was out the door before they finished talking. That was about half an hour ago. Elton called a few minutes ago. She is doing a lot better now, but is still holding on to him for dear life. Elton told him to just stay with her today."

"Oh no, I should go there," Zach got up.

"Not necessary. I think that she is settling down now. Just let Kevin take care of it. You know, there is no one she would rather be with," Harrington assured him. "I wonder what the hell happened with those crayons."

Kincaid hadn't moved. He was so busy thinking about himself and his good fortune that he neglected things with Miriam. He knew, too. Way down deep, he knew that Bible School would be a trial for the little girl. The voice in his head told him that he should be there. "Damn it all."

"Look. It's okay now. We have to realize it will just happen and deal with it as is does. She can't sit in a confined space all her life or those crazy people will have won and that's a blasted fact," Harrington was definite.

"I wonder if there's any way we could find out what happened?" Zach barely mumbled. "Hypnosis? Or something?"

Harrington thought a minute, "I doubt it. She's awful young. I don't know if we will ever know. Whatever it was, it must've been horrible."

"I wouldn't put anything past those parents of hers, but hell," Kincaid pointed out, "It could have been any one of the other psychopaths that they dumped her off on. Obviously, we have to get her over it before she goes to kindergarten. She'll encounter crayons in her life."

Zach was grim, "How the hell are we going to do that? She even sees a picture of one, like in Katie's book, and she curls up. I'll have to talk to Dr. Samuels about that."

Elton came in the office and grabbed his Coke. After a big swig, he asked Harrington, "Did you tell them?"

Harrington nodded. Elton shook his head dejectedly, "Awful business. Poor little girl. Kevin was out of here before we even found out what happened. When I talked to Marly a bit ago, she said they were rocking now. Miriam was crying into his shoulder and not curled up anymore. I hope she can get to sleep." Elton sat down, "I was so happy that she could to Bible School with all the other little ones. I even thought she might get to be in the program. I forgot all about the crayons!"

"Me, too," Zach said. "Never entered my mind."

"Well, she made it most of the day. And Ruthie said she had a good day. She was even singing with the other little kids and stuff. I hope she can go back tomorrow. How can we do that?" Harrington asked.

"Don't know, but she really should go back. If she stays home now, that'll be another big block she has to face," Elton pointed out. "You know, when Andy was little, I used to go to Sunday School class with him. Suppose that would work?"

The men all looked at each other. "Worth a try," Kincaid said, "But she panics around crayons when we're holding her."

"We need to have a powwow tonight to figure this out. We can't take the crayons out of the whole Sunday School area. That's not only unrealistic, but not fair to the other kids," Zach pointed out. "Maybe she should stay home. You know, I'm going to talk to Kevin and then call Dr. Samuels before we talk tonight."

"Good idea. And we'll keep thinking," Elton said. "See you all at dinner."

On the way home, the guys stopped in at the parsonage. Kevin was there rocking Miriam. She was just beginning to go asleep. Marly made them some coffee and filled them in on what she knew.

"The kids just got their papers handed out and Miriam was in her wheelchair. She was sitting there when the teacher took the box of crayons out and opened it. She let the crayons roll out on the table so each child could take one. As they rolled out, one rolled toward Miriam. That's when she panicked. Mrs. Sandvahl didn't know what to do. She called for Suzy and Byron. They came running. She was all curled up in seconds," Marly explained.

"Byron took her out of there and Suzy brought her wheelchair over later. That's the worst I have ever seen her. Byron couldn't get her to uncurl or to breathe regularly and that is when he had me call the shop. Kevin was here in minutes. As soon as he picked her up, her breathing was more relaxed. It took him awhile, but he got her to finally uncurl. She was so panicked that she has gouges in his neck from gripping on to him."

"They're better now. She was almost asleep with him rocking her, so I came out here to give them some quiet," then she looked at the men. She started to cry, "What are we going to do with her?"

Zach put his arm around Marly, "I don't know. We'll think of something."

After a couple cups of coffee, Kevin came into the kitchen. "I got her down now. I hope she sleeps a little. Got some of that coffee?"

Marly gave him a hug, "Sure. Thanks for coming right over."

Kevin looked at the guys. "What can we do with her? She won't be able to go to school like this. Marly said she had a good morning, sang and everything. She was going to be walking on her own pretty soon and I had visions of her being all better." He shook his head. "Then this. She's terrified. I've been scared in my life, but this is sheer terror. She just shakes and whimpers. I can hardly stand it."

Byron came in. "Hi, how's the little one?"

Marly gave her husband a kiss and poured him some coffee. "Kevin just got her to settle down."

"What are we going to do? I have never seen her so scared; and believe me, I have seen her scared," Kevin continued.

"I don't know. I'm going to go home now and call Dr. Samuels," Zach said. "I want to see what he says."

"You can use our phone. Call him from here. Then if he wants to talk to us that were here, he can," Byron said.

Zach got an odd expression on his face. "Okay."

He called and Samuels was with a patient. They were finishing their coffee when he called back. Zach told them what he knew, and Samuels asked to talk to Byron and Kevin. He asked a lot of questions and then said he'd call them back later when he had more time to think about it. He was glad that she was sleeping and suggested that they keep her in her comfort zone until she could regroup.

On the way home, Zach hardly said a word and before they parked his car, Kincaid said, "Okay, out with it Petunia. I saw that look on your face. Spit it out!"

"What look?"

"That odd look. Something's eating you," Kincaid was brutal. "I know you like a book. Out with it."

Zach dropped his head, "I'm supposed to be her guardian and her caretaker. Kincaid, I'm hardly with her. I hardly know her. What good am I? She would rather be with anyone else but me."

Kincaid patted his shoulder, "Stop. You can't be everyone's knight in white armor. We all have a part in her life. Don't kid yourself, she knows who you are and she trusts you. She just likes Kevin better. Hell, I like Kevin better than you and you aren't whining about that!"

Zach gave him a dirty look, "But I don't care if you like me! Do you think everyone thinks that I dumped her on you all?"

"You keep saying that. If you think you know how to change it and be with her more, change it. Otherwise, just appreciate the fact that she has all of us. Okay?"

"Okay, but it doesn't feel right."

"Your life must have been similar to hers when you were little, you just forgot it. But remember how you were six months ago? I haven't seen you throw up in at least a month!" Kincaid went on. "She'll be fine and if it takes all of us to make it right, then so be it. Don't make it be about how you feel. You know Zach. You're probably not the best to be taking care of her. It's too close to home for you."

"What do you mean by that?" Zach was taken back, "I'm her uncle."

"Yah, that's just biology. She doesn't know you any better than she knows any other of us. And one of the people in the world that you spent most of your life being terrified of was her mother! I can't see how either you or Ruthie can be objective about Miriam. You love her and no one would doubt that, but she brings up all the tortured memories of your past. Sure, in some ways it's good, but it keeps you from being objective."

"Am I that lousy of an uncle? Does everyone think that I'm not good with her?"

"I didn't say your weren't good with her. Not at all. No one else has mentioned it to me, so I have no idea what they think. I do know that they don't think about it as much as you do! It doesn't bother anybody but you and Ruthie."

"Well, Ruthie is pretty fragile herself. I mean, her life was a mess. I wouldn't expect her to be able to handle Miriam. She has enough on her plate," Zach pointed out.

"Listen to yourself! Why do you think that you're any different? What about that vomit machine I met a few months ago? I remember. Sure Zach, you're doing well and getting better. I'm glad that you are handling everything so well, but the old Zach isn't gone. He still hides when he can, and he does it to protect himself. Just like Miriam curls up. You hide in your work. Zach. You are an excellent doctor and you do a lot of great things for people. You've been a better friend to me than anyone in the world; but you have to realize that you dealing with Miriam's problems makes about as much sense as you becoming a rattlesnake handler! Shit man! You identify too closely with her."

Zach's expression changed, "Oh my God, is that what I have been doing? I think you're right." He thought a bit, "You might be right about that. But I wanted to be the one to fix things for her, because I understood. I guess it's an ego thing, huh?"

"Could be. Why don't you talk to that shrink you jabber to all the time. Hell, you pay him enough. Until then, don't beat yourself up about it. We can't all be all things to everyone. You're still her guardian and we all know you would do anything in the world for that little girl. But the best thing you can do, is let someone else do it. Everyone has a little something to throw in the pot. She just connects with Kevin. Look how she was so stuck to Elton in Shreveport, and she met Kevin once. Now he's her favorite. Who knows why, but thank God."

"You're right, you old Coot. I'll talk to Samuels. You're smarter than you act."

Carl laughed, "No one could be as dumb as I act!"

48

Nora invited the Ellisons over for dinner so they could all discuss the situation with Miriam. Carrie and Kevin came, too. Marly had a huge kettle of scalloped potatoes cooking when Nora called, and Nora thought they would go just dandy with her fried chicken.

Dr. Samuels called Zach right before they sat down to eat. After grace, they discussed the situation. Zach said, "Samuels said we need to get her to overcome the phobia and for our own sanity, we need to quit trying to figure out how it started. It may always remain a mystery, or we may find out. Either way, it makes little difference to the situation."

They all had to agree with that but how to do it escaped them.

"He said the first thing is that she needs to go back tomorrow. If she doesn't, she is well on her way to associating church and Sunday School with crayons. Then we will have another whole can of worms. The Jeffries have thrown up in enough churches! I told him that Elton had suggested someone going with her. He thought that was an excellent idea," Zach continued. "As far as the colors, he said if we can, start with her just getting used to seeing them. Then when she can handle that, let her be close to them and then hold them. Just a little at a time. It's going to scare her and there is no two ways about it; but unless she faces her fear, she'll never get over it."

They all went back to their eating; thinking while they ate, but no one said anything. They knew it was the right thing to do, but none of them wanted to be the one to put her through it.

After much contemplation, Elton cleared his throat. "I have an idea. Let's look at it from her point of view as best we can. She loves her Kevin.

He hasn't been to Bible School in years and I think he'd probably put use a refresher course. Harrington can help me at the station, if he's willing."

Ian was pensive, "I'd love to. I really enjoy being at the shop but with my bum arm, I'm useless."

Ken looked at him in amazement, "No you're not! You taught Rod and me a lot of stuff! Uncle Elton and Kevin are good too, but you have the time to show us how to do stuff. We need to learn how."

"Thanks Ken but that isn't much help," Harrington responded quietly.

"Today, you did all the ordering for me," Elton pointed out. "And you talked that Johnson dude into not raping us on the price of that transmission. Pepper and I've been trying to get him to come down on his prices for three months!"

"Ah, that was nothing," Harrington said. "But I will help out. I love the shop. It reminds me of my teenage years!"

"Lord and all the Saints!" his mom exclaimed. "Just so you're reminded and don't start reliving them! I hardly made it through the first go round! Zachie, best keep that shrink's number handy!'

Zach grinned, "I have it memorized, Mo! With this outfit, we need one on retainer!"

Annie suggested that she buy more colored pencils. She had seen some made by the Crayola company and they had the logo on them. The colored pencils that she had Miriam using before were generic.

"She colors with them all the time. Without a problem," Annie explained. "Remember that first time, Coot? That was horrendous."

"Yah, it was. She finally started to mellow about them when we were drawing the plans for the water diversion," the older man nodded. "It was just like that volcano!"

"The paints I bought were made by Crayola too, and she took one look and was all done." Pepper was quiet a minute and then giggled, "But when I brought out another brand of paints, she was into it up to her eyebrows!"

"And our eyebrows!" Annie laughed.

"That was one of the biggest messes I ever did see!" Ken shook his head in disgust. "You guys were terrible! You grownups were worse than the kids!"

"Yah, Ken," Coot agreed, "It was pretty bad."

Kevin was nervous. "Okay, okay. That's well and good, but what about tomorrow? What am I supposed to do? I'm not a shrink or a doctor."

Zach looked down at his plate and then back to Kevin. "As usual, Kevin, you have do the heavy lifting for me. I have four surgeries tomorrow. So, I'll be crapping out on Miriam again. I'm no help at all. But you're always with her, and you know her better than any shrink! You can work with her the best of anyone!"

"Thanks, but I don't know what I'm doing," Kevin swallowed hard.

"Yes you do. You know it innately. You don't have to look at a book, you just know. That's worth more than anything." Zach assured him. "You're a godsend to her. And she loves you."

"Well, she loves a lot of people," Kevin shrugged.

"But not like her Son," Elton pointed out. "We all know that. If she was going into an alligator pit, you're the one she would want there. And I know you. You would want to be the one who went in with her."

Carrie patted her husband's arm, "You know that's true, honey."

"Okay," Kevin cleared his throat, "I never said I wouldn't do it, but what do I need to do?"

Byron explained, "You can bring her to Bible School and stay with her."

Kevin nodded, "Can I let her sit on my lap rather than in the wheelchair? I think she feels more secure on someone's lap."

Everyone agreed.

"In the morning, is singing and that stuff. Then there's lunch. It isn't until the afternoon that they color," Byron explained. "What do you guys think?"

Everyone considered the situation. Ruthie finally said, "I think that Kevin should just play that by ear. If she can watch the other kids color, that would be great. I can talk to Mrs. Sandvahl again. She can pass out the crayons instead of putting them on the table. Maybe if Miriam sees that you aren't afraid of the crayons, maybe she won't be either."

Kevin chuckled, "What if I get scared!"

Pepper was sitting next to him and whacked him.

"Dad, are you going to let her do that?" Kevin whined.

Elton raised his eyebrows, "If she hadn't, I would have."

"Well, if that don't beat all!" Kevin grumped. "Okay so what are we going to color with? Her and I won't have colors."

"You know, I'll go to Merton in the morning and pick up some generic crayons at the store there. You can use those," Darlene suggested.

"That is a good idea," Mo agreed, "But I'd also take something that she is comfortable using already."

Coot nodded, "Our colored pencils?"

Annie said, "Of course. We'll get them for you."

Everyone went back into deep thought. Finally Kevin said, "I have one problem with all this."

"What's that, Son?" Elton asked, with concern.

"How am I going to have a cigarette? I'm going to be dying all day. When she gets so scared, it makes me a wreck. I won't be able to stand it without a break. That sounds awful, but I think I'll collapse," Kevin reported honestly.

Zach's heart went out to him, "I really understand that. I think what you're doing is above and beyond."

"No, it isn't, but I'll need a smoke."

Suzy offered, "Well, I'll break you. Miriam and I'll do fine and I can take her to the bathroom and so on. And if it is too hard to get her away from you; you guys could both go take a break. In fact, she might need one too."

Little Katie's eyes got huge, "Miriam will need a cigarette?"

Suzy giggled, "No Katie, but she might like a little break."

Katie nodded, "I was worried."

"I think you're right about that," Keith agreed. "If you think the pressure on you will be tremendous; imagine how it'll be for her. I think it's great that you are doing it for her."

"Ah, Dad's right. I think we all need a refresher Bible School once in a while." Then Kevin got his devilish grin, "Especially with a smoke break!"

That time, even Carrie whacked him.

49

The next morning was sunny. Coot spent a good share of the night stewing about his little Miriam. He wished that he could be there for her, but he also knew that she'd prefer Kevin. Carl couldn't imagine himself at that age even considering doing something like Kevin was going to do. On the other hand, no one would've asked him either.

Before milking, Kevin was a nervous wreck. Pepper harassed him unmercifully, but everyone knew that he'd have been more than willing to return the favor had the shoe been on the other foot. Harrington was nervous that he'd be able to help at the shop and Elton was trying to scrape him off the ceiling. What a bunch of petunias! Carl was certain that the Mafia planned a hit with less consternation and self-doubt than this outfit did taking a kid to Bible School! He listened to them and then had to smile as he thought to himself, 'I never realized it was such hard work being a petunia!'

Mo saw him grin. She put her arm around him and said, "What?"

Kincaid put his arm around her and whispered, "I'll tell you later." Then he kissed her cheek.

Just like that, everyone was silent and looked at them. He could have died, but instead he grinned. "Haven't you ever seen a guy kiss his girl?"

Everyone giggled and went on about their banter. Maureen gave him a hug and went back to stirring the waffle batter.

Ruthie walked with the other kids over to the church but Miriam seemed more than content to stay with Marly. Usually, she wanted to follow the other kids but today she just watched them leave without a flinch. It was obvious she had no desire to go anywhere near the church. Byron watched and shook his head. He kissed his wife goodbye and whispered, "This will be a bearcat."

She nodded back with a worried smile. Then Byron kissed Miriam and said, "See you later."

She shot him a look a pure panic and turned into Marly's arms. Marly patted her back and glanced at Byron. They were both concerned.

A few minutes later, Kevin drove up. He came to the door and knocked. Marly let him in. He was obviously a wreck.

"Good morning. You look like a basket case," Marly kissed his check. "It'll be okay. If it gets out of hand, just come back over here. No big deal. We can try again tomorrow. You know, Kevin, we can only do the best we can. The rest is in God's hands."

Kevin was not impressed, "Well, I think He should come here and do it then. He'd be able to handle it."

Marly winked at him, "What do you think He put you here for?"

"Thanks," Kevin said dryly. "Put pressure on the mechanic!"

While they were talking, the little girl had moved over to Kevin's arms. "You know what I want to do today?" Kevin asked with a smile.

Miriam studied his face.

"I'd like you to go to Bible School with me, okay?" Kevin asked.

Miriam tucked her head into his shoulder and shuddered.

"Would that be okay? We can go together and you can show me what to do at Bible School. Won't that be fun?"

Miriam shrugged and then put her arms around his neck. She started to tremble.

Kevin cuddled her gently and said, "But we don't need to go right this minute. Want to rest a bit?"

Miriam shrugged. Kevin eyes pleaded with Marly for a miracle and she just patted Miriam's back. "How about some hot chocolate?"

Kevin was almost crying himself by now, but said as cheerily as possible, "Doesn't that sound good, Miriam?"

The little girl shrugged.

They went into the kitchen and sat at the table. Kevin straightened her out on his lap and smoothed out her pretty dress. "Is this ever a pretty dress! Is it new? Did Marly get you ready this morning?"

Miriam nodded.

"I really like your bear tails. Those ribbons are just perfect," Kevin wiggled her little braid. "Did Marly fix those for you?"

Miriam answered quietly, "Ruthie."

"Ruthie did a fine job."

"Mighty fine indeed," Miriam mumbled.

Then Marly put the hot chocolate on the table and a bowl of whipped cream. Kevin grinned, "Look Miriam, we even get whipped cream for our chocolate!"

Miriam smiled weakly, "Lick?"

"You can lick it if you like," Kevin grinned.

She put her little finger in the bowl of whipped cream and got a tiny dab on it. Then she put it to Kevin's mouth, "Thank you Miriam."

"Thank you," she answered.

"Do you know where her class is?" Kevin looked to Marly.

"At the bottom of the stairs, first door on the right. You aren't late yet. They have a little kid's service first thing. That doesn't start for ten minutes yet. Ruthie was going to talk to Mrs. Sandvahl this morning before class. It'll be okay, Kev. If it goes sour, just come back over here. Rome wasn't built in a day."

"No but I think it burned down in one!"

"Okay, Mr. Pessimistic! But I think it took at least a day and a half," Marly patted his shoulder.

They sipped on their hot chocolate for a couple minutes and then Kevin took a deep breath. He put on his cheerful voice and said, "Okay Miriam. Let's go."

Miriam grinned at him, "Let's go."

They told Marly goodbye and went out the door. It wasn't until Miriam realized they were heading to the church, that Kevin felt her start to tighten up. He stopped and turned her so he could look into her tear-filled eyes.

"Okay little one. You and I are going to Bible school. You won't cry, will you? You're going to help me and I'm going to help you. Neither of us wants to cry today. Okay?"

Miriam's eyes were about brimming over, "If you want to."

"I want to, a lot. Okay? Will you do that for me? If it gets too hard, you can just tell me, okay?" He asked the little girl.

Miriam was very uncertain about his plan, but she wanted to be with him. She looked at him and then at the church door, and finally said, "Okay Son."

Kevin gave her a hug and he reached out to open the door. Hell, he wanted his break already and they weren't even in the building yet.

The other kids were already with their classes in the pews. Kevin and Miriam came in and sat down near the back. Suzy was by the door and patted Miriam's back and gave Kevin a kiss on the cheek.

Miriam wouldn't turn around and sit down on his lap, but stayed with her arms around his neck. Granted, she wasn't gouging him but it was definitely a good grip.

After they sang a couple songs, she started to relax and about half way through the service, she finally turned around to watch the little puppet show. At the end of the program, she even sang along when they sang *Jesus Loves Me.*

The teachers started to leave the sanctuary with their classes, the youngest first. Mrs. Sandvahl's class was the second one out. Kevin got up and walked out behind the last of Miriam's classmates. He could feel Miriam's breathing change. He started rubbing her back and saying quietly, "It'll be okay, Miriam. I promise."

By the time they got to the bottom of the stairs, Kevin's own breathing was no longer normal. He was convinced that his heart was not letting any blood through and he would pass out any minute. He felt dizzy.

Suzy was right behind them and brought in a folding chair for Kevin. Inside the door, Miriam was like stone. No sound, no movement and certainly, little breathing.

Suzy shot him an apprehensive look and left the room, while the other kids scrambled for their seats. Mrs. Sandvahl introduced Kevin to the rest of the class. "Mr. Schroeder came to visit our class, kids? Isn't that wonderful? Let's all welcome him."

All the kids clapped their hands, and Kevin smiled, "Thank you. It's so nice to be here. Miriam and I'll sit back here and watch you have your class. Will that be okay?"

They all yelled "Yes!"

Then one little boy asked, "Are you going to sing with us when we do our songs?"

"We just might." Kevin nodded, but thought to himself, 'Or be in the back room in convulsions.'

Miriam didn't move a muscle. They sat and listened while they went over their lines for the program. The whole class had two lines to say, "We are the animals of the world! We are going to ride on Noah's boat."

The class repeated it over and over. After the second time, Kevin felt her start to relax. By the last time they repeated the chant, he could feel her little lips saying it silently against his neck. He couldn't help but smile.

Then they sang a little song. Kevin had never heard it before, but it was about the animals going on the ark, two by two. Miriam lifted her head and peeked around a couple times. Before long, she was turned and finally was willing to sit on his lap and face the table. They sang the song over and over, so the little ones could learn it. By the time they were finished with 'rehearsal,' Miriam was singing along.

Kevin was so relieved he couldn't believe it. She had been sweating and had his shirt soaked. Then he realized, he had been sweating as much as her. Mrs. Sandvahl said it was treat time. He was so very grateful.

Ruthie came in with a plate of cookies and a pitcher of Kool-Aid. Mrs. Sandvahl served them each a little cup and a cookie. Miriam was now almost completely into the class. Mrs. Sandvahl caught Kevin's eye and gave him the thumbs up. That was the first time that he realized that she must have been as nervous as he was. He grinned back.

After their treat, it was story time. That went very well and Kevin even took part in some of the questions and answers. The kids loved that. Miriam was smiling and even giggled a couple times.

At lunch, they went to the hall and ate with their class. Miriam was comfortable enough so that she let Kevin help Mrs. Sandvahl serve the other kids their sandwiches. It was good. Byron came by and she smiled. He asked how it was going and Kevin nodded.

Then they all went back to their rooms. Now it was craft time. Miriam was unaware what was coming and was happily sitting on Kevin's lap, leaning her elbows on the table. Mrs. Sandvahl brought out the pages the kids were supposed to color. She handed them out and Kevin could feel Miriam begin to tighten up.

Then the teacher explained that they were going to color the pages to take home to their parents. Miriam let go of the paper, turned and immediately climbed up to Kevin's neck. Kevin tried not to let her know that he was panicking.

The teacher handed each child a color crayon and then handed Kevin a colored pencil. By now, Miriam's face was buried deep in his neck. He tried to ignore her. They all started to color, and he colored too. He tried to make happy conversation with the others in the class about their pictures, while the tiny girl clung to him in desperation.

After a few minutes, Miriam went from near panic to curiosity. When he asked the teacher if she liked the color of his ark, Miriam couldn't stand it and had to take a peek. One quick glance and she crawled back into his shoulder, but her body wasn't as tight as before.

She never looked around again or even acted interested, but she didn't cry either. For his part, Kevin thought that the coloring thing was at least eighteen hours too long.

Then one of the little kids dropped their crayon and it went rolling across the floor, under Kevin's chair and came out behind him. Miriam panicked immediately.

Kevin reached around to pick up the crayon and handed it back to the little kid with a smile. The little boy said, "Thank you."

Miriam stared. Frozen solid and unable to make sense of any of it, she stared at Kevin. He was certain his blood pressure had set some sort of world record and his stomach wall was devoured completely through by acid. He was almost relieved when she turned back into his neck and snuggled in. He patted her back.

As the teacher continued with the kids, Kevin said quietly, "I think we're going to take a little break. We'll be right back."

Mrs. Sandvahl nodded and looked like she needed a break too. They went out the back door of the church. The cool air felt wonderful. Kevin reached in his pocket and got out his cigarettes, lit one and replaced the pack. It was a couple minutes before Miriam moved. She turned and patted his cheek. He looked at her and grinned.

"Well, little one, we made it through part of the alligator pit! Huh?" He asked.

She looked at him, "Alligator."

He chuckled, "You don't need to tell anyone that, you know. We really needed this break huh, and I needed this smoke."

Miriam nodded, "Smoke."

Kevin hugged her with a chuckle, "You don't need to tell anyone that either."

They sat quietly until he finished his cigarette, and then he said, "Okay, Miriam. Let's go find Ruthie or Suzy to take you to the rest room and then we can go back to our class."

Miriam said, "No go."

"Yes, Miriam. We need to go. We did mighty fine indeed. Did you know that you are a very good singer? I love to hear you sing. Did you know that?"

She shrugged. "No go."

"I'm sorry, sweetheart, but we have to go back. Okay?"

Crestfallen, Miriam mumbled, "If you want to."

Soon they were back in their classroom. The crayons had been collected and the class was beginning to listen to a story. It was about a little puppy dog. Miriam was very interested in that. She even giggled when the rest of the class did.

Then the teacher passed out all their papers, which now displayed big gold stars on them, and told them to gather their things. When she started to pass out the papers, Miriam tried to turn into Kevin's arms, but he wouldn't let her. He made her face the teacher when she handed the paper to her. Miriam was scared, but she did it.

Kevin took the picture he had colored with the colored pencil and then pointed to the big star. He smiled to Miriam, "Mighty fine indeed."

She looked up at him and tried to discern what he meant. But he was grinning, so she smiled. She touched the foil star with her finger, "Mighty fine indeed."

Then Kevin folded the paper and put it in his pocket, "We'll show Marly when we get home. Okay?"

"Sharlee, Ginger, Katie, Mr. Bear, Uncle, Coot," Miriam started, obviously still very unimpressed with it.

Kevin chuckled, "Yes Miriam, we will show everyone!"

"Mighty fine indeed."

After the closing gathering where they sang more songs, they got to go home. Kevin had never been more glad to get anywhere in his life. He came in the house and gave Marly the biggest hug in the world.

"I'm so glad to see you! You have no idea. Can you hold Miriam for a minute, while I go to the bathroom?"

A few minutes later he came into the kitchen and Miriam was in the high chair. He nearly collapsed at the table, "I've never been through anything like that in my life! I thought I was having a heart attack all day today."

Miriam nodded to Marly, "Heart attack."

Both Marly and Kevin had to laugh. Miriam just smiled and drank her chocolate milk. The phone rang. Within the next few minutes, they had a call from Carrie, the guys at the shop, Coot, Keith, Darrell, and Zach. Everyone had been worried and praying. They're all relieved today had gone so well, but no one thought they were out of the woods.

Kevin took the paper out of his pocket and handed it to Miriam. She didn't like it, but he said, "Show it to Marly, Miriam. She wants to see the gold star."

Miriam held it out to Marly, "Mighty fine indeed."

Marly took it and looked it all over, "Miriam, that's just grand! Did you color it?"

Miriam pointed to Kevin, "Son."

Marly gave him a kiss on the cheek, "Very good work, Kevin."

Miriam watched as apparently everyone was very happy with that hateful piece of paper. She preferred her cookie. When Katie came back with the other kids, they all brought their papers in and showed them to Marly. They all had stars too.

Miriam watched as they showed their papers with pride to their Mom and Kevin. Then Byron came home and he lavished praise on their good work. He saw Miriam's paper and told her it was wonderful. She pointed to Kevin, "Son."

Byron then praised Kevin for his fine work. Miriam watched as all their papers were hung on the refrigerator with magnets. Byron stepped back and appraised the fine art, "I'm so proud of my whole family!"

50

That evening at chores, Kevin was very tired. He was happy about how things had turned out, but knew it was nip and tuck all day. Just because the little girl wasn't in a catatonic state or the fetal position, didn't exactly make it a success in his mind. He was glad though it had turned out as well as it did.

"I'm going home to crash and burn when we're finished here. I'm totally wiped out," he announced.

After chores and the grandparents were in bed, the older folks visited on the patio. The four were sitting at the picnic table, munching on some chips and dip with their drinks.

"I'm so relieved that today worked out as well as it did," Elton said. "I know Kevin is still concerned that it won't last or that it wasn't that much of a success, but I think it was a major success that he even got her to go in the church, let alone her classroom."

"Or be in the same room with the crayons," Maureen pointed out. "I remember the Wee One in Shreveport. It was unbelievable. He just doesn't appreciate how good he is with her."

"You know who else doesn't give himself credit?" Elton asked. "That Ian Harrington. He can handle the stuff at the shop like a pro and he has only been there a few times. He just thinks that because he can't get under the car with a wrench, he's no good. I would like to box his ears. Oh, guess what? Doug came in today and told me the news. Don Holloway, Chris' dad, is getting serious about retiring. You know, his back has been giving him a bad time for months. He wants Doug to buy him out! Isn't that wonderful?"

"Oh, that's great!" Nora beamed. "He's worked there forever. He'll do a fine job."

"That's good," Kincaid smiled, and he turned to Maureen. "Doug is a clanner. He is married to Julia, Nora's cousin."

They visited for a couple hours and then Nora and Elton went in. Maureen was going to follow, but Kincaid took her hand. "I need to talk to you."

"Okay," she smiled.

He asked her to come over to the swing. She grinned, "We always get into trouble on the cuddling swing."

Carl grinned, "That we do, but I have some important things to talk to you about tonight."

"Sounds serious. What is it?"

He took both her hands in his and gave her a little kiss. He looked deeply into her eyes and asked, "What kind of car do you like?"

She stopped short for a second and started to giggle.

"What?" Kincaid was taken back and a bit chagrined.

"That just wasn't what I was expecting. I'm sorry, I didn't mean to make fun," Maureen explained. "I don't know. I guess just one that runs, an automatic preferably. Why do you ask?"

"I need to get a car, or maybe two. When we're married, I thought you should help pick it out."

"Are we getting married?" Maureen was puzzled, "I don't recall that being a given. Is it?"

"Well, oh damn." Kincaid was embarrassed now. He had plotted and planned most the afternoon, and then messed it all up. He tried to think of what to say, but couldn't. "I got this all backwards. I kind of forgot to ask you, huh? I was going to do that first!"

Maureen smiled at him, "If I was going to marry you, I would say a four-door hardtop, automatic transmission, maroon in color and that we should start out with one and see if we'd have the need for a second car. And if you had asked me to marry you, I might have said yes. But, since this is all speculation, I guess I'll throw in white-walled tires."

Kincaid chuckled, "I love you. Will you? I mean, will you marry me?"

"Yes, Carl. I will," she grinned. "Now, when do I get the car?"

"Gold digger!" Kincaid teased. "I guess you get the car as soon as we go to town and pick one out. Elton would be the one to take along, huh?"

"I guess he would. So, then what?" Maureen asked. "You've been doing a lot of thinking the last couple days. Am I going to be privy to any of it?"

"I guess you might be interested?" Kincaid poked. "Well, here's what I've been thinking."

Carl explained how he had made up his mind that this is where he wanted to live, unless she was opposed. He discussed investing in Darrell's farm and about the property across the road. He knew she'd want to see her family a lot and he agreed that she should and they'd plan on that. Mostly he wanted what she wanted and for her to be happy.

She listened quietly to the whole thing and asked a few questions. She agreed with his idea about investing in the farm. She thought that living across the road would be better than in Zach's back yard, but that either would be good. She didn't want to live in Merton, Bismarck, or Boston.

"If I'm going to start a new life with you, I'd like it to be new; not live in my old life. This can be a new life for both of us that we can build together. Does that sound okay?"

"That's perfect," Kincaid embraced her, "Totally perfect."

Then she asked, "I have to ask you Carl. Are you going to want to turn Catholic?"

"Ah," Kincaid swallowed hard, "Honestly?"

"Yes, honestly. That works out best. No point in starting out lying."

"I guess, huh? No, not really. I've never gone to church much but I think that Byron's church is about as religious as I can get," he dropped his head. "I suppose if it means a lot to you, I will though."

"My faith means a lot to me but I wouldn't want to force it down anyone else's throat. I liked Byron's church too. Since we're past the age of having children, I wouldn't have a problem if you wanted to remain Lutheran, if you let me go to my church."

"No problem at all." Kincaid was so relieved. "I'd be glad to go with you now, and maybe sometime even change. Maureen, I was going to get you a ring before I asked you, but I had no idea what you would want. I thought we could pick it out together. Is that okay?"

"That's wonderful," Mo giggled, "I have to try them on anyway. My fingers are so short that some rings make me look like a midget."

Kincaid gave her a big hug, "We wouldn't want that. So, how soon will you marry me?"

"Whenever you want," Maureen answered. "I'm a little busy tonight. I have a date with my boyfriend. I think it would be tacky to sit on the cuddling swing with him and then marry you."

"You're such a tart!" Kincaid chuckled. "Really, what do you think?"

"Well, I need to tell to my kids, first," Maureen said. "All of them. And you should probably tell your Gophers."

"My Gophers! They'll probably want to be in the wedding!" Kincaid was worried now, "What if your kids say no?"

"I'm not going to ask them, Carl. I'm going to tell them. There's a difference. I never told them they couldn't get married and they better not think they're going to tell me that I can't. But I need to talk to them. I'd like to have my Matt marry us."

"Hmm, I suppose that would be in Boston, huh?"

"Well, I don't know. I suppose you'd like to have Byron marry us?"

"That'd be nice, but the wedding is up to you. I'll let you work that out. I just want my girl to be happy," Kincaid said sincerely. "Planning weddings are a girl's job."

"You are such a male chauvinist!" Mo giggled.

"Yes, and you love it," Carl grinned. "At least I hope you do. I think I'm too old to change. Maureen, I haven't shared a life with someone for years. I have no idea how to even begin. You'll have to help me, but I promise you, I'll try to be the best husband I can. That might not be very good but that's all I can honestly offer."

Maureen leaned back in the crook of his arm on the swing, "I know that you will. Carl, you're a fine man. A little rough around the edges but your heart is pure gold."

Kincaid chuckled, "I know this kid that can weave me all the gold I need."

They were involved in a loving kiss, when Harrington drove up in Ruthie's car. He parked it in the garage and walked back to toward the house. The couple never left the swing. When he got to the patio he teased, "I'm going to have to ask you Mr. Kincaid, just what are your intentions with my mother?"

"Well, I just asked her to marry me," Kincaid beamed. "And she said yes."

"Really?" Harrington ran up to them and shook Kincaid's hand and gave his mom a hug. "That's just great. Wonderful! Fantastic and that's a blasted fact! I'm so happy, Mom and Kincaid! This is just terrific! When?"

"We thought we'd wait until tomorrow at least," Maureen giggled. "I think you gave your approval!"

"Yes, I think it's great. I never thought I'd be saying this about this old miserable grump, but I think he'll make a great Dad," Harrington shook his hand. "Just don't take to me to the woodshed, okay?"

"Only if you misbehave. What do you think Matt will say?" Kincaid chuckled, "Will he be as happy as you?"

"Probably happier! He and Zach have been planning this since Shreveport! They both thought that you two were great for each other. That's just wonderful, you guys! So, what are the details?"

"We don't have details yet," Mo smiled. "We just made the decision. We want to get married soon."

Kincaid joked, "At our age, we can't be dawdling!"

Harrington laughed and sat down at the picnic table. "This is fantastic."

"How is the Wee One tonight?" Maureen asked.

"Good," Harrington nodded. "She was pretty tired out tonight. It was probably good that it was just Ruthie and me at Ellisons with her tonight. She ate a pretty good dinner. Ruthie made some green beans and chocolate milk shakes, so she was cool with that. She even let me rock her a while. I have a hard time holding her with my bum arm. Do you think that she will ever like me as much as she does Kevin?"

His mom looked at him, "Probably not; but Ian, she thinks a lot of you. She just thinks Kevin is special."

"That was really good of him today," Harrington pointed out. "He'll make a great father." Something in Harrington's voice was almost sad.

Maureen sat up and took his hand. "What is it, Ian? What has my boy bothered tonight?"

"Nothing, Mom. I just wish that things were different," he looked up at the sky. "Guess I should be just damned glad they're as good as they are, huh? I'm just being ungrateful."

Kincaid leaned ahead in the swing and looked directly at Ian, "Not really. Sure, you're lucky to be alive. So am I. But the lives we were left with were not what we had bargained for. It is hard to change your whole mindset overnight. I know. I fought this kicking and screaming. Babysitting!! Talking to addled old men!! Going to church and sitting around with Petunias!! Good grief, what could be worse!"

Harrington had to smile, "Yah, I'm sure that you did fight it. You're doing okay with it all though. Kincaid, you seem to have found your niche. I can't do that. I'm too young. I need to find something to do with my life. I can't ask Ruthie to marry me unless I have a life to offer her."

Kincaid gave Maureen a kiss, "Can I ask you to go in? I want to have a talk with Harrington. Cop to cop. Okay?"

She nodded and kissed them both good night. After they heard the door close, Carl said, "It's none of my business, but that doesn't seem to bother folks around here, so I'll just say it. Harrington, you can't not ask her to marry you."

"What do you mean?"

"Just what I said. She has been driving herself crazy about this nun thing since it they sent her out here," Coot said. "You don't want her to go back to the convent, do you?"

"No way in hell!" Harrington burst out, too fast and too emphatically to brush it off.

Carl raised his eyebrows, "So, what is that about? What else is going on, Ian? Don't try to lie to me. I can smell a lie a mile away."

"It really isn't my place to say anything. Ruthie would be upset with me."

"Well, what if we don't tell her we talked about it? Would that work? Apparently, you feel pretty strongly about it. It sounds like you need to talk about it."

"She can't go back to Philadelphia. I won't allow that!" Ian was adamant.

"What is with Philadelphia?"

"Never breathe a word of this, okay? She would die if I told you. Only Matt knows because she told him. I think she talked to Suzy about it too. She needed to talk to a girl. But no one else knows and she really doesn't want them to."

"What happened?"

"That Father Timothy blackmailed her into having sex with him so that he wouldn't expel her from the convent."

"Dammit! That kind of shit makes me just furious. No wonder she is so messed up about churches. I can't believe it. Makes me wonder what the hell the Lutherans will do to her?"

"I don't know. But that's part of the reason she was in such a mess. It happened when all this stuff with Naomi came up. Oh, she did tell Father Vicaro when she got here. He was really good about it and told her that being in a convent isn't all it's cracked up to be. He told her she didn't need to be there to do the Lord's work. That's why she was okay with working with Byron. She is still just glued together, Carl. Finally, she is getting some sort of a normal life. Living with Byron and Marly has done her so much good. She loves Grandma Katherine. She told me that she finally thinks that she knows what it means to have a real family."

"Yah, she and Zach have both been through the mill. Zach is still just barely past the glue stage. Elton is the one that scraped him off the ceiling. I don't know, but without this is crazy outfit none of us could have made it! Sad state of affairs."

Ian smiled and nodded.

"Does that bother you? About that Father Timothy. I mean, is that why you have put off asking her to marry you?"

"No. I just want her to start having a decent life. And having me loafing around wouldn't be good for her. I really want her to be happy."

Coot leaned back and lit another cigarette. As he did, he looked at Ian. "Don't tell your Mom or Magpie. I will get lectured for three hours about smoking. Agree?"

"Agree," Harrington grinned.

"Kid, I don't know much about love stuff. I realize you'd be shocked to hear that! But I have observed a lot of stuff over the years. I know you love her and want her to be happy. I love your Mom and want to be the best husband I can for her. But let's get realistic. Neither you or I can make someone else happy. We can do the best we can, but we can't assure that. Know what I mean?"

Ian thought and then slowly nodded. "I guess."

"I love that little Ruthie and I think you guys are great together, but cop to cop I need to say something. Okay?"

"Yah."

"I don't want you to marry her and think that it's all about you making her happy. That's too one way. She needs to want to make you happy too. If not, before too long down the road, it'll be a burden on both of you. I really hope you aren't doing that," the older man looked at Harrington.

Harrington thought a while, "No, I'm not. I do enjoy seeing her be happy. There are so many things she has never enjoyed before. You know, she has never even tried on a formal before. Now she is getting fitted for the dress for Zach's wedding and she is like a little kid. I enjoy that."

"I know, but what about the real stuff?"

"Carl, she understands me and how I feel better than anyone in the world. I think that she'd be there for me no matter what. Even if my arm stayed a dangling decoration."

"Well, so what are you waiting for? She loves you and you love her. Everyone knows it. I don't care if you get married right away but you need to make it official. Know what I mean? She needs to be secure that you intend to marry her."

Harrington studied his face, "I guess you're right. But what am I going to do for a living? I won't just sponge off her."

"I don't think you should either. But that doesn't mean that you can't get engaged first. Just don't set the date yet. You already made a commitment to her verbally, and I think it's only right that you make it official. As far as a job, something will come up for you. You need to keep your eyes open. It is hard to look for something when you don't know what it is."

"That's for sure. There are a lot of things I like, but without an arm, what can I do?"

"Oh for crying out loud! Eddie has a huge cheese business and he only has one arm. You'll find something. Just relax. I needed to quit thinking and trying so hard; then it kind of fell into my lap. Sometimes we try so hard that we miss what we are supposed to see."

Harrington's face filled with a grin, "I can tell that you have been hanging around these guys. It shows."

"Maybe it does, but I think they're right."

Harrington nodded, and then his shoulder's fell, "You don't know how it feels. I was a good cop. That was my whole life. I can never do it again."

Carl got up and sat on the picnic bench next to Ian. He put his arm around his shoulder. "Yah. I do know. I know exactly how it feels. But I'm here to tell you something important, so listen. You were what made the job good, it wasn't the job that made you good! Do you hear me?"

Ian turned and looked at the old FBI agent. He was thinking. "You mean that?"

"I sure do, and I didn't read it someplace either. I thought it up all by myself."

Harrington grinned, "That means alot, Kincaid. Thanks for that."

They sat without talking for a minute and then Kincaid said, "Let's hit the sack."

"Sounds good."

Before Ian went upstairs, he turned and gave Kincaid quick hug. "I really appreciate what you said. You might just be a pretty good Dad."

Then he turned and ran up the stairs.

51

The news from Byron that morning at milking was not that good. Miriam was restless all night and though she slept, she woke up crying many times. She went back to sleep, but obviously didn't get a lot of rest.

"Maybe we should just skip it today," Kevin suggested. "I don't want her to start associating me with the crayon thing. Then she'd be scared of me too."

"I'm going to defer to your judgment," Byron said. "However, I think that she needs to go to some of it. I don't want her to associate the whole thing with church either."

"Yah, I know," Kevin agreed thoughtfully. "I thought of that too. You know, I'm her godfather. Wouldn't be good if I terrified her of church! I don't think that I slept any better than she did. You guys don't realize how scared she was all day. There were only a few times that she even relaxed. Maybe we'll take more breaks today."

Byron winked, "When I was rocking her last night, she said 'Smoke'. I think she wanted a cigarette!"

"That little rat! I told her to be quiet about that!" Kevin rolled his eyes. "Now she's going to have people think I'm giving her cigarettes! I'm going to skin her!"

Byron laughed, "That should take her mind off the crayons!"

Kevin arrived at the parsonage as Ruthie and the other kids were leaving the house. Charlie had to give Kevin the lowdown on all that had gone on at their house and then Ginger filled him in on the gossip of Bible school. Kevin and Ruthie shared a smile.

"I went to Bible school many times and never knew all that stuff! Hmm. I guess I didn't pay enough attention," Kevin chuckled.

Inside Miriam was getting the last of her bear tails in. She had been crying and was not a happy little girl. She looked at Kevin and started shaking her head no. She didn't reach out to him like she always did. He was devastated.

Marly caught his glance and patted his arm. "Hello Kevin. Look Miriam, Son is here."

Miriam never looked up.

Kevin sat down next to her and smiled, "Hi Miriam. How are you today?"

She shrugged and squeezed Mr. Bear.

"Do you want to take Mr. Bear with us today to Bible school?"

"No go."

"He can come along. I bet he'd like that," Kevin persisted.

"No go," the tears started to flow quietly.

"Look honey, we'll go over for the music and the singing and then we'll take a break. Okay? We won't have to do any drawing or coloring today. I promise you."

Miriam looked at him without expression. Obviously she wasn't convinced. Marly finished her bear tail and kissed her cheek. "Want to go to Son now?"

Miriam shrugged. Kevin was sick. He was becoming angry at some stupid parents that he'd never laid eyes on! If he had those monsters there, he'd have kicked them black and blue.

He took the little girl and smiled, "We can goof off today. How does that sound?"

Miriam shrugged.

"Have you ever goofed off?"

"If you want to," she barely mumbled.

"Okay, here's how you do it. We can go over to the church and sing a little bit, we can check on our class and see what they're doing and then we can go for a walk outside or come see what Marly is doing. Then we can go back and check on our class again and just mess around. How does that sound? You can decide when you want to leave, okay? If you want to go, you just tell me and we will. Deal?"

Miriam watched his expression and then shrugged. Obviously yesterday had taken a major toll on their relationship.

"Okay, that is what we'll do," he picked up the little girl and then they hugged Marly good bye.

Before they went in the church door, Miriam put her arms around his neck and almost begged, "No go."

Kevin hugged her tight, "You must come in with me but when you want to go, you just tell me. Okay?"

Miriam put her head in his shoulder and started to whimper. He patted her back, "Please try honey. Will you please try for me?"

She patted his neck with her little hand. He didn't know what that meant, but he took it that she'd try. "Thank you sweetheart. You're my favorite little girl."

Inside they sat in the back pew and she didn't turn around until the service was almost over. When they sang *Jesus Loves Me*, she sang along into his neck, but she never looked up. After service, he decided not to go down to the class right away. He took her outside.

When they went out the door, she looked up for the first time.

"Bye Bye," she said clearly, obviously glad that was over. He took her over to the sandbox and they played for a little bit. She started to relax. Soon she was giggling and talking about Sharlee and Coot.

Then Kevin suggested they go check on their class, "We need to see if they remember the words for the program."

She ignored it and gave him no response.

Kevin tried a different tactic, "I think we're supposed to say, all the animals of the world are going for a ride in Noah's car!"

Miriam looked at him and giggled. He smiled back, "Isn't that right?"

Miriam said, "Boat."

Kevin grinned, "Oh, all the boats in a the world,"

She giggled right away, "Animals go boat."

"Hmm." Kevin said, "I guess I need to practice more. What do you think?"

She nodded, "Son practice animals."

"Will you come with me when we go practice?" Kevin asked.

Her eyes darted from him to the church and back. He could see her start to tense up again.

"It's up to you, Miriam. If you want to, we will. Otherwise, we can practice right here."

Miriam stared at the church. "Gopher Son go."

Kevin was so relieved. He brushed the sand off her dress and hands, "Thank you Miriam. We don't have to stay long, unless you want. Okay?"

Miriam whispered, "Okay."

When they took their seat in the class, Mrs. Sandvahl had just finished with their Bible story for the day. "We're just going to practice for the program. I'm glad that you made it in time."

They sang the song several times and Miriam sang along, but was leaning tightly back into Kevin's lap. Then they practiced the lines for the play. After the class said the lines a couple times, she patted Kevin's arm. He leaned down and whispered, "Thank you."

Miriam smiled.

At lunchtime, Byron came over and sat with Miriam's class. Miriam smiled at him, but didn't let Kevin help serve the sandwiches. He and Byron exchanged a few words.

"I have to admit, I didn't know if I'd see you today or not," Byron told Kevin. "It didn't seem like things were very good this morning."

"We've been goofing off most of the morning. We spent some time in the sandbox," Kevin admitted.

Miriam looked at Byron and nodded, "Goofing."

Byron gave her a hug.

After lunch was craft time. On the way back to class, Mrs. Sandvahl told Kevin quietly, "I got some finger paints today! Yesterday was extreme and unusual punishment! I don't think I could face it again so soon."

Kevin touched her arm, "I want to thank you so much for all your patience with putting up with us."

"Not a problem," Mrs. Sandvahl smiled, "Pastor Marv told me a little about the situation. Life is hard enough; it shouldn't be any harder than it has to be."

"Well, thanks again. I really do appreciate it. In fact, the whole family does."

Anytime a person thinks that ten three-year olds with finger paints seems like a better idea than what they did the day before, that person should seriously rethink their life! It was a fiasco, but the kids loved it!

Mrs. Sandvahl had brought old dishtowels which she and Kevin used as huge bibs to cover the kids. Then the table was covered with an oilcloth and papers were handed out. That part went fine.

Then, she passed out the jars of finger paints; green, blue, yellow and red. The moment that she showed the little ones how to put their fingers into the thick paint was the last moment of anything that resembled organization.

The next half an hour was filled with squeals of laughter and smeared paint on the paper, faces, or any other surface. Kevin and Mrs. Sandvahl were busy rerolling up cuffs to keep them out of the paint, wiping paint out of hair and admiring fantastic modern art drawings. The kids had a ball. Miriam giggled and smeared with the best of them. She was having a great time.

The next hour, the grownups spent washing up kids, the table and the floor. When it was all done, the kids were fine. Kevin and Mrs. Sandvahl were definitely worse for the wear, but much nicer than the day before. They had fun. They all did.

Then they left their papers to dry and went up to the closing service. The three-year-old class sat together. Kevin sat at one end and Mrs. Sandvahl at the other. In between, were ten wiggly, giggly little kids. Kevin looked at the women who had a class by themselves. His admiration for them had grown enormously.

After the service, they went back to their room and Kevin helped Mrs. Sandvahl put shiny gold foil stars on the paintings as the parents came to pick up their children. When it was all over, the teacher thanked him. "I'd have never been able to handle that alone."

Kevin raised his eyebrows, "If it hadn't been for us, you wouldn't have had to." Then he smiled, "It actually was kind of fun."

Back at the parsonage, Miriam couldn't wait to give her paper to Marly. Marly asked, "Did Son do this one today?"

Miriam patted her little chest, "Gopher."

Marly gave her a big hug, "It is beautiful Miriam!" Then she hung it on the refrigerator.

Kevin had a cup of coffee and waited until Byron came home. He looked at the refrigerator. He praised Ginger's drawing of the Ark and Charlie's colored page of the two sheep that had cotton balls glued on for wool and then he praised Miriam for her finger paints. The little girl beamed, smiling so hard that her face almost broke.

She looked at him, "Mighty fine indeed."

He chuckled, "Oh yes, it's mighty fine indeed."

Byron walked Kevin to his car a bit later, "You did very well today. She seems happier."

"Yah, but we avoided the whole crayon thing. She and I spent most of the morning, digging in the sandbox. I hope we can get her through this week, but I'd be shocked if she is over her phobia at weeks end."

"I would be, too. We'll probably have to work on it for a long while. Suzy got some generic colors for Coot. She thought maybe he could use those for the water diversion plans and then Pepper was going to buy the Crayola colored pencils."

Kevin laughed, "If Crayola makes finger paints that would be the thing! She loves it. Yea gads, what a mess! And she was just wallowing in it! I was so glad to see her happy though, it was worth it."

52

That night, Kevin and Carrie stayed for dinner. Carrie wanted everyone to try her side dish that had entered in the contest. It was deep fried artichoke hearts. "Poor Kevin has eaten them so many times that I'm embarrassed to serve it to him anymore."

He kissed his wife's cheek, "They're good, but I have to say I'll be glad when I can go two weeks without seeing an artichoke!"

"I will be glad when the contest is over," Nora giggled. "Maybe we can get back to some normal food. We have all been eating our entries so much, that we are about sick of them."

"For sure. Miriam and I are having one more practice session. I think Friday night, after all this Bible school stuff," Carrie said. "I was going to do it earlier, but this week has been a lot for her." She patted Kevin's neck, "And for my husband, too."

"I decided," Kevin stated, "My goal is to just make it through the week without her hating me or the church. To hell with the crayons. We'll just go outside when they color. I can hardly take the pressure. She was too funny today with those finger paints. She was like a little pig in a mud puddle."

Everyone agreed that was a good idea.

Then Carl took Maureen's hand, "Well, I have something to say tonight. Maureen and I have an announcement. We're going to get married!"

Everyone offered congratulations all around. Lloyd perked right up, "You? Married? You don't even own a car. Do you want to buy my car? I never get to drive it. I don't have a license."

"I'll get my own car Lloyd," Carl said, "But thank you for offering. That was very kind of you."

Lloyd nodded, "I know."

Carl chuckled.

"So, when is the big day?" Elton beamed.

"That's up to Mo. Whenever she says, I'll be there," Carl answered.

"Good for you," Darlene giggled, "You got him trained already, Mo! Will you be getting married here or in Boston?"

"I have to talk to my kids before we get too carried away. I'd like Matthew to marry us. I mean if you raise a priest that is that least they should do for you, right?" Mo asked.

"I'd think so," Nora smiled.

"So, after I talk to him, I'll know more about when and where," Maureen smiled. "Whenever or wherever, you're all invited."

Keith looked at his water glass, "I don't know. There must be something in the water. Everyone is getting hitched."

Elton raised his eyebrow, "Or having babies!"

A father-to-be himself, Keith chuckled, "There's a little of that, too!"

The next morning, Miriam was ready to go to Bible school. She smiled at Kevin and was in a pretty good mood. Kevin was encouraged, although wondered how she'd like it when they didn't do finger painting again, but he would take what he could get.

They sat with their class for the service. Kevin had more or less become a teacher's assistant when he could. The other kids turned to him too because they saw that Miriam did. He did the best he could to help with them.

After services, Mrs. Sandvahl read the Bible story. Everyone listened to the story of Jesus going to look for the lost little sheep. They all clapped when Jesus found the little sheep and brought him back home.

Miriam sat on the end of Kevin's knees, but was leaning on the table through it all. She was doing great. She clapped and cheered with the rest of the kids.

Then they practiced for the program and they all knew the lines. They yelled them out, and Miriam did too. Then the class went up to the sanctuary to practice for the program.

Mrs. Sandvahl said she had thought about it, since Miriam still couldn't walk on her own, that Kevin stand on one side of the group and she on the other. He could stand Miriam up in front of his feet during the program. It'd be nice for her, because he could help with the other kids on that side of the 'stage.' Kevin was less than enthusiastic, but had to admit, it made the most sense. The little kids loved the idea that the 'big boy' in their class was going to be in the program with them.

Kevin took a break during lunch while Suzy sat with Miriam. He went out back and had a cigarette. While he was looking off toward the ripening fields, Pastor Marv came up behind him. "Taking a break?"

Kevin nodded, "Today's been pretty good, but I have had more nervous breakdowns this week than you can imagine. That stuff really tires a guy out. I can't believe it."

"Yah, I can only imagine. Bible school's kind of fun though, huh?"

"Sort of. Better when Miriam is good. She is doing great today; of course, we haven't had to deal with a crayon yet."

"Awful what those people did to her," Marv shook his head. "Makes you wonder, huh?"

"I never figure out how you could hate someone you'd never met before," Kevin nodded. "But I do now."

"It's probably best to remember that they were damaged themselves," Marv pointed out. "Normal folks wouldn't do what they did."

"That's true."

"So, are you going to teach a class again at the next Bible school?" Marv grinned.

"Don't really see that happening," Kevin laughed. "This is a onetime adventure!"

"You're good at it," Marv smiled as he appraised him.

Kevin grinned at him, "I know what you're up to. No way, Marvin. Don't even think about it. Sometimes a guy has to do stuff, but don't get any ideas I'd do this all the time."

Marvin slapped his back, "Oh, we'll see Kevin. You know, guys teach Sunday school classes all the time."

The men moved toward the door. Kevin laughed, "Good for them!"

The craft time started out okay. Miriam of course, climbed right up into Kevin's arms when Mrs. Sandvahl said it was craft time. Then she took out pieces of brightly colored construction paper and handed them out.

Kevin had to forcibly turn Miriam around to take the paper. She was very surprised when it was a bright green sheet of paper. She looked at Kevin and smiled. She had fully expected a coloring page.

Then Mrs. Sandvahl handed out stencils. There were all kinds of animals. Each child got to pick one. Miriam wanted the duck and kept saying 'Splursch!"

The teacher told the children that she was passing out fat pencils so that each of them could trace around the stencil. Miriam started to tighten up, but Kevin acted like it was going to be fun. The teacher gave each kid a big fat pencil sort of thing.

The inside where the lead would be was a quarter inch in diameter black crayon, but it was surrounded by layers of brown paper. To sharpen it, one pulled on a string which unwound the end of the layers of paper.

Mrs. Sandvahl handed the 'fat pencil' to each kid and Kevin took theirs. It wasn't sharpened, so he had to unwind the end of it. He put his arms around Miriam who was on his lap and worked on it in front of her. She watched the whole thing with rapt attention, pressing back against his body with all her might. The little girl was very unsure about the whole procedure.

When that was done, she tried to turn around but he just kept on. He took her little hand in his and put them both around the fat pencil. He could feel her start to panic and try to pull her hand away but he didn't let her. Together they traced around the duck.

When they were finished, he put the fat pencil down and lifted off the stencil. There was the duck on the green paper.

Miriam turned and looked at him with surprise. She covered her little mouth and giggled. "Splursch!"

He was so relieved and he kissed her little cheek. "Splursch!" he returned.

The other kids started asking him to help them and pretty soon, they all had their animals traced. Then they glued things on the paper. There were little pictures of flowers, butterflies and bumblebees. Before long, they were all engrossed in the glue. Everything was stuck to everything and everyone was giggling.

As they went to the closing service, Kevin felt better than he had all week. He thought maybe they had turned the corner. When they got back to the room and he helped Mrs. Sandvahl put gold stars on papers, he asked her where she found those fat pencils.

"Those aren't what they are called. They are made by 'that company' that we can't say, and they are c-r-a-y-o-n-s. But I took off the outside paper and thought we could get away with it. I think it worked."

"I think it did too! I have to get us some!"

"After school is over, you can have a box!" she grinned. "I have a couple."

He gave her a hug, "I think you are an angel!"

The middle-aged lady giggled, "Well thank you so much. A person doesn't hear that every day."

That night at milking was the happiest that anyone had seen Kevin all week. He was almost babbling with joy. He made everyone promise they'd be there for the program. It was going to be at three o'clock at the church. If you weren't working, being dead was the only other excuse acceptable for not attending in Kevin's mind.

The morning routine was the same, except everyone was dressed up to the nines. It was a challenge to keep the little girls' dresses clean and the boys little jackets neat until three o'clock. Finally Kevin showed the little boys how to take their jackets off and put them over the back of their chairs like he did. They thought that was cool.

Rehearsal was upstairs with all the other classes. Mrs. Sandvahl's three-year-old class knew their lines and could sing the song. They didn't quite get how to stand in a straight line, but it was close enough.

Before lunch they had crafts again. This time, it was making a necklace out of yarn and Cheerios. Kevin thought it was a splendid thing to do! Lunch was peanut butter sandwiches, cookies and Kool-Aid. Everything was going along fine.

The classes all returned to their rooms for the last of the classes before the program. Their teacher read them the story about all the animals going on the ark two by two. The kids each got to stick a couple flannel animals onto the flannelgraph ark. They all liked that.

Then they got ready for the program. Kevin helped get the kids ready. He tied bows, wiped noses, helped the little guys with their neckties and got jackets on. He thought the whole class looked pretty neat as they were lined up to go upstairs. He marched at the end of the line of Miriam's classmates, with Mrs. Sandvahl in the lead.

It wasn't until they entered the sanctuary that he realized there were a lot of people there. He had known it intellectually but he never thought about it. He hated being in front of a crowd. And yet, there he was. There was half the county and he knew them all. He was so embarrassed. He wished that Miriam could have walked on her own, but she couldn't.

He walked in, looking straight ahead. He hadn't been this nervous in front of a crowd since his wedding. Miriam saw the people and started to panic a bit and his attention immediately went from himself to her. She put her arms around his neck and whispered, "Smoke."

He chuckled and gave her a squeeze. "We'll have a break later."

He was very relieved when they filed into their pew and sat down. He never looked around because he knew that would only make him feel worse. He was hoping that most people would think that he was an assistant teacher even though he doubted anyone would believe that.

The whole class was relatively well behaved; relatively. Not so most folks would notice, but he and Mrs. Sandvahl exchanged a grin of satisfaction. Only they knew what this group of short people was capable of; and by those standards, their behavior was exemplary.

Then the program started. Their class was second to march up front. The teacher led them and Kevin brought up the rear, carrying Miriam. They all stood in a line. He stood Miriam up in front of him. He didn't want to look out over the crowd, so he glanced over next to him.

One child over from Miriam was a little girl, Autumn. She was about to cry. She was so nervous that she had rolled her dress into a wad at her waist in front of her. He knelt down, reached over and patted her back. Then he helped her unwind her dress and straighten her skirt.

The little guy the next one over from her was picking his nose. Kevin handed him his handkerchief. Then they started their lines. The kids just yelled it. Kevin was sure that folks in Bismarck heard, "We are the animals of the world! We are going to ride on Noah's boat."

Then Miriam's class joined with the other three-year-old class that was standing the step behind them in singing the song about the Ark. The audience applauded and the kids bowed.

One little guy bowed so far down that he rolled off the step. Kevin reached down and helped him back up. Then he picked up Miriam and they all clambered back to pew. Kevin was delighted to sit down. Thank God, that was over!

They watched the rest of the program and it was fun. Charlie did a great job as a zebra walking into the ark, even though his partner zebra wouldn't hold his hand. Ginger did a fantastic job in the play as Mrs. Noah. She stood next to Noah and motioned for the animals to come in. When the kids didn't move fast enough, she said, "Step on it! We don't have all day!" That was not in the script.

On the way back to their room, Carrie met up with him and handed him the bouquet of flowers they had bought for Mrs. Sandvahl. In their room, Kevin presented them to her 'from her class.' All the kids clapped and she thanked them all. Then she gave Kevin a kiss on the cheek. "Thank you."

"We make a good team!" He chuckled. "If I'm ever in the trenches again, I'm going to look you up!"

The other kids waited for their parents and Kevin stayed until they were all picked up. Then he and Miriam went upstairs. There was the biggest share of the clan. Even Jerald had made it out from work. Everyone congratulated them and Coot gave each of his Gophers a cookie for their good work. He also had a cookie for Kevin.

Miriam giggled and grinned. She was a very happy little girl. They all knew that it was only a beginning, but it was a good beginning.

53

Friday evening after dinner, Annie called. She'd received a telegram from Andy. She was so excited she could hardly talk! He asked her to marry him in Honolulu. His R&R would begin July 26 and he had to report back to Schofield Barracks on August 2. He asked her to let Mom, Dad and Darrell know.

There was a lot of laughing, crying and excitement before Nora hung up. Then she went to Elton and cried into his arms. She was so happy. He let her cry a little and then said, "What are you going to do now? Cry, or call Darrell?"

She wiped her tears and giggled, "I guess I better call Darrell."

As she reached for the phone, it rang. It was Darrell. He was chuckling, "You sound like Annie! We just talked to her. She was babbling and giggling so much I could hardly understand her! I guess I have to pack a suitcase, huh?"

Nora bubbled, "It looks like it! If you need any help getting ready to go, just let us know. Help with the milking or getting the tickets, anything at all Darrell."

"I talked to Sammy and Joey before. They already said they'll do my chores. They're just waiting for the date. I can get the tickets, but I think I need to talk to you guys first. Right now, I need to talk to Kincaid."

"Oh certainly, here he is," Nora handed the phone to Kincaid. "It's for you."

Kincaid took the phone and Darrell asked, "Have you changed your mind on the partnership?"

"Not at all. I was waiting to hear from you. Did you decide?" Kincaid was holding his breathe.

"I talked it over with Jeannie and I, well we, would like to do it. Did you talk to Maureen?"

"Yes, she thinks it's a great idea."

"Where do we go from here? Do we need to get a lawyer?" Darrell asked.

"I got the number of Magpie's attorney, if that's agreeable with you."

"If Elton thinks is he fair; that's good enough for me. Jeannie's here with me now. If it's okay, we'd like to come over?"

"Nora, Darrell and Jeannie want to come over. Is that okay?" Carl asked.

"Well, of course," Elton grinned. "They are always welcome here."

Within a few minutes, they were all sitting on the patio. Everyone was settled with their drinks and Darrell said, "We have some news. I asked Jeannie to marry me and she said yes. We're going to get married this July!"

Everyone's mouth dropped open! "That soon?" Nora gasped. "Before or after Hawaii?"

"During," Darrell grinned. "Andy and I had talked about this for a long time but we thought it would all be different. We wanted to get married at the same time, a twin wedding."

"A double wedding, Darrell," Jeannie giggled.

"Yah, that's it. We never said anything because we didn't know how things would work out. But that's what we're going to do. The girls think it would be great too!"

Elton and Nora embraced the couple and they were all happy with it. Then Nora sat down, "What are your parents going to say?"

"Aloha!" Darrell grinned. "See, we were just waiting for Andy to get the dates to see if it would work out. It'll be almost perfect."

"We were worried because my school starts soon. Teachers have orientation in mid-August. So it was getting right down to the wire. My Mom and Dad are going to Hawaii on July 22 for two weeks. They planned to be on the big island anyway, but Mom said they'll get a day flight to Honolulu for the wedding. Darrell's Mom and Dad wanted to do something special for their anniversary in mid-September. They wanted to go to Aruba, but we talked them into Maui instead. They'll go earlier and spend the first couple of days in Honolulu to be at the wedding. Annie's dad and his girlfriend are going to fly over for the wedding."

"What does his girlfriend do?" Elton asked.

"She sews draperies. It's a business out of her home and she can work around the time off. Anyway, all the parents will be there. We'll have our double wedding and Darrell and I will have our honeymoon before we come home. Annie and I have spent a lot of time at the library researching stuff. Pastor Byron said he'll help us get a minister," Jeannie explained. "It got more complicated than we ever imagined."

"We're only going to do this if Andy got Hawaii. Otherwise, we're going to wait until he got home and then have a double wedding," Darrell grinned. "I was really worried how it would all work out because Dad is retiring you know. That is until Kincaid came over the other day. Should we tell them?"

Carl nodded.

"Carl and I are going into partnership! He is buying out Dad's share of the land and dairy. That really takes a load off me," Darrell clapped Kincaid on the back. "Of course, now I have to keep on the straight and narrow or he'll get me arrested."

Elton's face glowed with happiness! "This is the grandest news! I suppose you know that he and Mo are tying the knot! I think Keith is right. There's something in the water!"

Jeannie hugged Maureen, "Well, you better get a muumuu and come to Hawaii too! We can have a triple wedding!"

"Carl and I are going to watch things for Elton and Nora while they're learning to hula. But you kids can come to our wedding after you're old married folks!" Maureen smiled.

"Have you set a date yet?" Darrell asked.

"Not yet. Maureen's son Matthew is a priest. Mo would like him to marry us." Carl explained.

"That'll be so nice, Maureen," Jeannie said. "I can't imagine having my son perform my marriage."

Maureen chuckled, "Neither can I. I don't suppose I'll be able to use my spit and handkerchief to get a smudge off his cheek, huh?"

Everyone laughed. Then they visited a while about the weddings, Elton's lawyer and the plans for the cooking contest.

"We have a ton of things to get done tomorrow to get this contest set up. Annie and Marty both have this weekend off and Chris will be home. It will be a big deal. We can make it even grander by announcing all the weddings! And I am hoping every one plans on taking home tons of leftovers!"

"I'll be so glad when it is over," Jeannie said. "I have eaten so many Cornish game hens, I can hardly stand the sight of them anymore!"

"Good," Kincaid proclaimed, "That is one vote that I can count on!"

"Yea gads, Kincaid," Elton pointed out. "Little Jeannie has been my best buddy for years. She'll vote for me, naturally."

Jeannie giggled, "You two are worse than Andy and Darrell."

Nora agreed, "See what you and Annie have to look forward to!"

"Ah, hmm. Makes you wonder why we are go through all this fuss to get married, huh?" Jeannie observed.

"Because your life would never be the same without us," Darrell chortled.

Jeannie looked at him seriously and answered, "That is so true. Just think how nice it could be."

Darrell started to open his mouth and Elton grinned, "Might as well get used to it Darrell. You'll never win."

Darrell gave Jeannie a dirty look, "I'm beginning to see that."

Jeannie giggled and then said, "Hey, how 'bout that Miriam? She made it through the program. I was amazed that as scared as she is of some things, that she could stand up in front of a crowd. I think Kevin was more nervous about that than she was."

Elton nodded, "Kevin's always hated being in front of a crowd. And yet, when he is in the crowd, he's the one causing all the commotion! Go figure!"

"Suzy told me that Mrs. Sandvahl found these crayons wrapped in paper. Neat idea. I'm going to get some for Ginger's classes. We might have to draw some pictures of dirt."

Everyone gave her a puzzled look. Maureen was finally the one to ask. "How do you draw a picture of dirt?"

Jeannie's eyes just twinkled, "Probably with a brown crayon!"

Kincaid raised his eyebrows, "You might want to rethink those wedding plans, there Jessup. Your girl might be a tad wobbly!"

Darrell hugged her, "Not a tad, a whole bunch. Otherwise she would have never said she'd marry me."

"Good point," Elton laughed. "If it wasn't for women's poor judgment, most men would still be bachelors!"

That night, Lloyd only came to visit for about half an hour. He was talking about the Bataan Death March. He was yawning the whole time and then told Kincaid that he sure didn't know much. Carl walked him back to his room.

Later that night, Carl turned over in his bed and watched crazy old Elmer keeping watch by the gopher hole. "You might just get that gopher yet, you crazy old dog."

He pulled his blanket over his shoulder and watched as the shadows from the clouds crossing in front of the moon as they made their way across Schroeder's yard. He remembered how much he hated being there that first night. Bert was crabbing and coughing, and he himself was about as cantankerous as one can get. It seemed like years ago.

He wondered what Bert would say about all the goings on. He'd have half the guys down at the sales ring buying cows; that was certain. Carl could just imagine him smirking. He knew Bert would want to take credit for Carl's marriage. And in a way, Carl guessed he should.

54

Saturday was a crazy day. Between all the calls about Andy's wedding and the contest, there was hardly a minute that someone wasn't talking on the phone. Chris drove in from Grand Forks during the night and joined the family around the coffee pot by six am. Annie and Marty would be home around ten in the morning. Zach had stayed in town overnight and was going to make early rounds so he could get out to the farm for the weekend.

Ellisons came over and Miriam was delighted when her Son came in with Carrie. She had been over at their house that evening to practice their recipes for the contest. Byron stated he would be delighted to not have to drink anything resembling lemonade for the next ten years. Having three lemonade contestants in the same household was simply too much.

Chores went fast because there were so many helpers. Then Elton, Harrington, Chris and Kincaid began to work on the patio. The other guys all promised to help set up grills later that night, if they couldn't get them all done before hand.

The ladies were all busy making room in the refrigerators, getting prize ribbons done, starting their own cooking and setting the tables. It was pandemonium.

After lunch, they all decided to put their feet up for a bit and went out to enjoy the nice summer day. The phone rang and it was Matthew. Maureen and Harrington talked to him for quite a while.

When they returned they had some news. For the most part, Maureen's family was delighted that she was getting married. They had heard good things about Carl and her children all knew that she cared about him.

Matthew was able to qualm any of their concerns, so they were all happy about it.

Sean's family, on the other hand, was not. Maureen thought that would be the case. While she was hurt about it, she accepted it as predictable fact. Matthew suggested that since they all felt that way, his mom should get married in North Dakota. He would work out the ceremony with Byron. Most of their family wanted to make the trip out to the prairies anyway, to see where their mom was going to live. Maureen was very happy about with those plans.

Then Matt talked to Ian. He told him that he agreed with what Carl had told him about his job and getting married. Then he chuckled, "If you get married near the same time as Mom, I can do both ceremonies."

"You're a swindler and that's a blasted fact!" Harrington chuckled. "I don't know when Mom is planning to tie the knot. I certainly don't know how I would feel about having my baby brother pronounce me married. Yuk! I remember how the deal with my comic book turned out!"

"It was my comic book," Matt stated flatly.

"You'll never admit that you took it. How can you be a priest and still cling to that lie? But I suppose Ruthie wants you to marry us and so would Mom. I'm telling you though, I don't think I like it!"

"Well, since Ruthie works for Byron, I think maybe he'd actually make the pronouncement. You know, he is licensed in North Dakota. I'm not. So, either he or that Father Vicaro would have to officially do it."

"See what I mean? You're just going to mess it all up. You'll marry me and it won't even be legal!" Then Harrington got quiet. "Matt, do you think it'll be okay, I mean, marrying Ruthie? What if I can't find job?"

"Ian, it will be fine. I know it will," his brother assured him. "I got some news of my own."

"What's that?"

"I'm going to leave Boston."

"What? You leave Boston? I can't believe that. Why?" Harrington was shocked. "Oh, is this that wanderlust thing you were talking about?"

"Yah, sorta. I have had some problems with this Bishop, but I'll tell you about that later. Also, I got into a clash with some of the mucky mucks in the church over that deal with Father Timothy. I thought he should be reprimanded and they said no. Can you believe that? They wouldn't do it!" Matt was very angry. "I told them they shouldn't leave a priest like that in the position he had and they blew me off! They thought Ruthie was likely unstable and misinterpreted things. I know what Ruthie meant when she explained why she never reported the rape. They wouldn't have listened to her. You should have seen it."

"Well, I know that I sure didn't like that creep," Harrington agreed. "When Ruthie told me what happened, it didn't surprise me at all. What's their reason for keeping him in place?"

"Oh, political junk. I guess he has brought the school out of the red. I'm so sick of it. I just want to be a priest somewhere that I don't have to play all these games. I don't believe that is what the good Lord intended," Matt said thoughtfully. "Anyway, I'm taking a sabbatical right before Zach's wedding for six months. Mom doesn't know how long. I just want to get out in the world and see if I can find a niche someplace."

Harrington chuckled, "We can both live with Mom and Kincaid, and mooch off them. Like when we were teenagers! Then Kincaid will know he's really our stepdad, and that's a blasted fact!"

"Let's not tell him until after the wedding, okay? Mom would hang us out to dry!"

"She probably will anyway," Harrington laughed. "It was good talking to you. If you need an ear, call. I appreciate all the times you have been there for me."

"You too."

On the way back out to the patio, Ian tried to decide how much of their conversation he should share with his Mom. She already knew that Matt was considering leaving Boston, just not why, how serious or for how long. He decided not to say much right now. It was up to Matt to tell her about his decision and it would have to be Ruthie's decision about telling her about Father Timothy.

As far as skeletons in the Catholic church closet, he knew probably more of them than Matt did. He had long ago decided it wasn't his place to tell anyone. He wondered if Matt knew all the stuff that had come across his desk when he worked in Vice. He had originally been shocked, but soon realized that it was much more common than he ever imagined.

By evening, the patio looked like the lawn and garden department of the Home Improvement store and the kitchen looked like a restaurant. Everyone had sandwiches and potato chips on paper plates for supper.

No one was brave enough to open any refrigerator or cupboard for fear of being caught in an avalanche of casserole or sauces!

Elton was grumpy. "So much food and nothing to eat!"

"Poor baby," Nora teased. "Ham and turkey sandwiches with your choice of cheese isn't exactly destitution. Besides, tomorrow you'll be complaining about too much food."

He kissed her cheek, "You and the ladies have done a fantastic job with all this. But it isn't our fault, you know. Coot and I would've been happy, just our little contest between us."

"You and Coot happy?" Nora laughed like crazy.

55

Sunday, Pepper's alarm screamed expectancy! Every person in the clan had a dog in this food fight, directly or indirectly. All had prepared for the contest or been drafted as a guinea pig. There had been more preparation for this than the D Day invasion! The only moment of culinary agreement that morning was that the coffee was good. After that it was all bravado and insults.

There was only one person who ignored the whole thing. It was Lloyd. After he had won the prize earlier that week, he felt no need to continue to compete. After all, once one is proclaimed the best; there is nothing else. They're all very happy and relieved about that.

The family was on their best behavior when they graced the pews of Trinity Lutheran. Pastor Marvin's service was nice and everyone behaved, even Charlie. Miriam sat with Zach and Suzy. She sang along with the hymns. Seems most folks didn't know that the words to *Jesus Loves Me* can be sung with any tune. That morning, they found out it can.

After church, the clan began to assemble at Schroeders. The kitchen was a free for all. A horde of wannabe chefs slaving over their grills descended on the patio. Some approached the event with great seriousness and some with hysterical joviality.

Then it was time. The platters were all filled and the group was at the tables, holding hands and waiting for grace. Byron offered a wonderful prayer. He dared not mention the contest, or the preacher's reported 'in' with the Big Boss.

After the Amen, Nora made an announcement. Each person had a ballot by their silverware. The four tables were numbered and table one was to go fill their plates from the buffets first. After they tasted each of the grill entries which had been cut into very small servings, they were to rank them: first, second place and third place. Then Annie would collect the ballots.

Carrie would count the ballots under the watchful eyes of Megan, Pepper and Becky, to make sure the count was fair and square. The judges of the other food would turn in their decisions to Annie and Jeannie. They would check them over and the awards would be handed out by Nora. The self-appointed committee would then decide on any special awards. They would award all the prizes.

Lloyd wouldn't mess around tasting the entries. He took what he liked and that was it. Most of the little kids did the same and they zeroed in on the hot dogs. The Gophers told everyone they were voting for them, no matter if they had an entry or not. The clan decided they all had a career in politics.

Lucy Schroeder was the judge for the bean competition and those entrants were Maureen's Boston Baked Beans, Annie's Prairie Beans and Corn dish, Ruthie's Southwestern Chili Pintos, Marly's Northern Beans and Ham and the surprise entry from Ken Ellison and Becky Oxenfelter. They entered a Lima Bean and Sausage Casserole. After tasteful consideration, Lucy made her decision. Ken and Becky took first prize, Maureen second and Annie won third.

Everyone applauded when Becky and Ken received their blue ribbons, Maureen her red and Annie her white. Ruthie won a green ribbon for originality and Marly got a pink ribbon for best rendition of a traditional recipe.

Then was the deeply contested potato salad competition which was knowledgeably judged by Julia Anderson. The contestants were Carl and Katherine's Hot German Potato Salad, Charlie and Katherine's Mustard Dill, Greta Heinrich's Sweet Vinegar, Jeannie's Hawaiian Sweet Potato and finally, Katie's New Potato Salad.

Katie won hands down and accepted the blue ribbon. Greta's Sweet Vinegar Potato Salad took second place and Charlie and Grandma Katherine accepted third. While no one else gave an acceptance speech,

Charlie did. He thanked everybody, including the chickens for laying the eggs, and said, "Don't cry Agent Coot. Maybe I won't play next year so you can win."

Carl and Katherine won a green ribbon for Most Ethnic and Jeannie's Hawaiian won a purple ribbon for most original. The judge thought it was a winner, but that maybe the sweet potatoes were a bit too soft. Nora took photographs of the winners with their ribbons.

Jeannie had difficulty making her decisions on the side dishes. Greta won with her Au Gratin Broccoli, and Julia Anderson came in second with her Chilled Asparagus with Aspic. Third place was a tie. Lucy's Scalloped Corn and Elsie Oxenfelter's Fresh Creamed Peas shared third place.

Ruthie's Spinach Soufflé went flat and so was not as puffy as it should have been, however the taste was fantastic. Since Clark Olson and Charlie were seen poking holes in it, which led to the collapse, Ruthie won the award for the "Most Tampered With" Side Dish. Carrie's Deep fried Artichoke Hearts didn't last long enough to be tasted by Jeannie! The men kept swiping them from the platter before they all got to the table. When Jeannie got there, the plate was empty! Carrie won the "Most Tasted" ribbon.

The salad contest was interesting and everyone was surprised at the number of entrants. Elsie Oxenfelter had her hands full to make the decision. Jenny Schroeder won with her Waldorf Salad which was the clan favorite. Ruthie came in second with her Crab Salad and Carrie and Miriam won third with their Green Bean Salad. Miriam giggled and clapped when they got their ribbon. Lucy's Cole Slaw took the prize for Traditional recipe and Jeannie won for Most Unique for her Spinach with Hot Bacon Salad. Suzy's Carrot and Raisin Salad won for Prettiest Salad. She giggled when she graciously accepted her award, "Boy, that is scraping the bottom of the barrel for an honor!"

Annie handed in her choices for lemonade winners. Eve Jessup won first with her Fizzy Lemonade. It was an interesting lemonade with just enough soda to give it a fizz. Becky's Country Style and Katie's Tart and Sweet tied for second. Ginger won third place with her Raspberry Lemon.

Ken and Clark Olson had to withdraw because someone ate their fresh strawberries, so they just ended up with plain lemonade. They won the gray ribbon for "Might Have Won." Carrie commiserated and they decided that in their next contest, the FBI agent and the Boston PD detective should be assigned to guard the food. Everyone agreed.

After announcing that he'd never be the pickle judge again, Elton revealed he had uncovered a conspiracy. Some plan was afoot to try to see how hot the pickles could get before the judge's mouth bled. He thought those contestants should be disqualified, but no one else agreed.

Darlene won first place with her Watermelon Pickles and Greta shared second place for her Bread and Butter Pickles with Carrie's Kosher Dills. Jenny won third with her Hot Dog Relish.

Then the others contestants broke down like this. Marly won the 'Meanest Pickle Person in the World' award for her Hot Chili Peppers and Elsie's Tangy Dills and Julia's Pickled Beets brought them second runner up in a new category, Painful Pickle, just invented by Elton. He pointed out he'd never before eaten a Pickled Beet that made him cry!

Grandma Katherine made an announcement before she gave her list of winners for the rolls. "Next time, we need to divide these entries. There're several that are the buns for a grilling dish and I think that they should be judged together in a sandwich category. For today, they'll be judged as rolls or bread on their own."

Everyone agreed the change would be a good idea.

The winner was Jeannie Frandsen's French Bread, followed by a second place tie: Glenda Olson's Hamburger Buns and Elsie's Foot Long Hot Dog Buns. Katie's Caramel Rolls took third. Nora's Dinner Buns took the best traditional buns, Darlene's Sauerkraut buns won with best specialty bun, Ruthie's cornbread won in the category of non-flour bread, and Annie's deep fried squaw bread was the most exciting bread award. Ruthie giggled, "Wow! That's like the most tasty wall paper paste!"

The tension was building and everyone was anxiously awaiting the big prize, but there was one more to be awarded first. It was the coveted pie award. Most of the men in the clan knew enough to not take sides in this contest if they valued their happy homes, which they did.

Marly was the judge and she said it was very difficult to choose the best of the best. They would be judged on crust, filling and taste. After a lot of consideration she had decided there was a tie for first place. Megan Elizabeth's Wild Cherry Pie and Ruthie Jeffries Pecan Pie were the winners. Second place went to Maureen Harrington's Cranberry Apple Pie and the third place was Greta's Peach Pie. The other awards were Elton's Favorite Award which went to Suzy for her June Berry Pie, Katherine won the Traditional pie award for her Sour Cream Raisin Pie. There was a special award for Carrie and Miriam's Chocolate Cream Pie. "It was the most Licked Pie!" Miriam loved it!

Then it became silent while the women recounted the votes in the kitchen for the grilling contest. Perhaps only waiting for the final tally of the votes in the Dewey-Truman election of 1948 would've been more stressful. The only sound was that of breathing. When the ladies returned to the dining room, there were a few hushed whispers. The tension was almost too much for the little entrants who were beginning to squirm.

Lloyd looked around the table and shook his head, "Did somebody die?"

"Why do you ask Lloyd?" Elton asked.

"Never saw such carrying on. In my day, we didn't get ribbons for eating. We're just damned lucky to get fed!" The old man grumbled.

Elton clapped the old man on his back. "That's so right, Lloyd," Elton agreed. "We should all remember that."

"I'm going to take a nap," Lloyd announced.

"Are you sure you don't want to wait and see who wins for best cook?" Elton asked.

"Don't need to. I know I'm the best. I already know," Lloyd stated.

Annie intervened, "You're right Lloyd, but can you wait one second? The girls and I want to give you your award before you go to bed. Okay?"

He nodded. Annie could get him to do anything.

Darlene and Megan came out with a huge multicolored ribbon that displayed a huge number one on the front. They put it around his neck. He beamed.

"Now everyone knows I'm the best, right?" Lloyd grinned proudly.

"Yes Grandpa. Now they do," the girls assured him. "You're the best."

Everyone cheered and then he said, "I'm going to lay down now."

The girls helped him to his room. When they returned, it was time.

Nora explained that the judging was divided into categories to make it easier. She suggested if they ever did this again, they should divide them right away. The categories were: Beef, Pork, Poultry, Seafood and Sandwiches.

Darlene began reading off the winners by category, while Annie and Ruthie handed out the ribbons. In the Beef category the entrants were: Elton for his Spicy Rib Eye Steak against Marty and Danny Schroeder's T Bone Steaks. The prize went to the T Bone Steaks. The young men accepted their award graciously and Elton shook both their hands with sincerity. "Your steak was very good.'

Next was the Pork category. The entrants were Carl for his San Antonio Barbequed Pork Ribs; Eddie Schroeder and Dick Heinrich's Marinated Pork Loin and Rod and Ken's Grilled Ham Steak. Eddie and Dick took first prize for the Marinated Pork Loin. It was fantastic.

Poultry entrants were Doug and Little Bill Anderson's Drumsticks and Sauce, Chris and Pepper's Barbequed Chicken, Chatterbox and Clark's Dinosaur (Turkey) Legs and Kevin and Darrell's Cornish Game Hens. Doug and Little Bill tied with Chatterbox and Clark with their entries for best Poultry entries. The little boys were delighted with their awards.

The seafood category was rather contemptuous. The entrants were Harrington and Zach's Marinated Halibut Steaks up against Darlene and Glenda's Grilled Tuna Steak. Ian and Zach won first place in the category. They were pleased and offered their secret recipe to anyone that wanted it. No one asked.

Then came the Sandwich category. Since Byron and Marvin had invoked the Lord as their partner, the competition heated up considerably. Most folks thought they were taking unfair advantage. They had entered with their Hamburgers with Cheese, served on Glenda's second place Hamburger buns. Next, Jerald and Junior Oxenfelter's Chicago Foot Longs, served on Elsie's second place Hot Dog buns. Then was Keith's Wisconsin Brats served on Darlene's Sauerkraut buns.

The category winners were Jerald and Junior's Chicago Foot Longs. Almost every youngster in the clan had voted for them. Jenny Schroeder's Hot Dog Relish was probably a big help in the victory.

Then there were a couple more prizes before the grand overall winner. Rod and Ken won for the Most Original with their Grilled Ham Steaks with Plum Sauce. It was agreed that everyone really loved them. They also were appointed to cook their prize winning recipe the following Sunday dinner. Darlene and Glenda won the prize in the Girls Only category and Chris and Pepper won in the Couples Category.

Then there was another category. It was the Windiest Chef's category, It was a three-way, or four-way tie. Of course, everyone knew the winners: Elton, Kincaid, Byron and Marv. Byron and Marv got a special ribbon for 'Cheating the Most.' Marv tried to defend their behavior saying that anyone could have asked for the Lord's assistance but that fell on deaf ears. So, they just accepted the award under protest.

Elton had a special award, for the 'Most Whining Judge Ever.' He still insisted there was a conspiracy. The number one "Windiest Braggard" award went to Coot. The Gophers all cheered. They didn't care what the award was for, they were just happy that their Coot had won it! They couldn't have been more proud. Carl was insistent that he was just underappreciated.

Then, minus the drum roll, came the long awaited prizes. The Third Place award for grilling went to the team of Chatterbox (Merv) and Clark Olson for their prehistoric entry. The Dinosaur (Turkey) Legs were favorites of almost everyone.

Second place went to a single entrant, Keith Schroeder. He took home the prize for his Wisconsin Brats. He had served them with Simmered Beer Onions and Sauerkraut Buns. He definitely had earned the prize.

Finally, a team won the first place Grilling Award and cash prize of $75. It was for the Cornish Game Hens offered up by Kevin Schroeder and Darrell Jessup. Everyone knew they deserved the prize and Miriam got to go up with her Son when he accepted the award. Ginger, not to be outdone, walked up with her Uncle Darrell.

There'd been a lot of merriment and they had all learned a lot. Everyone had won a prize for something. Even Elton and Carl had won something. They decided they were all grand cooks and the rest of the world should be jealous.

By the time the family sat down to relax that evening, things had been put back into order. It had been quite a day. Besides the contest, there were announcements of an engagement, two weddings and Glenda Olson had received a good report from her doctor. She would not have undergo surgery after all and it seemed that her back pain was dissipating. They're also excited that Doug had signed the papers with Chris' Dad to take over the grain elevator. They were also glad to hear that Don Holloway's doctor thought that if he quit lifting those bags at the elevator that might resolve his back problems without surgery.

As he leaned back in a big chair on the patio, Elton observed, "These last couple days have been so good, it darned nears scares me."

Maureen grinned, "I was just thinking the same thing!"

56

Harrington was doing the ordering for Elton's garage when Doug came in to talk to Elton. A clanner for years. the dark haired man in his early forties had a friendly demeanor.

"Whatcha doing?" Doug asked as watched Harrington studying some papers.

"Ah, messing around. I did some ordering for the shops. A person has to do something to earn his bread and butter. You know, some of these vendors do a lot of fudging and are pretty shaky on their math."

"No lie. If you ever get bored, stop by. I've a stack to do myself. When I helped Holloway with ordering, I knew about the trouble we have. Even with the franchise! I was surprised that they'd be so shifty. Guess where money's concerned, folks are just that way," Doug shook his head. "It takes a lot of time to check them out and all that. I hate dickering with these guys. Is the Elton bird busy?"

"He's going over payroll, but I think he would be willing to take a coffee break," Harrington grinned. "You know how he loves his coffee."

"Ian, in case I never told you," Doug smiled, "I want to welcome you. Have you and Ruthie set any dates or anything? I hope you plan on hanging around in this area."

"Not yet. I know that Ruthie feels really at home here and that is very important. She needs to have some roots. Thanks for asking, Doug," Ian answered.

"What about you? What about your roots?"

"I had them growing up. I can set up any old place and be okay. And now that Mom will be moving out here; and my home is where my Mom's apple pie is. You know, Ruthie was cheated out of that and I'd like her to have a chance at it."

Doug studied him a bit, "You're a good guy."

Harrington looked at Doug in surprise, "Nice of you to say. You seem pretty decent yourself."

"What is this?" Elton interrupted, "A mutual admiration society?"

"Are you jealous?" Doug joked.

Elton looked them both over, "Nope. I have so many friends I'd hardly notice if you two weren't around."

"I was going to have a cup of coffee with you," Doug said. "However, I might change my mind."

"Oh come on in," Elton laughed. "You know you can't do any better than me."

"Yea gads," Doug groaned.

Harrington chuckled, "You might want to look into buying your own coffee pot, there Doug. You wouldn't have to endure the sarcasm."

"Good idea."

"So, to what do I owe this honor?" Elton asked as he handed Doug a mug of hot coffee.

"Nothing. I guess I'm just nervous about taking over the elevator. I mean, I'm going to do it and all. Hell, there is nothing else I'd even know how to do. But, it's a bit overwhelming. I think I'm in over my head. You know, I did mostly the muscle stuff and Holloway did the brain stuff. He was good at it. I can do it, but honestly Elton, I hate most of the business end of things."

Elton leaned back in his chair, "Yah, I do know. My boys are like that. They love the mechanical work and they can do the business well. But they totally hate it. That's why we have Pepper do so much of it. But that's going to change soon, I think."

"Why? Doesn't she like it?"

"Oh she does and does a great job. But you know, she and Chris-. It about drives them bats when they're apart so much. It's going to be a long time before he is done with school," Elton said. "I probably shouldn't asked her to do any of the shop stuff because I think she feels tied here now. She could easily get a job wherever with her physical therapy training. Then they could be together."

"I can see that. Pepper is outspoken enough, I think she'd tell you if she felt that way. Don't you?" Doug asked.

"Yah, I guess. I need to talk to her though. Anyway, that doesn't deal with your issue, does it? What do you plan on doing with the elevator?"

"I need someone to run the store part and help with the business stuff. I can do the elevator and that. I guess I need a replacement for Don."

"Hmm. Will he stay on?"

"He said he would but his back is so bad, Elton. The poor guy can hardly maneuver as it is. That's why he's selling in the first place. I thought about swiping Rod back from you, but I think it's good for him to have other bosses than me. Besides, he wouldn't be any help with the business stuff."

"That's true. Well, I'll keep my eyes open," Elton grinned.

There was a knock at the door and Harrington poked his head in, "I got the ordering done and am going to the post office. Do you have anything for me to take or pick up?"

"No, thanks a lot Ian. When you get back, we can go home for lunch. Okay?" Elton asked.

"Sounds good. I'm mighty hungry and that's a blasted fact!" Harrington teased as he closed the door.

Doug smiled, "He's quite a guy. Boy, Rod thinks he hung the moon! Rod says 'and that's a blasted fact!' all the time! He knows a lot about mechanics from what I gather from Rod, huh?"

"Yah. Too bad his arm is bummed up. When he was here before the shooting, he helped here one day and did a great job! He knows his way around an engine. He is a bright guy. I can't understand his accent half the time, but . . . I sure hope that his arm gets better. This has been hell for him and Kincaid. Hardly seems fair, they both did their very best at their jobs and both ended up without a job! Seems like a rotten deal. I know Carl has had a time adjusting to not being a detective, but now that he and Darrell are going into partnership he seems to be happier. Of course, he has his Gophers!"

Doug chuckled, "That's quite the crew! I don't think I could stand it! The kids idolize him."

"Mo told Nora that she thinks they should build a six bedroom house!"

"What on earth for?" Doug frowned.

"For all the Gophers. She said he wants cribs and rocking chairs! Mo told Nora that he's looking forward to Carrie's baby, Darlene's baby and already has plans to take care of baby Matthew. He watches Clark and Maddie whenever Olsons need him."

"Does that make Mo crazy?"

"No, honestly, she's as bad as he is. She's raised enough kids to populate a country."

"Who'd have ever figured a grizzled old FBI agent would be a babysitter? Doug asked.

Elton grinned, "Probably the only difference is the age of the people he's babysitting!"

"Well, you got to get to work and I still have to face that pile of papers. Thanks for the coffee," Doug went out the door.

As he was leaving the front of the station, Harrington had gathered the mail. "Got anything you want me to take over to the post office? I can take it along as long as I'm going that way?"

"Actually, I do; if you wouldn't mind."

"No problem."

Harrington followed Doug into the grain elevator and back to his office. While Doug was getting the mail, a vendor came in with a delivery. Doug said he had not ordered anything and the vendor was adamant that he had.

Harrington stood quietly and listened to the heated discussion. Finally he said calmly, "Excuse me, but is there a purchase order?"

The vendor looked at him blankly, "Well, no," he stammered. "We just always deliver it every other week."

Doug said, "We use a lot of it in the winter, but we sell none of the product in the summer. What are we supposed to do with all of this?"

"That's your problem," the vendor said smugly. "I brought it out here, so you have to take it."

Harrington appraised the situation, "If you have no PO number or any signed order, you have no sale. Doug is not obligated to take it."

The vendor squinted his eyes at the young Bostonian, "Really, where did you get your knowledge of the law?"

Ian shrugged, "Boston, Massachutes."

The vendor looked at him blankly and said, "Okay. Mr. Anderson, you call us when you want to reorder. Maybe we can set up a standing PO for the winter months." With that, he abruptly turned and walked away.

The two men watched him in silence as he got in the car and drove off. Then they turned and broke into laughter. Doug guffawed. "I think he's afraid of Boston lawyers!"

"Too bad he doesn't know all the law I know is as a detective. I wish I was a lawyer!"

"I'm sure you know more law than most. Anyway, thanks a lot. That saved me a pile of money. You'll have to explain all this purchase order stuff to me when you have time. We only use them with a few companies. I thought the vendors used them, not us."

"No. You use them. I'd be glad to show you what little I know about them this afternoon, if you have time. Although Pepper or Elton might be more help. I don't do anything but collect dust anyway and that's a blasted fact."

57

Back at the house that morning, Kincaid and Mo were abuzz with plans. Zach's construction man was coming over in the afternoon to talk to them about their house. The Gophers spent the morning giving their input.

Carl had taken out some paper and the drawing pencils so that he and Maureen could sketch up some of their ideas. Once the kids saw that and since they always helped with the plans on their water diversion; they figured it their responsibility to help with the house plans.

Needless to say, many were made and many were vetoed. Charlie couldn't understand why a chicken coop couldn't be put in a house like any other room. It would make it a lot easier to feed the chickens in bad weather. He also pointed out to Mo that she could just go down the hall to gather the eggs! The only saving thing was that Ginger was against the idea, thus swaying the vote in Mo's favor. Charlie wasn't a big fan of democracy.

However, Kincaid and Mo did agree to a huge patio with a built-in sand box. The kids envisioned at least a two acre sandbox and notably, the adults never explained how small a ten foot square sandbox was by comparison. They simply hoped the kids wouldn't pay attention to that detail.

Maureen would have a large kitchen with an eating area. She'd also have a very large dining room, but not as big as the clan required. "We'll have to set up folding tables for clan gatherings, when it's our turn."

"That's a good idea," Carl agreed. He was actually secretly proud to think that he'd have the clan come to his home! It was amazing that someone who never invited even one friend over for potato chips was even considering inviting over forty people on a fairly regular basis.

"You know," Kincaid said, leaning back in his chair. "We could build a good sized dining room next to a big enclosed porch. If we made big doors from it to the house, we could just open it when we had dinners. The rest of the time, it would be a good place for the gophers to play in bad weather."

Mo and the Gophers all agreed, and the suggestion passed unanimously. All sorts of turmoil broke out over the bedrooms. Mo and Carl wanted to build a three bedroom house. That would leave room for Ian and still have a guest room. Pouts and tears immediately broke out among the Gophers.

"Where I'm going to be when I sleep over?" Charlie demanded. "I have to have a room so I don't have to carry my stuff back and forth. I need to have a bed for if I get tired. You don't 'spect me to sleep on the floor, do you? Aunt Nora always keeps extra clothes for me in case I get dirty and—"

"Down boy," Kincaid laughed. "We'll have one more room. Alright?"

Gingers arms immediately crossed and she was huffy. "What about Miriam and I? Don't us girls get a room! That's not fair! We are mad, aren't we, Miriam?"

Miriam shrugged her shoulders, nonchalantly.

Ginger hit the ceiling, "I know you are not so frad jelly, Miriam! You're mad too! I told you to be! We need to have a place too, or we will be mad!"

Miriam's eyes got huge and she looked at Kincaid crossing her arms like Ginger, "Ginger wants to."

Maureen just cracked up. "Okay, girls. Coot and I will figure out how many rooms we're going to have. You don't mind sharing, do you?"

"We think it's okay. Right, Miriam?" Ginger relaxed. "We share all the time anyway, right?"

Miriam was nodding in agreement and patting her chest, "Ginger Gopher share."

"Okay. You guys can think about what color you want to paint the walls and stuff," Mo smiled. "Would that make you happy?"

"That would be neato, huh Miriam?" Ginger giggled, relishing the fact that she controlled two votes. "We think we want fairies and tulips and rainbows. Right, Miriam?"

"Neato," Miriam agreed.

"Looks like a five bedroom house," Maureen giggled.

"Yea gads," Carl groaned. "I can see this all now. We should see if we can borrow the floor plans from a Federal penitentiary."

Charlie looked at him seriously, "Do they have a slide and a swing set in that pen cherry place?"

"No," Carl groaned. "They have cages."

Ginger's eye opened widely, sparkling with delight, "Are we going to have lots of pets? We don't have any. Aunt Nora and Uncle Elton have Elmer, but he lives outside and Twiggy, Pepper's kitty. She is nice but she hides all the time."

"That's because you guys scare her half to death," Coot pointed out. "And no, I don't think that we'll have pets."

Charlie piped up, "Why do you need cages then? Are you going to put the chickens in the house? See, Ginger. I told you it was a good idea!"

Miriam looked at him in wonder. Then she turned to Coot and patted the back of his hand, "Splursch!"

Maureen started to giggle, "Do you want a duckie, Miriam?"

Miriam patted her chest and nodded yes, "Splursch!"

"Heavens to Hermatroid! Is it too early to start drinking?" Carl turned to Maureen in despair, "For our own sanity, I think we should consider moving to Texas."

Mo laughed, "You asked for it."

"Why do you want to go to Texas," Ginger asked. "I got dirt from Texas. Did you know there is a lot of sand in Texas and oil lives under the dirt—!"

By noon, Carl felt like he had been in a tag-team wrestling match. He couldn't wait to talk to someone over fifty. Even Lloyd wouldn't want to have chickens in the house. Well, he couldn't be certain about that, but he wasn't going to ask him either. This whole place was filled with lunatics.

Pepper drove in shortly before the guys and Ruthie. Soon they were all saying grace at the table. After the Amen, Elton asked innocently how Carl's morning went.

He answered very quietly, "Don't want to talk about it, thank you." Then he became extremely interested in his lunch and didn't return Elton's look.

Elton gave a worried to look to Nora and mouthed, "What?"

Maureen saw it and stifled a grin. "He's just pouting. The kids were helping with our house plans this morning. I think he's at his wit's end."

"Oh no," Charlie stated innocently, "Coot didn't have red coming out his eyes! He just gave us ten to life!"

Harrington started to laugh and pretty soon, he and Elton were laughing so hard they both had to leave the table. Kincaid glared at them. If only he was allowed to bring his gun to the table.

Pepper was in a good mood. She was off until the following Monday. Chris had come home for the Fourth of July and had the week off. She was going to meet up with him right after physical therapy to go fishing with Eddie and Denise. She had done Carl and Miriam's therapy in the morning, and just needed to work with Harrington for a while before he went back to work.

While they were exercising his arm, she asked, "What did Dad have you doing this morning?"

He told her about the ordering and then about Doug asking him to help him out. She listened, "Hey, I have some of my books from the commercial college out here. Would you like to look them over?"

"Ah, I don't do that much," Ian answered. "Although, I'd like to know more about some of those PO procedures. If I knew more about it, I thought maybe I could write up a cheat sheet for those guys to follow."

Pepper stopped what she was doing. "That's a fantastic idea, Harrington. If you want to do that, I'd be happy to type it up for you. It could be sort of primer for the two shops and for Doug. What do you think?"

Ian grinned, "I wasn't thinking of anything that extravagant. Just a few notes."

"I know. We can just put them in an easy notebook for them or they'll lose them. That's a great idea! I feel bad that I can't help Dad more, but I'm just too busy."

"Pepper, you're Roadrunner. I don't know how you do it!"

"It is just because otherwise I miss Chris so much. If I keep busy, I'm too tired to be lonely. Know what I mean?"

"Yah, I do at that." Ian started bending his arm again, "You know, I think I'd like to read up on that stuff, if you don't mind."

"Sure, I'll get the books right after therapy."

Carl was extremely glad that his Gophers went home before the contractor arrived. He was certain he would've had an eighteen bedroom house with chicken pens. As it was, the couple ended up with a much larger home than either had anticipated.

Since Carl wanted it to be Maureen's dream house and since neither of them wanted stairs, they decided on a sprawling ranch style over a full basement. The house was a U shape and all three wings overlooked a common outdoor garden in the middle. There would be room for Maureen's flower garden and sitting area. Her flower garden was her pride and joy in Boston.

One side of the U was bedrooms and bathrooms with the master bedroom's huge patio doors opening onto the garden. The other side of the U contained Maureen's sewing room and their den. Then there was an extra room. No one knew what it would be used for, but both Mo and Carl had no doubt it would find a use.

The bottom of the U was the most fun. The front of the house had an entry that opened into a large homey living room which opened to the garden, the kitchen and eating area.

It was next to the large dining room which opened onto the enclosed patio. This room would be the play room and double as the expanded dining room. Off to the right was another attached room which housed a craft room, a place where the kids could do their projects. This room boasted of tile floor and sinks. Carl had learned after the volcano episode that any place where kids were going to be, had to be durable and washable. He wanted to put in a fire hose and drain, but the contractor talked him out of it.

The house would boast of a few things most houses did not have. All the doorways were wheelchair accessible. There was a bathroom off the playroom that had a child-sized toilet and sink. Carl just couldn't understand the virtue of trying to get a small kid to balance on the side of huge pool of cold water! As he put it, "It is bad enough to have to take a kid to the bathroom, let alone to help them teeter on a ledge."

The sandbox was outside the patio door. That end of the yard had its own 'tool shed,' where the kids could hang their shovels and hard hats.

After dinner, while the couples sat on the patio enjoying their day, Elton and Nora listened to Carl and Mo tell about their plans. Carl was very excited. Finally, Mo said, "Coot, why don't you tell them the secret? They won't tell."

"You think I should?" he looked at his fiancée with delight.

"Yes, I know you're about to burst!"

"Okay. Now, promise you won't tell anybody, especially the kids, okay?"

"We promise," Nora smiled. "Tell us."

"I didn't say I'd promise," Elton smirked.

"But you will," Nora said pointedly.

Elton grimaced, "Guess I will then."

"I remember the night of that bad storm when we had to get everyone downstairs. It was awful. It took so long, we could've all been dead," Carl said seriously.

"That's the truth. That's one good reason to have a basement in tornado country," Elton agreed.

"Yah, but I got to thinking. If we had the Gophers all there and had to get them downstairs pronto, we'd have a heck of a time. Then Charlie said something that made me think."

Elton started to laugh, "Charlie always makes me think! Or is it panic?"

"He asked if a penitentiary had a swing set."

Nora and Elton both looked at him curiously. Nora shook her head, "I don't get the connection."

"You kind of had to be there, but I thought; why not have a slide that went from the playroom to the basement? Then we could get the kids downstairs in a real hurry," Carl watched them expectantly. "Well, what do you think?"

Elton's mouth fell open. "That's a darned good idea. Weird, but sensible."

Nora was frowning, "I don't know. How're you going to keep the kids from going down the slide all the time?"

"That's the first thing I asked," Maureen said. "But Carl said we would put a latch at the top of the door so the kids couldn't use it unless we opened it for them. Then downstairs, they'll land on a mat. I think it's a brilliant idea."

"I have to say, Kincaid," Elton was thoughtful, "I think so too. And don't worry, I won't tell a soul. I'm just sorry I didn't think of it."

While they were visiting, Ruthie's car drove up. She waved and kissed Harrington goodnight. Then he came over to join the group.

"You seem very happy tonight," Nora observed. "Would you like a soda or something?"

Harrington smiled, "I'll help you freshen up everyone's drinks. I have something to tell to you."

"Okay, come with me," Elton got up to help refresh their drinks.

After everyone was seated with their drinks, Ian cleared his throat. "Tonight, I officially asked Ruthie to be my wife and she agreed."

Everyone rejoiced and toasted the event.

"I'm so happy," Nora said.

"My last baby is going to get married," Maureen embraced her son. "I'm delighted and Ruthie will be a fine daughter! You guys belong together."

Carl shook Harrington's hand. Suddenly he sat down and grimaced. "That doesn't mean you two are going to live with us, does it?"

Harrington laughed, "Ah gee Dad! Are you throwing your son out so soon?"

"No, but I just spent the day building a house with fifty bedrooms! I figure you should get your order in right away!" Kincaid joked.

"So have you any idea how soon and all the details?" Nora asked.

"Oh Lordie, here she goes," Elton beamed. "She'll have the rice thrown before we get in the house!"

"Not yet. We have so many things to think about," Ian was serious. "I really need to get a job."

"But Ian," his Mom pointed out, "You get the disability-pension thing from the department. It isn't like you don't have an income."

"I know Mom, but I need to do something with my time," then he winked. "Otherwise I might start chasing women."

"Holy Mary and all the Saints," Maureen gasped. "I'll have one son that is a priest and the other is a philanderer!"

Carl wagged his head with a grin, "At least it isn't the same son!"

The men thought it was very funny, but Maureen was not that amused. "Twas a mournful day when these made acquaintance!"

58

The next morning around the old coffee pot, the family talked about their Fourth of July plans. They'd be going to the county fairgrounds. Everyone was home except Marty and Annie who had to work. Some of the young folks had been snagged to help out with the games at the fairgrounds in the morning. The women had arranged for a picnic lunch. Zach and Harrington were put in charge of grilling the hot dogs and hamburgers for the clan, much to the dismay of Elton and Carl.

"Well, if that don't beat all!" Elton grumped.

"Dad," Pepper giggled, "We want to eat, not listen to you two squabble."

"He always starts it!" Carl pointed at Elton.

"Do not," Elton retorted.

Miriam covered her mouth with her tiny hands and giggled, "Goats."

The day was a lot of fun. Jerald's team won the very close softball game in the afternoon, which also meant that Ken's team lost. No one was very upset about it though. It was all in good fun. In the afternoon, Pepper and Chris took Lloyd home to nap and then he decided not to go back to the park.

While watching the game, Doug and Julia sat with Ian and Ruthie. Ian had read some of the literature that Pepper had given him. He told Doug about their plan to make a cheat sheet for him if he was interested.

"That'd be great! If I just had something like a guide or a system, things would go a lot faster. That is really a good idea! You'll probably still have to teach me how to use the guide!" Doug chuckled.

Harrington raised his eyebrow, "Don't kid me. You know most of it already."

Doug shrugged, "I guess I do but Ian, I really hate it."

"That is more like it," Harrington clapped him on the back. "I don't know how soon we'll get it done. I made some notes and Pepper volunteered to type them up. We're going to do that for the shops too."

"I would be glad to pay you for it," Doug offered.

"Don't be stupid. We just want to do it."

"Hmm. Well, you'd make more money if you charged for it."

"That's the hooker's excuse," Harrington laughed. Ruthie whacked him.

The weather was perfect and it wasn't even windy. The young folks dashed home to do the milking and then returned for the evening's festivities. Everyone danced outside at the fairgrounds. The prairie sunset rivaled the fireworks in splendor. The fireworks were very nice that year because it wasn't so dry that there was a huge worry about setting the prairies on fire. After the fireworks, they all went home. By the time the family arrived home, they were all tired out. It had been a great day.

The following morning, Elton took Carl to town. They're going to meet up with Darrell and sign the papers for the partnership. Darrell and Jeannie were meeting with the contractor that afternoon about their house.

While waiting for the attorney to finish with his other client, Darrell was nervous. Elton had rarely seen him like this as he was usually a pretty relaxed.

When Kincaid went to the restroom, Elton asked him, "What is it? Do you have reservations about this partnership? If you do, it's usually best to hold off. No one will be upset with you."

Darrell dropped his head, "No. I like Kincaid and this is a godsend, but I feel like such a failure."

Elton put his arm over his shoulder. "Why do you want to feel like that?"

Darrell grinned, "I don't want to. I just do. Hell, I haven't accomplished a darned thing. I live in a sheepherder's cabin and milk goats! What is that?"

Elton shrugged, "Sounds like a real person to my notion. You've a lot going for you, young man. Carl's no fool. He knows quality when he sees it. And so do I. I'm proud of you."

"Yah, yah, yah."

"Don't yah, yah me!" Elton snapped. "What exactly is bugging you?"

"I just feel like he's giving me the money like a charity case. I wouldn't have even been able to afford to go to my best friend's wedding if he hadn't offered this! What does he get for it?"

"Half ownership in the land, barn and livestock and the land for his house," Elton said sternly. "And mostly, he gets a place to belong. There is no price for that."

Darrell studied Elton's face, "Do you think that's really important to him?"

"You know it is," Elton said quietly. "He's not had that since his wife died when he was in his late twenties. It's very important to him, though he may never admit it. The more you include him in your life, the better he feels."

For the first time, Darrell grinned, "Maybe I should teach him how to milk goats."

Elton was serious, "It probably wouldn't be a bad idea."

"Really?"

"Really."

Kincaid rejoined the men, "So when are you and Jeannie going to meet with the contractor about the house?"

"Gee Carl," Darrell began, "We're thinking to maybe not do that. We can't really afford it right now."

Kincaid frowned, "That would be foolish. The contractor is giving us all a discount because our place is so close to Zach's and with yours in the mix, he won't have to shuffle his crews all over creation. That's why he wanted me to get my land deal done ASAP so that he doesn't have to move his dirt crew away and then bring them back. You will never get that good of a deal again and besides, it'll cost me and Zacharias money! Our partnership is paying for the houses anyway. Otherwise, I'll have to cough up the shekels on my own. Hell after the Gophers got through, I'll need million bucks just for shingles!"

"Oh, I forgot about the discount thing. What do you think, Elton?" Darrell asked.

"I don't want to tell you how to run your finances, but it sounds like a good deal. If you wait, you'll have to pay that much more plus inflation. A twenty percent discount on a house is nothing to sneeze at."

"No, it sure isn't," Kincaid agreed. "Ian and I talked about it, too. He is holding off until he gets his settlement from the department and he and Ruthie got married. I told him he might want to do it right away. Whether or not he gets married, he needs a place to live anyway. This is a good deal. The contractor will only give us this deal if we all do it at once."

"When should he get his settlement?" Darrell asked.

"From what I understand, it won't be until the docs sign off on his arm and that could be a long time," Kincaid answered. "Over a year."

"Zach told me that he was going to talk to Ian. He said he and Ruthie have all that money from Abraham, so they should just build." Elton pointed out, "But you know, he needs to keep his pride too. He just doesn't want to feel like he is mooching off Ruthie."

"That's silly," Darrell stated. "No one thinks that."

Elton turned and looked straight in his eye, "Yes, but you know how people are."

Darrell stopped, absorbed the message and then nodded. "Yah, I do."

When the guys got home, Pep asked to go for a walk with her Dad. They went for a long walk out the end of the pasture.

"It sure is a nice day, huh?" Elton grinned. "Slow down there, girl. Your Dad is an old bird."

"Let's park on this hill, huh? I need to talk to you. Mom and I talked already, but I want your input," Pep said as she sat on the ground.

"Good, because I want to talk to you about something too."

"You do? Am I messing up somewhere?" Pepper gave her Dad a worried look.

"Not that I know of, but first," her Dad lit a cigarette, "What is it you want to talk to me about."

Pep bummed a cigarette and then cleared her throat, "Dad, this last year has been great and I have appreciated how close we have become more than you'll ever know."

"Me too."

"But I feel like things are getting away from me, again."

"How so?" Elton questioned his girl.

"Chris and I can't stand begin apart any more. I mean, if we knew it was only going to be another year, yah. But we're facing at least three more years. I'll go nuts, and so will he. I love being with my family. I don't want to let you guys down, but he is where my heart really is," she started to tear up. "Are you upset with me?"

Elton put his arm around her neck and pulled her head toward him to kiss her forehead. "Not at all, you goofy kid. That's what I wanted to talk to you about. I want you to know that I really love you being so involved in the business, but I don't want you to feel tied to it. I know you do and I don't want that. You'll always be a part of all decisions of the family business, but more than anything, I want you to live your life. This shouldn't be a burden."

"I don't feel like it is a burden. I really enjoy it, but I can't do it from far away."

"I know. You and I talked before about how long you and Chris were going to be able to make this work. You know, education is great and I am so glad that you and Chris are doing what you are doing, but it's totally against biology. You're both ready to start nesting and you have to put it off. It doesn't work that well."

Pepper hugged her Dad, "Did I ever tell you that I love you?"

"Hmm, dunno. Maybe once," he grinned. "I suppose you could do it again."

"Well, I do. Chris found an application to the orthopedic center in Grand Forks. If it okay with you, I'd like to put an application in there. Only if you are okay with it. The job doesn't start until their expansion project is done in late January. I thought maybe we could get Carrie or someone to handle my work at the shop. Or have you thought about Ian?"

Elton looked at her and broke into a huge smile, "Actually, I did. I think he would be a great fit. Carrie would be good but she'll have the baby. She might be pretty busy. Besides she has a great job at the bank."

"I know. She said they were talking about promoting her to branch manager. Wouldn't that be fantastic?"

"Wow! It is. She is a good kid," Elton looked off toward the horizon. "I hope that someday, Pepper, you can look back over your life and feel you made some good decisions. They won't all be, but I want my kids to be content."

Pepper patted his hand, "I think we will be, Dad and because of you and Mom."

"Look kiddo," he smiled. "You and your Mr. Cassidy make whatever decisions work the best for you. You have our support. I think Ian would be a great choice."

Harrington spent the day at the shop. He did a lot of Doug's paperwork that morning. In the afternoon, Doug asked him if he'd watch the store at the elevator while he was in back unloading some hog feed. Harrington thought that was a fine idea.

He was busy that afternoon, crazy busy. When Kevin stopped by for a minute to get a candy bar, Ian confided, "There must be a notice up somewhere! Come to the elevator and harass the Bostonian. And that's a blasted fact!"

"Yah, there is," Kevin teased gleefully, "Put it up myself! How's it going?"

"Alright. Really, it wasn't that busy; it was just that I didn't know where everything was. I'm starting to figure out where things are now."

"You look good behind that counter!" Kevin laughed. "Especially with your hand in the till."

"You're such a jerk."

"Hey, Keith asked me to have you call him. He has a problem with some of the young people that are hanging around the station at night. He needed some advice."

"Don't know what I'd know about it but I'll give him a call," Harrington said. "Kevin, can I ask you something?"

"Sure," Kevin said as he sized up his candy bar.

"How did you know when it was the right time to get married?"

Kevin smiled thoughtfully, "I didn't."

"What?"

"Nope, and I still don't know. I mean I wanted to be with Carrie all the time and she seemed to be so inclined. We couldn't stand being apart anymore. So, that was it."

"Really?"

"Look, the way I figure it, we decided to take a chance and face life together. It's too hard to be on your own; so you sort of need a cohort. We don't know what will happen. Neither of us believes that anyone ever really does. So, we weren't looking for a guarantee. I know I drive her to distraction sometimes and there are times, I'd like to skin her. But she's my trusted Tonto in everything. So, even if she makes me mad, I have to get along with her. I'm still certain she is my best bet. Why do you ask? Ruthie?"

Ian chuckled and shook his head while he listened to Kevin talk. "Yah. I really want to be with her, like you said; but my arm is no good."

"Hell Harrington, my brain is no good! I didn't let that stop me!"

Ian laughed, "And that's a blasted fact!"

"Look, she knows about your arm and I am pretty certain that she doesn't care. She wants to be with you. A word of warning though, if you use the arm as an excuse too long, she'll start to doubt everything you say."

"Huh?"

"You heard me. Don't use it as an excuse because you're afraid to make a commitment. She'll see right through it. I saw it. You don't want your lady to turn vicious. What are you planning if it never gets any better than it is right now?"

Ian's face paled with the realization, "I dunno. I guess I never thought about that."

"What if your arm gets better, you get hitched, fall down the stairs and break your back? Will you leave her?"

"Of course not."

"Doesn't that tell you something?"

Harrington sat on the stool and thought a minute before he answered, "You aren't really as goofy as you'd like people to think, are you?"

"Don't know. Sometimes I'm worse. Hey, just think about this. What else have you go to do with the rest of your life?" Then he put his change for the candy bar on the counter and waved goodbye.

Harrington had to admit, Kevin had seen right through him. Sure, he was worried about his arm and not having a job. Sure, he didn't have his settlement yet, but seriously, he was mostly just worried about making a commitment and having it fall apart. Harrington was deep in thought about it and said aloud, "Dammit Kevin."

"Did I interrupt something?" Doug asked.

"No, just that Kevin made me think."

"I hate thinking too," Doug laughed. "Wanna take a break?"

"Sounds good," Ian said as he went to the pop machine, "My treat. What's your poison?"

"Coke," Doug answered as he sat down and put his feet up on a stool. "You've been a real help today. I'd have been stuck behind the counter and never got that truck unloaded."

"I can see where that could be," Harrington agreed. "Sort of like the shop. All you have to do it get under a car and someone will drive in and want gas. Sure as shooting."

"What time is Elton expected back today?" Doug asked.

"He said about four, but if he and Kincaid get loose in a store, who knows!"

Doug laughed, "So I've heard. Is Carl planning on retiring now? Or does he have any plans?"

"I think that he is retiring, but honestly Doug, he has the kids with him all the time. He and Mom talked to the contractor and you would think they were building a nursery school. Mom is bad that way too, but she doesn't hold a candle to him. Do you know that he's even having a tool shed built near the sandbox for the kids to hang their shovels? I think he is out of his mind."

Doug broke into a long laugh, "He is a character, that's for sure. Mr. Gruff and Tough. I can't imagine him being an FBI agent."

Harrington got serious, "He was a darned good one and tough. He handled almost all of the church scandals in the country. He was considered the expert in the agency. He'd focus like a laser and never let up until he got the bottom of a case. That's why he devoted his entire life to the agency. He is just playing catch up now on the rest of his life that he missed before."

"Makes sense. I figured he was a good agent. He seems to read people like a book. I imagine he could be brutal if he set his mind to it."

"Yah, and I know he did a time or two. You can't do that kind of work all your life and end up fit for much else," Harrington pointed out. "Those skills aren't too useful in common society."

Doug leaned forward, "Now are you talking about Carl or Ian?"

Ian swallowed hard, "Both."

"I'm sorry," Doug apologized, "It's not my business. I just don't know when to put a sock in it."

"No problem," Harrington answered, "You know, I was reading some of Pepper's books and I got to thinking I might take some of those classes at the Commercial College. Too bad they're all night courses. Ruthie works all day, so then we would never get to see each other."

"No, they have them all day, too. Pep took night courses because of her schedule. That'd be a great idea if you did that. You have a knack for it. Only thing is then you'd charge me for advice."

"Ah, I'll do a trade," Harrington chuckled.

"Advice for hog fodder! Sounds like a heck of a deal to me!"

59

The next couple weeks were crazy. Ian had talked to Ruthie and they decided to take advantage of the contractor's discount. They purchased a piece of land from Kincaid and Darrell that was a couple miles north of Kincaid's place, almost directly across the county road a from Danny and Jenny's home.

The land overlooked a gully that was quite pretty, even though it was not that good for pasture, the deer seemed to love it. Ruthie saw a doe and her fawn there and that finalized the deal. They made plans for a four-bedroom house with an attached garage and a full basement. Since Zach, Coot, Darrell and Ian were building; almost every conversation seemed to revolve around home construction. Elton whined that he was left out. "If you guys had done this sooner, I could've got a discount for my addition."

He received no sympathy.

Everyone was getting ready for Zach and Suzy's wedding on the fourteenth. Coot took his Gophers to the church to practice walking down the aisle. It was still rather shaky on how Charlie would fare. Some days he was great, and some days—well, not so much. Even though no plans had been finalized, Coot did announce to Mo that he didn't want Charlie to be the ring bearer when they got married. She just smiled and suggested he be the best man!

Harrington and Ruthie worked on the house plans together, but had not set a wedding date. Ruthie was very content working at the church and Harrington didn't want to upset that apple cart. He spent most of his time helping out at the shop and elevator and doing his therapy. His physical progress was unbelievably slow.

One afternoon, he and Pepper went to the commercial college and Pep introduced him to the school. By the time he left, he had signed up for a couple mornings of classes each week. He thought he could check in with Keith to help at the Bismarck shop those afternoons.

Four days before Zach's wedding, Elton returned to the shop but went over to the elevator office to see Doug. About fifteen minutes later, they called and asked for Kevin to join them. Keith called and asked for his Dad. Ian told him that they were over at the grain elevator. Pepper drove in and parked her car out front of the station.

Harrington watched as she got out of the car and he thought she'd be coming in to the shop. He was going to ask her something about a contract. He was surprised when she went over to the elevator. He decided he'd talk to her that evening and went back to a stack of invoices.

His concentration was broken by Kevin, "Hey, they want to see you over at the elevator office. It's important."

"Me?" Ian was taken back, "I hope I didn't screw up something."

Kevin laughed, "Well, if you did, they haven't discovered it yet. They just want to talk to you."

When he went into the office, there was Doug, Pep and Elton. He felt like he was about to be given detention for throwing spit wads in high school. "You wanted to see me?"

"Yah, grab a chair. Want a Coke?" Elton smiled.

"I'm okay," Harrington became nervous. "This is ominous. What's going on?"

Doug cleared his throat, "We have an idea, but only if you are cool with it. Pep wants to tell you something."

"Pepper?" Now Harrington was certainly confused.

"See, Chris and I have decided to get married on winter break before he goes back to school. I just found out that my application was accepted in Grand Forks at the orthopedic center there."

"Congratulations, Pepper. That's really great," Ian was even more confused.

"Thanks, but this isn't for publication yet. So mum's the word. You know, Chris has to buy a cow!" Pep giggled.

"I'm honored to be among the trusted few," Ian smiled, still bewildered.

"And you are," Doug agreed. "We were talking about you. We have an offer to make to you, Elton and I. We know you are going to school and we can work around it."

Elton explained, "Harrington, we'd like to have you work for us. Neither of us can afford a full time manager but we can split the cost. You'd have to handle the Bismarck station, this shop, the grain elevator and store. We could work it out though so you could go to school, but Pep can tell you more about that. What do you think? We have health insurance and vacation, long, thankless hours and unlimited grief. It would be hard to find a better deal."

Ian was dumbfounded. "Ah," he stammered, "I'm shocked. I need to think, I mean, I should talk to Ruthie. I'd like to but I don't know if I know enough about it."

"Oh yes you do," Pep said. "You certainly know more than I do. I know you can do it, I just don't know if you want to work with these guys."

"No," Harrington mumbled, "I like them, but then again they weren't my bosses so I could ignore them."

Elton shrugged, "Never seemed to make a difference with anyone else; don't expect it will with you either."

"I want to thank you guys for considering me. I hope you aren't just making this up for my benefit."

Doug frowned, "Look, you're a nice guy but I don't go around paying out health insurance to every nice guy I meet. You are a tremendous help."

"When do you need to know by?" Harrington looked at Elton.

"By the time that Chris comes to ask me if he can marry my girl," Elton chuckled. "So I figure any time now."

"Okay, I'll talk to Ruthie tonight and get back to you tomorrow," Ian stood up. "Thank you guys. You realize that my arm still isn't any good."

"We didn't know that!" Doug shook his head. "You idiot."

That evening, Ruthie and Ian talked about the idea and she thought it was a wonderful idea. "Gee Ian, it is close by so you wouldn't have to drive all over the countryside, you know the guys and it's something you are interested in. It'll fit in with your school. I think it is great, but I sense that you aren't too sure."

Ian took her in his arms, "I know this sounds stupid and I should be delighted, but I guess I was still hoping my arm would improve and I could go back to law enforcement. I feel like by taking this job, I'm giving up."

Ruthie embraced him, "I understand. I don't want you to feel like you are giving up on your dream. I'm pretty sure that if you took this job and your arm got better; those guys would be the first to expect you to go back to police work. They all know that you loved it and were good at it."

"Wouldn't that be unfair to them? I mean to work for them and then leave when I got better?"

"Not if you do a good day's work every day. Why would you feel that way? You didn't think I was being unfair to Marv and Byron when I took the job at the church. They both knew that I'd have gone back to the convent if I had the chance. They knew they were second choice."

Ian's looked deeply into her eyes. "Is that the way you feel about me? Second choice?"

"Not at all. You're the most important person in the world to me. I have to say however, that had you not asked me to marry you before long, I would have gone back to the convent."

"Really?" Harrington smiled, and then mumbled. "They're right."

"Who?"

"Oh, Kincaid and Kevin. Carl told me that if I kept messing around, that is exactly how you would feel. I was so afraid of asking you because of my arm, that I was going to put it off until I got well. He told me I was all wet."

"He was right. You egghead! What if you never get any more movement back that you have now? Would I still be waiting?" Ruthie giggled, and then hugged him. "We're a pair, you know."

"I prefer to think of it as a team."

Ruthie kissed his cheek, "I think I do, too. Hey, what time does Matt get in tomorrow? I'm anxious to see him!"

"I hate to admit it but I am too. Please don't tell him though," Ian laughed. "He is coming in on the 7:15 pm flight. I think that Zach is picking him up on his way out, so we aren't going in. Mom is bananas to see him."

"How does she feel about Matthew taking a sabbatical?" Ruthie asked.

"You know, she is okay with it. I don't know if she knows all the details though. I thought she would spazz out or something, but I think she read the handwriting for some time. She thinks he just needs to get away from all the church politics. You know Ruthie, I think it's almost worse that regular politics. At least the politicians don't cloak it in religious terms. I think there is more to it than a sabbatical."

Ruthie leaned back in the crook of Ian's arm, "So do I. It is more like a nice way of saying a suspension. I feel bad about it. I know he got into hot water with the Bishop over my business with Father Timothy."

Ian bolted straight up, "Listen here. He got in to hot water because he couldn't stand their cover up. His break from the church is not just about you. Don't you even start with that. Hear me?"

"Yes, I hear you. In fact, almost anyone within a mile radius heard you," Ruthie's eyes filled with tears.

"I'm sorry, but just I don't want you to blame yourself. I personally think it's a good thing. I know a lot about some of the stuff other priests have done and how the church closed ranks to protect them. Believe me, I'm not nearly as enthralled with the church as you guys are. I believe for good reason."

"What do you know, Ian?"

"No, I'm not talking. It is part of legal cases and I sure as hell don't want to be the one that spills the beans. I'm happy you all find peace with the church. I really am. Just leave it alone. If a time comes when I can talk about it, I will," Ian was adamant. He became silent for a minute, and then smiled with his big dimples, "Hey, how did your dress for the wedding fit? I think Nora mentioned that Marly was altering it."

"It's very nice. Marly is quite a talented seamstress. I asked Katie if she will do the beading on my wedding dress when we get married."

"Cool. She does beautiful work." Ian grinned, "And you're becoming a master baking lady! Grandma Katherine must've taught you all her secrets. I'll get fat on your caramel rolls. And that's a blasted fact!"

60

The family was waiting eagerly for Zach to arrive home from Bismarck. He would be off work now for two weeks and it was three days before his wedding. On his way out from town, he met Father Matthew Harrington at the airport. He was Maureen's youngest son and Ian's brother. Father Matt was taller than Ian and a thin build. He had become a good friend of the family while they held vigil at the Shreveport hospital. Even though he knew quite of few of the family, this was Matt's first visit to North Dakota.

Zach pulled up in front of the house and the folks began pouring out of the old farmhouse to meet him. He got out of the car and was immediately engulfed in a big hug from his Mom. Then Elton held out his hand and welcomed him to his home.

While Zach got the bags from the car, Elton introduced his wife Nora. She was as nice and as gracious as Matt had heard.

"I've been anxious to make your acquaintance and I feel like I already know you. Would you like me to call you Father or Matt?"

"Matt, please."

"Okay Matt. Call me Nora. Make yourself at home."

"Thank you," Matt said. "I've been equally as anxious to meet you."

Kincaid shook his hand and Father Matt chuckled, "Hi Dad. Did Ian tell you that he and I are going to hang out in your basement when you and Mom get married? We'd like pizza every day about eleven."

It pleased Kincaid more than he'd ever admit, but he replied, "Of course, my son. And all you have to do is get your butts out of bed and bake it; right after you take out the garbage and weed the garden."

Matt laughed, "I might want to talk that over with Ian. We'll get back to you."

Then Ruthie ran up to him and gave him a big hug, "It's so good to see you. I really missed you and have been looking forward to it so much! I have so much to tell you! There are so many things I need to talk to you about!"

Matt grinned, "Slow down girl, we don't have to do it all tonight, do we?"

"No, you gotta see Ian," she drug him over to where Ian was standing.

"Hello, did you bring my comic book?" Harrington laughed as he hugged his brother.

"Nope and I not gonna either," Matt chuckled. "It's mine, fair and square. You look like you got a little sun. It looks good on you."

"If you ever get your collar off, you might get some sun too."

Zach had to say goodbye because he was expected at Heinrich's. Suzy's brother had arrived that afternoon and they were going to meet for dinner. Then he and Suzy would come back to the farm. Suzy was anxious to see Matt, too.

Byron greeted Matt and walked into the house with him. In the kitchen, he was introduced to Marly, Grandma Katherine and Grandpa Lloyd.

Lloyd was in a good mood and feeling rather well. When the dark-haired young priest with bright blue eye and a disarming smile that betrayed near dimples was introduced, Lloyd eyed him up and down. "You another preacher? We got some already. Don't know if we need any more."

"No, Mr. Engelmann," Matt replied. "I'm a priest."

Lloyd sat back and studied him a minute. "Good. At least I don't have to find you a wife! You know," He motioned for the younger man to lean ahead as if he was whispering to him in confidence, even though he was speaking loudly, "Elton keeps dragging these guys home and I gotta find them a woman. That last one was really tough. He is old and has a cantankerous nature. Had a hell of a time finding someone to put up with him."

"That lady is my mother," Matt grinned.

"You don't say? She's the mom to the cop. He got my car back. Do you know him? Yah, the cop guy is going to marry my daughter. I always forget her name. What's it again, Elton?"

"Ruthie."

"I feel bad about that. A guy shouldn't forget his own little girl. I try real hard but I think I wore my brain out. Elton says it is because I have too many things to remember. Do you think he's right?" the elderly man asked.

"It well could be. You seem to have a lot of people to watch over."

"Yah, I do. It's a hell of mess most the time. Like trying to get chickens to stand at attention." he whispered to Matt, "They are decent enough, but most of them are a little wobbly, if you get my drift. Don't tell them; it might hurt their feelings."

"I won't, Mr. Engelmann," Matt squeezed his hand. "Your secret is safe."

"I'm going to eat now. There's this guy's coming to visit and now I have to wait for my dinner. Damned near starved to death. Folks should show up at a decent time, don't you think? It's not right to make folks go hungry."

"I agree."

Pepper came up to help Lloyd to the table, "Hello Father Matt, I am Victoria, Elton's youngest. I go by Pepper."

"I've heard about of you," Matt smiled.

"That's frightening," she said as she helped Grandpa to the table. "Just believe the good stuff."

Matt was introduced to Chris, Pepper's fiancé, and Pastor Ellison's kids. "I've heard so much about all of you. I feel like I already know you."

"Pleased to meet you," Ken nodded and Katie gave him a big smile.

Little Charlie took his hand, "I'll show you where to sit, but Coot said I have to keep my socks on so you can eat a piece of pie."

"What?" Matt tried to contain his merriment.

Kincaid heard it, "That's not what I said. I told you to put a sock in it, so the man could eat in peace."

"I know," Charlie agreed. "That's what I told him." Then he looked at the young priest in exasperation, "Coot's really nice, but sometimes he just says crazy stuff. When you want to see the chickens, I'll show them to you. I am the Uncle Elton's Chicken Man. Have you ever been a Chicken Man?"

"No, I never have."

"That's too bad. I can show you how. My Dad's a preacher. He said you're like a Catlick preacher. Is that right? Ginger and I want to know about some stuff," the young boy rattled on.

"What's that Charlie?"

"Who cleans up the messes at the Catlick church?" he asked innocently.

Matt broke into a laugh. "I don't know."

"Seems like you'd get skinned for leaving a big mess every Sunday," the little boy said seriously.

Maureen came over and rescued the situation. "Come on Charlie. Shall we let Matt sit down so he can eat? He hasn't had a good meal all day and he is hungry."

Charlie climbed up in the chair next to Kincaid, "Okay. But he probably should've cleaned his plate. Then he wouldn't be so hungry."

"Yea gads, Charles," Kincaid said. "Settle down. You will talk a leg off him."

"Aren't your legs good either? Coots aren't so good, so I have to be his legs. I am his Goer and Getter Guy. If you need a Goer and Getter Guy, don't worry. I'll be it."

"Okay, I think I'll be fine," Matt nodded. "But thank you."

Byron raised his eyebrows, "Charlie, please be quiet. Let someone else have a turn talking to him."

The little boy looked at his Daddy, "Yes sir. Whose turn is next? Is it Ginger's? She hasn't talked to him yet and she can't wait to find out his stuff."

"I get to say that," Ginger was huffy. "I get to talk now."

"After we say grace, okay?" Byron said.

Then Kevin brought Miriam to the table and up to Matthew. He held out his hand to introduce himself while holding her. "Hello. I'm Elton's son, Kevin and this is my wife, Carrie."

Matt stood up and shook their hands. "And is this little Miriam?" he said as he gently touched her back. "Do you remember me, Miriam?"

She stared at him and then turned suddenly to bury her head in Kevin's shoulder.

"Miriam, it's okay if you can't remember. He is a good guy. His name is Father Matt. Tell him hello."

She turned around and he held out his hand like he was going to shake hers. She looked from him to Kevin and then back. After a bit, she reached out, touched his hand quickly, drew it back and turned to Kevin.

"We can talk later," Matt smiled. "Okay, Miriam?"

Miriam answered without looking, "Okay Fodder."

Dinner was fun and everyone was jabbering away. Ginger finally got her chance to find out his 'stuff' and was most disappointed to learn that priest didn't have either children or wives. "That's just stupid. No wonder there isn't anyone to clean up the messes at the Catlick church. If you had a bouncer, she could do it."

"You might get into trouble with women's libbers," Matt's eyes sparkled.

"I don't like liver. Mom cooks it with onions and I just eat the potatoes. Yuk!" Ginger answered.

"Neither do I," asserted Charlie. "I sneak mine in my pocket so Mom can't see and then feed it to Elmer. Do you know who Elmer is?"

"No, I don't," Matt replied.

"He is Uncle Elton's dog. He will dig up gaskets unless you make them deep enough. Coot and Mo are going to get cages for their new house so we can have a bunch of pets. Then they can eat our liver. Cause we kids don't, do we Ginger?" the boy looked at Matt seriously, "Ginger and me tell Miriam what to do because she is frad jelly. Have you ever eaten frad jelly? I wonder if it tastes like grape?"

Marly raised her voice, "Ginger and Charlie. No more. You have jabbered long enough. Now be quiet."

Charlie grimaced to Matt, "I've to be quiet now. Mom is at her wits end. Did you see the red come out of her eyes? That's never good."

Ian reached over and touched Matt's arm. "Didn't I tell you?"

"It has to be experienced," Matt grinned.

Then everyone turned to their dinner and no one was talking. Miriam was sitting between Kevin and Carrie. She seemed to take the silence as her queue to step in.

She patted her chest and looked at Byron. "Gopher turn."

"Sure, you can have a turn honey," Byron winked at Elton.

"Mr. Bear, Gopher, Cawwie, lick," started to tell Father Matt.

"Can someone explain?" Matt asked.

"Cawwie, Mr. Bear, Gopher, Oops! Lick." Miriam repeated. "Chocolate."

Carrie explained about the practice with the chocolate pie and Matt said, "I bet that was fun, huh Miriam?"

Miriam nodded, "Fodder lick?"

"I think I might try it."

Miriam nodded, "If you want to."

By the time dinner was over, everyone had a chance to visit and Miriam even showed Matt how to lick the whipped cream off the top of a banana cream pie. After dinner, while everyone else was cleaning up, Matt and Ian took Matt's bags upstairs.

Harrington showed his brother his room that overlooked the backyard of the Schroeder home. "The bathroom is the second door down to the right. If you need anything, don't be afraid to ask. These folks will expect you to. They're really great."

"They seem to be. Those kids are a riot. I can't believe how good Kincaid is with them. He really seems comfortable here."

"He does. But then again, if you can't be comfortable here, I don't know where you could be. I hope you enjoy them as much as I do. I love it here."

"I can tell."

"We need to get down there again. Ellisons will be leaving."

Later after Ellisons and Kevins had gone home, the Grandparents were in bed and Chris and Pepper had gone for a walk, the rest relaxed around the picnic table.

Kincaid had his whiskey, Ian and Matt a beer and the others had sodas or ice tea. They all fell into comfortable silence, full tummies and peaceful company. Matt leaned back in the cushioned redwood chair, looked at the starry sky and sighed, "This is the life. Can't even hear a car. Only crickets."

"Isn't the sky astonishing?" Mo crooned. "I can watch this amazing sky for hours. I only caught a glimpse of those incredible Northern Lights one time."

"It really is something, Mom," Matt agreed. "Do you see the Northern Lights often?"

"Seems to go in stretches. Sometimes we do. They are quite mind-boggling. Even those born and raised here never fail to stop and look," Elton agreed. Then he added, "Unless it is forty below."

"I am not looking forward to that," Kincaid grumped. "That tornado scare was enough for me. I may have my house up for sale come spring."

"Ah, just fill your freezer with food and make sure you have heat. You'll do just fine," Elton advised. "It isn't bad if you don't have to go out in it."

Nora smiled, "The cold isn't the bad part; it's the doggone wind! That's what causes the trouble."

"You're so right, Nora," Elton agreed. "Just think, a couple days from now Zach gets married. Hard to believe, huh?"

"He seems really cool with it," Matt stated. "No jitters."

"I doubt either he or Sue have any doubts, do you?" Elton asked Nora.

"No. I'm so happy for them," then Nora cleared her throat, "By the way, gang, tomorrow we got things to do. So I don't want anyone slinking off on me."

"Oh, oh. Nora is in wedding mode. We'd best tow the mark," Elton teased.

"Hush. We all need to do our share. We have to get the barn decorated. Annie will be home and she, Chris and Pepper are going over there to help Greta and Linda. It would be nice if more could help. Mo and I are cooking up to our ears and Darlene is going to help us. Kincaid has to practice with his Gophers going down the aisle and then start cutting potatoes for salad. Marty is bringing out the tuxedoes and Carrie, Katie and Marly are doing the last minute alterations. So, you guys all have to try on your suits as soon as Marty gets here."

"Yes, Ma'am," Kincaid mocked. "You ever in the Army?"

Nora gave him a quick glare, "We can't all get by with being windy like you do!"

"Wow!" Harrington laughed, "Guess you got told!"

"You know, when I first met Nora I was really jealous. I thought she was the sweetest, gentlest thing in the world. But since then, I have felt the crack of her whip. Trust me, Magpie has his hands full!" Kincaid blustered.

Elton nearly choked, "Man, should I kiss you or what? I never thought I'd live to hear you say that. I tried to tell you, didn't I?"

"Ah hell, she was probably real nice 'til she started hanging around you."

Maureen laughed, "By my mind, you two both are hovering dangerously close to the chasm. And not a body of us would make any move to save you."

"That is so true," Harrington agreed. "You should just hush up."

Matt laughed, "Or 'put you socks on' as Charlie said!"

Then Zach and Suzy drove in. Suzy jumped out of the car and ran to give Matt a big hug. "I'm so glad to see you again. Thanks for coming out! I hope you're having a great time."

"Nora was just telling us about some of the plans. Decorating a barn and all that. It sounds exciting! You look grand and Zach looks happy. I'm so pleased for you both."

"What do you think of our little Miriam? Zach and I can't take any of the credit, but isn't she doing well?"

"She sure is. It's heartwarming to see."

61

The morning light was already flooding the prairie when Pepper's alarm shattered the slumber at the Schroeder household. Matt had a pretty good idea of the routine from what his Mom and brother had told him. He was anxious to see it in person. Although, nothing really prepared him for seeing so many zombie-like humans staring at a single coffee pot, cups in hand.

He entered the kitchen late and there they were. No one was speaking, nine people, just standing there staring vacantly and listening to the perking of a huge coffee pot. He had to laugh.

"What?" Elton asked indignantly. "Ain't never seen folks ready to start their day before?"

Matt chuckled, "Not like this. You guys are funny."

Grandma handed him a cup and said, "Get in line, young fella. Since you are so perky, we will be expecting great things from you today."

"Yah," Kevin said as he entered the kitchen, "Who are you going to milk?"

"I thought I might help decorate the barn," Matt stuttered.

"Buddy, that is after the milking is done. It isn't either-or," Kevin chuckled. "I'm thinking Esmeralda. Huh, Dad?"

"You shouldn't be so bossy, Kevin," Pepper reprimanded her brother. "You're always so bossy. He should milk Snowflake."

"Now who's bossy?" Kevin argued. "You want to be the boss all the time."

"Dad! Make him stop!" Pepper whined.

"Esmeralda would be good," Elton shook his head. "But so would Snowflake!"

"You always let her get away with it," Kevin pointed out. "Just because she is a girl."

"Does not," Pepper grumped.

"Oh dear lord, some days I'd like to skin you both," Elton said. "Zach is the only one who is normal."

"I beg your pardon," Harrington asked indignantly.

"Huh?" Elton said. "Yea gads, not another one!"

"Here's your coffee. Elton. Just ignore the kids. Someday they'll grow up and leave home," Grandma suggested.

Elton looked around, "It hasn't worked so far."

After chores, the family settled down to a huge breakfast of homemade smoked sausage, buttermilk pancakes, fried eggs and canned peaches. Matt couldn't remember the last time that he had such a big breakfast or ate so much. He knew the fresh air and exercise down at the barn had increased his appetite, but the food was fantastic. He raved about it and then Ruthie explained that she and Grandma were making caramel rolls for breakfast the next day. They were even better.

At seven-thirty, the decorating committee began to assemble at the Heinrich barn. Pepper, Annie, Matt and Ian were met by several of the neighborhood young folks. A bit later, Jeannie and Darrell arrived and were introduced to Matt.

"It's great to meet Boston's brother," Darrell said. "Did they make you help with chores this morning?"

"Yah, I even milked a cow," Matt grinned proudly.

"Come over to my place and you can milk goats," Darrell chuckled. "Actually, I guess I should get used to saying our place. Kincaid's my partner now on the farm and the dairy."

"Oh, Mom mentioned that. I'd love to come over to your place. I told Kincaid yesterday that I was planning on mooching off him once he and Mom got married, living in the basement. He is trying to figure out how to squirm out of it."

"I'm sure he'll figure a way!" Darrell laughed. "Well, then we'll be neighbors! That's cool. This is my wife to be, Jeannie. We're getting married ourselves in a couple weeks."

"Congratulations!" Matt smiled. "Is Pastor Byron marrying you, too?"

"No," Jeannie said, "We're having a double wedding with Annie and Andy Schroeder in Hawaii. But Byron helped us line up a minister there."

"That sounds exciting," Matt said. "Will there be a lot of folks there?"

"No, only our parents," Jeannie said. "It is too expensive for everyone else to get there. But we'll enjoy Smitty's wedding dance."

"Smitty?" Matt asked.

"That is what some folks call Zach," Harrington explained. "Darrell does that. He calls me Boston."

Matt laughed, "Hmm. Oh, I heard about you! The boy that named the nanny goat Arnold."

Jeannie kissed Darrell's cheek, "See honey, your reputation precedes you."

"I better go help Eddie bring the ladder up the stairs. He and Denise are the best decorators in the country," Darrell changed the subject.

The group hammered, strung, hung, taped and glued, but when they finished; the hayloft had been transformed into a gala ballroom. Matt was impressed.

"I've never been in a hayloft in my life, let alone one that's used for dances. This looks like it will be great fun," Matt said to Darrell as they took a break sitting on a hay bale. "Do you do this often?"

"Minus the decorations, we used to do it almost every weekend, except Lent," Darrell explained, "Most of us kids learned how to dance here. But it's been less in these last years. Gilda and Bill, Suzy's folks, are getting older and it seems like everyone is so busy. I can't really figure it out. We have all these time saving devices and less time! Makes no sense."

Matt nodded, "That's so true. I'm really looking forward to this. I don't know why. I don't even dance."

Jeannie came up to sit next to Darrell and overheard him. "We can remedy that, right girls?"

Before he knew what hit him, the radio had been cranked up and everyone was dancing. By the time the next hour had passed, Matt had been given the seal of approval by all the women there.

Pepper laughed, "I think you had better wear your clerical collar to the wedding."

"Why is that?" Matt asked innocently.

"All the single women will have designs on you!"

He looked perplexed, "Do you really think that I should wear my collar?"

Harrington laughed, "Whatever you look best in."

Darrell realized that Matt was honestly concerned, "Really, do what feels comfortable to you. You came to have a good time, so do. If someone has a problem with it, tell them to go suck an egg!"

Matt's eyes got huge and he burst out laughing, "I've never heard that expression before!"

The decorators all arrived back at the farm and entered the busy kitchen. Kincaid was just getting his Gophers ready to head over to the church. They were squirrelly. He'd planned on leaving Miriam with the women, but she was having none of that.

Ian offered to come along with him and bring the little girl, so she wouldn't be left out. She patted his neck when he picked her up and said, "Gopher—Hawwie go."

"Are you going with or helping peel the potatoes?" Grandma asked Matt.

Matt looked over the situation, "I'll go with. I want to see the church."

"Oh tell the truth," Grandma giggled, "You just don't want to peel potatoes!"

"That's part of it," he chuckled.

Byron met them at the sanctuary and explained to the kids how important it was to behave. It would've been obvious to any passerby that he was wasting his breath. Charlie couldn't understand why Zach couldn't just put the ring in his pocket. It wasn't that big or heavy. He didn't need someone to carry it for him. He wasn't doing anything but standing there anyway.

Ginger was pretty good, but thought that since the lavender petals were so pretty she should throw them all over the church. That way, everybody would get some. Kincaid explained to her that it was just for the bridesmaids and bride to walk on. Besides, they would run out of petals. Then she was good with it.

Charlie had decided that he shouldn't have to stand there all the while his Dad talked. He knew how much he talked and thought it would be boring. Kincaid reminded him that good Agents always did the hard stuff. That helped, but Charlie still couldn't see point of it.

Finally his Dad and Kincaid told him if he was going to cause trouble, he'd have to sit in the congregation and not be in the wedding. Charlie's bottom lip came out, "But then I'd have to sit still and I promised Suzy and Smitty I'd do it and I'm so short, I won't get to see anything sitting there and it will be just awful. I'll be good. Cross my heart."

Byron knelt down by his son, "I know Charlie. But you can't goof around. It's important to Suzy and Zach. You have to do a good job."

"Yes sir," Charlie grumped. "I thought this would be more fun."

Once back at Schroeder's, Charlie was very quiet. He sat on the grass petting Elmer, not talking to anyone. Matt happened to see him from the window and went out to him. "May I join you?"

Charlie shrugged, "Okay. This is Elmer. He's helping me think."

"Hello Elmer," Matt said and patted the dog's head. "It's good to have someone to think with."

"Yah, a guy can think pretty good under his bed too," Charlie advised. "Have you ever tried that?"

Matt looked off to the vast horizon of the prairies, "No I haven't. I might do it though. It really works, huh?"

"Yah, Dad and I had a long talk under my bed one day. I like it because then nobody can see if you are stupid."

Matt nodded, "That sounds like a good idea. I'll keep that in mind."

They sat silently and patted Elmer. After a bit, Charlie asked, "Why do grownups have to be so grumpy about everything? They have so many rules about stuff!"

"Don't know, Charlie. It's a pain, huh?"

"Yah. Kind of. I thought I'd have fun at this wedding but it'll be just a bunch of rules and stuff I hate."

"That is probably because it is a solemn occasion."

"What is solomon?" the little boy looked at Matt in surprise.

"It's called solemn. I means that it's very, very important and serious. Zach and Suzy are making a promise to God in front of all their family and friends. They are promising they'll stay together from now, until they are older than Grandpa Lloyd and Grandma Katherine. It's a hard promise to make. That is why we have to all be serious while they make the promise to God. If we goof off, they might not do it right."

"I didn't know that. Why didn't anybody just tell me that?" Charlie asked.

"Don't know. Sometimes grownups forget to tell kids stuff. We just think that you know it already, I guess." Matt rubbed Elmer's ears.

"I like you," Charlie smiled. "I'll be solomon for the wedding. Will God be upset if I make a mistake? Will that mess up Zach and Suzy's promise?"

Matt turned to Charlie and reassured him, "No, God will know that you tried your best. He never expects us to be perfect. He knows better."

"Boy, that's good," Charlie said with relief, "Otherwise He'd be at His wit's end all the time!"

Matt chuckled. "I think He's probably close to that anyway. Hey Charlie, I like you, too."

"You can be one of my Secret Project Buddies if you want. But you have to be on 'promotion' first. Coot and I have to keep an eye on you to see if you are any good. Then we'll give you a project ring."

"That sounds cool, I'd like to try," Matt answered.

Eton drove in from the shop to get lunch, "You guys coming in to eat with us?"

"Yes," Matt answered. "We'll be right there."

"Father Matt," Charlie was very serious, "Will you help remind me at the wedding so I don't mess up?"

"I'll do that. I'm sure you'll do a great job, Charlie."

"Okay, let's go eat. Aunt Nora is having turkey salad sandwiches. She makes good ones but you have to pick out the onions. I'll show you how, okay?"

During lunch, Marty came with the tuxedoes. So, everyone who had a tux was expected to get fitted after lunch.

Kincaid asked Matt if he'd like to go over to see where their house would be. Pepper offered her car. Kincaid, Matt and Mo took her car and drove across the road to the place. They got out and overlooked the stakes that were placed to mark out their future home.

Matt smiled to himself when he saw how his Mom and Kincaid nearly burst with excitement sharing the plans for their home. He had never seen his Mom so happy and Kincaid was almost bubbling. And he was not, by nature, a bubbler.

After they walked around the property, Carl asked if he wanted to go over and see Darrell's place. When they drove into the yard, they were met by the dirt crew from the construction company working on the basement.

Darrell and Jeannie had decided to build about a half mile west of the little sheepherder's house inside an already established windrow of trees. It was a beautiful location. When they drove up, they found Darrell looking it over.

"This is so exciting," Darrell related. "You guys came to ooh and ahh over my foundation?"

"That we did," Kincaid said. "And we wanted to show Matt the lay of the land."

"What do you think?" Darrell asked.

"It looks fantastic. I can't wait to see the dairy barn."

"Well, you'll have to wait with that," Mo pointed out. "Darrell, the tuxedoes are at the farm and if you want to be alive at daybreak, you might be thinking on getting fitted."

"Thanks for reminding me. If I forgot, Nora would have my hide," Darrell chuckled. "I better clean up. Hey Matt, come over anytime next week and I'd love to show you around."

"That sounds good," Matt smiled. "Thanks, Darrell."

When they arrived at the house, everyone was eagerly awaiting their return. "What's going on? We were just gone an hour."

Nora explained, "It's Charlie. He tried on his suit and it only took a little fixing. But now he won't take it off until Matt sees him. I don't know what is up with him."

"Where is he? I'll go talk to him," Matt offered.

"Would you please?"

Matt found Charlie in the nursery, sitting like a statue on a stool. "I hear you want to talk to me?"

"Yes. I was waiting and being very careful. Do I look solomon enough in my suit?" the little boy asked with tremendous gravity.

"Let me see," Matt said somberly, "Stand up and turn around."

After inspecting him, he pronounced, "You look very solemn to be sure. And you kept your suit neat and clean! Maybe you should hang it up now so that it'll be neat for tomorrow, huh?"

"Oh good! I was worried. I didn't want to mess anything up," Charlie stated with relief.

That night the whole crowd descended on the Heinrich residence after rehearsal for dinner. It was great fun and there was plenty of food. They had a sing-a-long, while Terry, Suzy's brother, played piano and her dad, Bill played his accordion. Everyone sang along and suggested songs. The Bostonians had not ever heard Elton and Byron sing their duet rendition of *I Fall to Pieces* before, and laughed until they were in tears!

Even the little kids sang along. Miriam did too, but the only words she knew were to *Jesus Loves Me* or the song about Noah's Ark. So those were the words she used. The tune was secondary.

62

The next morning, the group that gathered around the coffee pot looked even less lively than the day before. They were paying the price for their joviality the night before. But it was worth it.

Zach was beginning to get nervous, and of course, Kevin had to zero in on him. During milking, there was no let up. The only saving grace was that Keith was home. Keith took it upon himself to level the playing field by reminding Kevin what a basket case he was before his wedding.

"I wasn't nervous for me," Kevin pronounced. "I was worried that Carrie would mess up. You all know how she can be."

Everyone turned and frowned at him. "Even the cows won't buy that one!" Elton said.

Keith laughed, "If I had your track record, I'd be a basket case. You're a groomsman. You're the one to mess up. Remember, you'll be standing up there in front of a church full of people, all staring at you, looking you over and watching your every move."

"Shut up, Keith," Kevin turned pale. "That isn't funny. You know how much I hate that stuff. Dad, really. Make him stop."

"Keith, even though he deserves all the grief you can dish out," Elton agreed, "You might want to back off. He might pass out or something."

"Yah, you lucked out Kevin. Next time, though." Keith smirked, obviously pleased he got Kevin to yell uncle.

Ruthie was so excited to serve her caramel rolls that she didn't even sit down until everyone had tasted theirs. Grandpa Lloyd took a bite of his and then smiled, "See, she's my girl. My Katherine showed her how to make caramel rolls. They're really good, Girl. What's your name again?"

"It is Ruthie, Grandpa. Thank you so much," she gave him a hug. Then she sat down by Ian to eat her own.

Grandpa Lloyd looked at Harrington, "When are you getting your cow? I let you get by because you got my car back but you can't marry my girl until you get a cow."

Chris just cracked up, "I was waiting for that."

Grandpa Lloyd turned and looked at him sternly, "Did you buy your cow? You should have one already. Maybe you and the cop need to go to the sales ring."

"Oops," Chris grinned. "I thought I skated on that one. We aren't getting married right away, Grandpa."

"You won't be getting married ever if you don't get a cow!" the old man was adamant. "Elton, make him understand. He has to take care of our girl. We didn't let my tall relative get married 'til he got his cow."

"Okay, Grandpa," Chris patted the old man's hand, "Harrington and I'll get a cow."

"Two guys, two cows," the old farmer stated.

"Okay, two cows," Harrington assured him. "We need to talk to Elton though. He'll have to keep the cows at his place."

"Well, Lloyd, I'd rather the boys bought their cows after we get back from Hawaii. I won't be home for a while," Elton explained.

Lloyd started to panic, "Who's going to take care of me? You promised, Elton. You aren't going to put me in a home, are you? Is Nora going to be here?"

Elton went over to the old man and put his arm around him, "Lloyd, you'll be right here. This is your home. Okay? Nora and I are going to Hawaii for Andy's wedding. Then we'll be right back. The other kids and Kincaid will be here to watch out for you. I promise it will be okay. Byron will be here every day to check on things. So don't you worry."

"Is that right?" Lloyd looked around the table.

"Yes, Grandpa," Pepper said. "We all give you our word."

"Okay then," Lloyd relaxed. "I don't think I'd want to get married on Iwo Jima, but it's his wedding. Who's he marrying?"

"Me, Grandpa," Annie smiled. "I'm marrying Andy."

Lloyd frowned, "Does Bert know? He'll be really mad about that."

"He knows," Nora said, "And he said it's okay."

Katherine patted his hand, "Don't worry so Lloyd. You can relax."

"I need a nap. This just tires me out."

"I'll help you to your room, okay Lloyd?" Zach said.

"You're a good relative. I think these people are my relatives too, don't you?

"Yes, Lloyd. I think you're right about that."

That afternoon, Ian asked Matt if he'd go for a walk with him. The two headed out to the pasture. After crossing the creek, Ian asked, "Have you talked to Mom yet about your sabbatical?"

"Only briefly," Matt said. "I can't believe how Lloyd relies on Elton. Can you?"

"They have quite a relationship," Ian agreed. "You know, I don't know what it would have been like if our Dad had lived but I really feel comfortable with all these guys. They are different. I was surprised about how they always hug each other and stuff. No one else seems to do that. But you know, I think I like it. They really care about each other. I had a good talk with Kincaid the other night about cop stuff. He's surprisingly easy to talk to. I thought he might be judgmental but he really isn't. I still wouldn't want to cross his path in a big way," Ian pointed out.

"No, that wouldn't be good."

Matt walked in silence for a while and said quietly, "You know, some of those higher ups in the church get so full of themselves, they treat everyone else like imbeciles. No one is very pretentious around here. This is such a great relief. I can see why Ruthie was able to adjust. Of course, a lot of it is because of Byron. He's a great guy."

"Yah, he is. Have you met Pastor Marvin yet?"

"No, I don't believe so. He works with Byron right?"

"Yes. You'll meet him at the wedding tonight. Both guys are doing the ceremony because Suzy works for both of them." Ian looked at his brother, "Hey, is Dad's family really all torqued that Mom is remarrying?"

"It's downright frightful. You would think that she was having the marriage ceremony on Dad's grave before the dirt was settled. Hearing them talk, you'd never believe that he passed away fourteen years ago!" Matt shook his head. "I tried to calm them, but only got barraged with how shameful it all is. I think they overlooked that 'until death do you part' thing. I guess you just can't confuse some people with the facts. Did you notice? Mom didn't seem surprised by their attitude."

Ian nodded, "I imagine she's lived with it a long time. She knows them pretty darned well. Heck, even if she had tried to tell us before, we wouldn't have understood."

"No, I'm afraid we wouldn't have. Anyway, I'm glad that Mom has the courage to break away."

"So, baby brother," Harrington said, "Where are you with your spreading your wings? Ruthie is afraid that your situation is her fault."

Matt looked down, "No. I'll have to talk to her about that. I've been getting more and more disillusioned with the politics of the church for a long time. It gets difficult to do anything. This deal with Father Timothy was only another nail in the coffin. The church will protect him! I'm sure Ruthie was not the first nun he got to and she won't be the last. The powers that be won't do a thing. And Ian, between me and you, that isn't as bad as some of the stuff I've seen. I'm almost embarrassed to be a priest sometimes. The worst that happens is that they get sent to a different location. If a regular citizen did some of those things, they'd be in the penitentiary."

"Matt, I know about a lot of it. I've known since I worked Vice. I never said anything because it isn't up to me to debunk the church. I've talked to families that have left the church because of molestation and the church won't even acknowledge them. That is part of the reason I won't go to Mass at some places. I know what a few of these guys have done. And don't kid yourself, Kincaid knows too."

"You knew?" Matt looked at his brother, "I guess it makes sense. Why don't the people press charges?"

"Mostly because the church closes ranks," Ian stated. "Also, few folks are willing to put information out there about their children. You know, it can be devastating. Personally, I've wondered why some of these priests didn't just get a bullet in the head. There a two in particular that I know of that are really bad. I wouldn't let my kids anywhere near them. I personally took reports of about fifteen cases against this Father Butterton. Nothing was ever done. I think once he was sent for some sort of therapy, but he was right back at it within the month."

"How long do you think it will take the truth to come out?" Matt asked.

"Years, if ever." Ian pointed out, "I hoped with all the kids this Rendall character hurt, that he'd get caught. Instead I think the Cardinal sent him to Florida or something."

"I know who you're talking about," Matt nodded. "It's horrible. They aren't only allowing behavior that damages children beyond reason, but they're also putting the reputation of the entire Church at stake. They seem oblivious to the fact that the vast majority of us would never consider doing that stuff. They're letting a few perverts ruin it for everyone."

"Is that why you're thinking about getting out of the priesthood?"

"Some of it, but it's all symptoms of the same problem. The guys in power do whatever they want, and reason has nothing to do with it. I still want to serve the Lord, just not inside the church. I don't know, maybe I should go to Africa!" Then Matt became quiet for a minute, "Ian, don't tell Mom please, but I was, shall we say, encouraged to take this sabbatical. It's really a leave of absence. I was forced to go 'think over my position on issues' and more or less told that if I couldn't trust the judgment of the Bishop, I should reconsider my vocation. I have to learn discipline."

Ian hugged his brother, "Ruthie and I already figured that. You're not the first on that ran up against that wall."

"I really don't know what to do, Ian. What do you think?"

"I think you should take some time and don't think. Just give it a little time and go with the flow. Your answer will come. And Matt, even though Mom is proud as punch of you, if you told her the square of it and Kincaid and I backed you up, you know that she'd back your choice. She'd have no part of covering up child abuse or raping nuns. Good grief, we'd probably have to tie her down!"

"I guess, huh?"

When the brothers got back to the house, Kevin and Carrie arrived with Miriam. Carrie carried her in the house and the guys followed.

In the kitchen, Elton asked, "Did you and Carrie come to see me?"

Miriam patted her chest, "Fodder, Son and Hawwie."

Maureen almost choked on her coffee! "I was expecting her to say Hawwiespiwit!"

Matt looked at her, "Mom, sometimes I worry about you!"

"I thought the same thing," Grandma giggled.

"To be honest, so did I," Elton chuckled. "Anyway, I'm glad you came to see us. Guess what I got, Miriam? Chocolate pie with whipped cream!"

Miriam patted her hands and then held them out to him, "Gopher lick."

63-

After their coffee and pie, the women started getting ready for the wedding while the men got the chores done. The wedding party left for the church early for pictures and the rest followed shortly.

By seven o'clock, everyone was in place at Trinity Lutheran Church. The medium oak walls of the sanctuary were polished and the evening sun danced through the stained glass windows across the oak pews. The church was decorated beautifully with lavender and mint green flowers. There were some accents of dark purple and deep green.

Terry Heinrich started the music at seven promptly. Grandma and Grandpa Engelmann were seated in the place of honor on the groom's side. Suzy's one surviving grandmother was seated on the bride's side with her brother. The grandmothers were wearing floral dresses of lavender, deep purple, and mint green. Grandpa Lloyd had a rented dark charcoal gray tuxedo. Then Marty, who was an usher, escorted Nora and Elton down the aisle to be seated as the parents of the groom. Nora was devastating in her dark green satin dress. Wearing his dark charcoal tuxedo, Elton carried Miriam who sat with them during the service. Of course, by then Elton's eyes were already tearing up. But that was Elton. He was by far the most openly emotional guy in the neighborhood.

Miriam wore a mint green dress with dark purple ribbon around the waist. She had purple ribbons holding her bear tails and was carrying a little bouquet of lavender flowers. She looked like a little doll. Mr. Bear sported a purple bowtie.

Another usher, Dick Heinrich escorted Aunt Gilda, in her dark purple dress, down to set on the bride's side. Then the music changed and the two ministers took their places at the front of the church.

Terry Heinrich began to play Canon in D by Johann Pachelbel while Suzy's cousin accompanied him on the violin. Pepper started down the aisle. She wore a lavender dress with a full skirt, boat neck collar and puffed sleeves. She looked fantastic with her hair up in a crown of matching flowers.

She went slowly down the aisle to meet Darrell. He was wearing a charcoal gray suit with a lavender boutonniere. They went up the first step and separated. They were followed by Suzy's sister, Greta who was met by Kevin; and then the maid of honor, Ruthie Jeffries started down the aisle.

Ruth had never been in anything like this before in her life and was overcome with emotion. The experience was something that she had only imagined a princess in a fairy tale must have felt. When she came down the aisle, she was a nervous wreck until she saw Ian, who was best man. Their eyes met and she was okay. She was gorgeous and so very happy.

Everyone stood up at the signal from Pastor Marvin. The next to appear were Ginger and Charlie.

Ginger stepped out onto the aisle. She wore an identical dress to the one that Miriam wore. Theirs was the same as the bridesmaids except that the bridesmaids wore lavender instead of mint green. She walked as straight as she could and threw the lavender petals as she had been told. She looked simply precious and with the help of a bit of makeup, her scars were barely noticeable. She didn't even fuss about having ribbons in her mahogany curls.

Tow headed and slightly freckled, Charlie wore a white tuxedo, like Zach's and was neat as a pin. He walked next to his sister, carrying a satin pillow with lavender and mint green ribbons. He stood as straight and tall as possible. No one had ever seen him so serious. The entire congregation was holding their breath.

Coot was fighting back a stroke and even though not a praying man, he was fervently asking God to keep things under control. Other than Lloyd, only one other person wasn't hanging by a thread. That was Matt.

When Charlie passed Matthew who was near the aisle, he gave him a grin. Matt gave him a thumbs up and the little boy continued on.

Terry switched to pipe organ and began playing Air on G String from Bach. Then Bill appeared with the beautiful bride on his arm. Suzy was every bit the vision of a fairy princess. Her dress was the same pattern as the other girls, but of white taffeta with almost a rainbow sheen. She had beading around the bodice and sleeves. Her floor length veil was attached to a tiara. She was amazing.

Zach almost lost his breath when he saw her. He always thought she was beautiful, but today she was even more so. As she came down the aisle, he thought about all the times she had been there for him, handing him towels while he threw up, rocking little Miriam, painting his apartment and comforting him. Many times, he wouldn't have been able to face next day without her. He remembered how devastated he was the day she was late to join him in church. He was sure she'd broken up with him. When she finally came to sit by him, drenched in communion wine, he was so relieved. He got a silly smile.

She took his arm as her father said that he gave this woman to be Zach's bride. She gave him a quizzical look as she wondered why he had such a silly smile. He was pretty sure he would have gotten whacked if she knew he was thinking about how she smelled like a brewery that day!

Suzy and Zach went up the steps to the altar and Byron began the service. Suzy looked at this man standing next to her in his white tuxedo. He looked so neat and self-assured, even though she knew all his doubts and insecurities. She knew she loved him. She'd never forget how he sat with her outside that sleazy bar that winter night when her then boyfriend stood her up. She thought about how he called to check on her when she and Eric broke up and how patient he was to listen to her feeling sorry for herself. Suzy also appreciated how he had assured her father that he would respect her after her sister's death and he never violated that trust. Even during all the trials he had to overcome, he never was anything but great to her, rarely even getting mad at her. She was very fortunate.

The ceremony was not long and when it was time to exchange rings, Charlie came forward like a perfect gentleman and held the pillow up to Ian. He was very solemn and his behavior was flawless.

When Pastor Byron said Zach could kiss the bride and Ruthie put Suzy's veil back. Zach gave her a kiss and that was too much for Charlie! He turned to look at the congregation and crossed his eyes and stuck out his tongue like a gag. Kevin grabbed his hand and pulled him over beside him.

Terry began the Mendelssohn Wedding March and the wedding party marched back down the aisle and out to the waiting cars. Zach and Suzy were married. Ginger didn't stumble and Charlie was almost perfect. It was amazing.

At the top of the stairs at Heinrich's barn, the wedding party formed the receiving line. Everyone came through the line and then hit the huge buffet, found a place and sat down. There was no head table.

Kincaid was so relieved and delighted. His Gophers had done well and he was able to go up the steps under his own steam, without sitting in the farmhand. He was with his favorite girl and surrounded by great friends. Besides all that, his potato salad turned out pretty darned good.

Ian, Ruthie and Matt came to sit with them at the table along with Kevin and Carrie. Miriam latched on to her 'Son' when Nora and Elton joined them. It was a great dinner.

The wedding cake was rolled out and after Ian gave a toast, the bridal couple cut the cake. Then they came over to join the rest of the family at Kincaid's table.

Zach gave Elton and Nora big hugs. "Remember the first dance I came to here? You had to keep me from throwing up. I love you guys so much. You'll never know how much you mean to me. And you shared your whole wonderful family with me."

"You just don't know how much you mean to all of us," Nora replied.

Lloyd was sitting beside Nora, "Well, why wouldn't you? You are my relative and we should all get along. Right, Elton?"

"That is right, Lloyd."

The grand march started and everyone in the wedding party danced. Even Lloyd danced around with Nora while Elton danced with Gilda and Zach danced with the only grandmother he had ever known, Grandma Katherine.

Then Annie and Marty took Lloyd and Katherine home and Holloways went over to visit with them in case Grandma needed any help with Lloyd.

The dance then began in earnest. Matt had chosen not to wear his collar and wore a regular suit instead. He felt very comfortable with his decision. He visited a while with Darrell and Jeannie. Then Jeannie decided she needed to move around and she and Darrell started to dance. Pretty soon, Matt was on the dance floor.

He was used to sitting and visiting with the older folks as a priest at this sort of event. That was not the case tonight. He danced with almost every girl in the county, from Miriam to Gilda. He was included in conversations with the folks he was beginning to recognize as the clan. He made some friends outside the clan also.

He was introduced to a girl that Keith knew from Bismarck and they danced a little. Then he met a few paramedic friends of Annie and Marty's from the fire hall.

When he was about worn out, he visited with Dr. Lassiter, a colleague of Zach's. They chatted for a long time and really hit it off. During their conversation, Dr. Lassiter revealed that he had gone into the priesthood as a young man and then left it after a few years. He went to med school and ended up happily married and working as a doctor in Bismarck. "I was so worried I wasn't doing the right thing when I left; but you know, I've never been sorry. You might disagree; but I think there are many ways to serve the Lord besides being a priest."

"How did you know to tell me that?" Matt asked in awe. "I've been struggling for a while about that very thing you just told me. Amazing."

Lassiter laughed, "God works in strange ways, my friend. If you want, we could have lunch someday. Zach has my phone number. Call me when you have time."

"I might just do that. Thank you," Matt said sincerely. "I guess we need to mingle. This isn't the time to delve into my psyche."

"Yah, I guess not. I heard there are some sandwiches over on the buffet table. I might need one for the long trip home," Dr. Lassiter smiled.

Matt danced with Ginger before her parents told her that she had to go rest with the other kids. She bucked, but Zach explained that she didn't want to overdo it and she was already up for three hours past her normal bedtime. Ginger knew she was getting tired. This was the day that she had looked forward to for so long! The one when her best friend Smitty got married. She had an exciting day and it ended with Zach taking her to the coatroom to find her the best coat to sleep on.

Katie had been sitting quietly most of the evening, visiting with a few friends and dancing with the clan men. Matt sat down across from her with his turkey sandwich. "Did you like the wedding?"

"Yes," she answered politely. "It was very nice but I get nervous when I do the beading on a dress. I dropped the tie on one of the beads on Suzy's dress and hadn't found it again to knot it well. It would've been horrid if it broke."

"You did all that? It was wonderful work. You are very talented," Matt told her.

"Thank you Father Matthew," Katie said.

"You can call me Matt."

"I think it would be easier. Are you been having fun tonight?"

"Yes, I have had a wonderful time. How about you?"

"Yes. I like these things. Charlie was good at the wedding, wasn't he?" the teenager giggled.

"He behaved very well. I was so proud of him."

"I was too. You know, sometimes he's such a lizard head. He should have four middle names, because you need them all when you scold him!"

"I bet."

Just then a slender, young lady came up to the table, "Hello Katie. How are you?"

"Hello Mrs. Waggoner. I'm fine. How are you?"

"Good. Are you enjoying your summer?"

"Yes. Mrs. Waggoner, I'd like you to meet our friend. He is Matt Harrington from Boston."

"Hello, Mr. Harrington," the young lady shook his hand. She wore her short brown hair in shag cut and had big brown eyes. "I was Katie's American Literature teacher last year. She's one of my favorite students."

"I would imagine so," Matt said and motioned for the lady to sit with them. "Would you like to join us?"

"Oh, I really shouldn't. I'm with fiends and should return to the table."

"Well, if you change your mind, we'll be here, right Katie?"

"Yes," Katie smiled. "Are you coming back to teach school this year?"

"I am," Mrs. Waggoner nodded. "I just had to take off the last part of last year. But things are okay now, so I'm back. I'll be teaching junior high."

"Good, maybe I'll have you for some of my classes."

"I hope so, Katie. Nice to meet you, Mr. Harrington."

After she left the table, Matt asked, "Was she ill last year?"

"No, her husband got blood cancer so she quit school after Christmas to help take care of him."

"How's he doing?"

"He died about Easter time. I was afraid she might move away because she's from Maine. I'm happy she didn't. I might get her again for some classes. Well, I promised Mom and Dad I would go check on the little kids, so I had better do that."

"Thank you for visiting with me," Matt said. "Maybe we could dance a little later."

After she left the table, Matt went over to refill his plate. He came back and sat with his Mom and Kincaid. Coot asked, "You having a good time?"

"I really am, Kincaid. Were my eyes deceiving me or did I see you out there dancing with my Mom?"

"You did. She's a good dancer."

"Gee, Mom. Maybe we should dance after I finish my sandwich."

"Shamrocks and Leprechauns! Isn't there a Harrington alive that can just ask a girl to dance without beating around the bush?" Maureen shook her head.

"Mom," Matt put down his sandwich, "Will you do me the honor of dancing with me?"

"I would."

Matt rolled his eyes to Kincaid, "Watch my sandwich, will yah?"

"You got it."

That night Gilda and Elton did a mean polka, and of course, everyone watched while Byron and Elton danced to the *Beer Barrel Polka*. Matt, Mo, Ruthie and Ian were in stitches. It was about one-thirty when Bill's band played *Good Night Irene* and everyone headed out for home. It had been a lot of fun and everyone had a good time.

64-

Matt thought that Pepper should definitely throw her alarm clock away. It had the loudest, most annoying sound he'd ever heard. The thing seemed to go off earlier and louder every morning. He couldn't imagine what it would be like to be in the same room with it!

He dragged himself out of bed and once he put his weight on his feet, he was in agony. Good grief! His calf muscles weren't much better! He had danced way too much. He realized that he wasn't in as good shape as he had thought.

He looked back at his bed longingly. It was so soft, warm and comfy. The pillow just right, the blankets—. It would've been so easy to just crawl back in. Then he heard the doors begin to open and weary footsteps stumble down the hall. He decided to be a good sport and join them.

That morning, he stood numbly with his coffee cup watching the coffee pot perk in silence like the rest of them. Matt only hoped that Kevin would be very quiet, too.

The door burst open and his hope was shattered. "Good morning, Gang!" Kevin bounced in. "Carrie stayed home this morning, but I wouldn't let you down! You can count on me to be here. Right, Dad?"

Elton turned slowly and mumbled, "It's a real thrill. What can I tell you?"

Kevin clapped his Dad on the back. "Slowing down there in your golden years?"

Elton growled, "Watch it!"

Undaunted Kevin saw Matt. "Well, what have we got here? Is Fred Astaire moving a little slower this morning? That's what you get for being a dancing machine! Bet you wore the soles right off your shoes!"

Kincaid glared at Kevin, "Don't you ever quit? There should be a law."

Kevin was almost energized by the scowls, "Nope. Not even close! Come on guys, we're burning daylight!"

Keith filled his cup with coffee, "I have an idea. Why don't you go down and start. We'll catch up with you."

"I'm not falling for that, again. I learned when you conned me into cleaning out that granary by myself. This dirty bird was in the house stuffing his face with cookies! I was left with all the work," Kevin was indignant all over again. "See if I hang around you guys anymore!"

Pepper jeered, "Oh, you will. We couldn't be that lucky,"

"Dad, make her stop!"

"Yea gads," Elton groaned. "I can't believe I ever wanted a family."

Matt was expecting the whole day to be very inactive and mostly a day of rest. He was looking forward to just sitting around. Ellison's didn't come over which was usual for a Sunday. Ruthie came down to the barn though, but that surprised no one. She still had her head in the clouds from the wedding. She was on cloud nine.

"I never had such a fabulous time before in my whole life! The music and the dresses, my Ian," she effervesced. "And my brother! Zach got married to my best friend! Do you guys realize that I have a best friend? I never had a real friend in my life until this summer. Now look! I could just cry."

Elton chuckled, "If these were all the friends I had, I'd cry too! You better get to work on Buttermilk before she isn't your friend anymore."

"Okay, come on Buttermilk," undaunted, Ruthie sat down with the pail. "Ian, what kind of cow are you going to buy? I hope it isn't a Holstein. We don't need another Percifull. I think the Jerseys are so pretty. Don't you?"

"Lloyd said I only had to buy a cow if I'm going to get married. What makes you think that I need to get one?" Harrington taunted.

"Dad," Ruthie whined to Elton, "Make him stop! He's being so mean."

"Better settle down, Harrington. We don't want to burst her balloon. The fallout could be a fright." Elton intervened.

"Besides you guys," Ruthie went on, "I got my wedding all planned out! I'm having four attendants. Suzy, Pepper, Annie, Katie and Carrie and I want Byron, Marvin and Matt to marry us. I think I want to carry white and deep yellow flowers with dark green ferns. I really like them. I'm going to wear my hair up with a gold tiara. And the girls will have dark yellow dresses and-,"

Carrying his pail of Petunia's milk, Kevin started to chuckle, "Put a little thought into it, did you?"

"Of course, what were you thinking about while you were standing up there? Listening to the sermon?"

"Doesn't sound like you were doing much listening," Matt pointed out.

"Just don't you guys worry. And then Elton will give me away or Zach, I'm not sure because he might be the best man, huh?" She continued. "Of course, Mo and Kincaid will be the groom's parents! And Elton and Nora are mine. It will be so much fun! Do you think that Heinrich's will let me have my dance there?"

Elton shook his head, "Your wedding, your dance? Does your husband to be get a say in anything?"

Ruthie stopped abruptly for a second. "I'm sorry. I never thought about that. I suppose he'd want to have some input, huh? Ian, can we go for a walk this afternoon?"

"Sure honey. Whatever you say," he laughed.

"Better take a towel with you. It sounds like the spit will be flying!" Keith teased.

"I wasn't that bad, was I?" Ruthie asked.

Everyone answered "Yup!" in unison.

After chores, everyone returned to the house for breakfast. Darlene said grace and they ate Grandma and Kincaid's breakfast, which featured Kincaid's homemade blueberry muffins. Matt was thinking that after dishes, everyone would be taking a nap.

He couldn't have been more wrong. Ruthie said she would run home to change, saying she'd pick up those who wanted to go to nine o'clock Mass. Then they could go to the eleven o'clock service at Trinity, if anyone wanted. She was trying to figure out which place would be better to have her wedding. It should be in the Catholic church; but she really liked Trinity. It was a dilemma. She thought she should look at the sanctuaries to figure out which would be the best. She had almost decided they should just get married twice, once in each church. Everyone just let her babble on to her hearts content. They didn't feel much like talking and she certainly did.

Lloyd had been watching her with rapt attention. Finally he had to say something. "What's your name again?"

"It's Ruthie, Grandpa."

"Look Girl, I see you have a problem. Since you can't make up your mind, I'll do it for you. I need to do that for my girl," he said as he added two more tablespoons of sugar to his coffee.

Without saying a word, Elton reached over and removed the sugar from his reach. Lloyd gave him a dirty look, but never responded.

"So, which church do you think I should get married in?" Ruthie asked.

"Get married outside," Lloyd pronounced.

Ruthie dropped her fork and her mouth fell open, "Grandpa! That's the most wonderful idea! Isn't it, Ian? What do you guys think?"

They all agreed it was a great idea and that became the plan. Lloyd was very pleased with himself. His day had been a success.

After breakfast, Chris took Grandpa off to shower and get ready for church. Maureen and Nora put the last touches on their dinner. The men helped the ladies by setting the table. Matt had attended banquets smaller than this family dinner. At one point he caught Ian's glance and looked at the table. They both smiled. It was amazing.

By eight-thirty, Ruthie returned and the Harrington's loaded into the car to go to Merton. They promised they'd go to Trinity's eleven o'clock service. Kincaid would just go to that one and meet them there. Suzy and Zach would be coming out from Bismarck to church, too. They had stayed at the apartment on their wedding night but were coming back out to the farm.

Matt felt good attending Mass and thought that Father Vicaro was a good speaker. He had chosen to wear civilian clothes and keep the fact that he was a priest quiet. However, as they left the church, Father Vicaro shook hands with Ruthie and she introduced Matt as Ian's brother. "You must be the guy I talked to on the phone, huh?"

"Yes, I am. I am pleased to meet you," Matt was embarrassed that he had forgotten they had spoken about Ruthie.

"I see you are undercover. I won't blow it for you," he winked. "Maybe we could have lunch or something one day."

"I'd like that," Matt answered honestly. "Should I call?"

"Yah, Wednesdays are out, but I can finagle something on the other days," Vicaro responded. "You staying at Schroeder's?"

"Yes."

"How about I give you a call?"

Matt nodded, "That would be nice. We'd better move on. We are backing up the line."

While crossing the parking lot to their car, Matt felt a tap on his elbow. He turned to see Mrs. Waggoner. "Hello, Mr. Harrington," she smiled.

"Hello yourself," Matt grinned. "A pleasure to see you again. Have you met my family?"

"No, I don't believe so. I do recognize the best man and maid of honor however," she said sweetly as she reached out to shake their hands.

"This is my brother, Ian and his fiancée Ruth. This lady is my Mom, Maureen," he said with pride. "Mrs. Waggoner was Katie's American lit teacher last year."

"I was a teacher also," Ruthie smiled. "And Matt has taught too, right?"

"Yes I have. High school math and physics," Matt said. "Ruthie taught elementary."

"And how about you, Ian?" Mrs. Waggoner asked.

"I was with the police but now am studying business and accounting."

"How exciting," the pretty lady smiled, "Well, I had better get moving. 'Miles to go-,"

"Before you sleep?" Matt finished the line of the poem.

"I see you are a fan of Robert Frost also. He is one of my favorite poets. It was nice to see you all again. Bye." The young woman waved gracefully and turned toward her car.

"Good bye," Matt said as they moved on.

Ian couldn't wait to get into the car. "Spill the beans, baby brother. What is the story on the pretty lady?"

"There is no story. I was talking to Katie last night when she came by to tell her hi. All I know is that her husband died this spring."

"Well, she seems like a dandy in my book. Nice girl," Maureen decreed.

Ian and Matt looked at each other and shook their heads. Ian asked, "How can you determine all that with that little bit of conversation, Mom?"

"I didn't get this old by being stupid," Mo smiled smugly.

As they turned into the parking lot at Trinity, Ian started to laugh. "You know, I had missed Mass a lot before, but I think Ruthie here is catching me up fast! Twice every Sunday."

"I'm sorry, Ian. I never thought of how you feel about it. I've been so selfish lately," Ruthie apologized.

"No need to be sorry, my little Ruthie," Mo giggled. "Don't hurt him even a smidgen to get some Bible learning! And I think it is good for Father here to find out how it looks from the other side of the pulpit!"

"I guess if you say so. I went to six Masses every Sunday," Matt explained.

"And you still haven't learned a thing!" Ian chided.

Matt raised his eyebrows and answered seriously, "No, I doubt that I have."

The Harringtons sat with Coot and Charlie in the pew behind Carrie and Kevin. Of course, Miriam was sitting on her Son's lap. Ginger was sitting with Darrell and Jeannie as usual. Zach and Suzy sat with her parents, Bill and Gilda. Pastor Byron gave the sermon and it was quite good.

As they were leaving the service, Mrs. Sandvahl came up to Kevin. "May I ask you a favor?"

"Of course," Kevin said, "I think I owe you about a hundred favors. What is it?"

"Well, I was wondering if you'd help me with my Sunday School class this fall. It is at the earlier service, the same grade that I had at Bible School. The three year olds plus the four year olds! Last year I had ten kids and this year, there'll be eighteen! I know I can't handle that alone. Honestly, Kevin, no one else wants to help. If you don't want to, I'd understand. We could either divide the class into two or do one large one together. Please think it over."

Kevin grimaced, and then he squinted, "Did Pastor Marv talk to you?"

"No," Mrs. Sandvahl said, "Was he supposed to?"

"No, it's just that he brought it up to me while at Bible School. Well, I guess since Miriam will be in that class, it might be a good idea. She can be a handful all by herself. What do you think, Carrie?"

Carrie smiled broadly, "I think it would be great! I think you should do the class together. In fact, I'd be happy to help out if you need an extra pair of hands, at least until the baby arrives."

"That would be wonderful. I'll let Suzy know then that you'll do it."

"Suzy, huh?" Kevin's eyes narrowed, "I smell a dirty rat."

Miriam patted her chest and nodded, "Doity Rat."

"Yah," Kevin said as he gave her a squeeze, "Now look what you go me into!"

"Gopher Son Cawwie into!"

"Oh Kevin, since we're going to be partners, you should call me Joan. Okay?"

"Thank you, Joan. Let me know what I need to do, because I don't know anything."

"I will. And thank you Carrie. I'll call and we can get together."

Miriam waved good bye and said, "Bye Bye, Joan."

Elton had come up behind them while they talked. He patted his son on the shoulder and said quietly, "I'm so proud of you." Then he walked on with his wife.

The Engelmann clan all arrived at the farmhouse bearing more food. They were joined by the Heinrich's, although that only added Bill, Gilda, Terry and Linda because the rest were all clanners anyway.

After the smorgasbord dinner, the bridal couple opened wedding gifts. They received several wonderful gifts which they decided to store in Schroeder's basement until their house was finished. The contractor had hoped it would be completed in a couple weeks.

There was excitement about the impending trip to Hawaii and those weddings. Annie and Jeannie were very secretive about the plans but assured everyone they would have a photographer to take a Super 8 of the ceremony. They'd all get to see it when they returned.

Jerald leaned back in his chair, "I think there'll be a flood of hitching up in the next year and then it should cool down again. Remember the year that we got married? There was Greg, Doug, Byron, Elton and me! Now it's another whole batch. Makes your head spin."

Grandma laughed, "And then come the babies."

Keith grinned, "Well, Danny, Kev and I are doing our part in that department! I'm sure Zach will too."

That evening when the family relaxed around the picnic table, it turned out to be the first time that Matt got to rest. He had to smile to himself. It wasn't a napping day, but he felt good. He had plans the next day to go with Annie to Darrell's for a horseback ride. He was looking forward to that, even though he didn't know how much he would hurt after he did.

Suzy and Zach walked over to their house while Ian and Ruthie went for a walk in the pasture. Everyone knew that by the time they got back, Ruthie would have confirmed every last detail of their wedding.

Matt leaned back in the cushioned chair and looked at the sky. It was a perfect evening. They were able to enjoy a glorious, panoramic sunset in the western sky. It was a beautiful end to a wonderful weekend.

Matt watched his Mom as she and Nora visited about the Hawaiian trip. It was the most relaxed he'd seen her in years. He wished that his father's family would be happy for her. She deserved that. He felt confident that she was doing the right thing.

He wished he knew what he was going to do. The last few days he'd lived not being an active priest was good. He felt some guilt about it, but it had been a great respite. Even if he went back after six months, he knew it would have been worthwhile to get away.

"Matt?" Elton was saying, "Earth to Matt?"

"Huh," he jumped when he realized that he had been off in his own world. "I'm sorry. I guess I my mind was far away."

"I hope we didn't tire you out too much," Elton continued. "We can be quite overwhelming and you haven't had a minute to yourself."

"No, I'm having a great time," Matt smiled. "I really did. I loved that sing-a-long, the wedding dance and the dinner today. It was all really good."

"I hope you don't get in trouble for coming to our church," Nora asked.

"From whom?" Matt grinned. "I enjoyed your church. You have a warm and friendly congregation. There is sort of unity about it,"

"I hate to admit it," Carl groaned, "But even I like it."

Elton chortled, "Hallelujah! Can I quote you?"

"Just keep your mouth shut, Magpie!" the old FBI agent warned. "Hey, did you take Matt down to see the new airplane yet?"

"Not yet. I figured when he heals up from the dance. You were really cutting a rug the other night," Elton observed.

"He is a fine dancer," Nora complimented him. "I think he might be even better than you."

"No. He isn't, but it gives him a goal to aim for," Elton boasted.

"Don't be blowing up your head, there, Magpie," Coot grunted. "I think my kid will win that battle hands down."

"He won't."

"I'm not competing," Matt laughed. "But I had a lot of fun. That Schottische is really fun."

"So, did you get to talk to a lot of folks?" Elton asked. "I mean besides us guys."

"Yes, I did. I have a tentative lunch date with Dr. Lassiter. He seems to be a nice man. And then I met Mrs. Waggoner, Katie's teacher from last year. When we came out of Mass today, she was there and said hello. She is going to be teaching again this year."

"I really like her," Nora said. "Diane's husband had leukemia and she took care of him in his last months. It was really hard on her. She seems like a gentle soul, although I don't know her very well. She ended up losing their house because she had to quit work to care for him. She lived with the Waggoners. I think she's still with them. Her family all live out east, so she's very dependent on her in-laws."

"I liked her," Mo agreed, and then said thoughtfully. "I hope that she doesn't get tied to his memory and can build a new life for herself."

They all knew that Mo would know about that.

Elton asked, "Does she have any little ones?"

"No. It was very sad. They lost a baby about a month before her husband took ill. She had a very bad year," Nora explained. "I worried for her. That is a lot to take in."

They all agreed and then sat in silence thinking about it.

Finally, Carl broke the silence, "So, Mrs. Harrington, when are we planning to go out to Boston to get your things and all that?"

"I thought we could have to wait until after the Hawaiians come back and the house is done. If the wonderful Mr. Magpie lets us keep hanging out here until then?" Mo fluttered her eyelashes at Elton.

Everyone laughed, except Elton, who teased, "I think a little rent would help the convincing, but flattery goes a long way!"

Matt cleared his throat, "Well, I really have to talk to you all about that."

"About what, my Mattie?" his Mom was concerned. "You don't have to pay this Magpie person rent. He is spoofing."

Matt grinned, "I know. What I want to talk to you all about is,—well. Ian knows, because I have talked to him about it for a while now. Mom, Carl. I took a long sabbatical. Longer than you think. It's for six months. I am considering a great change in my life."

"Like what? Moving?" Mo asked. "I know you'd mentioned leaving Boston."

"Yes, but more than that. I'm not so certain that the priesthood is where I need to be. I may leave it. I don't know yet. I do know that I need to get away from it for a while to think. I was hoping that I might be able to think here with you for a time. Really Elton, I'd be happy to pay you rent if I you'd let me stay 'til the folks house is done."

Everyone was dumbfounded and speechless. Then Nora smiled, "Of course, Matt. You're welcome to stay here as long as you want. That's a huge decision and you can take all the time you need. Elton and I'd be happy to help you with whatever we can. Consider this your home, but there's absolutely no rent required."

Matt's mouth fell open, "I wasn't expecting that. I can't believe that you would offer me that. I just wanted to know I'd have a place to hang my hat a while. I planned on paying rent."

"Why?" Elton grinned. "We kind of like having you around. You're welcome here, if you want to be. Just know that."

"Only until our house is done," Kincaid snapped. "We're his family. Everybody doesn't have to stay with you!"

Elton smirked, "I know, but he'll probably be as sick of you as we are before long."

"I don't know why I put up with all this abuse," Carl grumped.

Elton clapped him on the shoulder, ""It's the best deal you'll ever get. Besides, it looks to me like you are here now. Unless you expect this young man to go sleep in that pile of dirt you call your house."

Maureen giggled, "Gee Mattie, I don't know what you expected but it looks to me like these old buzzards are fighting over you!"

"That is very kind and I honestly appreciate it. I don't know what I'll end up doing. I might go somewhere else too. I do know that I'll leave Boston though, that I am certain of." Matt said seriously, "Thanks you guys. Please don't say anything to everyone until I know for certain, okay?"

"Of course we won't," Nora said. "I think we've all had things in our life that we have to think over. Sometimes if too many folks know, a person gets so much advice it makes your head explode."

Mo started to laugh, "Amen to that! You'll stay a priest long enough to marry your old Mom off though, right? I mean I'd never want to make that kind of a decision for a silly reason like that, but I kind of looked forward to it."

"Motor Mouth," Carl took her hand, "We'll have to move up our wedding date so he can do it. How's that?"

Matt smiled, "You guys can take your time. I'm not making this important of a decision that quickly. I just wanted to let you know because I was thinking I could move my stuff out here when you move."

"Mooching already! Good grief," Kincaid grumped. "I thought if the kids were grownup, I wouldn't have to feed them."

Elton grimaced, "It didn't work out that well for me!"

"That's your own fault," Kincaid shook his head. "What do you expect? You're such a Petunia. You drag every stray home!"

"Sometimes I have to remind myself that you guys are friends," Matt stated.

Both men responded, "We're not!"

The next day after lunch, Darrell rode over to Schroeder's on his horse. He came in for coffee while Annie and Matt got ready to join him.

"Cabbage rolls? I really planned this wrong. I should've come before lunch! I'm slipping!"

"It's not too late. Help yourself. I'll grab you a plate," Nora smiled.

Annie looked up from pulling her boots on, "I have to go bring up Crenshaw and Moonbeam anyway. So chow down."

"Thanks," Darrell grinned as he filled his plate. "I've been cleaning house. I have to get stuff straightened up before Jeannie sees all the stuff

I hid under the bed. She knows I'm not a neat nut, but I doubt she really knows what a slob I am."

Elton laughed, "That is a secret that doesn't need to be shared. The wives will clean everything once you are married anyway."

That earned Elton filthy looks from every woman at the table. Even little Charlie knew that wasn't a good thing to say. "My Mommy whacked my Daddy once when he said making beds was women's work. Didn't he, Ginger?"

"Yes. He never says that anymore," Ginger affirmed.

Miriam shook her head slowly with dead seriousness, "Bywon no more."

"Yea gads," Elton laughed and then kissed Miriam on top of her curly head. "Come on Harrington. We got to get back to the shop."

"Yah, I think it'll be safer there," Harrington chuckled. "Watch out for my baby brother, Darrell. He's a city slicker."

"Oh, not to worry," Darrell grinned. "Friar Tuck is safe with me. Besides Annie is a paramedic."

The ride was fun and Matt proved to be a natural horseman. The three rode almost all the way to Merton. It was a wonderful summer day and the weather was perfect. As they were heading back to Darrell's place, they came upon a Chevy with a flat tire. There was a lady jacking up the back end of the car to change it.

Darrell waved and said, "Hold it there, Ma'am. We'll do that for you."

The lady turned around in surprise. "Well thank you." Then she noticed who it was. Diane Waggoner grinned. "Hi Darrell. Hello you guys. We keep running into each other everywhere."

Matt smiled. She really looked cute and he noticed more than he should. The gentle breeze was playing with her hair just a little. She wore no makeup but was pretty as could be. She was wearing blue jeans, a tee shirt and tennis shoes. Matt thought she personified natural freshness and beauty. "Hello Mrs. Waggoner."

"Please call me Diane."

"Okay Diane. I'm Matt."

"I remember, Matt," she smiled and handed the jack handle to Darrell. Matt had never seen anyone hand someone a jack handle with more poise in his life. It was amazing.

The men took over the tire changing. Annie and Diane visited about the dance and upcoming Hawaiian weddings. "So, what brings you out into the country?"

"I was visiting with Mrs. Schulz. She and I serve on the same committee at St. John's. I'm afraid I'm not much good at maintaining my vehicle, obviously."

Darrell responded, "This wasn't maintenance. There was a jagged piece of metal in the tire. You must have picked it up on the road. It wasn't your fault."

"Well, thank you. That is encouraging. I'd hate to tell Wag I messed up again."

"Wag?" Darrell asked.

"Mr. Waggoner. He'd pull his hair out, except that he is bald already! He always says he can't figure where his son found me!"

"That isn't very nice," Annie said.

"Oh, no. He means no ill by it. I have to admit, I'm pretty uncoordinated mechanically," Diane answered quickly.

"I am too," Matt added. "Mechanics is something that escapes me. Now Ian, he just seems to automatically understand it."

"I prefer animals myself," Darrell grinned. "Which reminds me, we had better get back to my place. I got chores to do."

The men lowered the car onto the spare tire. "You might want to get the air checked and then replace the flat," Darrell warned.

"I will. What do I owe you?"

Darrell shook his head and Matt put up his hand, "Absolutely nothing."

"That doesn't seem fair," Diane repeated.

"Yes, it does," Annie said. "Sometime, you can do us a good turn."

"I can handle that," Diane held out her hand to Darrell to shake it. "I'm in your debt. Tell Jeannie I'm looking forward to seeing her next week at orientation. And congratulations on your weddings."

"Thank you," Annie and Darrell answered in unison.

"Gee, I feel left out," Matt grinned.

"Oh quit feeling sorry for yourself, Friar Tuck. Get on you horse and let's get back to work," Darrell joked. "We have goats to milk!"

Matt rolled his eyes, "Methinks I milketh thine goat herd this eve."

Diane waved, "Sounds like it. Thanks you guys. You were lifesavers."

Annie giggled, "Not them, that's my business."

65

Matt stayed and helped Darrell milk the goats. They had a ball! After chores, Darrell invited him to dinner with him and Jeannie. Matt thought he had better call Nora before he did that.

"Sure, Matt, you can eat there," Nora said, "Or, you could bring Darrell and Jeannie over here. We have chicken fried steaks, mashed potatoes and—,"

"Excuse me Nora," Matt interrupted, "I'll let you talk to Darrell. I'm drooling so much now I can hardly talk."

Darrell took the phone and before she finished her sentence, he accepted. "I'll call Jeannie to stop there on her way home."

As the two young men went out the door, Darrell chuckled. "I'm so glad you were here, Friar Tuck. I'd hate to have missed the chicken fried steaks!"

Matt chuckled, "Glad to oblige. How long have you all been friends?"

"I was five when we moved here from Arkansas. Before the first year was up, my sister Marly was married to Pastor Byron. Andy Schroeder is my very best friend. He and I almost share the same brain, we're so close."

"The guy in Vietnam?"

"Yah. We've done almost everything together, except him going to Vietnam and me having a heart attack."

"You had a heart attack? Wow! You're kind of young for that," Matt was amazed.

"It was a freaky deal. I had kinks in one of the main arteries, hereditary I guess. Anyhow, I had a couple surgeries. As usual, Schroeders were here for me every bit of the way. You'd have to look hard to find more loyal people," Darrell said as they drove down the gravel road.

"From what I hear, they feel the same way about you," Matt offered. "Even Coot thinks you're great and he's a tough nut."

Darrell laughed and then said seriously, "I hope I don't let him down. He's a decent sort. I know he really cares for your Mom. 'Course, she'll have to dig through all his bologna to find it!"

"I think she knows."

"Yah, so do I. I've watched him with the little kids and he's more patient with them than I could ever be. I can't believe it."

Matt laughed, "He gave Charlie ten-to-life the other day!"

"I'm sure he deserved it. He's quite the kid. If he couldn't dig, I think it would nearly kill him. He's definitely headed for a life of heavy equipment!"

Matt looked at Darrell, "Do you think that you can tell what a person will be by what they like when they are young?"

Darrell thought, "Sometimes. Not always. I have loved goats since I saw the first one. I was every bit as bad as Charlie is about digging. Course it's a lot different. He could make a career out of digging. What the heck is it to milk goats?"

Matt studied his friend, "It is a decent and honorable profession, farming and milking goats. I hear you also work at the Cheese Factory. Why do you think it's not enough?"

"I guess you wouldn't understand, being a priest and all," Darrell tried to explain. "You have a real vocation and it's a great calling. It doesn't even compare to milking goats."

"Darrell. That's not true. We aren't all supposed to preach or dig, someone has to farm so we can eat. It's all important. Every bit of it. We all have a place," Matt said.

"Thanks, but we both know that to be a priest is a great thing."

"I've only told a few folks, Darrell," Matt said earnestly, "But I feel I can trust you. I'm not so certain I made the right choice in becoming a priest. I've taken a leave and using this time to rethink my decision."

"Really? I won't tell anyone, unless you say. May I ask why? Do you doubt your beliefs? Don't need to answer if I'm intruding."

"No. That's the problem. I still believe very strongly. What I've seen go on in the internal workings of the church and things that priests have done that have been covered up, makes me sick. Don't get me wrong. I'm no saint but a few of them behave atrociously. What gets me the most is that the church covers it up! We get into hot water over tiny infractions and then major things are swept under the rug."

"You mean like messing with nuns and little kids?" Darrell blurted out and then said quietly. "I'm sorry. I've heard rumors. I'd no right to say that."

"You're right. Sometimes, I'm downright embarrassed to have anyone think I'm a priest because they might think I'm like those few! If I was a parent, I wouldn't let me near my kid!"

Darrell drove in silence, "I think I can about imagine how that would feel. I think. Is that why you wanted to be just Matt at the dance?"

"Not really, well maybe. I just don't know. I want to be me for a while and see if I can decide what I should do. Father Vicaro at St. John's knows I'm a priest."

"He's a good guy. He has a great reputation and I'd have a hell of a time believing he'd never do anything like that. He's been around a long time. I bet he'd help you work it out. But so would Byron, even if he isn't a Catholic."

"Byron and I became friends in Shreveport. I know I could talk to him and plan on doing that."

"Well, you're in good hands then. Matt, you can always talk to me. I wouldn't be much help, but I'll listen. That you can count on. Listening and goat milk! Hell of an operation! Gee, I think I'd better change your name, huh?"

Matt was puzzled, "What?"

"Yah, I think you're just Tuck," Darrell grinned. "We will keep the Friar in reserve. How's that?"

Matt laughed, "I think I really like that."

A bit later, they were seated in the dining room of the Schroeder home. Jeannie had come bopping in and greeted Darrell with a kiss. Then she hugged Matt and Coot. She took her place just before the family joined hands in grace.

"I got some more books for you today, Coot," she grinned. "One is really fantastic about water diversion. I brought them along."

"Thanks," the old FBI agent grinned, seeming unbothered or simply resigned being called Coot. "Charlie's done with all his other books. Did you get Ginger some more dirt books?"

"Only a few. We've gone through so many, I can't believe it," Jeannie giggled. "She got four more jars of dirt today! Byron is going to ban me from his house soon!"

"She's learning so much from you, Jeannie," Nora said as she passed the mashed potatoes. "She wasn't very excited about school before. Her tragedy might have turned into a blessing for her." Then she hesitated, "Well duh! I can't believe I said that. Of course it would, huh?"

Keith smiled at his Mom, "Don't know, but that's what you always tell us!"

"Well so far this year, things have turned out that way," Elton said. "At least I think so. I still haven't come to grips with that gnarly old FBI agent that hangs around here. Other than that, it's been mighty good."

"Be nice to him, Elton," Grandpa Lloyd said. "He was shot, you know. Between you and me; I think if he doesn't start acting nicer, he'll probably get shot again!"

Everyone just about choked on their food; they were laughing so hard.

"I don't know what it is about you people," Coot blustered. "Even if you are nice, you aren't."

"Oh now Carl," Mo patted his hand, grinning from ear to ear. "It isn't so bad."

"You say that because they're nice to you."

"Speaking of being nice, guess who I saw today?" Jeannie smiled. "Diane Waggoner. She said you guys helped her with her tire on the road."

"We did," Darrell said. "It was flatter than a pancake."

"I'm so glad she's back this year. I was worried that she would go back east. She told me that she'd signed a contract for three years, so she still has another one to go. As she put it, 'it wasn't the school board's fault that Dean passed away.' I told her I thought that they'd have understood, but she felt that a deal is a deal. I'm glad she did though. She is a good teacher and I like her."

"Is that the lady that we met at the church, Mattie?" Mo asked.

"Yes, Mom," Matt answered.

"Hmm. Fine young gal, I'm thinking," Mo said. "The thing the girl needs the most is to be able to get her life back. She needs someone to appreciate her for her own self. I hope she has her own place."

"No, she lives with Waggoners," Jeannie said. "She moved in there while Dean was dying."

Mo looked down at her food. "Well, maybe it'll be okay. I hope she has a good group of friends that she can be with besides them. She needs to not lose herself."

Jeannie absorbed what Mo said. "I never thought about it before. I'll make it a point to do things with her. Thank you for mentioning that to me. We've always been friendly although she was pretty tied up this last year. You tell me more about what you think I should do, okay? I mean, I don't want to offend her, but I sure want to be a friend."

Matt looked at Ian and he caught his glance. Matt wondered if Ian was as taken with the conversation as he was. He had rarely heard people talk about going out of their way for someone like that. If he had heard it from most folks, he would have thought it was so much hot air. But from Jeannie, he felt that she meant it sincerely.

The rest of the conversation was about the plans for the Hawaiian wedding. They were getting things set up so everything would be taken care of while the wedding party was gone. Darrell's brothers, Sammy and Joe, were doing his chores. Keith and Kevin would handle the milking at Schroeders. Katherine with the help of Mo would keep the home fires burning. Coot would be overseeing all the building projects. Ian was keeping an eye on the business end of the shops and Zach would keep them all healthy. There were plenty of people to take up the slack, so no one was too worried.

It would be another two weeks before they left. The houses were coming along fine. After Ian and Ruthie signed with the contractor, it took them little time to decide on a house. Of course, Ruthie already had her wedding all planned down to the last toothpick on the appetizer tray. All they needed to do now was to set the date.

Ruthie would continue living with Ellisons until she got married, as would Miriam. The family thought she should stay at least until school started. Coot already volunteered to keep her during the day. He'd miss his Gophers when school started as much as they'd miss him. Jenny was getting ready to go back to work, and Kincaids would care for Baby Matthew. Glenda of course, would still drop off Maddie Lynn every so often. Coot grumped, but he was pleased. He thought it was his secret; but he fooled no one, not even the kids.

66

The Schroeder household fell into a routine. Morning and evening chores of course, and cooking three meals a day, Coot watched the Gophers and everyone else went to their jobs. Ian was working at the shops and going to school. He seemed very enthusiastic about it. He seemed happier than he had since the shooting. Mo was in her element working with the ladies and planning with her new house.

Everyone seemed to have a new direction except Matt. His main assignment was to take Lloyd and sometimes Katherine for a drive in the morning. It was important to Lloyd and that made Matt feel good, but he really thought he should be doing more.

He helped the Schroeders in the morning with chores, but very often helped Darrell at night. He was pleased one evening when Darrell was delayed at the Cheese Factory. He started the milking on his own. He was a third done before Darrell arrived!

Matt liked Darrell. They had fun together and Darrell taught him to do different things on the farm. Darrell never pressed Matt, but as he'd promised. was always ready to listen.

One evening while they were milking, Jeannie called. She and Pepper wanted to go bowling and had reserved an alley. She asked Darrell and Matt to join them. Pepper was bringing Katie and Ken. The guys were tired from haying, but thought it might be a nice change. Matt went home to clean up and would ride in with Pepper.

As they drove out of the yard, Pepper grinned, "I suppose you're a closet bowling champion, huh? You'll wipe us all out when we aren't looking."

Matt chuckled, "Not hardly. Ian used to be good but I rarely bowled. You know, Pep, I've done more stuff in these last few weeks than I've done in my life!"

Pepper giggled, "Darrell is a good egg. He'll keep you occupied, if that's what you want. It's easier than thinking sometimes."

Matt was quite taken back, "Thinking about what? What did you hear?"

Pepper looked at him and smiled, "Nobody said anything, you doorknob. But I do that all the time. I keep busy so I don't miss Chris so much. You've been as busy as a gerbil in a pile of grain dust. To me that means you're trying to avoid something. It is just that when you're together all the time like we are, a person picks up little glimpses of sadness or discontent." Then she stopped a minute, "Matt, I'm sorry. I have to apologize right here. I have a big mouth and if I think it, I say it. So, please forgive me. If I say too much, feel free to tell me to put a sock in it."

Matt laughed, "Keep your socks on, as Charlie says? I see you come by your name Hot Pepper honestly, huh?"

"Yah, sorry to say. I can keep a confidence though, but not a thought. If you know what I mean. There are two things my Dad will not abide; lying and breaking a confidence."

"Pepper, do I act like I need to talk to someone? Am I a basket case or something?" Matt asked.

"Not at all. I just happened to notice it. Mom always says that sometimes it is better to work things out for yourself, but sometimes you need to talk. I just wanted to tell you that Uncle Byron is a good listener. If you only knew all the blabbering I've done to them, you'd be shocked."

Matt ginned, "I doubt it!"

"I'm mad at you now! What are you saying?" Pepper was immediately indignant, "You're as bad as my brothers! They're always picking on me! Now you are too! I think I'm going to bowl a 300 and leave your ball in the dusty gutter!"

Matt laughed, "I suppose you think you will. We will see."

Annie and the Ellison kids arrived before Matt and Pepper and rented their shoes and balls before going to the alley. Jeannie and Darrell brought over some sodas and a bag of potato chips. They were ready to start when Jeannie suggested they wait a few more minutes.

"I asked Diane to join us. She didn't know if she would come since Waggoners felt she should stay home out of respect for Dean's memory," Jeannie said. "I told her there was nothing disrespectful about bowling with us guys."

"Unless they know how badly we bowl!" Darrell teased and then he frowned, "I don't understand those people."

Annie piped up, "Well, I do understand how some folks are. It's a mess. I felt that way when I tried to get over my husband's death. Granted, I didn't live with the Grovers, but a lot of friends seemed to think that smiling or laughing is a no-no after your husband dies. I wondered sometimes if they didn't think the old Indian tradition of the widow sitting at the end of the grave waiting for death, wasn't appropriate."

"Wow!" Pepper said, "I never realized you felt that way, Annie. I guess I never thought about it. You've always seemed to handle everything so well."

"I was lucky," Annie smiled. "I had a job that kept me away from a social life. I could be busy, so I didn't have time to think."

Pepper looked at Matt and then said, "That's a good plan for awhile."

Just then, Diane came hurrying over to the group. "Hi! I hope you all didn't wait for me."

"Not at all," Darrell grinned, "We're just getting the treats lined up. What sort of soda pop do you like? I'll go get it while you put your shoes on."

"I like Coke, thanks. I can pay for it," Diane reached in her jeans pocket.

"Put your money away," Pepper giggled, "Darrell bought all of ours, so he can buy yours too."

"Seems I'm always having you do something for me," Diane smiled.

Darrell chuckled, "Your day's coming, Tinkerbell. I'm keeping track!"

"Well, are we going to have teams or what?" Ken asked.

"Teams. Who's going to be on what team?" Pepper asked, and answered before another breath. "Tuck and Darrell will be the head of each team. Then Tuck's team will be Jeannie, Ken and me. Darrell can have Diane, Annie and Katie. Okay? Sounds good, huh?"

Everyone laughed. "You're certainly decisive," Matt said. "What would you do if we would say no?"

"But you won't," Pepper giggled. "Will you?"

Darrell returned, "What trouble are you in now Pep?"

"Why does everyone always think I'm in trouble?"

Ken shrugged, "Because you usually are."

"Well, while you're all talking, I'm going first!" Pepper said as she took her ball and went to the line.

The four hours went by quickly and they had a good time. The rules of the game were fudged mercilessly but no one seemed to care. The others were all good bowlers, with the exception of Diane and Matt. They were assured it was only due to the lack of experience. Neither believed it but they decided to accept the encouragement anyway.

At one point, the two were sitting at the scoreboard moaning over the scores, when Diane looked at Matt. "We're pretty much losers, huh?"

Matt smiled with his faint dimple, "Why do you say that? Just because we have scores in the minus range?"

"Probably the main reason," Diane giggled. "I've had a great time tonight."

"Do you get out much?" Matt asked.

"I don't go out very much because it isn't inappropriate. I really caught hell about going to the dance at Heinrich's that night. I shouldn't have gone."

"You didn't do anything wrong," Matt pointed out. "There's no law that says you have to mope around for the rest of your life because you had the misfortune of losing your husband. You did nothing out of place at all. Just how much trouble did you get into?"

Diane studied he score papers, "It was nothing, really. Please forget it, okay?"

Matt watched her a minute. She was unusually uncomfortable. It made him extremely curious what sort of trouble she had encountered. Then he became uncomfortable, knowing he was tempting fate by giving her too much attention. He knew better.

Thankfully, Darrell came over, "Did you guys see that great score I got? Write it down, Tinker, before you forget. I'm watching to make sure you get it right! You are up next, Tuck. Out of the way gang—here comes the king of gutter balls."

Matt frowned at him and then chuckled. “Oh yah? If I win, you can buy hamburgers and fries, Mr. Jessup.”

Darrell took the pencil, “I’ll take everyone’s orders so you can buy our food after you lose miserably.”

67

That night, Matt couldn't sleep. Something about Diane was bothering him. He was worried for her; but maybe it was just projection of his Mom's situation. After all, Diane's situation was very different. She didn't have eight kids. He tried to tell himself he was making too much out of a situation he knew nothing about. He was also concerned about his attraction to her and knew he had to get it under control.

After an hour of tossing and turning, he went downstairs to get a glass of water. When he came to the bottom of the stairs, he encountered Carl walking Lloyd back to his room. They nodded and Matt went on into the kitchen.

He was just putting his glass in the sink when Carl came back into the kitchen. "Hey, I want a cigarette if you'll go outside with me? I am afraid of the dark," the older man grinned.

"We wouldn't want you to be scared, now would we?" Matt chuckled. "Want some water?"

"No, but I could use some of Nora's iced tea. How about you?"

"Yah, I'll get it."

Soon, the two men were sitting at the picnic table. Matt looked around the peaceful prairies, "It sure is quiet here. Only the sound of crickets."

"Yah. I could hardly stand it at first," Kincaid agreed. "Now, I don't know if I could take the hustle and bustle of the city anymore."

"I know what you mean."

Carl looked at the younger man, "How's it going for you? You look like you have a lot on your mind. Doing okay?"

"Yah, I feel bad. I shouldn't have plunked my troubles on you guys."

"Well who else would you plunk them on?"

"Don't know. I should keep it to myself. It isn't anyone else's problem."

"So, are you going to tell me what is really going on, or are you going to keep handing me this mumbo-jumbo stuff?" Carl raised his eyebrows. "Look Kid, I probably have more experience with liars than you have at lying. So don't waste our time. I can see right through you. What's really going on?"

"I'm not lying," Matt watched Carl's face, "I just didn't tell you all of it."

"Same difference," Carl grinned.

"Not exactly."

Carl raised his eyebrow, "Depends which end of it you're getting."

Matt looked at the man, "Kincaid, I was 'encouraged' to take a six month leave of absence so I could rethink my priorities and decide if I was willing to accept the church's decision on certain things."

Carl didn't say anything, but sat quietly while he smoked his cigarette. "And are you?"

"Am I what?"

"Willing to buy their bullshit?"

Matt was shocked, "How do you know it's bullshit?"

"Because I know them, I know you and I know Ian. If Ian thought you were wrong, he'd have said so long ago. Apparently, he doesn't think that you should accept whatever it is. Has it anything to do with Ruthie?"

Matt squinted his eyes, "What all do you know?"

"Let's just say, I know what that Timothy did and how she was 'encouraged' to rethink her commitment. Seems to me, the Catholics must have an overabundance of priests and nuns. They're pretty willing to throw out so many good folks to cover up the shenanigans."

"You are good. Well, Dad," Matt smiled at Coot, "I guess I might as well tell you. I complained to the higher ups about the Timothy thing. I ordered to keep my mouth shut. They said Father Timothy's doing a good job where he is, made the school there fiscally sound and he is dealing with his weaknesses. The Bishop knew that Ruthie had some emotional problems and thought that she may have just misinterpreted things. He told me to basically shut up."

"Figures. You know, the trouble with sticking your head in the sand that far is the only part you leave exposed is your ass!"

Matt started to laugh, "Funny but correct. To be honest, though, Carl, it isn't just the deal with Ruthie. I might as well tell you. One of the priests in a nearby parish is a pedophile. It came to my attention a couple years ago. When I found out, I reported him, but nothing was done. Then another situation with the same guy came up later, and I reported him again. Still nothing. Then I started to make a lot of noise. Boy, they came down on me like gangbusters. He's still there. I know he has been reported at least five times, each time a different boy! I can't believe that they aren't stopping him. He's destroying the lives of these young people, and the powers that be aren't doing a thing to stop it."

"I know about some of it. Boston has a big mess. There are a few other cities that have some big messes too. The FBI knows about some of it, but I'm sure not all of it. No one is ever willing to put their kids on display to stop this crap and the church pretends like it isn't happening. It is as hateful to those kids as what happened to Zach's family."

Matt nodded, "I know. And Carl, this sounds selfish of me to say, but it makes it hard to be a priest. I can see how some people look at me. I know they're wondering if I'm one of those creeps, some kind of a pervert."

Carl turned his attention toward the young man. "Matt, I know I'm partial to you, but I still don't think that's selfish. How are you going to do your job if everyone is afraid of you? We had a bad case of a rogue FBI agent who was on the take and working for a drug lord. When his story hit the press, we couldn't get a citizen to talk to us for months! They thought we're cut from the same cloth. I didn't blame them."

Matt looked at him for the first time, really appreciating that he might know how he felt. "When I talked to my superior about it, he told me that God's work overshadows the misdeeds of a few bad priests. He told me that I was just being self-centered."

"Ah, I bet he didn't deal with the public, did he?" Carl asked.

Matt thought, "No, he didn't."

"These hobnob church types all think the general population is stupid. Those people whose kids are molested have friends and families. People will believe them long before some pompous jackass expounding from a gold plated pulpit!"

"Don't hold back there, Kincaid."

"Sorry, I'm new at this being a stepdad thing. Since I happen to love with your Mom, I guess we're both stuck with the situation. All that aside, I'd feel the same if it was someone else. I know what I'd do if I was you, but I'm not you. For that, we can both be thankful. You're a good priest. I knew that from down in Shreveport. I'm sure you'll make the right decision."

"Don't you dare leave me hanging!" Matt said emphatically. "Don't get chicken and back off your advice. I need to hear what you think."

"Okay. You asked for it." Kincaid cleared his throat. "I'll be straight and to the point. I'd have never been a priest in the first place. So, I can't very well tell you what to do. But since you asked, I think you should tell them to stick it and go make a different life for yourself. Find yourself a good woman, have a couple kids and do God's work in the trenches like the rest of these folks. That's where the real work is, you know. Or like Byron. That poor bastard not only worries about everyone else in his church, he has to deal with his own family. I have to say, I've a lot more respect for someone who tells me to try to lead a child on the right path, when I know he has to deal with Charlie on a regular basis! But listen, if you want to stay, I can't understand it; but I'll support you. You do good work and will do anything I can to help you."

Matt sat quietly thinking over what the man said. "Thanks Carl. I appreciate your honesty. Can I tell you something?"

"Why not? I can either listen to you or Lloyd."

"It has never bothered me about not marrying. I mean, I notice the ladies, of course. However, it's been nothing but a passing fancy. Definitely something I could deal with. But lately, maybe it's my age, or Ian's relationship with Ruthie or whatever. Maybe it's because I'm doubting so much about my vocation, but I'm starting to feel that I'd like to have someone to really care about me, as a person. Does that make sense?"

"Yes, Matt, it does. Between you and me, I did the same thing. After Cecelia died, I put all that stuff away. I buried myself in work, day and night. It works pretty good. Sure, once in a while I'd weaken, pick up some broad and get laid, but I had no one. Nobody really gave a damn about me and I didn't give a damn about anyone. It worked pretty well until some psycho shot a hole in me and my little world. When I was in that bed in Shreveport, I had nothing and no one. I was so damned scared and lonely, you can't believe it. It was one of the lowest points in my life. I really know now how people feel who kill themselves. Then in waltzes

Petunia, dragging Magpie behind him. Well, we know how that worked out."

"I guess it's somewhat the same. I do have my faith and all that. I never thought I'd feel all alone in the end, but then I never thought much about there ever being an end. You know?"

"Yah, Matt. Sadly, I do know. It might have to do with you coming smack face to face with mortality with Ian. Then you saw how important Ruthie is to him. But what the hell do I know? Being around folks who love each other, makes a person realize what they're missing."

Then both men yawned. "My word, Carl, it is three-thirty in the morning! We have to get up in a few hours! I'm so sorry to keep you up all night."

"Don't be," Carl grinned. "This is my life now. Doddering old goats wandering around all night talking to me about some damned war, little gophers in the day and now I got me a whole batch of step-gophers to listen to besides! I just hope it helped some."

"It did, and I feel better knowing I can talk to you. You did good, Dad." Matt put his arm around Carl.

"Hey Matt. Can you do me a favor?"

"What would that be?"

"Go in Pepper's room and throw out her damned clock!"

Matt nodded, "I know, huh? That is a miserable thing. But she's home tonight, and I might get my clock cleaned if I broke in her room!"

When Matt and Lloyd got home from their morning drive, Nora told him that Father Vicaro had called. Matt called him back and they set a date for breakfast the next morning. Though torn about the meeting, Matt felt that he needed to go. Father Vicaro had been good to Ruthie. He seemed a sensible sort.

After lunch, Matt went over to Darrell's place to help grind feed. It was an itchy job. As they sat down at their coffee break, Darrell said, "You've been very quiet this afternoon. You know, don't feel like you're my farm hand. You can say no."

"I know. I want to build up my muscles so I can beat you next time we bowl."

Darrell looked down at his coffee cup, "I wanted to talk to you about that. Tuck, I think there's something wrong over at the Waggoner place. Jeannie and I went around with Dean and Diane last fall a little bit and kind of knew them. Tinker just didn't seem right, last night. You know, that and what she said when we changed her tire. It might be the normal sadness a person has when they mourn, but something is eating at me."

Matt was floored, "Why do you say that?"

"A few things that Jeannie said and then that the day we changed the tire. I hope she doesn't get in trouble for last night," Darrell worried.

"Do you know Waggoners?" Matt asked. He was quite surprised at Darrell's insight, but then decided he shouldn't be.

"Not really, but I'm going to see what I can find out. Dean was an okay guy. I knew him from stuff with Jeannie at school, but I don't know his family at all. Jeannie told me before that she was worried about Diane when Dean was so sick. But she never said exactly why except his parents seemed very domineering. But she worried me, a few of the things she said."

"Hmm. Me too. I just don't want her have trouble," Matt agreed.

"Me either, but I think she needs more than a friend," Darrell stated. "I'm going to try to find out what I can without setting off any alarms."

"Can't she get her own place? She probably shouldn't be living with Waggoners."

"I asked Jeannie about that last night. Diane's trying to pay off the medical bills and all with Dean's death. She had to borrow money from his folks. She is hardly making ends meet. I guess we all know how that can go."

"I'm glad that you feel that it needs to be looked into, too. I'll see what I can find out from Father Vicaro." Matt said, "Of course, it's none of my business. She's not in my parish or anything."

"Where does it say that you can only help people in your parish?" Darrell looked at him slyly. Then he stood up straight, looked Matt in the eye and said, "You like her, don't you?"

"Huh?"

"Don't huh me. I know you like her. Nothing wrong with that."

"Well, Darrell, I like a lot of people. You know, priests can't think like I think you think I'm thinking."

Darrell laughed, "I can't wait to hear you give a sermon!"

Matt frowned, "You're impossible."

Darrell got quiet, "Matt. I know that priests aren't supposed to think that way, but men do. You're a man, a human one. It'd be wise for you not to deny that. God made you, so He must've wanted you that way. Anyway, I like her and so does Jeannie. And if you were honest, so do you."

"Yah, I do. Between you and me, more than just a friendly way. I should get back into my collar very soon or I could end up down the path of sin and treachery. When I saw her that day on the road, I have to admit I haven't felt that way in a long time."

"Feeling that way isn't a sin. It's what you do with your feelings," Darrell answered seriously. "Of course, you know all that."

That evening while they sat on the Schroeder patio, Zach asked Matt if he wanted to go to town with him the next afternoon. "Dr. Lassiter called and said that he and you had planned to get together. He and I are having lunch and he wondered if you would like to join us."

"Gee, breakfast with Father Vicaro and lunch with Dr. Lassiter. I'm quite the socialite," Matt smiled. "I accept."

"Good for you," Coot grumped. "Cuts down on your mooching off us."

68

Matt was unbelievably nervous to meet with Father Vicaro, but didn't want any of the family to know. He seemed to be well respected by the community, but Matt knew they'd meet on a different level. Father Vicaro was a priest and so was he. He was hiding from his vocation and Father Vicaro knew it. The conversation could be quite contentious.

That morning while milking, Charlie sat down beside Matt during break. "Mr. Tuck," the little boy patted his hand, "Don't worry. Us special project guys always do the hard stuff. It'll be okay."

Matt looked at him in shock, "What will, Charlie?"

"Whatever," Charlie grinned. "And when you're done, you can have chocolate chips cookies."

Matt chuckled, "Thanks Charlie."

"If it gets really bad, go under the bed, like I told you. It really works."

"I'll remember that."

Before he left the house, Carl took his arm. "Be strong in your principles. Don't back down on them. You're the one you live with."

Matt looked at the older man, "Thanks."

On his way to Father Vicaro's home, Matt wondered if the entire clan was psychic. He finally decided it was because they're all tuned in to each other and weren't afraid to say something. He could understand why Ian and Coot felt so comfortable there. He knew that he was only a guest, but he felt comfortable there too. Those guys were definitely fortunate to be part of the clan.

Sister Abigail greeted him at the door and showed him into the library where Frank Vicaro was seated behind his desk. It was a beautiful room with dark walnut bookcases and a huge fireplace. Father Vicaro was a short man of Italian descent. His dark hair was graying slightly at the temples and his brown eyes peered out from behind his bifocals revealing his senior age, approaching seventy. He met him with a huge smile, reached out his hand and offered Matt a chair in front of the fireplace.

Matt sat down, still very nervous. Sister Abigail brought them some coffee and said breakfast would be ready in a few minutes. Matt took a sip and leaned back in the large rusty brown leather chair.

"I imagine you have already drunk at least two pots of coffee, if you are at the Schroeder's, huh?" Father Vicaro laughed. "Their coffee pot is legendary."

Matt chuckled, "Yes, I believe I did. I wasn't aware that you knew of their coffee pot."

"Ah, I have lived here so long, I know most folks, Catholic or not. Schroeders are a good bunch. Sometimes, I actually wished they're Catholic!" Father Vicaro chuckled. "But Ellison would be all bent out of shape then."

"Byron's a good guy."

"He is and I think that your soon to be sister-in-law is doing very well under his tutelage. I hope you're pleased with the results," the old priest put down his spoon and studied him.

"Yes. I am. Her childhood was hell. She has been through so much and I'm so happy that she had you and Byron to help her. I know that you might not be pleased with her decision to leave the convent, but I think for her it is the best. The convent wasn't good for her."

"I agree. You know, Matt,—may I call you that?"

"Of course."

"I've been around this game long enough to think that some things aren't the way they should be. Please, promise you'll never tell Rome, but there are some real good folks out there that have never been to a Mass and never will be either!"

Matt laughed gently but felt so much relief it was overwhelming. "I'm so glad to hear you say that. This whole business with Ruthie and her crazy family has really made me think. I was so grateful that you cut her a lot of slack while she was here."

"Not a problem. I couldn't in good conscience have done anything else. I'm not happy that she is working at the Lutheran church, but she fits there. I could use her expertise myself. In her world, that's not what she needs. She wouldn't get it here. She sure didn't get it in Philadelphia at the convent. Father Timothy's a piece of work."

Vicaro continued, "I had the unpleasant experience of trying to talk to that Timothy. I want to tell you upfront, so we don't need to beat around the bush. I have heard about the trouble you got into over his actions. You have my complete support. The powers that be can hurt you, but they can hardly hurt me. No one thinks that central North Dakota is a priest's dream job, so they're all content to leave me in the hinterland. I wanted to tell you I understand your situation. That is why I never made an issue about you going incognito."

"I do feel better that you know. I'm learning that folks up this way don't do a lot of beating the bush. Do you think I should be more up front about being a priest?"

"Look," the old priest said thoughtfully, "That isn't something easy to answer. I've no idea what you're thinking. All I know is that you took a 'suggested' leave after you got into hot water with that Timothy, some renegade pedophile priest and the Bishop in Boston. I'm in total agreement with you about that, too. Some of those guys should be expelled; at least removed from their present jobs. I cannot fathom that covering up some of that behavior will come to any good. Having said that, I'm also very glad that it isn't my decision to make."

"I can honestly tell you, Father Vicaro I don't know what I'm thinking either. I wanted to be a priest since I was a child. I still think that it's probably where I should be. But if you knew all the garbage that's going on in Boston, well. I just don't know how to deal with it. I hate to admit it, but sometimes I'm embarrassed to say I am a priest. I just don't know what else to do with my life."

Sister Abigail called the men to breakfast and they continued their conversation. After they were served their cheese soufflé and toast, they resumed their talk.

"How long is your leave?"

"I was given six months."

"Will you be here the whole time?"

"Don't know. I thought so. Schroeder's have offered me a home."

"They're like that. Good folks. You'll do well there. I've known Elton since his bachelor days. He's made more changes in his life than most and seems to have done it without getting a big head. Can I be frank?"

Matt teased, "I think you are Frank."

The older man laughed, "Some folks make changes to become a better person and get such big heads that their conceit is overbearing. They think they have a direct route to heaven just because they finally got around to doing what they should've been doing in the first place! Sometimes, I'd like to tell them that. Of course, I can't, but I'd sure like too! Have you ever thought about the ultimate sermon? All the things you would say if you knew you were going to die before the Amen? I have stayed awake nights planning it!"

Matt laughed so hard he had tears in his eyes. "You are as crazy as Ellison!"

"Must be the cold winters up here," Father Vicaro laughed. "Seriously though, is there anything I can help you with? I'd be glad to help out. I've heard some of the scuttle from Boston, New York and I have a friend in Manchester, England. It makes you sick to hear. But I know. I can't imagine serving in some of those parishes."

"It isn't easy. I feel like a fraud and a hypocrite. I've no control over anything. It's almost untenable."

"Sounds grim. So is that why you're thinking about your future?"

"Yes. I know that at least I'll be leaving Boston," then he lowered his eyes to his plate and was quiet.

"And the priesthood, possibly," Father Vicaro finished.

"Yes. I didn't intend to be incognito; it just sort of happened. I feel guilty about it, but I still feel that I need to get this worked out in my head. Is that reasonable?"

Father Vicaro thought while he jellied his toast, "Don't know. It's playing with fire, you know. You'll have a lot more temptations if people don't know you're a priest. On the other hand, it's hard to make a comparison, if you have nothing to compare. How about you promise you won't lie about it but we agree it isn't necessary to advertise? Will that work?"

"Yes. The clan already knows that I'm Ian's priest brother, and I really don't know too many other people."

"From what I understand, that's a pile of folks. What do they think?"

"Nora told me that we all need to think things out sometimes, Mom wants me to stay a priest long enough to marry her off to Carl. Ian never thought I should be a priest because he is still mad I wrecked his comic book when we were kids!" Matt grinned.

Father Vicaro laughed, "Good sound reasoning! Do you need to do penance over the comic book?"

"You know, it's been so long ago, I doubt if either of us even remember exactly what happened!"

"We'll take our coffee in the library, okay Sister Abigail?"

The men went into the library. "Well, young man," Father Vicaro started and Matt panicked. "What're we going to do with you?"

"What do you mean?"

"We can't let you just go to waste for six months. I've a couple of ideas. I would like to run them past you. I only wish you had an entire year instead of six month, but no matter. We can make this work."

"What work?"

"I'd like to use your talents. I was wondering if I'd ask you to help teach CCD. We have classes on Wednesday nights here at St. John's. I teach some, but I need help this year. If you could help at least until you leave that would mean a great deal. And you know going over our doctrine might help you too."

"You are an old fox, aren't you?" Matt grinned wryly.

"Look, I let Ellison get Ruthie but I'm not handing to have you over too! I need to get something out of this deal!" the older man teased.

"I understand. I won't be teaching at Trinity, but I don't know if I should teach here either."

"Think about it. I teach the oldest class and have a very reliable couple that teaches the middle class. However, my beginning class is a disaster."

"What happened?"

"I had a lady that taught before. She had to quit last year, and I got his guy to help. He did a good job, but he is involved in so many things.. He can't do it this year because he's all tied up with sports. I think it might be too much for one person. I'd be uneasy to take on twenty four ten-year-olds by myself too! I asked the lady from last year if I got someone else to help if she would reconsider. She said she'd talk it over with her family."

Matt was felt that it was a responsibility he should accept. After all, he wasn't doing anything as it was. He squirmed a bit and then said. "Okay.

You got your man. I'm going to Boston in a couple weeks to move my Mom out here and then I'm free. I'll say okay. You're a conniver."

"I find it kind of goes with God's work, huh?" the older man grinned, "We don't start until after Labor Day. My day was a success. Now if I can coerce someone to work with you, it might do us all some good."

Matt felt comfortable. Really comfortable. He was glad he had talked to Father Vicaro and very relieved he was so understanding. He wasn't at all like some of the guys he had butted heads with in Boston. He was a bit upset about getting conned into teaching a CCD class, but felt that he should. Father Vicaro was right. He might do well to have a refresher course in church doctrine.

Before he got home, he had realized he hadn't asked about the Waggoners, but decided he could do that later.

69

Matt was pretty jazzed as he returned to the Schroeder household. When he came in, Charlie ran right to him. "Was it solomon? Did you go under the bed?"

Matt grinned, "Didn't have to Charlie. It was all good."

"Too bad, it might've been better under the bed."

Matt laughed, "Might have been, but I'm saving that for when I need something special, okay?"

Charlie thought a minute and then grinned, "Good idea."

"So what did you get to eat?" Coot asked. "We had apple pancakes and sausage. They're mighty good."

"Cheese soufflé," Matt grinned. "It was good too."

"Ah, soufflé is pretty and all that, but it's filled with air." Carl pointed out. "Most likely not much good if you are pitching hay. How did it go?"

Matt looked at him, "Good, Dad. I'll tell you about it later, okay?"

Carl hoped that his deep pleasure at being called Dad wasn't apparent to everyone, but he was very pleased.

"Darrell called and wondered if you'd have time to see him before you go to lunch. Guess it's important."

"Hmm? It's only ten, so I'll run over right away if I can borrow the station wagon again."

"You have the keys," Nora smiled.

"Jeannie called this morning all excited," Darrell grinned as he climbed down off the piece of machinery. "I had to call you before she calls me back."

"What's so urgent?" Matt asked.

"She's been at orientation for the new school year all week. This morning she heard that Mr. Morley had been hospitalized. He teaches physics, chemistry and math. They need a temporary replacement. She thought of you right away. If you call, she could get you a meeting with the principal. She was so excited, she could hardly talk. She said she thinks this is for you!"

"Me?" Matt was shocked, "Can't I just coast?"

Darrell looked at him with a bewildered look, "Why on earth do that? No one gets to coast."

"Father Vicaro drafted me to teach CCD this semester."

"What is CCD?"

"Like your catechism classes."

"Oh you mean like confirmation? That's good, don't you think?" Darrell asked excitedly.

"Yes, Darrell, I said yes. It is only on Wednesdays, but teaching would be like a full-time job."

"Only until Mr. Morley gets well. He needs to have someone fill in for one semester. The doctors think he can come back. Jeannie and I thought that would be a perfect fit for you, if you're interested."

"Gee Darrell, I don't know. I don't teach chemistry and I mean, I wanted to think. I wanted to decide if I'd be comfortable serving the Lord in a different vocation," Matt mumbled.

"Well, seems to me this would be a perfect opportunity. We need someone with your qualifications. You need something to do. It's a public school. Anyway, please call Jeannie before she has a conniption fit. Let her know either way. She felt like she was sent on a mission to let you know!"

Matt answered thoughtfully, "I have to say, it does seem to be a ready-made solution all around. I'll call her. Do you have her number?"

Matt went in Darrell's house and called. Jeannie was just bubbling over with delight. She told him the particulars and said she had tentatively set up an appointment with him to meet with the principal the next morning at eight. Matt chuckled. "Women in this neck of the woods don't mess around."

Jeannie laughed, "I hope I'm not pushing you. Honestly, just say no if you don't want to do it. But will you please go talk to the man tomorrow? What can it hurt? Except that you'll have to drink his lousy coffee."

"I'll do it. Jeannie, thank you for thinking of me," Matt grinned.

After he hung up, Darrell thanked him. "I appreciate you talking to the man, even if you say no. I know that means so much to Jeannie."

"You guys," Matt shook his head. "You're forcing me to think."

Darrell took his arm and said in dead seriousness, "Matt. Seriously, don't do anything that you think isn't right because of us. Neither of us would want you to do that."

Matt looked at his friend sincerely and said, "I know Darrell and I wouldn't. No, I have to admit that I agree with Jeannie. It seems like there might be a reason in all this. I just had visions of doing nothing for a while. Apparently, that's not what the good Lord has in mind. Well, I'd better get back, Zach is waiting for me. Gee, this has been quite the morning."

"Tomorrow you might want to clean barn, after your meeting with the principal?" Darrell laughed.

"I might at that. See you tomorrow with my shovel in hand."

On the way to town, Matt shared the news of his morning with Zach. "I don't know, Zach. I feel like I should do all this but I'm not certain."

"Changing your life's direction could lead to uncertainty. How could it not?"

Matt grinned, "You should be a politician."

"I'll leave that to Coot's Gophers. You should've heard those little devils before the cooking contest; selling their votes for treats like pros! They're a corrupt lot," he chuckled.

"I heard it was quite the contest. Coot and Elton get along real well, don't you think?"

Zach smiled, "Yah. Elton can get along with almost anyone, but Coot's more particular. When I knew those two would be together, I admit I was worried. I was afraid that Carl would be thrown out in a heartbeat. I guess I underestimated them. They both read people and I think they saw through each other right away."

"I'm glad it worked out," Matt agreed. "We should still be working out this dowry thing. After all, we were way ahead on our matchmaking!"

Zach chuckled, "Yah, we sure were! Have you ever thought about being married, Matt?"

"Me?" Matt thought, "No. Not really. I mean I always wanted to be a priest and I knew they didn't marry so I never imagined myself with a wife and a dozen kids."

"But how do you feel about not being with women?"

"Well, Zach. You got married, supposedly be with only one woman for the rest of your life. Do you plan on having affairs with every pretty girl you see?"

"No, I don't. But you know what I mean."

"Zach. I recognize a pretty girl when I see one. Of course! I'm celibate, not dead." Matt chuckled. "Why do you ask?"

"Oh, I was wondering if that's why you're trying to decide about your future."

"Who told you I was?" Matt asked, suddenly doubting all the talk of respecting confidence he had heard.

"You just did! You told me you might take this teaching job in a public school for a semester until you thought things over. That's what you meant, right?"

"Yah, I guess it is. I suppose I should just be square with everyone. Zach, I'm doubting my career choice, shall we say. I'm thinking about leaving the priesthood but I haven't decided yet."

"Do you want me to keep it quiet? I will, if you want," Zach said.

"You know, only until Sunday. I think I'll mention it to all the clanners then. Some of them know already and I imagine the rest have guessed. What do you think they'll think?" Matt asked.

"Not much. Most realize that it's a serious decision and will give you the space to decide. They wouldn't expect you to stay in something that you aren't comfortable with," Zach said. "Anything that I can do to help in anyway, let me know."

"Thanks, Zach. Did you know that Dr. Lassiter left the priesthood when he was young?"

"No, I didn't." Zach thought a bit, "But I can see it in him. He is a real gem. I think the world of him. Ginger likes him and she's a pretty good judge of character. You could talk to her!"

"So is Charlie," Matt chuckled. "You know, this morning he picked it up right away that I was nervous about going to see Father Vicaro. He told me we could have chocolate chip cookies when I got home and not to worry!"

"Sounds like him. Are you off 'promotion' yet?"

"Not yet. He told me that he and Coot have to talk about it yet and they have been busy. The tension mounts."

"He is really a tough task master. He had Darrell on 'promotion' for over a month!"

The men had a great lunch with Lassiter. After talking with him, Matt felt a bit more confident if he should decide to leave the priesthood. They made plans to meet again in the near future. He was thankful that the Lord had put these people before him; an understanding priest, a man who had made a similar decision and also very good friends and family. He was extremely fortunate.

He was also aware that he shouldn't be too quick to put aside his commitment. He still wanted very much to be a priest. He just needed a way to do it without feeling that he was betraying his principles.

70

It was after eleven when Matt drove into Darrell's yard. Matt had just completed his meeting with the principal. Darrell was finishing the barn and taking out the last load of manure. He looked up and grinned at Matthew, "Perfect timing! Did you think to bring some coffee?"

"No, I didn't, but I'll buy you lunch at the Chicken Roost or whatever that place is in town. You interested?"

"I'd be if you promise to tell me all your news," Darrell laughed. "Just give me a minute to clean up. Oh, it is the Little Hen Cafe."

Matt laughed, "Okay. Sounds good."

A half an hour later, the two men sat down in a booth at the Little Hen and were looking over the menus. After they placed their orders, Darrell leaned back, "So Tuck. Are you now known as Professor?"

Matt laughed, "I think Tuck would be preferable. I took the job. It sounds really interesting and I think I'll like the challenge. I'm going to go meet with Mr. Morley next week. He's in St. Anne's Hospital in Bismarck."

"What are you going to do about the Chemistry?" Darrell asked.

"The Biology teacher is going to teach it," Matt replied. Then he became very quiet. "Darrell, can I ask you something?"

"Sure. Don't know what kind of an answer you will get."

"Well. After I talked to the school, I went over to Father Vicaro. We had to talk. Man, it was treacherous," Matt said sincerely.

"What do you mean?"

"I told him about the job and he peered at me over his bifocals and nodded. He pointed out that he could use a math teacher at St. John's high school. I didn't know what to say and just sat there. Finally, he leaned back and then grinned, before he got very serious. He'll run interference with my Bishop, if I promise to teach Adv. Algebra and Calculus at St. John's."

Darrell grinned, "He is a con man in a priest's robe!"

"Yah, for certain!" Matt agreed, "But he is no one's fool. He wants me to keep my foot in the door while trying to give me space to work out my problem. I do need his help me with the Bishop. Personally, I think the Bishop is glad to be rid of me and would just as soon dump me. Father Vicaro doesn't want me to leave the church unless I'm certain. Anyway, after a long distance phone call that lasted an eternity, my sabbatical is extended for the entire school year, until June 15. However, I'll not receive any pay after December."

Darrell watched Matt's face, "Is it because Father Vicaro thinks it'll take you that long to decide or because that's how long he needs you?"

"Happens to be how long he needs me. He made no bones about it. That's what I like about him. After the holidays, he'd like me to help at services once in a while and some other of the priestly duties; hearing confession and stuff. I don't know if I want to go down that path."

"Seems to me that you'd just be a priest again, huh? I don't know if that would do you any good."

"Father Vicaro understands that but he said to think it over. He said I wouldn't have to do any of that until after Christmas."

"I don't know if you should do it. You'll be back to being a priest the first time that you help with a service or hear a confession. You know that. If I was you, I would really think before I did that."

"Good idea. Thanks, Darrell. I'm really causing a ruckus, huh?"

"Not hardly. You haven't lived until you have seen some of the real ruckuses we have around here!"

"You know, maybe if I just became a straight out priest, I could stay at the rectory with Vicaro."

"I guess," Darrell grinned. "Pardon me if that doesn't sound appealing to me! I can't imagine anything less interesting. Oh Tuck, did you find out anything about the Waggoners?"

"No. Every time I talk to Father Vicaro, the conversation takes wheels of its own. But I will, I promise. Why? Did you hear something?" Matt asked with concern.

"Maybe, or maybe it is just my overactive imagination. Jeannie told me last night that Diane came to orientation yesterday with a swollen jaw. She looked like she had taken a big jab in the face. She said that she had an impacted tooth and had to go to the dentist today."

"You don't believe that?" Matt was uncertain that he did.

"I don't know why, but really don't. I know a person can get a humongous swelling from a bad tooth, but," he stopped and shook his head. "I don't know, Tuck. I'm just picking up on something."

"Me, too." Matt played with his French fry. "Darrell, between you and me?"

"Yah man."

"Way down deep, I wonder how much I want to take that job because I'm worried about her. Why am I so worried about her?"

"Hell, Tuck. I'm worried about her too! So what if you are? Look, Jeannie is worried too, so don't think it's all a generous dose of testosterone!"

Matt started to laugh until the tears rolled down his cheeks, "You're a crazy person, Jessup. I would say I loved you, but that is probably doesn't fit in this conversation either! "

They both laughed.

"Let's get home before we get kicked out of here," Darrell said. "Jeannie will be dying to hear what you decided."

She was delighted when the men told her that Matt had taken the job. She gave him a big hug and kiss on the cheek! "I just knew it! I'm so happy!"

"Thanks, Jeannie," Matt grinned. "I'll be depending on you to help me out. The principal said that I can come to 'second orientation' in a couple weeks."

"We have two every year. Teachers have had problems with the dates, so the school just runs them twice. I think that Diane will have to finish hers on the last part of the second one. Someone said that she had dental surgery today. I guess it really was her tooth. Darrell and I were letting our minds run away with our reason."

"He told me and I went to the same place," Matt nodded. "Do you think that she's okay?"

Jeannie thought, "You know, I just don't know. She says all the right things and it seems okay, but there's something amiss. Maybe she is just having a hard time finding her way as a single person again. I don't know. I guess we just have to be her friends and if she is having a problem, we can help her."

Matt looked at Darrell, "Do you know how lucky you are, Darrell? Yah, you do."

"Nobody ever lets me forget!" Darrell teased. "They just don't know my Jeannie that well!"

"Poor baby," Jeannie laughed.

Everyone was very congratulatory at Matt's news that night. He only told them about the school jobs and the CCD class and never mentioned that Father Vicaro wanted him to help out with clerical things. He didn't know why he didn't, but he just didn't feel right about it.

After dinner, Matt asked Carl if he could bend his ear. "Sure, we can let these folks do the dishes without us tonight."

Outside, Kincaid asked, "What is it?"

Matt explained to him what Father Vicaro wanted him to do. Carl listened carefully and then said. "You've asked Darrell about it and now me. That leads me to think that you doubt it's a good idea yourself. I think you should go talk to Byron. This church stuff is out of my league. You have some serious doubts, my friend. However, you know, by Christmas, you might know exactly what you want. That is still a ways away and by then you will have spent some time in public school."

"You think so?"

"Yup, I do."

71

The following week was exciting and filled with the last minute arrangements for the Hawaiian trip. Zach took the family to the airport Thursday morning for their exciting ten days on the Islands.

The remaining folks settled into their routine and even Grandpa Lloyd was relaxed after he realized that no one was moving him out of his home. He looked forward to his morning drive with Matt and became the tour guide of the Merton area. Matt felt he had learned things about the region that few people in the world ever knew.

One day, Matt and Byron had a long visit. He talked to him about his doubts with Father Vicaro's plan. Byron listened carefully and then suggested that he should take it one thing at a time.

"Matt, you suffer from the same disease as alot of us. We all want to know the end of the story before God is finished working things out. We have to learn to be patient and keep faith. You have four months before you need to tell Father Vicaro and the Bishop your decision about doing some priestly duties. At least, take some of this time and not think it to death. By the time you need to make those decisions, you'll have your answers. Maybe you will want to be back in the robe and collar.

"Your time at the school and with this new schedule should give you a lot of insight. We don't begin to understand God's will or what He has in store for us. You know, I think we have a good boss, but He isn't too keen on letting us know the end of things until He thinks we need to," Byron pointed out.

"Amen to that!" Matt laughed. "I'm so thankful for my friendship with you all and especially with Darrell. He is a good guy and very practical. He can read me like a book. That's rather eerie sometimes."

"Yah, Elton is like that too! Downright creepy sometimes, but I rely on that now. When I'm about ready to flip out, he is always the one to say, "We need to talk." I usually don't like what he has to say, but he's usually right on the mark," Byron grinned.

"I can understand that now that I know Darrell. I feel like I really shouldn't be asking everyone to help me," Matt confided.

"Matt, don't allow yourself to fall in that trap! I've done it. I remember telling Elton one time that since I was a preacher I should know the answers. He opened my jacket and announced he didn't see any wings! He told me I was just a human and should quit trying to be a saint because everyone including God knew better."

Matt laughed, "Darrell almost said the same thing to me! Are we that bad?"

Byron thought and then nodded, "I think it comes with the territory of our jobs. Our church isn't as demanding as yours about what is expected, but I think that attitude is a very real downside to the profession."

"Byron, my church is very demanding about some things, but then turns a blind eye to others. I'm not of a nature to keep my mouth shut when things are wrong and I know that's what the Bishop wants. I don't think that Vicaro is that way at all but I am thankful that he knows my situation."

"Do you think he'd keep quiet about some of the stuff you have told me those guys out there are doing?"

"I don't know. He said once that he was glad the decision wasn't up to him."

Byron shrugged, "I guess that makes sense, but I doubt he'd accept your situation. I know I'd have a heck of time dealing with it."

"No, but as he pointed out, he has a rather secure place and so he can have that attitude. I'm still new and in the wrong place to have that luxury," Matt got quiet. "I feel like I'm just a burden on everyone."

"Ah, no more than the rest of us. You need to relax. Enjoy life and let the answers come to you."

"Thanks Byron."

"Matt, if you need to talk again, don't ever feel like you can't ask me. Okay? Have I got your word?"

"You do. I really appreciate it."

That evening the family received good news. Zach's house would receive the final walk-through the next day and then they could move in. Suzy was beside herself and Zach was relieved because he had to head back to work the following week.

The next day was moving day. Everyone was on hand to help and by sunset, things were somewhat moved in. The following day, the furniture store delivered the furniture that the couple had bought. They were so excited and volunteered to have a cookout when they were all settled.

Coot and Darrell's foundations were dug and the crew was starting Ian's. The concrete men were pouring Coot's basement and had the frames up for Darrell's. It was getting very exciting to watch the new homes take shape.

That Sunday, the clan met at Ellisons. Matt attended Mass incognito again. At dinner, Glenda Olson asked if Coot could keep an eye on the kids on Tuesday because she had another doctor's appointment. He said he'd be glad to.

Tuesday morning, she brought the kids over. She was concerned because Clark had chicken pox. Everyone assured her it was okay because everyone had had them. It was the only childhood disease that they knew Miriam had.

Clark was tired and his face was badly broken out, as was his arms and chest. The poor kid was miserable. They put him in the nursery on the daybed before the Ellison kids arrived, and lowered the shades so he could rest.

Miriam was beginning to take a few steps on her own and everyone was very excited about that. She had now attained her desired weight and looked the picture of health. She had a smile most of the time and her nightmares had almost disappeared. They all felt she was on her way to a full recovery, as long as there were no crayons around.

About nine-thirty, Clark woke up crying with a sore throat. Grandma brought him something to drink. Mo was carrying Miriam and went into the dimly lit room to see how the little boy was doing.

Miriam took one look at him and screamed bloody murder. She instantly curled up into a tight little ball. Carl was right there and tried everything he could think of to get her to calm down. Nothing worked.

Matt called the shop and Kevin came right over. Kevin tried to get her to relax, but it was the worst they'd ever seen her. Her breathing was so very irregular that Grandma called Marty who came right over.

Marty and Kevin took her right to the hospital. Kincaid and Matt went along. Zach and Dr. Samuels met them at the emergency room and took her in immediately. The men paced the floor until Zach came out. He was devastated.

Carl gave him a hug, "What is it?"

"She is going upstairs, in ICU. We don't know what's going on. She is heavily sedated and has to have help breathing. Dr. Samuels thinks this is the most severe case he has seen in a while and is afraid that she is almost catatonic." Then the young doctor cried. "Jesus, you guys. I should've done more for her. I just let everyone else do everything and was so wrapped up in myself. I never paid any attention. I forgot what she had been through."

Carl stood to his full height, "You royal jackass! We all thought she was better. Every single one of us. And she was! If this had happened a few months ago, she'd be dead. What the hell gives you the right to think it is all about you? I'm with her every day!"

Just then Byron came in, "All of you, knock it off! She lives at my house. Look, she was better. We can't be responsible for what we don't understand. We have figured out a lot of her problems."

"God only knows what she was subjected to before she came to us," Marty stated. "I wish we knew more about her past. Then maybe we'd know what to do."

Kevin was sitting on the vinyl sofa of the waiting room, "I for one, am going to do just that. I love that little kid and I'm not about to let every little thing blow her world apart. There has to be a way to find out more. Isn't there?"

Coot sat on down next to him in deep thought. "I'm going to Texas."

"What?" Zach asked. "Why?"

"I'll call Diaz and tell him we have to get to the bottom of it. I can pull in some markers from my years at the Agency. I know this isn't their job, but they know all the players. They can help us. They can line up all the folks that they know that worked with those morons. It shouldn't even take that long. I'm going to find out if it's the last thing I do."

"How do you plan to do that?" Kevin asked.

"Some of Ezekiel's gang are in the slammer. I think they need a little visit from me. I'll call Diaz as soon as I get home. I'm going down there."

"You're crazy," Marty said. "You can't be traveling around the countryside. You aren't that well yet."

"I'm well enough. If you think that I'm going to lose that little girl without at least bashing a few heads in, you're crazy," Coot stated.

Byron put his arm on the man's shoulder, "Carl, we appreciate how you feel, but you can't do that."

"Watch me! She's my little Gopher. She has to get better."

Zach asked, "Do you think that Diaz will help you?"

"Yah, I have a few friends. A lot of the guys liked that picture I sent of the Gophers the day we got all that pipe. They'll help me. We might not find out much, but we can find out more than what we already know!"

Zach frowned, "But Carl, you can't travel alone."

"Well then someone will have to come with me."

Matt said, "Count me in. I have another week until orientation. I can go."

"So can I," Marty said. "Since my partner is off, I'm scheduled off. I can travel with Carl. Okay, Zach? Just tell me how to resuscitate this old geezer."

"Should I come too?" Zach said.

Everyone answered, "No"

Byron said, "You need to be here for her."

"No. I'm going, unless Miriam needs me here," Kevin was adamant. Everyone knew that there would be no talking him out of it. "She's my little God daughter. This time I'm going."

"Okay, but you know who'd be the best to take? Coot decreed. "Harrington."

"What about I talk to Dr. Samuels and we all meet at Schroeder's in a couple hours and figure this thing out," Zach said. "If there's any way we can to get to the bottom of this, we should do it."

Over homemade chicken noodle soup at Schroeder's, the family talked it over. After consoling Glenda who felt responsible for the whole thing, lots of tears and a generous share of profanity, they came to a decision.

Carrie, Suzy and Marly would keep vigilance at the hospital. Doug would keep an eye on the both the elevator and the shop in Merton with the help of Ken and Rod. Keith would handle the chores with Pepper and the shop in Bismarck.

Kevin, Ian and Carl were definitely going to Texas, as was Marty. Matt was going too and was assigned to keep the lid on everyone in Texas. Byron and Marv were assigned to the North Dakota crew. They'd all have their hand's full.

The following afternoon, before they left for the airport, Charlie wanted to talk to Matt alone. "Tuck, Coot and I had a special meeting. We decided you'll be a good special project guy. Mom got your ring. You want to keep it in your pocket, because it falls off your finger. Some of us guys keep it by their keys. Okay?" the little boy handed him the plastic ring from a bottle. "We know that you can help Miriam from being frad jelly. I don't like her to be frad jelly anymore." Then he started to cry.

Matt took the little guy in his arms, "Thank you, Charlie. I'm honored and I'll do my best."

"If it gets too bad, crawl under the bed. Okay?"

By now, Matt was crying, "I will."

"Tuck, will Miriam be okay?"

"I don't know Charlie. We can only do everything we can to try to fix things for her. Okay? But she knows she has people who really love her, like you do."

Early the next morning, the five men left for Texas. As they left, Miriam was still in ICU and not able to maintain her breathing on her own. Dr. Samuels and her team of doctors were baffled what to do. Zach and Byron were with her as much as possible.

Carl called ahead and Diaz promised as much help as he could give. All the guys were willing to help even though they were busy. Carl and Mo had gathered a bunch of pictures of their little sweetheart with the express purpose of tweaking the heartstrings of the agents and hopefully, some of Ezekiel's cohorts.

The men took a cab to the motel near the FBI office. It was familiar territory to Carl and Harrington. Marty had everything he could do to keep Carl from bursting his blood vessels and keeping his blood pressure under control. Harrington wasn't much better than Carl. Matt and Kevin were not familiar with all the FBI stuff but were very definite about what they wanted from this trip.

Diaz had gathered a list of the known acquaintances of Ezekiel and Naomi, Miriam's parents. There was a list of who was in which jail and who was out, and their addresses if known; or where they could be found. All the agents at the Texas offices had Miriam's picture on their desks and it worked as Carl had hoped. She was a sweet, innocent little girl and that sort of thing really made the adrenalin flow in a FBI agent. Diaz pulled as many strings as he could and managed to twist enough arms to get Kincaid and Harrington visitation with the jailed people. The others would have to be questioned unofficially and that would be left to Kevin and Matt.

The men rented some cars and Marty went with Kincaid and Harrington, to monitor them. They went to the local jail in the morning and then to the prison in the afternoon. Kevin and Matt were left with a handful of addresses, bars, and strip joints in San Antonio and strict orders to keep the names of any policing agency out of their questioning. However, if they got any leads, they promised they'd call Diaz and he could check them out.

So after breakfast and a word of prayer, the men headed out. They didn't have a lot of time and needed to find out as much as they could.

72

At the local jail, Harrington and Kincaid had visitation with five of Ezekiel's people. The first two were worthless. They were only hired for outside jobs and knew little about their boss. They did give them a few names.

One of the men, while staring at the little girl's photo, said, "You know, that bastard should have been shot. If I had a kid like that, I'd think I was the luckiest man in the world. He was really a piece of work. All I ever heard is that he was with this prostitute. I can't remember her name though. She was a junkie and dumber than a rock."

"If you think of her name, will you please, please give this number a call?" Harrington asked. "It is very important. This poor little girl is in intensive care and we need to know what happened to her. Anything will help."

The man looked at the photo and took the card. "Yah, I will."

The third man was obnoxious and cared less about anyone but himself. "If I do know something, and I'm not saying I do; what's in it for me? Do I get a reduced sentence? I need a deal."

Carl was immediately furious, "You slimy bastard, you'll be lucky if I don't smash your head in!"

Marty reached over and grabbed Kincaid's arm. "Calm down."

"Like hell I will. Leave me alone with this creep. We'll see about a reduced sentence!" Carl's face was red and his fists were clenched.

"No, that is not a good idea," Marty restated.

Harrington looked at Marty, "You know, maybe it is. We got this room for half an hour. I say you and I go get a cup of coffee."

Marty swallowed hard. He wasn't worried about the prisoner; he was about Kincaid. "I don't think so."

"Now," Harrington said sternly and Marty got up.

"I hope you know what you're doing," Marty stammered.

The prisoner was as worried as Marty but in a different way. Once out the door, Ian reassured Marty it would be okay. "We can go in this room and watch everything that goes on. Kincaid knows what he's doing."

"I hope so," Marty said reluctantly. "His blood pressure is sky rocketing."

They went into the room next door and stood in front of the one-way glass. Kincaid sat and stared at the man for a complete ten minutes, not saying a word. The man started to sweat and became very nervous, but Kincaid never moved a muscle. Finally, the man almost collapsed, "What the hell you planning to do, sit there and stare?"

"Thinking of what I should do. I have time, you know. Which are you most partial to, your eyes or your groin?"

"What are you talking about? You can't do anything to me. I'm protected. You aren't allowed to hurt me. I'm cuffed and it would be police brutality."

"I'm not a cop. I have no rules to go by. I've nothing to lose and I might figure it is worth a little trouble to teach a punk like you a lesson."

"What the hell? What do you want to know anyway? Ezekiel is dead from what I hear."

"That's why I'm talking to you. Apparently you knew him during the time we're interested in, about sixteen months ago. I want to what you know about his family at that time. Tell me something believable or I'll vent some of my frustrations. It'd make me feel better and I really don't give a damn about you."

The man stared back at him and tried unsuccessfully to get him to weaken his cobra-like gaze. Finally, the man said, "Okay. I don't know much. Honestly. Moses was hanging with this prostitute. About the time of the Vance job, he was griping because his wife said his kids were sick with measles or chicken pox, or some damned thing. He was furious with her. He told her that she had better get the hell out of the house before the day of the job, or there would be hell to pay and hung up. He laughed and said the house would be empty for us to use after the job. Honestly, that's all I know."

"That's better. See, that wasn't so hard, was it? Was the house empty when you got there?"

Whining, the man pleaded, "I never got there. I was picked up after the job and before I got to the house. I've been in jail ever since. So I really know nothing about it. You have to believe me."

"I don't have to believe a damned thing that you say. I'm going to cut you a break. I'll check this out and if you've been square, I won't come back again. How is that?"

With that, he got up and left the room. On his way to the next room, he told the guard to return the man to his cell.

In the room, Harrington shook his hand. "Good work. You scared the hell out of him,"

"And me too, I might add," Marty said. "Don't do that again! I almost had a stroke."

Carl grinned. He loved this. He was in his element. This was his life and he was good at it. "What do you think? Think he told the truth?"

Harrington nodded and even Marty agreed.

The fourth prisoner was a hooker who had hung around the gang at that time. She'd talk to Harrington only and Marty watched while he turned on the charm to this pathetic creature. Watching from behind the window, he shook his head and confided to Carl, "I don't know about you guys. You really work it with anything you can, don't you?"

"Yah," Carl agreed. "It's disagreeable until you get worked yourself a few times. Then you sort of figure turnabout is fair play. These ones today aren't the real hard core. They're the wannabes. Some of the hardcore can twist you so fast that you don't know which end is up."

"I wouldn't be able to do your jobs," Marty said.

"You would, but you don't want to. I couldn't do your job either. But Marty, I have seen you be tough when the situation calls for it. You don't always baby a patient, either. Sometimes you have to be less than sympathetic to help them."

"You're right. I guess that is true. I still wouldn't like your jobs."

Kincaid smiled, "I'm glad. We need you to be a paramedic."

Meanwhile, Harrington was able to learn the name of the hooker who was with Moses at that time. She was Mina Dendrill. The hooker confirmed the phone call of Moses and his wife. She said that his wife came there later that day. Moses never actually went on the Vance job, as was his usual pattern. Mina was mad because Moses told her to get lost until after the wife left. The only other thing she knew was what Mina had told her. His wife showed up without the kids and was there for four days. Then she left and Mina went back.

That afternoon, the men went to the penitentiary. They had two people to see but had to be accompanied by prison officials.

Harrington talked to Lee Pearson. He was arrested a week after the Vance job. He was quite talkative and had nothing good to say about Ezekiel Moses. Pearson said that he knew the kids were sick and that he had told his wife to leave the house. That is where they always met to get paid off by Moses and he never wanted his family underfoot. After the job went awry, those members of the gang that weren't arrested went to the old house to meet up. When they got there a couple days later, one of the other guys, Frenchie, was whining because he had to dig a grave for one of Moses' kids. Apparently the kid was dead in the house. Everyone complained the house stunk from the kid being dead in there. That is all he knew about it. He had no idea what Frenchie's real name was or where he was.

Carl Kincaid talked to a man named Pierre Amante. Pierre's cousin was the man Pearson had referred to as Frenchie. Pierre was serving time for a crime totally unrelated to Ezekiel Moses. All Pierre knew was that his cousin was really mad about the dead kid. He told him that he got to the 'safe house' and met Larry Gregory. Gregory was the first one there. He had found the kids. He said the boy was dead and the girl was almost dead. He told Frenchie to bury the kid while he took the girl to his sister. He wanted no part of dead kids. Pierre's cousin was dead and he had no idea where his sister could be found. All he knew was that was the last job his cousin did with Moses.

The men returned to the FBI station with the new names and waited for Kevin and Matt to return. Diaz thought they had made great strides in one day.

"Yah," Marty said, "But Miriam is still in ICU."

"I appreciate that, but this business isn't all worked out in an hour like on Dragnet. Real life takes longer." Agent Diaz pointed out.

73

Meanwhile, Kevin and Matt took the list of addresses and names and headed out. They drove to some of the more beleaguered areas of the city.

"We'll see the sights of San Antonio that most people miss. I'll bet on that!" Kevin said as they walked from one bar to another. "I have seen more pole dancers today than on any leave the Navy could muster up. Some real high class joints, too."

"It's a real eye opener today," Matt confided. "Yah, I was glad for my clerical collar today. I think it helped."

"Did it keep you from being tempted by the classy dames?"

"Yea gads no. I could see the diseases oozing all over. I could never get that desperate. I only meant that a few ladies were more willing to talk to me." Then he grinned, "I had to reel you back in though. Wonder what Carrie would say?"

Kevin shook his head, "She'd hope I had my vaccinations! Gads, that one place was the filthiest place I've ever been in my life."

They turned into a bar-strip joint. The men went to the skinny bartender with a runny nose and blood shot eyes, "Have any idea where we could find a lady named Pauline?"

"What for?" The man sniveled.

"We need some information about a little girl," Matt explained. "It will cause no one any trouble."

The man sized up the priest and his friend. "That hooker is back there, draped over that end of the bar. No trouble, you hear?"

"No trouble," Matt promised.

The men approached the unkempt, but overly made up woman. She looked them over and immediately became seductive. She was flirting outrageously with Kevin, but also offered she was willing to satisfy a man of the cloth.

Matt smiled and said, "All we're interested in Ma'am is some information."

"I can't waste time giving information when I have prospective customers."

Kevin looked around the sleazy bar. It seemed doubtful there was anyone in the place either interested or capable of being her customer, but he reached in his pocket, "We understand and wouldn't want to waste your time. Will $20 make it worthwhile?"

"That's an insult," the woman responded. "I'm worth more than that."

Kevin pulled out another $20 bill and put it in her hand. She shrugged, "Another tequila would help."

The men ordered her a tequila and she sat down. She remembered she'd gone with this Pearson who was on the Vance job. He was arrested a week later. He told her that Moses kid was dead when they got to the safe house. His head had been bashed in. He said that this Frenchie-guy had to bury the boy. This Larry Gregory took a girl to his sister, a Lucette something or other. But that's all that she knew."

The men thanked her and got up to leave, feeling disappointed. At the door, a very skinny woman came up to Matt.

"You a real priest?" she asked.

He assured her he was.

"I know this Lucette. She's dying now and needs a priest. If you promise to give her the Last Rites, I'll show you where to find her."

The three crossed the street to a flop house. The building stank of stale tobacco, body odor and cheap whiskey. The woman led them up to the second floor and down the unpainted hall with uncarpeted flooring. She opened the door to a room and the smell nearly overpowered them.

A nearly naked woman was lying on a filthy bed coughing and covered in oozing lesions. It was horrible. Kevin immediately went to call the paramedics while Matt gave her the Last Rites. The skinny woman disappeared when she heard the paramedics were called.

Kevin returned and they waited until the ambulance got there. The woman was drifting in and out of consciousness, but in one of her more lucid moments, Matt showed her the photo of the little girl. He asked her if she remembered her. The lady took the photo in her emaciated hands and tears rolled down her pallid face, while she nodded.

"My brother was the first one in the house after the job went bad. Half the guys were arrested and the rest scattered. It was two days after the job. He went to the house. It reeked so bad he vomited. He went out to get some air and he heard a whimper. He looked for the noise and opened the door to a room. He said the curtains were pulled shut in the room so it was almost dark. He found two kids in a crib. A little toddler was in the corner of the crib whimpering. She had chicken pox and was sitting in a messy diaper with half a bottle of sour milk. The boy was older and dead. He'd been dead a couple days in the summer heat. Larry said he had chicken pox but didn't die from that. His head had been smashed in. Her brother said he never forgot it. What really got to him—there was a bunch of crayons in the bed, like they were supposed to play with them or something.

"Someone else buried the boy and Larry brought the girl to me. I fed her and got her cleaned up. She had pretty black curly hair, but boney as hell. Then Larry took her to Moses. Moses was madder than hell at him,and said that he could've been rid of her if he had left it alone. Moses' wife took the girl but Moses belted her. He said, "You had the sense to get rid of the boy, why didn't you finish her off too?" Larry told me he remembered how the Moses woman cried and said that she had to punish the boy for coloring in the crib. That is when Larry left. He decided they were both crazier than hell and he wanted no part of either of them. He didn't wait to get paid for the job.

"I was there when my brother died a few months ago. He had been beaten in a bar fight. Before he died, he told me he always wondered what happened to that girl. Do you think Father, that he knows she is okay now?"

"I imagine he does, Lucette. He did a fine thing, and so did you. We want to thank you both for taking care of her."

She looked at them and nodded weakly, "I really miss Larry. He looked a lot like your friend, Father. Yah, this guy looks like him. Take care of her for us, I know Larry would want that."

Then she fell asleep. She died in the ambulance while they followed the ambulance to the hospital.

The men talked to the paramedics who said she had died peacefully about a block from the hospital. They went in and washed up before they headed back to the FBI office.

Over coffee, the men shared what they had learned. Everyone sat silently for a time, just absorbing the information. It explained a lot, but solved little.

Ian shook his head, "Jesus, I'm surprised she is as good as she is."

Carl muttered, "Me too. We'd better tell Zach right away."

Finally, Diaz said, "Well, you guys did a good day's work. I'm sorry the answers aren't more comforting, but they are the answers. Do you need to look any further?"

Carl wiped the tears from his eyes, "No. Thanks. I just hope this helps her. But now, at least we know."

"Yah," Diaz said, "At least you know. When are you heading back?"

"We'll get our return tickets and head back as soon as possible," Harrington said. "Thank everyone for us. It really means a lot and we appreciate all the extra work you guys did for us I'll leave some cash so you can have Ricardo's deliver those ribs for the office tomorrow. Okay?"

"No problem. The guys will love the ribs. Thanks Carl. Please keep us informed on how the little girl is doing. Thanks to Kincaid, we all kind of feel responsible for her. What is it that you guys call him?"

Kincaid interrupted, "Never mind that. Thanks. We'll keep you informed. If you ever get the dizzy notion, come and visit in the Dakotas. I have a house there. Stop by to see my wife and I."

"You're getting married? Carl Kincaid?" Diaz almost passed out.

"Knock it off. Don't act so damned surprised! These two men here are gonna be my kids". Kincaid grumped. "You know what? Don't come. Maybe you won't be welcome after all,"

"I wouldn't miss it."

"Oh my god, I bet you'll show up."

Back at the motel, the guys divided up. Harrington called Zach so he could tell Dr. Samuels. He received a good report. Miriam was breathing on her own and seemed to be doing much better. She was still tranquilized but not as sedated anymore.

Kevin called Carrie. He started to tell her and ended up crying so hard that Matt had to talk to her. After they hung up, Kevin sobbed, "I feel worthless."

"No need to, Kevin," Matt said as he comforted his friend. "This has been really torturous for you."

Kevin shook his head, "Can you imagine how she must have felt? I wonder what she thought? Stuck there next to your dead brother for two days, starving and sick! With crayons. Jesus! I bet she saw Clark and it brought that whole thing back to her. It explains so much. Honestly, between you and me, Matt, sometimes I have wondered about Zach and Ruthie. Now I can understand. They didn't have weak constitutions, but really strong ones."

"I know. Come on Kevin. Let's get some food into you. Marty was going to get our tickets. I think we're all ready to get home again."

Kincaid had called the farm and Byron was there, too. Everyone was dismayed and horrified but sadly not too shocked at the report. As Grandma said, "I wish it would solve the problems, but maybe we can avoid them further down the road. You know, I may not ever like crayons again myself."

Kincaid agreed. "Well, we're going to get some sleep and be home as soon as we can tomorrow. We can't wait to get home."

Dinner was quiet but the men couldn't help feeling like they had accomplished something. Ian poured the dressing on his salad and then stopped. "You know, for a while this afternoon, I really wanted to be back in law enforcement. But by the time we left the penitentiary, I decided I'm glad to be done with it."

Kincaid studied him a minute and then nodded, "I have to admit, I felt the same way. This morning, I'd have paid my soul to get my job back. By this afternoon, that feeling of futility had come back. I remember all the times I had walked out of an interrogation so frustrated that nothing ever seemed to get better. Now I know there are things that are better."

Marty smiled, "Well, I know I sure don't want to end up on the other side of the bars. One visit was all I needed. I sometimes think that my job is all gore and gunk, but I think I like it better than dealing with all the dregs of society."

Kevin smiled slightly, "I've no idea what I thought we would find out. I just wanted it to be a simple thing we could fix. Now I know it isn't simple and we probably can't fix it. I'm so thankful that Miriam wasn't any older when all this happened."

Ian nodded, "Like Zach and Ruthie were. Zach told me that Dr. Samuels thinks that he and Ruthie have a hard time being objective about Miriam. I can believe that. Every time they hear something, it reminds them of things that happened to them. Some of that was no picnic. I remember not long ago, when all you had to do was mention their childhood and they'd both throw up. I heard when we saw that shed where their brother was forced to put his hand in that bag, Elton almost lost it himself! Ruthie passed out. Zach threw up his innards. Those people they dealt with were some sick bastards. How anyone could inflict that on anyone in the name of God like that Abraham did, is beyond me. He destroyed a lot of lives."

Kincaid nodded, "That's why I'm not much of a church person."

"I know, you guys," Kevin said, "But it isn't the churches fault. They didn't condone it. I don't think that it was even a real church. It was some insane bastard."

74

A very bedraggled bunch of guys arrived at the Bismarck Airport. No one had said much of anything on the trip home, all deeply engrossed in the lessons of the trip. Ruthie was the first one to land in Ian's arms. She had been so worried about him. She knew only too well the treachery that her family was capable of inflicting.

Marty was met by his Greta and they were heading to her parent's house. Marty had been a real help to them all and teased that he had never used a blood pressure cup more in his life. Mo waited at the farm for Carl and Matt, who were going to ride home with Zach.

Kevin was met by Carrie. She had come from the hospital and was pleased to report that Miriam was awake a little more and seemed to be doing better. It was like a major step backward for her, but she was coming out of it.

Dr. Samuels felt that each time that it happened, it would be less traumatic and eventually go away. Now that they knew what they were dealing with, he had called some of his colleagues and they were working on a treatment protocol for her. They were glad she was as young as she was when it happened, but that was also a double-edged sword. It meant that she had to get a little older to be able to work out some of the issues.

Once in their car, Kevin asked Carrie, "Honey, would it be okay if we stopped and saw her before we went home?"

Carrie gave her compassionate husband a huge embrace, "I already planned on that. I knew you wouldn't go home without seeing her."

Kevin hugged his wife. "Honestly Carrie, does it bother you that I'm so worried about her while we are expecting our own child?"

"Kevin Schroeder! You big numb skull! Of course not! I love you because you are a caring person. I know that you'll love our baby as much as you do Miriam. We have enough room in our lives for this little sweetheart. I love her too."

"I know you do," He put his arm around her neck as he kissed her, "I'm sorry. I always act like it is just me. You know, she probably likes me only because I look like the guy that saved her from that crib."

"Kevin," Carrie took both his hands in hers and looked directly in his eyes, "Listen to me. That may be why she first took to you, but she loves you because she knows she can count on you. No matter what you look like. If you hadn't been so good to her, she wouldn't depend on you. I know that for a fact."

"Really?"

"No, I made that up."

"Carrie, you know I do a lot of stupid stuff, but the one thing I'll never be sorry for is marrying you."

"That works out well, because I am not sorry I married you either," Carrie kissed him. "Now let's get to the hospital and see our girl so I can get you home."

"Okay."

At the hospital, Kevin and Carrie came in the room where Byron and Marly were. Byron shook Kevin's hand and then said quietly, "She is semi-awake now, but they want her to sleep soon. Carrie insisted they let her stay awake so you could see her. I want to take the ladies for a cup of swill, so you can be alone with her."

Kevin hugged his Uncle Byron. "I appreciate that. Byron? I'd like to talk to you in the next day or so. This has been a bearcat. I think I need to talk some of this out."

Byron patted his back, "Whenever you can."

Alone in the room with the little girl, Kevin took a deep breath. He walked over to her bedside and looked at the monitors flickering. Then he looked at the tiny kid. He reached down and patted her curly mop of black hair. "I love you, Miriam."

Miriam opened her eyes and then closed them again. Kevin kept talking softly. "Honey, I don't know how to help you but I want you to know that you are so precious to Carrie and me. We want you to be happy, healthy and have a good life. You can count on us to be there for you whenever. Okay?"

She opened her eyes again and then moved her lips, "Mr. Bear?"

Kevin smiled through his tears, "Yes, Mr. Bear too."

Kevin leaned down and tried to hug his little sweetheart as much as he could. She moved her free arm around his neck. "Son. Cawwie, Gopher?"

"Yes honey, you, me and Carrie and Mr. Bear. And guess what? We are going to have a baby too, remember?"

Miriam smiled drowsily, "Gopher's baby."

"That's right. Gopher's baby." Then Kevin took Mr. Bear from the bedside table, "Do you want to hold him?"

"Okay."

Kevin tucked Mr. Bear in her arm and then said, "Honey, I have to go home now to take a nap and the nurses want you to take one too. Can you take care of Mr. Bear for me?"

"Okay, Son."

"Miriam, you get well really fast so that you can come to our house so we can lick chocolate."

"Okay Son. Mr. Bear and Cawwie?"

"Yes, they'll be there too. Miriam, I love you."

Miriam looked at him and was silent a minute before she said, "Love Son."

Kevin fought back the tears, "You try to sleep now. I'll stay here with you for a while. Okay?"

"Okay Son. Son love Gopher."

When the three returned from their coffee, they found Miriam and Kevin asleep. Miriam had one arm around Mr. Bear and the other on Kevin's head. He was sleeping precariously, leaning on the edge of the bed. He was holding her hand in his.

Byron gently woke him and told him that he had better go home and get some rest. He and Marly were going to stay a little longer until Elsie and Jerald came to stay with her.

Ian and Ruthie rode home in near silence. When they turned off the highway to Merton, Ruthie said, "Was it as bad as when we were in Arkansas?"

"It was all second hand information this time. God only knows what else she has gone through," Ian watched her as she drove. "You know, you're doing very well, and except for a few really bad things, so is she. Zach is almost over it. It can be overcome. You're living proof. I'm so proud of you every day. I see how you handle things. I love it when I see you enjoying life. I missed you so much when we are apart. Ruthie, can we set a date to get married?"

Ruthie was surprised, "Set a date? I mean, I thought you asked me to marry you to get Coot off your back."

"No. Coot just knocked me off my box of stupid."

"Seriously Ian, I think we should wait until after your Mom gets married. That would be proper, don't you think," She giggled.

"I don't know about properness! But okay. If you want Matt to marry us, you better not wait too long. I think he has about made up his mind to leave the priesthood."

"Did he say something?"

"No, I saw the look on his face when Kevin said something about no real church would condoned hurting children. Matt never had to say a word. I know him pretty well. I think that since Kevin didn't know what Matt was thinking and just gave an honest answer to a straightforward question, it hit Matt right where he lives."

Ruthie drove in silence, "Ian. I'd like him to marry us, but that's much less important than him making the right decision. I'm certain that Father Vicaro and Byron can handle our wedding. In fact, sometimes, I think we should just go to the Justice of the Peace."

Harrington laughed, "You've got to be kidding! I thought you had this wedding all planned out already. Everyone is looking forward to the gala event. I really want you to have that."

Ruthie got serious, "Of course, I'd love all that; but I'm not quite that juvenile. I love you and I want to be with you the rest of my life. I really don't think that a ten foot veil could make me love you any more than I do now."

"Ruthie, when we get to Merton pull into the parking lot of the Retirement Home. Please."

She looked at him in surprise, "Sure, but why?"

"Never mind, just do it."

She pulled into the lot and parked the car in the darkened lot. Ian scooted over, put his good arm around her and drew her close to him. He gave her the most passionate kiss they'd ever shared. Then he said, "Ruthie Jeffries. I want you to be my wife, whenever and however you say. Okay?"

"Okay. I love you Ian. I know we are meant to be together."

"And that's a blasted fact!" Ian moved back to his side of the car. "Now, we'd better get on home before the entire Merton police force descends on us."

"Maybe I don't care if their one tired policeman comes by," Ruthie grinned.

"Neither do I, but this Engelmann outfit has been through a lot lately. I don't think we need any more right now."

After his shower, Matt went to bed. He said some prayers and before he crawled in bed, he looked out over the back yard. He felt so alone. He had rarely felt this alone before. He was surrounded by good friends and a loving family. What more should a man need? As he thought that, it came back to him what Darrell had said to him that day. 'It would be wise to remember you are a man and a human one at that. The rest of us know it, and so does God.'

Had that been his problem all along? Had he wanted so much to be the perfect priest with wings under his coat? Did he expect too much of himself, or put himself on too high a pedestal? Did he think that he was above everyone else?

No, he was pretty sure that wasn't the case. He knew better than that. He knew himself well enough to know that he was even less good than many people thought he was.

He thought about what Kevin said. He was absolutely right. He himself would feel the same way if he was asked the question. While he knew the church didn't condone that behavior; they certainly were covering it up and thus, allowing it to continue. That was the same as condoning it. Then why was he having such a hell of a time just telling the church no? Was it really that big of a decision?

But there was something else. Something he had never felt or recognized before. He knew in his heart what he really wanted to do, but he had never admitted that, even to himself. He wanted to have a human being love him. Not his Mom and not a good friend. He had that. Not the love of God. That was wonderful, but sometimes, there was a lot to be said for the human touch.

He thought about that dying woman, covered in lesions. She reached out to hold his hand. He knew in his heart she wanted a real hug and a human to say I love you and really mean it. He had tried to bring her peace and he had done some of that. He gave her forgiveness and hope for the next life, but she still needed a loving embrace from another human being who truly cared. She had been there for her brother when he died, and no doubt, he would have been there for her if he had the opportunity. But she died without anyone.

He had to admit that when they arrived at the airport, he was jealous. He was jealous of Marty when Greta came to him, Ian when Ruthie jumped into his arms, Kevin when his Carrie embraced him, and even Coot who was met by Zach, but had his Mom waiting for him at home. He had no one waiting for him. He thought about Darrell and Annie and how they each must be married by now. It had never bothered him before, but it really did tonight. What was going wrong in his head?

Matt realized that he had tears rolling down his cheeks. 'Pull yourself together, you big dope. You're just fine. Things are a lot better for you than for most people on the planet.'

He flopped on his bed and had a cry. He had rarely felt so desperate. He was shocked when there was a knock at his door. Had he been loud enough to be heard? He had tried to be quiet. He got up, wiped his tears and answered the door.

It was his Mom. She never said a word but put her arms around her boy and gave him a hug. He returned the hug and then cried.

"It was a difficult trip for my boy, huh? Tell your Mom about it. I know you don't want to. You have always been like that, but just humor me this time."

Matt sat down on the side of his bed and his Mom sat down next to him. She took his hand. "To make it easier, I'll start. Okay? Carl told me about the trip and what happened with Kevin's comment."

"What comment?" Matt was flabbergasted.

"About belonging to a church, Coot told me. Dumb old me, I didn't know what he was talking about, so he explained to me about all the stuff you have been wrestling with. I want to apologize to you. I should have seen some of it. I was blind. He told me about Ruthie and that Father Timothy."

"How did he know?"

"I guess he and Ian had a long talk about the church one day. Ian never straight out told him, but Carl figured it out from what he didn't say. You know, he's no fool. They both knew a lot from their work in law enforcement. I have to admit, I have heard some of the rumors before about priests and women, but I never imagined about priest's molesting little children. Although, when Carl told me, I started to put things together. I knew a family that had twin sons. They were devout Catholics until their children took their first communion classes. Just like that, within a month or so, the family left the church and soon after moved to Oregon. I'd heard some terrible rumors then, but never believed them. Mattie, why didn't you tell me?"

"Mom, I didn't want to ruin your faith."

"Give me some credit, young man! This doesn't hurt my faith in God at all! I have no problem with God. It is humans that cause the trouble! And priests are humans. Even you, Matt."

"Mom, I've never ever even thought of doing anything like that! I can't believe that you would-," Matt was indignant.

"Matthew Harrington. I don't and would never think that! I know my boys better than that. I also know that you don't like to keep your mouth shut about injustice. You are outspoken like your Mom and I'm quite proud of you about that. I don't think that you should be quiet either."

Matt gave his Mom a hug. "I'm sorry I thought you'd think that of me."

"Don't be. Coot says that you are worried that folks might think that, huh? Don't underestimate the sense of the common folk. We all aren't so dumb you know. We spend our lives deciding who is good and who is bad; what is right and what is wrong. You priests seem to think that we all just buy your advertising without thought. We don't. I have to tell you something that I haven't been honest about. Okay? I'm not trying to bend you one way or the other, but I want to give you the benefit of my opinion."

Matt kissed her cheek, "I will value it."

"Don't be impertinent! I've been proud as punch about you being a priest. I'll back you one hundred percent. In my heart, I always wanted you to be a teacher and a husband. I wanted you to have children because you'd be a good parent."

Matt's mouth fell open. "Why did you never tell me that?"

"Honey Chile, I talk big, but I really don't know everything. I wanted to support your decision and I felt it was your heart's desire. Besides, I need another pile of grandkids like I need a hole in the head."

Matt chuckled, "Especially since you have all these Gophers now!"

"Yah, how did that happen? From kids to rodents!"

"You're as bad as Carl; you know that, don't you? He is doing real well at being a stepdad. He's helped with some big problems for Ian and me. How do you think he will handle it when he meets the rest of us? I really feel sorry for him, don't you?"

"Yah, I do. Mattie, I really love that big bruiser. I loved being you kid's mom, but this time, it's for me. Do you understand?"

"Yes, I do. Ian and I both do and we approve wholeheartedly. He is a softie."

"Don't ever let him know you know that. His whole façade would crumble."

"I know. I won't. Mom, thanks for talking to me."

"Oh Sonny, I'm not done yet! Now you listen to your old Mom. I want you to make a solemn promise that this time, you do it for you! Hear me? I want you to be a bit selfish. Think about yourself and what you truly want. You can serve God all over the place. Look at your friend Darrell. Have you ever met a better heart?"

"No, I really haven't."

"And Elton, Nora and even Grandpa Lloyd. I challenge you to ask Lloyd what you should do! He would give you an unbiased answer!"

"Mom, I might just ask him. He sure had the best answer for Ruthie's wedding."

Mo giggled, "Yea gads! I thought she was going to hire Queen Elizabeth's wedding planner!"

Matt replied, "You know, she has never had anything even remotely like that before. Zach's wedding was the first time in her life that she ever had a formal dress!"

"I know. I love her to death. She deserves a good life. And Matt, I think that there is a life out there for you too; one that you can be comfortable with and really enjoy. Don't rush it. If others want to push you one way or the other, hold your ground. I want my boy to be happy."

Matt put his arm around her, “Mom, I love you.”

“Well, I need my beauty sleep. Oh and by the way, Carl and I can get married without you doing the work. Will you give the bride away instead?”

Matt’s eyes filled with tears, “Thanks Mom. I’d be honored. You’re the best.”

“Remember that on Mother’s Day.”

75

Carl couldn't wait to talk to his Maureen. It was the first time that he really kissed her with a big embrace in public, and he didn't care one bit. He loved her and he knew that he needed her. He wasn't embarrassed by it at all. In fact, he was proud of it.

While he was gone to Texas, he did a lot of thinking. That was where his life had been forever. It was in his blood. He got a brief chance to recapture some of his past and found it sorely wanting. He realized that he only wanted his Mo, and his little Gophers. Hell, he even missed Magpie! He was so proud to be able to tell the guys at the Agency that he was getting married and that Harrington and Matt were going to be his stepsons! He could hardly believe it when he heard his own words. He tried to be a sort of father to these two guys; and they didn't even balk at it. Matt even said he was good at it, and both of the boys had called him Dad. That really meant a lot to him.

Later that night, when he went to bed, he looked around the room. Elmer was still sitting by his gopher hole, listening and digging every so often. And waiting patiently for the day. Carl had spent such a long time thinking that dog was nuts. Now he admired him. He knew what he wanted and wasn't about to give up until he had given it his best shot. Even if he never got the gopher, he could go to his grave knowing he had put forth his very best effort.

He missed his grumpy roommate, Bert. There was no question that the old Goat demanded his wishes from Carl for his own sake. He didn't do it to be nice to Carl, because Carl believed the man when he said at he didn't really care if Carl was happy or not. He wanted a backup. And the miserable cuss connived and weaseled until he extracted an unwilling promise from him to get what he wanted.

But now, Carl figured he got the last laugh. He did give in to Bert and do his bidding. However, he found more happiness than he had in his life. He actually won. He had to concede, they probably both won.

Sure, the Gophers had their problems yet, but they always would. Carl was lucky to have found a mate that would help him with them and their problems. He knew it. He was certain that Ginger would turn out to be just fine, and he figured he might be able to keep Charlie out of a maximum security prison. Even little Miriam would be okay. Clark and Maddie Lynn would be getting their hard hats any day now. Soon, when school started, he would have his new batch. Baby Matthew, Dan and Jennie's little boy and soon, Darlene and Keith would be adding to the rodent nest. Yes, he was confident that with the young men he had come to know, he would have plenty of gophers to teach the joys of irrigation and Lord knows what all.

His new stepsons were working their way through their problems, but they had a great support system and a wonderful Mom to help them. He was confident that Ian was making steps to a happy future and that while Matt's problems were still up in the air, he was sure he would make a sound decision. He didn't know what Matt would decide, but Carl figured he would do his best and they could be proud of him. Whatever it was, his family would support him. He really thought a lot of both the boys.

Ruthie and Zach were overcoming the damage of those deranged people. All the horrible things they had inflicted on everyone's lives, was now being erased. Instead of destroying them all, they had all found more joy and happiness that they had imagined. The victims had really, with the help of the good Lord, become the winners.

He didn't know how Maureen would handle the difficulties with her in-laws, but he would be there to protect her. She had some great friends now, with Nora, Marly and Grandma. She would be fine. He would dedicate his life to making her life as good as possible.

Carl turned over and pulled the blanket over his shoulder. After Matt finished his orientation at the high school, the family would fly out to Boston. There they would load and pack their things from Ian's apartment, Matt's few things and Mo's house. Ian was going to drive his car back, but Matt had to leave his vehicle behind because it belonged to the church.

Mo was going to bring her car back and they were going to rent a moving van for the rest. They planned to be back home in a week or so.

Home. Carl now had a home. A stupid, barren place in the middle of nowhere where he had been humiliated mercilessly and even hauled to a dance in a piece of farm machinery! He had been subjected to a torturous and humiliating physical therapy with a bunch of girls by a tiny little therapist who was barely five feet tall. Pepper had forced him to get his strength back and been there to knock some sense in him when he needed it. He got more advice from that eighteen-year-old hothead about life than he cared to repeat.

Hell, his new home was out in the middle of a goat pasture! But it was his home and he loved it. Every bit of it.

He was very happy to have Darrell as his partner. No man could be more fortunate. Darrell was one of the most decent caring people Carl had ever met; and fun too.

And then there was Zach. He was like a son to him. Not that he knew anything about having a son, but Zach was like his own. He could tell that guy anything and shared more private information with him than anyone in the world. Zach treated him with respect, but never hesitated to 'give him the business' when he needed it.

Now he was part of the Engelmann Clan. He had a group of people who were dedicated to each other and not just in lip service. Byron had always been there for him and actually depended on him too, sometimes. In fact, all the clan expected and gave the same treatment to him as to any other clanner and he loved it.

And then there was Magpie. Carl knew that Bert had wanted him to help Magpie when he had no desire to do that. However lately, he was beginning to enjoy it. Now, he had started to think that Magpie might allow him to help. Hell, he still didn't like the man. They really had nothing in common. He was annoying and a blow hard, but Carl had learned to understand him. In his whole life, he had probably never met a more genuinely kind human being. He was way too petunia for his blood and couldn't cook worth a damn, but he had a few good points. He had decided that he could even tolerate Magpie.

He turned again and beat his pillow into submission, "Yah, okay Bert. You miserable old Goat. You win. You knew you would, didn't you?"

Carl watched out the window. Elmer was sitting there with his head between his legs. Suddenly, he jumped up and dug like crazy.